doing it RIGHT

HARLOE RAE

Copyright © 2022 by Harloe Rae, LLC

All rights reserved. No part of this publication may be reproduced, distributed, or transmitted in any form or by any means, including photocopying, recording, or other electronic or mechanical methods, without the prior written permission of the copyright owner and the publisher listed above, except in the case of brief quotations embodied in critical reviews and certain other noncommercial uses permitted by copyright law.

This is a work of fiction and any resemblance to persons, names, characters, places, brands, media, and incidents are either the product of the author's imagination or purely coincidental.

Editor: Infinite Well
Cover designer: Book Cover Kingdom
Photographer: Rafa G. Catalá
Model: Victor
Interior design: Champagne Book Design

For my sisters—Heidi and Kirstin.
And to those who love without limits and take chances,
even after the heart is broken.

playlist

"Mercy" by Brett Young
"Missing Piece" by Vance Joy
"Happier" by Olivia Rodrigo
"With or Without You" by U2
"Walking in the Wind" by One Direction
"Ghost" by Justin Bieber
"The Good Ones" by Gabby Barrett
"'Til You Can't" by Cody Johnson
"All These Years" by Camila Cabello
"Happier Than Ever" by Billie Eilish
"Dancing with Your Ghost" by Sasha Alex Sloan
"Perfectly Wrong" by Shawn Mendes
"Out of Love" by Alessia Cara
"Us" by James Bay
"Mess is Mine" by Vance Joy
"Afterglow" by Taylor Swift
"Love You Goodbye" by One Direction

"Give me sunshine, but don't steal the clouds. For the brightest spots are truly appreciated after several days stuck under muted hues."—Presley Drake

"This doesn't have to be the end for us."
Except it was.

What did we know about happily ever after at the age of eighteen?

Mason Braxter was a football legend—destined for glory far bigger than the confines of our small town.
Meanwhile, I had dreams of my own—a simpler life that included staying put and growing roots.

And all those plans of mine were going splendidly.

Until one drunken mishap a month before college graduation left me staring at two pink lines.
Then I was sharing custody with the most unlikely baby daddy.
We've figured out a system. Kind of.
I'm rocking this single mom gig. Mostly.

If only I could get a boost in the romance department.

As if summoned by my dry spell, Mason Braxter makes a sudden reappearance in Meadow Creek.
Six years have gone by, yet I can still remember every stupidly sculpted muscle on his body.
How easy it would be to fall back into old habits.
But I'm not that foolish girl anymore.

That doesn't deter my all-star ex from trying to prove we can do it right this time.
For all his efforts, I might let him scratch my itch once.
Maybe twice.
Definitely not thrice.

doing it
RIGHT

prologue

Presley

THEN (SIX YEARS AGO)

A BLISTERING FLOOD CLOGS MY VISION AND I SWIPE AT THE resulting tears. Even through the blur, I catch Mason's handsome face. He's almost too perfect under the breaking dawn. His stark features are still chiseled in shadowy beauty.

This man has been mine since we were thirteen. He's all I've ever known. My first for everything that truly matters to a girl. The love of my life. And now, my soon-to-be-ex.

The sun is just beginning to rise on this dreadful day that's ripping us apart. Glowing streaks crack across the horizon, putting an end to the darkness. That approaching light promises warmth and comfort, but all I feel is the shattering of my own heart.

Another swollen beat passes, the internal countdown

slowly nearing zero. A raw ache threatens to steal my breath. These last moments are the most painful. It's been easy to deny the upcoming separation—this detrimental force that will irrevocably split us into two separate pieces.

I sniff at the burn in my nose. "Why is this so hard?"

Mason's lopsided grin wobbles ever so slightly. "Because we love each other."

My grip on his shirt tightens, a throb pulsing through my fingers from the effort. "I don't want to let go."

"Me either, Pep." His lips dust my forehead with the words.

"But it's for the best." I'm not sure who I'm trying to convince with that statement.

He hugs me impossibly closer until I can hear the thundering riot in his chest. "You could come with me."

Across the country. Away from my family and the town we grew up in. Ditching the plans I've made for myself.

The offer still tempts me, even after I've already decided against it on countless occasions. I can't leave everything behind to follow Mason's dreams while discarding my own. We've discussed the possibilities for months, ever since he accepted the full-ride scholarship in California. It's the best deal, offering a solid shot for him to play professionally after graduation. That's his ultimate dream—I'd never hold him back. But I also won't blindly follow him.

I recently acknowledged that there has always been an expiration date on our relationship. He's destined to find legendary glory under the stadium lights. There's no guarantee I'll find a permanent place for myself in his next chapter. A visual of me fumbling in unfamiliar territory assaults my mind and I shudder. Mason hasn't vowed to remain with me always, not that I want him to.

We're too young.

Too different.

Too stubborn with our own goals.

That selfish drive is what makes us who we are, and I refuse to let either one of us surrender. I don't want there to be a reason we eventually resent each other.

We could try long-distance, but he doesn't need the tether of a girlfriend rooted halfway across the country. I'd hate to question his fidelity for even a second. It's better this way, even if we're suffering right now. The pain will fade, though. I love him enough to put an end to us.

"A life without you is going to suck, but I can't leave." My tears stain his shirt with agony as I refuse him.

"I know," Mason murmurs against my temple. "You're meant to stay here."

Determined resolve pumps into my slumped form as I push away from his embrace. "And you're meant to be a star."

He tucks some loose hair behind my ear. "Will you still watch my games?"

The idea of that sends a stabbing pang into my stomach. But there's only so much I can deny him. "Of course."

"Then you'll catch my signal." He curves his hands into a makeshift heart, then flares the symbol outward in an arch. It's meant to represent an explosion, as if his chest can't contain his love for me. That's been our shared celebration since middle school.

Another slice cuts me deep. "You don't need to do that anymore."

Mason scoffs. "It's tradition after a completed pass."

I roll my puffy eyes. "From high school. I won't be cheering with my squad on the sidelines anymore."

Hell, I won't even be in the stands.

He adjusts the hat that's seated backward on his head. "That doesn't matter. You'll always be my good luck charm."

A knot squeezes my throat and I wheeze. "No, Mason. That's too—"

"Yes," he insists. In a practiced move, he dips down for a chaste kiss. His lips are salty and wet and mine for only a bit longer. "It's important to me."

I find myself nodding, our noses bumping with the jerky motion. "Okay."

"I'll miss you, Peppy Girl. You'll always be my first love." His voice hitches with the admission.

Fiery moisture pools in my vision. "Ditto, Ten. I'll never forget you."

He swipes at a stray droplet trickling down my cheek. "Too bad things couldn't be different for us."

"I wouldn't change anything."

"Me either, besides this part." Mason threads our fingers together. The soothing gesture is already losing its effectiveness. "I'll try to visit whenever I can."

But he won't. That's just an empty promise to soften the blow of him leaving. He doesn't have a reason to make the trip, since his parents moved to the west coast earlier this summer.

"I won't hold you to it," I murmur.

His chuckle is brittle. "You wouldn't."

With defeat pressing on my sternum, I reach to cup his scruffy cheek. "I'm glad you were mine, Mason Braxter. Even just temporarily."

He cringes. "Damn, that's sad."

"Why?"

"Because I can't picture us as over."

I shrug. "Then don't. Imagine we're floating in two opposite directions and drifting apart naturally."

A groove dents the space between his brows. "That's even worse."

"There are only so many positive spins I can make," I retort.

"You don't have to put on a brave face for my sake." He's memorized my coping methods.

There's no point in disputing the truth. All I can manage is a weak lift of one shoulder. "I have to turn this pity party around or we'll be miserable for years to come."

"I'll be miserable regardless. You're my daily dose of joy, Pep."

"Don't," I plead in a strangled whimper. "This is hard enough already."

"You want me to pretend that I'm okay with this? That leaving you isn't destroying me?" His scowl thrashes at my raw wounds.

I squeeze my eyes shut, scalding tracks burning my skin as more sorrow leaks out. My nod is disjointed. "Yes."

"Fuck that." Then he yanks me against him again. I collapse into his warmth without hesitation. Mason's familiar body molds to mine as he cinches around me. I'll no longer have access to the luxury of his comfort in about five minutes. Soaking him in feels vital, one last time. I bury my nose in the crook of his neck and breathe deep. Woodsy pine, reckless decisions, and starry nights console me.

After several stolen beats pass, I pull away from him again. His sole focus is latched on me. Mine mirrors his just the same. Our broken hearts bleed, the rivulets streaming down our cheeks. The inevitable looms at the edge of my vision. No more delay.

"All right." That limp surrender begins the separation process for what feels like the umpteenth time.

"Not yet." Mason's palm flexes on my hip.

I wiggle against his hold. "This is bigger than us. You can't have it all, Ten."

He peers at me with solemn regret reflecting in his gaze. "That won't stop me from trying."

I attempt a smile, but the edges fail to lift. "Tomorrow will be brighter."

"Not sure about that."

"You won't know until you try." I lift my chin at his truck in the driveway.

He glances over his shoulder to where I'm staring. "Is that my cue?"

My gaze trails to the horizon, which is now painted with vibrant hues revealing the morning hour. Anguish perfumes the air with a pungent waft. That stale, hollow scent signals what I've been dreading. Our time is up. This is it.

I blink against the flaring heat behind my eyes. "You'll be late otherwise."

Mason recognizes the resignation on my features. His posture goes rigid as he glares at the rising sun. "Fuck, Pep. I don't wanna leave you."

"But you have to. This is when we say goodbye," I choke.

With a thumb under my chin, Mason forces me to meet his penetrating gaze. A glassy sheen covers his vibrant green eyes. "I don't want us to say goodbye. That's too final. This doesn't have to be the end for us."

"If you insist," I relent. There's no point in arguing.

His touch ghosts along my jaw. "You'll be okay?"

"Always, right?" That's the response he expects, and I plan to follow through.

"Our paths will cross again, Peppy Girl."

My exhale is thick while I paste on a grin. There are no more tears to shed. "I'll never reject a reunion invite."

Mason flashes me his signature smile—framed by both dimples—that's reserved just for me. "Then I'll be seeing you."

chapter one

Presley

NOW

A POP SONG WITH A HYPNOTIC BEAT BEGINS BLARING FROM the speakers. It's one I instantly recognize from every other playlist and borders on being a broken record. That doesn't mean I'm able to resist the snappy rhythm. I shimmy my hips while mouthing the provocative lyrics. My seated dancing earns me a laugh from the snarky redhead beside me.

Vannah wiggles her brows. "Shake it, baby. You're damn hot."

"Better be careful or I'll jump your bones." I nudge my bestie with a wink.

She pouts. "Still treading sand in the Deprived Sea?"

My dramatic sigh says it all. If I don't laugh, only tears

wait to be shed. This dry spell could use a good quenching, and not for lack of trying. "Unfortunately."

"I bet Mr. Right For Tonight is about to walk in and sweep you away."

"Maybe." But my reply lacks conviction.

Her gaze trails behind us to the bar entrance. "Speaking of, are we placing wagers on when the happy couple will arrive?"

I flick my wrist to check the time. "Another hour, at least."

Vannah blows out a loud breath. "They're such horn balls. Don't they care that we're waiting on them?"

Amusement bursts from my lips in a sharp cackle. "Oh, you're one to talk."

She doesn't bother denying my soft jab. Instead, her ruby-stained lips curl into a knowing grin. There are no secrets between us. Savannah Simons is one of my closest friends. Along with Clea and Audria—who have yet to arrive—we form a tight-knit four-pack.

We all met during freshman orientation in college and just clicked. They're my dependable gal pal tribe that I can always rely on. I'd lose my luster—not to mention be horrifically lonely—without them.

Clea doesn't have a clue as to why we're gathering at this swanky joint. Her suspicions were stroked by our choice in bar. The downtown location is almost an hour from my home, but totally worth the drive. Knotty Knox reserved their entire patio for us without much fuss. The expansive area is currently covered with a tent structure as the fall season kicks in. Any hint of a chill is warded off. It's toasty, private, and damn cozy.

"At least we're waiting in comfort." I'll make the trip again for the top-notch service alone.

"The ambiance is rather polished. That doesn't make me any more patient, though." Vannah tosses her sleek hair over one shoulder with a grumble. Her restless irritability stems from genuine anticipation.

Nolan should be proposing to Clea at any moment, if all is going according to plan. He might be down on one knee right this second. I can perfectly picture the waterworks streaming down her cheeks while unyielding devotion spills from his lips. A jolly thrill flutters in my belly, and I'm not even the one getting engaged.

I stir my margarita with a smile, leaning forward to swallow a healthy gulp. "Just relax and enjoy your drink. We have the entire place to ourselves until the others get here."

Vannah takes a dainty sip of her vodka concoction. "Is there time for me to take Lannie in the bathroom for a quickie?"

Tequila gets stuck in my throat when I giggle. A very unladylike croak follows close behind. "You just finished telling me about the nerve-numbing orgasm that's still curling your toes. Has that already worn off? Landon might be losing his touch."

The man in question scowls at me from his stool next to Vannah. They just got married in June and are very much coasting in the honeymoon phase. He clears his throat pointedly. "That's never going to happen."

A dreamy glint highlights her flawless features as she ogles him. "He's right. The guy is extremely talented. That's why I can't get enough."

"Must be rough." I cluck my tongue, jealousy no doubt tinting me in a green hue. It's been too long since I've gotten properly laid. My dating life came to a screeching halt when those two lines appeared on the pregnancy test. My son will be three in January. Attempting to crunch the numbers isn't doing me any favors. At this point, my hymen is probably forming a reconstruction plan.

I wave that buzzkill off with a swat. "Anywho, we should sit tight and be ready to celebrate our friend's exciting news."

"Not sure why we can't start the party early. Everyone knows the best events start with a bang." Vannah gnashes her teeth with a purr. Sheer lust and hunger waft in every direction as she continues leering at her husband.

"Clea doesn't know she's the guest of honor. Well, maybe she does by now." I blow out a long breath to counteract the horny fumes secreting from her pores. As if I need to give my neglected hormones another reason to rage. "That's beside the point. They have Tally with them. You shouldn't be all flushed and mused."

She bats at the air. "That adorable little girl is seven, and clueless as to why I'd be disheveled."

Before I can provide an opposing—yet uplifting—response, movement in my periphery distracts me.

"Peppy?"

I swivel on my stool, jaw already halfway to the floor. The joint unhinges completely when I lock eyes with the owner of that alluring voice. My ex is hovering mere feet away in all his statuesque glory. His features are slack with a shock that mirrors my own.

My mouth goes dry at the sight of him. I snort at myself. *What a freaking cliché.* But the man is smoldering hot. I'm almost afraid to get scorched by his intoxicating heat at this range. The magnetic attraction that's been lying dormant explodes to the surface. I shiver involuntarily, goosebumps pebbling my skin despite the warmth enveloping me.

It's been six years since I've seen Mason Braxter, yet in this moment it feels like just yesterday. He's broader and more filled out—the toned definition of a professional football player. Time has been very kind to him.

The staple backward hat is tucked on his head. His cotton shirt is worn and faded, in the effortlessly casual style he always preferred. Dark stubble dusts his square jaw, somehow making the sharp angles more pronounced. I recognize him like a favorite pair of jeans. It would take zero effort to slip him on and let our history wear me out for a date.

I easily recall that devastating smile he offered as a parting gift. Mason is grinning now, but his features appear weary and strained. The edges of his mouth waver as if he isn't sure how to feel. Either that or he's forcing himself to put on a happy face. Probably the latter. This throwback clash might not be a blissful occasion. That reminder calms the giddy cartwheels wreaking havoc on my nerves.

Vannah sputters and begins hacking up a lung, effectively knocking me from the reverie. A mixture of vodka and soda shoots from her lips. "Peppy? Holy shit, if that isn't the greatest nickname I've ever heard. Please tell me he's talking to you."

Mason's brow furrows as he glances at her. The confusion clears when his focus returns to me. "This is quite a pleasant surprise."

My lips part with a soundless gasp. I try again, gulping at the knot lodged in my throat. "What are you doing here?"

His piercing green stare threatens to incinerate me. "In Minnesota?"

"This bar, more specifically." I jab a finger into the wood counter for emphasis. Last I heard, he was still in California recovering from an injury.

He hikes a beefy shoulder. "It's been a long-ass day and I need a beer. This place has excellent curb appeal."

I squint at him, scrutinizing the honesty in his eyes. "What are the odds?"

My question is rhetorical, but he humors me with a response. "Heavily in my favor."

A hum rises from me to agree with him. "This is definitely a surprise. Not to mention an extreme coincidence."

Mason steps forward. "Can I join you for a drink?"

I glance at my empty glass. A refill wouldn't hurt. "Are you alone?"

"Does it matter?"

My gaze strays to him without permission. "Not really."

"I'm all by myself. Take pity on me?" he cracks with a smile. Even after all these years, those dimples are still the death of me.

I laugh and shake my head. "Never have. Never will."

"That's my girl," he croons.

The all too familiar sentiment grates on old wounds and I wince. "Yikes, Braxter. Just diving right back in?"

"Force of habit." He holds up a palm in apology. It's probably my imagination, but a shimmer of pain passes through his gaze. "Let's catch up. I won't make it weird."

"Excuse me," Vannah interrupts. "This reunion special is super cute, but I missed the entire original series. I'm going to need a brief, albeit thorough, recap."

"Oh, whatever. I've told you about Mason." The rebuttal is weak, even to my own ears.

"Not a chance. I wouldn't forget stories about this one." She makes a zagging motion down his muscular physique.

"I did. He was my high school sweetheart. Right, Brax?" I bat my lashes at Mason for added impact.

Vannah snorts. "And that's about all the details you provided. He deserves far more."

Landon is quiet. Alarmingly so. His assessing gaze is pinned on my ex. "Are you the Mason Braxter from Central Cal and the 86ers?"

"The one and only." His monotone response lacks the enthusiasm I'd expect.

"Damn, you've cost me a lot of money."

"Shouldn't bet against me."

Landon chuckles. "Yeah, I figured that out. Learned my lesson last season. That arm of yours is a nuclear weapon."

"If only my knee didn't blow from the impact." A noticeable slump curls Mason's shoulders inward.

In a rare show of compassion, Landon cringes. "I saw that. Sorry, man. Those two pro seasons were killer, though. Your rookie year broke records."

"They're bonding," Vannah murmurs from the corner of her lips.

A cramp pinches my chest. "I hope Landon doesn't get attached."

"He's not a keeper?"

I sigh to release the brewing strain. "Not anymore."

She slurps at her cocktail until the contents are drained. "I can't believe you kept him a secret."

"Not on purpose." But that's a lie. After Mason left, just thinking about him ripped at my heart. I couldn't bring myself to reminisce about our relationship, even years later.

"Tell me about him."

"Later," I promise.

"Fine, fine. In the meantime, take a long stroll down memory lane and get reacquainted." Vannah mimics stroking a phallic object.

Fire stings my cheeks. "What? No. That's a terrible idea."

"Scratch that itch, girl," she hisses with a gleam in her eye. She tips her head toward him in an entirely unsuccessful attempt to be subtle.

I allow my eyes to land on him again. There's no denying that the suggestion is tempting. But this isn't Mr. Right For Tonight. This is Mason. Our past is messy.

That's when I notice the deep shadows swirling in Mason's eyes. A hollow gleam replaces the vibrant charm I couldn't resist. This isn't the boy I used to know. I've memorized the subtle cues from his facial features well enough to note that the man standing in front of me is carrying baggage. He's more jagged and broody. I find myself wondering what haunts him, but that's none of my business.

Mason must feel my blatant attention, putting an abrupt

end to his conversion with Landon. My temperature spikes with his gaze back on me.

"Can we talk, Pep?"

Vannah giggles in an uncharacteristic fashion. "Peppy Presley. Wow, that's better than my imagination could ever conjure. Just wait until Clea and Audria hear about this."

Mason narrows his eyes at her. "It's not a joke."

The bite in his tone makes me blanch. His blatant hostility is unexpected and new. Not that I can claim to know him anymore.

I break the tension cracking off him with a huff. "Don't mind her. Vannah is a brat."

"Pardon me for trying to lighten the mood." She mumbles under her breath about me gnawing on a bone.

"Why don't you see about that quickie?" The urge to shoo her twitches my fingers.

Her gasp is dripping with exaggeration. "Are you trying to get rid of me?"

My shoulders bounce as I laugh at her dramatics. "Yes."

"Fine, I can take a hint." Vannah digs in her purse. "I'll call Clea for an ETA."

Mason towers over me, bending forward until our cheeks almost brush. "Does that mean we have a minute alone?"

"I suppose." As if it's a hardship.

Relief crosses his expression, tension bleeding from his rigid posture. "So, this is unexpected."

"To say the least."

"Do you come to this bar often?" His watchful gaze scans our surroundings.

I can't stop a laugh from spilling. "Idle chit-chat? I thought you weren't going to make this weird?"

"Give me a second to recalibrate. It's been years since I've seen you."

The reminder is painfully unnecessary. "I'm well aware, Brax."

He has the decency to appear flustered. "Right, of course."

A nagging thought wiggles to the forefront of my brain. "Shouldn't you be with the team this weekend?"

"Keeping tabs on me?" He sounds far too pleased about that prospect.

"Just through the grapevine." I'll never admit it, but I follow the game schedule religiously. These fibs will catch me eventually. That's a worry for another day.

Vannah snaps her fingers, appearing out of nowhere. "Oh, it's all making sense."

Her pesky disruptions are beginning to irk me. Mostly due to this squirmy desperation to be alone with Mason. It wouldn't take much for me to collapse against him in a hormonal heap.

Just for a few minutes.

Or an hour.

Maybe the entire evening.

But by morning, we'll part ways.

I berate myself. Who knows if he'd even be interested. He likely already has a girlfriend back home.

Home.

That used to be in Meadow Creek, with me. That frigid reminder is enough to sober my wayward exuberance. Dammit. I can't let prior attachments keep me clinging to him.

My lovely bestie doesn't appear to notice my internal crisis. The look she pins on me is pure trouble. "No wonder you always make me watch football."

I squish a finger against her lips. "Hush."

But Mason catches her comment. Those tired emerald eyes brighten while remaining fixed solely on me. "You watched my games?"

"I might've caught a few."

"Quit playing coy, Press." Vannah swats my arm, then turns her gleeful expression to Mason. "This girl is your biggest fan. Has your jersey and—"

Now I clap a palm over her mouth, already stammering out an excuse. "That's, um. We don't need to get into—uh, she's joking."

"Do you?" The hope resonating from his voice shatters my denial.

I tip my face to the canvas ceiling with a silent curse. "Maybe. That doesn't mean I'm still pining after you or anything. It's just kinda cool that I had a personal connection to the star quarterback once upon a time. Call me sentimental or deranged or whatever. Just… don't read into it more than for vanity's sake."

He winces at my past tense phrasing. "I'm flattered."

"Good. It's a fairly large ego boost I suppose."

"That means you saw—"

"Yes," I blurt. However he intended to end that sentence had the potential to crush me.

His gaze burns into me. "Good."

Vannah fans her face. "Wow, this is getting steamy. You two have some serious unfinished business."

Mason ignores her yet again. "Can we talk, Pep?"

I bite the tip of my cocktail straw. "Aren't we already?"

"Somewhere with more privacy." His gaze strays to the couple pretending not to eavesdrop on us.

Landon chuckles and grips Vannah's elbow. "Let's give them some space, Sugar."

She pouts but allows him to steer her away. Before they're out of earshot, she points at me. "You better tell me everything."

I offer a wiggle of my fingers and a wink. "No promises."

Once they're out of sight, Mason slides onto the stool next to mine. He expels a loud breath. "She's a bit intense."

"Oh, that's just Vannah. You get used to her brash attitude. It's mostly a defense mechanism. She's come to my rescue more often than I can count. There's no one more protective or dependable."

"Not sure about that."

I quirk a brow. "You can't possibly be referring to yourself."

"And if I was?"

It's my turn to release a thick exhale. "Then I'll require a lot more liquor to survive this conversation."

chapter two

Mason

OLY FUCKING SHIT.

The expletive plays on repeat while I gawk at the raven-haired beauty sitting close enough to kiss. I still can't believe my luck. Presley Drake is in my presence. Not a day has gone by in six years without visions of her running through my mind. My thoughts wander to her almost automatically, regardless of the situation. That fascination has caused quite an inconvenience on several occasions.

But my obsessing finally conjured her.

Walking into Knotty Knox is one of the best decisions I've ever made. The likelihood of stumbling across her was almost impossible. It helps that I'm in Minnesota, fifty miles from Meadow Creek where we grew up, but the chances were still delusional at best. That overwhelming doubt was misplaced.

Static has replaced all common sense since catching sight

of her across the room. That crackling noise only gets louder when I lean in. A burst of wildflowers, summer sunshine, and reckless passion drags me into the past. Damn, she still smells the same.

My ravenous hunger bores into the woman responsible for every fantasy I've dared to dream. There's no other term to describe my undivided attention.

Presley dips her chin, peeking up at me through black lashes. "You're staring."

"Can you blame me?" I refuse to take my eyes off her in fear she'll vanish. She's far sexier than my memories gave her credit for. Blood rushes south at an alarming rate, creating a bulge behind my zipper.

She sucks in a sharp breath. "Wow, you're being awfully forward."

That's when I recall what she said before my brain nose-dived into the gutter.

"But you haven't left. Does that mean you'll humor me and accept another round?" I gesture to her drink.

Presley hums with a nod. "Yes, please."

"What're you drinking these days?" Not like I have the slightest clue what she prefers where alcohol is concerned.

"Margarita on the rocks."

I bob my head and signal to the bartender without removing my gaze from her. "Solid choice."

Her lips twitch. "Good thing it's strong. Sitting with you after all this time is very… exhilarating. In the best possible way, of course. I'm going through a kaleidoscope of emotions just being near you again."

A smirk of my own forms on reflex. "Sunny as ever, huh? I'm glad you haven't lost that sparkle."

Her blue eyes narrow on me. "Why would I?"

"Reality has a way of adding harsh complications." A dull

throb presses against my temple, attempting to snatch the joy she unknowingly provides.

Presley makes a noncommittal noise. "Aside from losing you and our breakup, I haven't had a reason to wallow."

"That's incredibly honest. And refreshing." Not to mention bold to admit. Although her filter has always been flimsy. That's one of the things I always loved about her.

She accepts her fresh margarita with a grin, pulling the straw between her teeth. "What did you expect, Brax?"

I tip the bottle of Coors to my lips. "Certainly not bumping into you at a random bar."

"That reminds me," she drawls. "Why are you in town? You haven't told me."

My sigh is rife with defeat. "Business, not pleasure."

"That's vague."

I grunt and sag lower in my seat. "It's not a simple answer."

"I'm not going anywhere."

A rock settles in my gut. "This isn't what I wanted to talk about first."

"You'd rather have me assume?" She taps her chin. "Maybe you're stalking me."

"If only I were that mysterious."

"You're stall-ing," she sing-songs.

"Okay, okay. It's reassuring to know you haven't gotten any less stubborn."

"Uh-huh." She lifts her brows, motioning me onward.

"Well, after I took that hit during playoffs, the doctors told me that I'd never play professionally again. My knee can't handle the pressure and I've been forced to consider other opportunities." At the mere mention, a blunt ache pulses through the joint.

It's been nine months, yet the pain feels fresh on occasion. My therapist assured me the sensation is mostly mental. I'm still not sure if that makes it better or worse.

"Oh, no. I had no idea your injury was so severe." Her hand rests on my arm. "That really sucks. Are you okay? How are you handling it? When did they tell you? Is it definite? Can you get a second opinion?"

Presley's barrage of questions eases the strain between my shoulders. That immediate concern rising to the surface is such a welcome relief. It's not the artificial sympathy I'm accustomed to. Her version is sincere and compassionate. The glassy sheen glittering in her gaze reveals that she truly cares. This tender display has nothing to do with prematurely ending an expensive contract. It's not about losing a lucrative client or valuable team member. She's just worried about me. Period.

That knowledge fills me with a warmth I haven't felt in over six years. Forget rehab and meditation and wishing my body didn't quit. All I need is encouragement from Presley to get me back on even ground.

"I'm all right. Better now," I confess with a smirk.

She rolls her eyes at my blatant flirting, but a noticeable blush blooms in her cheeks. "Such a charmer. You rebound fast, huh?"

If only. It's been an uphill struggle coping and adjusting to my new normal. There wasn't a spare second to prepare. Getting ripped from the highest peak of my life without warning causes a lot more than physical damage. Tension builds in my chest as oppressive shadows threaten to ruin the significant progress I've gained. I flex against the force, fighting the urge to punch a wall. Those dark thoughts don't get to intrude on us.

With a deep inhale, I chase the demons off. I can fake it for her sake. Besides, I'm suddenly finding that it's no longer a challenge to look on the bright side.

Presley is studying me with a keen awareness, taking notice of the shift in my mood. "Don't leave me hanging, Brax.

Tell me more about these other opportunities that I'm beginning to suspect brought you here."

My next exhale resembles a whoosh. "Perceptive as always, Pep. Since getting the bad news about my football career ending, I've been training to be a coach. If I can't play, then that's the next best thing. Isn't that a famous motivational phrase?"

"Seems legit." She appears riveted to my story, edging forward until our knees brush.

I sip at my beer. "There was a conference this past week in Minneapolis. I couldn't miss the chance to visit my old stomping grounds."

"Interesting."

"I aim to entertain." I paste on the wide smile that's made me popular with the media.

Presley frowns in return. "Any idea where you want to coach?"

Uncertainty slithers in my veins and I ditch the grin. "Not specifically. At the college level would be ideal. I've had a few approach me, but nothing set in stone. There's no chance I'll get offered a position in the NFL without experience."

"Makes sense. I'm sure you'll find just the right fit."

"Me too." But I'm no longer talking about a job.

She must catch my underlying meaning. Presley shivers and rubs the pebbled bumps on her arms. We sit in silent limbo until the tension swells to stifling. I tug at my shirt, suddenly desperate for a breeze. The last thing I want is to give her an excuse to leave.

"So, uh, what're you doing for work?"

"I'm actually my own boss."

"You started a company?"

Pride beams from her stretched grin. "Sure did. Clean Sweep. I'm a professional organizer."

The beer in my mouth dribbles out when I choke. "What?"

"Are you laughing at me?"

I press my mouth into a firm line. "Nope."

Presley pokes my chest. "It's a valid career. People need help getting rid of clutter. I'm very successful."

I glance down at her finger that's now tracing a tantalizing line along my pecs. Desire coils in my gut from that relatively innocent touch. "I believe you."

She catches my husky tone and snatches her hand away. "Good, you better. It's an incredible gig. I set my own hours and choose how many clients to take a week. The flexible schedule allows me to be with Archer whenever I have him."

"Who's Archer?" I lift my bottle, feigning cool and calm.

"My son."

I spew another mouthful of Coors. At this pace, my shirt will be little more than a wet rag by the end of the night. "You have a kid?"

Presley's smile radiates joy. "I do."

"Where is he?"

"With his father." Her casual tone reveals this to be common practice.

An acidic churning swirls in my stomach. This is the worst blindside I've ever experienced. "Do I know him?"

"I doubt it." Then she tilts her head in consideration. "Well, maybe."

"You're not going to tell me?"

"It's none of your beeswax, Brax." She flutters her lashes, more than comfortable calling me out on my shit.

A muscle tics in my jaw. "Are you together?"

Her giggle borders on shrill. "Oh no. Not even a little bit. We're good, though. Our system is fluid after two and a half years."

That response doesn't appease the riot that's surging into my veins. "Were you ever dating?"

Presley polishes off her cocktail with a slurp. "You're wading dangerously close to invading my privacy again."

"Fuck," I spit. My eyes clench shut while the storm inside of me rises. I don't know what I was expecting. It's not as if Presley would remain single and unattached in my absence. She's been busy living, just like me. That doesn't stop the selfish and primal urges from pummeling me. I can't come to terms with her moving on.

"What's this about?" She winces while making a circular motion around my face.

"I thought we'd always have kids together."

"So did I, once upon a time. But we haven't seen each other in six years. The tide shifted, Brax."

"Damn," I mutter.

Maybe she catches the gut-wrenching agony in my expression. She huffs. "If it makes you feel better, Archie is the product of too many shots and a really terrible social experiment. Total accident. A big ol' whoopsie. But I'd never take it back. Not even for a second."

I rip on the brim of my hat until it's facing forward. The sting blurring my vision is completely uncalled for. "Well, congratulations. I'm happy for you, Pep. Even if I'm having a tough time accepting it."

Her nod is slow, understanding ripe with the motion. "Want to see a picture of him?"

"Of course," I blurt.

She whips out her phone and opens an app. "I just took this yesterday."

A grinning toddler beams at me from the screen. Warmth spreads through my chest at the sight of him. Dirt smudges stain his cheeks. There might be some food speckles mixed in too. That startling blue gaze pulls me in with such a familiar potency. His mop of dark hair is in disarray, sticking up in numerous directions and resembling a faux hawk. I can admit he's adorable. "What a handsome fellow. He has your eyes."

"Thank you. He's my entire world." Presley sighs in that

way only a proud mama does. "Archie loves people and getting attention. Soaks it all in with a huge grin. Such a lush. He's getting to the point where he can verbalize his needs and communicate. Most of what he says doesn't really make sense yet, but it's fun to play along."

This strange sense of attachment takes root with a yank. "Maybe I can meet him someday."

She lowers her cell, tucking the device in her dress pocket. "Aren't you leaving soon if the conference is over?"

I blow out a heavy breath at the reminder. "Tomorrow, actually."

A realization seems to strike, a deep furrow creasing her brow. "You weren't going to call me."

"Pep," I start.

But she shakes her head. "If we didn't accidentally bump into each other, I wouldn't have known you were in town."

"It's complicated."

"Enlighten me." Her wounded expression could bring me to my knees.

"I wanted to see you, to the point of distraction. I could barely concentrate on anything else. But it's been so long. Any attempt I could've made felt futile without even trying. Besides, I wasn't sure how to reach you." The pitiful excuses weigh heavily on my shoulders and I slump. I'm such a fucking coward.

She crosses her arms. "My number is the same. Did you forget it?"

"Never." My fast response loosens the tension vibrating off her.

"You should've called. Years ago," she adds.

Failure brews into a putrid fog and I avert my gaze. "I didn't want you to see me like this."

"In fear I'd hump your leg?"

"In my dreams," I mutter.

"Oh, please. As if you're oblivious to your appeal. Don't take me for a fool."

"It's all an act."

"You can't fake these." She squeezes my biceps.

I flex on masculine instinct, and she laughs. "But that's just a polished exterior. I'm a disaster on the inside, Pep."

Presley tosses waves of glossy hair over her shoulder. "Lucky for you, I handle messes for a living. But that's beside the point. You didn't want to see me."

"Only because I'm ashamed."

The humor fades from her features. "Of what?"

"Who I've become." It pummels my pride to admit that, but I can handle the pain for her.

"Rich and famous?"

"Shallow and empty."

She recoils. "I don't believe that."

"Things haven't been the same since I left. Fame comes with pressure and expectations. I had to fit the mold. It's exhausting. Then I got hurt and everything went to shit." A groan escapes me. "I have no right to complain."

"Don't discredit your feelings. You're allowed to be disappointed. Feel free to vent."

I scrub a palm over my mouth. "But not to you. Not after all this time. I shouldn't drop my problems on your lap."

"Eh, I'd be more worried if you didn't."

"Still too fucking good, Pep."

Her expression brightens. "Thanks."

"I'm an idiot."

Presley winks. "That's correct."

"Still so damn honest too."

"It's one of my better qualities."

"Oh, I'm well aware." The temptation to bite my fist is powerful. "And that's a long list."

"It's only grown with your absence," she purrs.

A deliberate lob like that can't be ignored. "Damn, you're sexy."

"Thanks for noticing." She nibbles on her bottom lip. "At least that attention to detail hasn't changed."

"Not where you're concerned."

A rosy hue stains her cheeks. "Good one, Brax."

I can't hold back another second. "Would you have met me if I called?"

"Yes." There's no hesitation. Then she pauses. "But only if Archie was with his dad."

The fact she's protecting her son from me is troubling. Not that I have any room to protest. "It would've been a grave mistake to miss this. Forgive me?"

"There's nothing to forgive. You're right about us being different people, and I can't blame you. I'm the past. Why would the all-star athlete want to slum it with his ex-girlfriend who stayed behind in their small town?"

"It's not like that." Does she really think so little of me?

"If you say so." But she doesn't sound convinced.

"This was meant to happen randomly," I state with conviction.

"That's adding a positive spin." She waves her hands as if clearing the air. "Speaking of, enough gloom. I don't want to focus on the bad stuff. We're here by chance and should take advantage."

"There's the eternal optimist I love."

"Careful," she warns.

"Right, sorry." I guzzle what's left of my beer. "I'm forgetting myself. You're just so damn refreshing. I've missed being, well... me."

Presley's gaze is fixed on my throat as I swallow. "What, uh, time is your flight tomorrow?"

"Not until late morning."

A gleam enters her gaze. "Do you have plans for the rest of the evening?"

"Are you suggesting I stay?"

"Maybe."

I adjust on my seat with a scoff. "Now who's being vague and ominous?"

Her eyes roll skyward. "Talking to you has been nice, that's all. I wouldn't mind if you stuck around for another drink."

"I'm not going anywhere."

"Good," she exhales.

I feel that relief deep in my bones. With a raised arm, I blindly signal to the bartender. There's no removing my gaze from her captivating presence.

My foot taps a rapid beat on the wooden rung. I barely hear the stool squeak in protest against the agitated motion. The fact that I'm jittery is telling. I've felt the pressure from thousands of spectators without buckling, yet this woman has the power to unnerve me. "Are you dating anyone?"

"I wish," Presley mutters.

"Oh?" I lean in, erasing most of the distance forcing us apart.

"It's an inside joke. Never mind."

"So, there's no special guy in your life?" I need her to confirm it.

She shifts forward with an exhale, close enough to touch. "Other than Archie? Nope."

That mends a wound I didn't notice was still festering. The persistent throb in my temples ebbs. "I'm tired of pretending, Pep."

"Then stop," she whispers.

On pure instinct, I curl a palm around her nape and pull until she collides flush along my chest. Our mouths meet automatically. We melt into the intimate embrace, achingly familiar even after years apart. Our bodies remember what we were willing to ignore. Never again. I'm instantly transported to the days when this was as natural as breathing. It's everything I've been missing, yet not nearly enough.

Her tongue slips out to tease my bottom lip. I part my mouth on a groan. Teeth gnash while the heat builds. Hands wander with tempting touches, stoking the flames. She scoots to the edge of her seat, nearly straddling me. With each passing second that we spend tangled together, the unknown between us disappears.

My fingers spear into her hair and guide our movements. Presley is mine again, at least for a moment. That's a heady sensation and I haul her tighter against me. Feverish lust floods me when she nudges my cock with her pelvis. I'm hard and reeling, ready to suggest we ditch this public space.

Before I can do just that, Presley rips her mouth away with a gasp. "What was that for?"

"The last six years without."

chapter three

Presley

A SPUTTER ESCAPES ME AS I GAWK AT MASON. I LIFT TREMBLING fingers to my mouth, trapping the buzz lingering there. My lips are puffy from his rough treatment. A smile takes shape and I drop my hand. It's been so long since I've felt desired. That's an addictive high I want more of.

"You kissed me."

His heated stare is locked on mine. "I did."

"And you want to kiss me again." There's not a hint of doubt wavering my voice.

"I do."

My grin turns cheesy at his bold admission. "I can't believe you just went for it."

"Don't act surprised." He's right to call my bluff.

One thing hasn't changed—Mason has always gone after what he wants without fail. When we were together, that was a trait I admired, even when he stooped to reckless levels. His determination is what drove him to success. It certainly didn't bother me in this case.

I resist rolling over quite yet. "What if I dodged you?"

He grunts. "That would've hurt."

"As if I could deny you," I mumble under my breath.

Mason hears me, his smoldering expression gaining momentum. "I'm glad the attraction is mutual."

Is he joking? My chest is nearly heaving from a quick kiss. "You don't have to play the modest game with me. Chemistry has never failed us."

A rusty chuckle slices the tension. "That's a relief."

My brain trips over the gruff tune still rolling from him. "Ah, you can laugh."

"What?"

I flail an arm in his direction. "You've been so… serious. In a concerning, tortured hero sort of way. I was beginning to wonder if you'd lost that bottomless sense of humor."

"There hasn't been much to laugh about lately." His solemn tone deflates the ballooning need between us.

"Is it that bad?" From where I'm perched, he looks better than ever.

Mason shrugs, his eyes busy eating me for dessert. "I can't seem to recall at this very moment."

There's no controlling my squirm. "You're giving me a lot of credit."

"That you've earned. I'm cluttered junk and that just so happens to be your specialty." His wink is paired with a playful smirk. This man knows exactly how to push my buttons. Years of practice have honed it to an exact science. Am I falling for it? Maybe.

"You can hardly be considered work."

"Or you're just that good."

A pleasant tingle erupts over my skin. "Okay, Mr. Flattery."

"Will it get me everywhere?"

I fan my flaming cheeks. "Jeez, someone is laying it on thick."

Mason draws in a breath. "Would you prefer I go back to pretending?"

"Obviously not."

"Then you have to deal with my shameless flirting."

"Such a hardship." I accept my fresh drink from the bartender with a smile, whirling to focus on my ex again. "You're really twisting my arm."

"That's not where I want to touch you." He bites his bottom lip.

"Uh, wow. You're cranking the heat." I press the cool glass to my flushed skin for a brief reprieve. "We're reaching a point of no return."

Mason scoops up my palm, lacing our fingers together. "It's easy to get lost you in, Pep."

Flutters wreak havoc on my system. I tuck some hair behind my ear, a visible tremor making the move sloppy. All pretense that I'm not flustered has long flown out the window. "What happens now?"

"You tell me."

The answer waits on the tip of my tongue, but I hesitate.

My body is practically vibrating with desperate need. I shake off what's left of the fog that he put me under. This decision requires logical thinking, which has all but fled the building. I mean, this is Mason freaking Braxter. He's not just a random dude I'll forget once the afterglow wears off. Our history adds layers of complications, but also a comfort I won't receive from a one-night stand.

I bite my lip, glancing to the far corner where Vannah is talking on the phone. Her animated hand gestures suggest she might be trying to hurry Clea along. There's still time before the happy couple arrives.

The desire in my veins regenerates with a hot surge. Those smoky tendrils of lust will only grip me tighter and tighter with every second I continue to sit beside him. That hollow ache won't be satisfied by my own methods.

Letting him scratch my extremely chaffed itch wouldn't be a challenge. The somewhat practical reasons rise to the forefront. First, we've been intimate often enough that it won't be awkward. Second, there's zero doubt Mason will get me off. And last, but certainly not least, the man is a prime example of what fills my clit closet. Big shocker there.

He's always been the one I could see a future with. The true object of my affection. But now? Mason tests the strength of that cotton shirt whenever his muscles bunch. Drool pools in my mouth. Holy sex on a stick. This is like an updated version with extra sides of secrets and brooding.

Yes, please. I'll have a heaping serving of that.

Am I actually considering this? Without a doubt. If Vannah finds out, she'll never let me live down the hypocrite status. I can't find one shit to give.

Mason watches me process the options with a silent contemplation of his own. He tightens his grip on my hand, as if I'm about to fly off this stool. A whimper lodges in my throat as his finger gently traces circles on my inner wrist. Damn, I really need to get laid. That indisputable fact settles my mind.

I rub my bare calf against the denim covering his. "We could continue reminiscing."

"And how might we do that?" His voice drops several octaves.

"What are the chances you want to get reacquainted in a more physical sense?"

A fiery blaze ignites in his eyes. "Peppy Girl, are you suggesting we sleep together?"

"Very much so."

"Do you live close by?"

"Not really, but in the general vicinity. I was thinking somewhere even more convenient, though." I hitch a thumb over my shoulder.

His focus trails to where I'm pointing. "Inside the bar?"

"The bathroom is very spacious—and single capacity."

"There's room for two?" Mason rubs my knuckles that are bent around his.

"Uh-huh."

"So, we're doing this?"

I nod with conviction echoing the action. "One more time, as closure? Get rid of this… unresolved tension?"

"You don't want to see me again?" His hurt expression threatens to douse the fire in my lower belly.

"Never said that, but I also don't expect to. No promises, right?"

"Okay," he concedes.

"Don't agree strictly for my benefit."

"Trust me," he assures in a growly tone. "There's little else I've thought about over the past six years."

I could make the same statement, but that isn't wise. I have to keep emotions out of this or I'll never recover. Mason lives halfway across the country. We're just having a quick one and done.

With yet another internal debate nixed, I gulp at my margarita for liquid courage. "Ready?"

Mason mirrors my actions. "Should I toss you over my shoulder and haul ass to the hallway?"

That image elicits a molten throb and I knock my knees together. "Maybe a little less conspicuous."

"If you insist." He stands and steers me with a palm on my ass to our destination.

I peek up at him. "Staking your claim?"

His fingers dig into my flesh with a possessive squeeze. "I'll use any excuse to touch you, Pep. This is just the beginning."

For tonight, I remind myself silently. To him I say, "You're going to get me riled up."

"Isn't that the point?" Mason glances behind us to check for followers, then shoves the bathroom door open. "Ladies first."

I saunter in with added sway to my hips. After a flawless whirl on my heel, I beckon him forward. A startling realization strikes me, one that didn't concern us before. It almost pains me to ask. "Please tell me you have protection."

His gaze leaps to mine, a lashing from my own hand reminding us of our years apart. That silent exchange lingers and ebbs between us. Then he nods and digs out his wallet. A sharp jab hits me at the awareness of him carrying around condoms, but we wouldn't be doing this if that weren't the case. I shove the harmful thoughts away with a huff.

Mason notices, lifting his brows in question. "Problem?"

"Not at all. Suit up, Ten."

He pauses deft fingers that had been unbuttoning his jeans. "Oh, it's been a long time since I've heard that."

Dammit, that's what I used to call him in high school. His jersey number was still ten last time I checked. "It just slipped out. Don't overthink my flimsy filter."

"I never do."

Rather than roll the rubber down his length, he prowls forward and kneels in front of me. Mason skims a palm up the back of my leg, sliding under my modest hem. Goosebumps rise in his wake and I shiver against the rising heat. His hum is steeped in approval. "This dress was a smart choice."

"Without the intention of getting laid," I quip.

He peers up, his earnest green gaze imploring me. "Does that make me special?"

"Of course." Truth serum drops off my tongue with the easy confession.

A rumble escapes him. "Fuck, that's sweet."

Mason tugs at my thong and I shimmy to help him along. Once the scrap of lace is untangled from my ankle, he shoves the bundle into his pocket. I watch his deliberate movements with a squint.

"Really?"

A lazy shrug is his immediate answer. "Am I not allowed to have a souvenir?"

A sour gurgle passes through my stomach. "I can only imagine how many trophies you've collected over the years."

"Just yours." His quick response sounds like a placating line, but it appeases my territorial needs all the same.

"Yeah, okay."

In a tight fist, he collects the flouncy material that's maintaining my modesty. Mason hitches the bunched fabric around my waist and exposes me to the chilled air. He leans in, smelling me in lewd fashion. "Delectable."

A moan escapes me. "I see your mouth is still dirty."

"It's your fault." He drags his tongue through my folds and I nearly collapse.

My palm slaps the tile I'm leaning against. "Get inside me. I can't handle foreplay."

His nose bumps my clit as he dismisses my command. "Just a taste."

"If you insist," I recycle his easier phrase with a giggle. But who am I kidding? There's already a pleasant warmth thrumming in my veins. If the man wants to take the edge off, I'm going to let him.

My feet leap from the floor at his next swipe. Mason chuckles and I almost whimper. My libido is singing his praises and wants to be petted.

Down girl. Relief is coming soon.

"So sensitive," he murmurs against me.

"It's been a while."

His lips tease me with gentle suction. "How long?"

"That's personal."

"More personal than me on my knees, giving you pleasure?"

I spear my fingers into his hair, guiding him onward. "Forty-one months and some loose change."

"That's oddly specific."

"Less talking. More licking." I wiggle my hips in impatience.

Mason clucks his tongue. "What the lady wants, she needs to ask for nicely."

Did he develop a begging kink? I can work with that. "Please, Brax. I want you to make me come."

"Say my name," he demands.

"Mason," I exhale. "Please."

He shudders, then swoops in to do my bidding. Sizzles erupt along my limbs while he feasts on me. I should probably feel somewhat self-conscious with his face buried between my thighs. The guy is getting an extreme close-up with my lady bits, but I can't find the mental power to care.

His groan bounces around the small space. The salacious noise makes it sound like he's devouring his favorite meal. My cheeks sting, but the burn is instantly forgotten when he latches on my clit. A tightly wound coil snaps inside of me. I open my mouth to scream, slapping down a palm to trap the sound. My babbling nonsense must encourage him. He begins really getting after me—deep pussy diving style—with a newfound frenzy. Sparks shoot across my vision as I topple off the peak.

"Oh, Sweet Mother of Orgasms. That's incredible." I tip my head back while the prickling relief thrums through me.

"Good?" Mason straightens from his crouched position, wiping over his grin.

"Better than I remember." I haven't felt this relaxed in ages. Every bit of me is sighing in relief. "Well worth the wait."

"Fuck, babe. Keep those compliments coming. You're good for my ego."

"And you're about to be bad for my unnecessarily long celibacy."

"Yeah," he grunts. "Let's put an end to that."

I walk my fingers up his chest. "By all means, go ahead."

That's all he needs to hear. Mason whips out his dick and rolls the condom on. I barely get a look at my long-lost friend before he's hoisting me up. My legs instinctively wrap around him, crossing at the ankle against his ass. I'm effectively boxed in a cage of his arm's creation. His broad frame towers over me.

"I've missed you." He cups my jaw in a tender hold, sincere affection shining in his gaze.

A lump instantly forms in my throat. "Don't, Brax."

His eyes search mine for answers I refuse to give. "I can't be honest?"

The noise I emit is pitiful. "Don't make me regret this."

"As if you ever could."

"There's the cocky boy I know."

"That's where you're wrong, babe." His smirk is pure trouble, a warning to heed. "I'm all man."

Any chance of a retort is cut short as he plunges into me with a punishing thrust. I'm slick with arousal, making his rough entry a smooth glide. The smoldering embers within are being stoked as he forces me to accept each steely inch. My mouth gapes open on a breathy gasp. I bang my head against the tile wall, letting my lashes flutter shut as the forgotten burn settles into me. An ache streaks out from my center in a fiery rush. The dull throb is a painful pleasure that has me rocking against him. When he pulls out, I hiss between my teeth. My body stretches to accommodate his next harsh intrusion.

"How I've needed this," I purr while going limp in his grasp.

Mason dips his face into the crook of my neck. "Did I break you already?"

"Hmmm," I sigh. I was right earlier—he slides on like my favorite pair of jeans. "Just taking it all in."

"Yeah, you are." He draws his hips back and slams in, a steady rhythm being coordinated. His cock is buried to the hilt and I clench around his length.

"You're so big," I mewl.

"It's a tight fit, but just right." His correction makes my toes curl.

Giddy zings ricochet in my belly. I shouldn't let the whimsy get to me. A passionate breeze carries the resistance away. His woodsy cologne assaults my nostrils while I drag in a deep breath. I'm choosing to enjoy every aspect—temporary reprieve or not.

Our tempo is rushed and fast, a furious pounding to provide instant gratification. I'm all for it. Can't get enough, really. His huge palms latch on my ass, spanning me in entirety. Those massive paws are responsible for clinching national championships and awards, but he handles me as if football was merely practice. He uses his grip to thrust in and out at a punishing pace. I'm just here for the ride, and he's proving to be more capable than ever at delivering a thrilling spin. It won't be a shock if I get bucked off.

"Damn, you're good."

"That should never be up for debate." Mason nips my chin.

"It's been a long time."

"Too long."

The reminder pierces the blistering fervor, a sting sharp enough to ruin the mood. I clench my inner muscles until he grunts. "Who's fault is that?"

"Let's not argue over details while I'm balls deep inside of you, yeah?"

"Just keep going." I squeeze his hips between my thighs, locking him in.

He pumps forward with a savage thrust. "Nothing could stop me."

Tendons flex and bulge as we chase relief. I roll my pelvis when he hammers forward, flesh slapping against the cool wall behind me. Mason seduces me with each stroke. I'm ready to surrender. The empty gnawing in my belly is sated as he glides into me with a long stroke. I thrash in the confines of his arms. A shout rips from the neglected depths inside of me.

Raw hunger is ripe in the air. I inhale the heady scent of our combined desire. Each grunt and moan prods at my bubbling lust. My nails scrape against his scalp as I haul him closer. The smoke billowing between us could cause a fever. Tingles are fast spreading, the impending orgasm within reach. My core cinches him in a punishing grip while I race for the edge.

"Fuck, you're so responsive to me. Not gonna last," he grits.

"That's fine. I'm about to…"

My words trail off in a loud moan as relief pours over me. I tumble into the luxury of him wrapped around me. The pleasure is a hot sweep, knocking me from reality. I soar on a rippling wave as the crashing tide takes me under. The spasms still have me in their hold when Mason goes rigid against me. With a final thrust, he stills with a muffled curse. Heat washes over me anew. That liquid warmth flows through my veins.

"Um, wow." I'm lulled into a calm state as Mason pulls out and cleans up.

His chest rises and falls at a rapid rate. "I don't hear you complaining now."

My gaze is riveted on a trickle of sweat streaking his skin. I have the sudden urge to lick him. "Check later. All rational thought was screwed out of me."

He presses against me again, a pillar to ensure I don't fall on my butt. "Satisfied?"

"Yep." I pat his chest. "That's how you end a dry spell."

His chuckle fondles my overly sensitive bits. "I'm glad I could be of service."

"Me too, champ. It was great catching up."'

Mason rests his forehead against mine. "We should do this again sometime."

"Like in an hour or two?"

He searches my gaze, brushing our noses together. "Sure, let's go with that."

chapter four

Mason

"ARE YOU LISTENING TO ME?"

I'm yanked from another salacious replay by Paul's nasally voice. The vision of Presley squirming in pleasure is replaced by his bored scowl. What a damn boner killer.

The grin I force is faker than his tan. "No."

"You could lie."

I slouch lower in the leather chair, sprawling my legs wide. "Not my style."

My agent—and so-called friend—pinches the bridge of his nose. "Yeah, yeah. You're always walking on moral high ground."

There's no trapping my scoff. "I'll take that as a compliment."

"As I was saying," Paul drones. Then he proceeds to pick up where he left off, which is apparently LSU.

He's been pressuring me to choose a job since the anesthesia wore off after my surgery. The fog had barely lifted before he started shoving new contracts at me. The man is a shark—one of the best in the business. He's driven by being served his piece of the pie. All I've received from him is a list of possible options, yet his commission will be a hefty percentage. The fucking red tape never gets cut.

I feign enough interest to be sure Paul won't question me again, but my mind is already wandering right back between Presley's thighs. Damn, she's sweet. Her tangy honey flavor still peppers my tongue.

His beady gaze narrows on me, catching my drifting attention once again. "Where's your head been lately, Braxter?"

In Minnesota with the memory of screwing Presley against the wall, but he doesn't need to know that. Her moans have haunted my every waking moment for the past week. Don't even get me started on my dreams. If it weren't for Paul's expectant gaze latched on me, I'd be popping wood hard enough to rip seams. An uncomfortable tightness spreads across my lap and I adjust to hide any awkward evidence.

Another vision forms to further distract me. Fuck, I really am a mess. When I'm not obsessing over our bathroom tryst, I find myself wondering about Presley's son. A displeased and disgusted grunt escapes me. I scrub a palm over my mouth. These whiplash musings make me seem like a creep. That doesn't mean I stop the boomerang from taking flight. It all boils down to me missing too many years and experiences. I refuse to lose more. The details on how to accomplish such a feat are still fuzzy.

I force my concentration to land on the task at hand. At least, what Paul wants me to focus on. He's been yapping for an hour and I can't recall more than a few words. The papers piled on his desk give the gist. I'm supposed to choose five schools from the stacks and visit their football programs. From where I sit, the colleges and universities he gathered don't make my cut.

"I'd like to do my own research."

He recoils as if I'd slapped him. "Why? You're paying me to do the initial surveys."

"And I may be regretting it if these are the best options."

Paul sputters, adjusting the glasses on his face. "Come again?"

That's precisely my plan with a very specific woman in mind. "None of these feel like the right fit."

"But these are the best programs in the country." He lifts his bushy brow. The curious expression doesn't fit with his typically mundane disinterest. One clear point has manifested from this drivel—something needs to change.

I've been wallowing for too long. More than enough time has passed, but I'm still stuck in a rut. I realize now that my motivations were lost. After getting hurt, the future was a black void. I didn't know what direction to turn. It was a bottomless pit, the drop a painful spiral that I couldn't control.

The only thing that eased that ache in my chest was her. Since I returned to California last week, that pressure has flooded back tenfold. My goals have shifted, whether planned or not. The sport no longer takes priority. I need substance and roots.

A beautiful, sunny smile pops into my mind. Presley defines stability and value and meaning. But more than that, she represents what I've lost. The sacrifice I never should've made. I shouldn't have left her. She shouldn't have let me. That fateful morning, we tossed out a shot at true love. But we're in this together again. I'll make sure of that.

Presley is the path leading I was meant to take, but I ignored the pull. Now she's a mother with responsibilities I can't fathom. It's nothing short of a miracle that she's single. Somehow. I'll only add a complication to the fluid system she mentioned. But maybe I can do more. I can fix this and be better. For them.

Football has been good to me. Unbelievably so. Every athlete dreams of playing professionally and I had that chance. My career was cut short, but two years is more than most will have. I'll never take the opportunities gifted to me for granted. That being said, the last six years have been filled with destructive turmoil. Between my contract and sponsorships, I'm set financially for at least three years. I'll get a job where I want. The freedom to choose is mine to take.

"Let's narrow our search to the Midwest." The seat creaks when I recline.

Paul's brows hike skyward. "Why would we do that?"

"I want different scenery. A fresh outlook," I explain.

"Weren't you raised in Minnesota?"

"Your point?"

"This is an important decision that shouldn't be taken lightly. You're being reckless and impulsive."

"I'm serious." And won't cave on this decision.

He scoffs. "Oh, please. I've seen this situation play out countless times. Something—or someone—is calling you back there. The heart is a foolish organ. Use your brain, kid."

"You have no idea what you're talking about." I'm choosing to ignore the fact that his assumption is spot on.

"I do," he insists while puffing out his chest. "And you need to listen. The most lucrative positions are on the coasts. I've found several bowl-caliber teams willing to take a chance on you. Take your pick from east, west, or south."

"I'm most interested in the north." My thumb points to the ceiling for emphasis.

His refusal is a disapproving frown. "That isn't an option."

The force in his tone has me sitting upright. My knee jerks

at his words. I should leave. Most would. But my reputation is already tainted. I don't need to give the press another reason to cast me as rotting trash.

"This isn't your choice, Paul."

"Take my advice. I have your best interest in mind."

I almost choke on the stench of artificial sincerity. "Either you look where I'm pointing, or I'll do it myself."

"Damn stubborn pride," he spits. "Don't let the past cloud your judgment. You'll regret it."

"The present company is doing a fine job of that."

"I thought you wanted to coach at the professional level? The NFL has astronomical standards." His smug expression isn't appreciated.

"Well, sure. That doesn't mean it's going to happen."

"It could, but the odds will plummet if you accept a backseat role at some Podunk school in the middle of nowhere."

"There are plenty of excellent schools in Minnesota."

"Not of the same caliber," Paul counters. "Clearly you're not prepared to be logical about this. Take a few days to reconsider. This is your future, remember. You don't want to throw it away."

He won't let this go without a fight. I don't have the patience to argue. Nor do I care enough about his opinion. I made the worst mistake of my life six years ago. Repairing the damage is long overdue.

"Sure," I relent while getting to my feet. "We'll talk again soon."

Paul's expression brightens with victory. "Good. Tell Jill to get an appointment on my schedule for later this week."

"Will do." But that's a lie. I stroll from his office without a single regret, feeling lighter than I have in ages.

Paul might believe this is career suicide, but I couldn't care less. I'm finally seeing ahead clearly. Presley waits at the end of this dark tunnel. There's no convincing me otherwise.

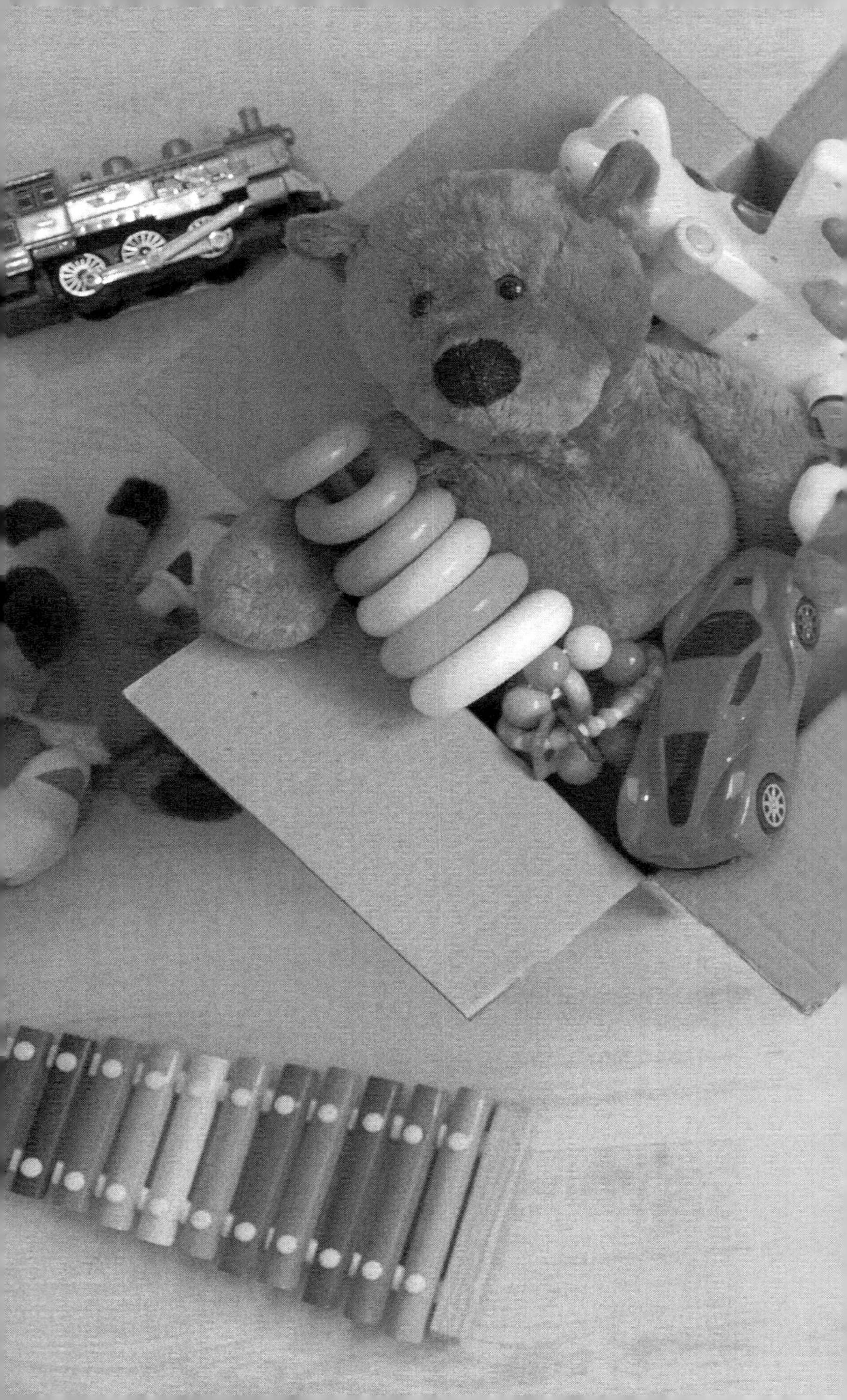

chapter five

Presley

CLEA TILTS HER HEAD, POINTING A FORK AT ME. "You had s-e-x."

I laugh at her not-so-subtle spelling method to avoid little listening ears. A sideways glance shows Archie scribbling on his paper menu without pause. The stickers he got from my purse provide cartoon accents. Or problematic roadblocks for his crayons. Either way, he's entertained.

My focus shifts forward to address Clea's knowing grin. "Like a week ago. It's old news."

She collapses into her chair with a huff. Her platinum bob glitters under the afternoon sun. It's a warm fall day, allowing us to eat on the patio. "I'm losing my touch."

"Did you have a keen just-got-laid sense to begin with?"

"I might've just lost my virginity two months ago, but that

didn't make me blind to the signs. Especially when the person is glowing brighter than Rudolf's nose."

I slap a palm to my cheek. "What? No. Am I really flushed?"

She winks at me. "Eh, not even slightly. But your reaction further proves my point. It must've been a good bang. Who was he?"

"My ex." It takes Wonder Woman strength to maintain a level tone. The reminder of what Mason did to me at Knotty Knox is sure to get a real blush rising to the surface.

"The one at my party?" She'd been too high off getting engaged to notice many other details. Or guests. That also kept her off my hussy trail.

Mason and I snuck off once more after our initial romp. The five orgasms he blessed me with are still pulsing under my skin. That buzz might stave off my cravings for another three years. I suppress a grin, gnawing on my bottom lip. Or until he visits again.

Clea's gasp knocks me from the memory. "You did it at the bar."

There's no use denying the obvious. "So?"

"That's why you disappeared during Nolan's toast."

I wince. "Bad timing. Sorry I missed it."

"Oh, it's fine. You're forgiven, and properly satisfied for a change. Or I hope so." She narrows her eyes.

"Yes," I laugh. "He took exquisite care of me."

Clea wags her brows. "I bet he did. There's a fragrant spritz of reconciliation in the air. Does this mean the flames are rekindling? Second chance romances are my favorite."

I shrug, feigning indifference. "Ah, nope. Mason lives in California."

She pouts. "That's unfortunate."

"It's a bummer, but that's one of the reasons I agreed to sleep with him."

"Um, that's a weird deciding factor. Why does it matter?"

A complex tangle tightens in my belly. "Next time we have a girls' night, I'll give you all the details. Vannah has been hounding me all week and I'd prefer to retell the tale just once. The gist is that there's a complicated history between us. I wouldn't have waded into those turbulent waters if he lived here. Too messy."

"Wait." She holds up a palm. "You wouldn't have let him shag you dirty if he was local?"

I chance another peek at Archer. His tongue is sticking out as he concentrates on doodling elaborate swirls. He couldn't care less about what we're talking about. That means I can continue pleading my case until I'm blue in the face.

"No, definitely not." But the thrum in my veins betrays the lie. There's little doubt I would've jumped his bones regardless of where he sleeps at night. Thankfully, I didn't have to make that choice.

Clea gapes at me. "I'm failing to see how him being readily available is a bad thing."

That's not surprising considering her true love lived right next door for years. It doesn't get more convenient than that. But her journey with Nolan was riddled with challenges. I can't easily explain my hesitation without shoving a foot in my mouth. Talk about a slippery slope.

"It took me years to mend my heart after he left. This way I'm not looking forward to potentially seeing him again. There's no chance. We had a great time, and it's over. Cut and dry. No plans to be made."

"That's rather pessimistic of you. I'm usually the Blue Belle of our bunch." She quirks a brow.

"No, it's realistic. I won't be disappointed when he doesn't call." The smile I showcase is all teeth and exaggerated enthusiasm.

She scoffs at my antics. "How sad. You looked so happy with him."

It hurts to acknowledge that I was. He's always done that for me. But I need to let go, permanently. "That's just our past tying us together. Mason is familiar and easy to be with. We click, you know?"

"Mhmm, do I ever." Her wink is way over the top.

"Don't make it sound so salacious," I giggle.

"The sparks were flying across the room. You almost stole my thunder."

It's my turn to huff. "That's ridiculous."

"Well, yeah. It's hard to overshadow me when Tally is my personal amplifier. That little turkey retold the proposal story a dozen times. She even shouted it once or twice. But the fact remains. He made you shine really bright."

My grin wobbles at the edges. "It was nice to see him again. I got my closure. Our story feels more complete now."

She must sense my brewing distress. "Okay, fine. Mason is out of the picture. We'll find you someone better."

There's no masking my cringe. Sadly, Mason Braxter is the best I can imagine. Anyone else will be a poor substitute until I can get over him. Again. "Uh, that's not necessary. I'm good. The kitty has been properly scratched."

Clea is already shaking her head. "Nice try, Press. I refuse to watch dust collect in your flower. A bee needs to pollinate you with his big stinger."

I snort out a very unattractive laugh. Our creative language is cracking me up. "We don't need to discuss my coochie cobwebs. Shouldn't we be planning your bachelorette party or something?"

"Or something is right. We're focusing on your happily ever after, beech. You're the last one standing single."

"No need to remind me. I'm already planning my spinster tattoo," I tease.

"Then make this easy on me. What's the next stop in your dating life? What can I do to help? I'll gladly sit in as your wing woman."

My son smacks the table and sends crayons flying. Saved by the toddler. I almost wipe my brow.

"Mama," Archer coos. He holds up his paper. "'Ook! So pity."

I give him a wide smile. "Very pretty, sweetie. Great job coloring."

"Oh, yes." Clea leans closer to get a look. "You're such an artist, Archie."

He beams at her. "I did it!"

"You did it," we say in unison.

"Ah done. Stomp, stomp!" He stands on the wooden seat and begins pounding his feet.

"Oh, little man wants to dance?" Clea gets up and reaches for him. "I've got you handled, Archie."

I watch them spin and twirl, soaking in the cheerful joy. "Gosh, who needs hired help when I have friends like you?"

"Just practicing." She squints at some random spot in the distance. "Or refreshing, I guess. Tally gave me a solid introduction."

I drop my cup to the table with a clank. "What? Are you trying?"

"No," she scoffs. But her blush reveals the truth.

"You eager beaver," I spew. "I'm so proud of you."

"Only you would be."

"Not even. Vannah and Audria will sing your praises in tune with me. Heck, Audria will probably plan to get preggers with you. She wants to fill an entire classroom with Reeve's babies. I think all that country air is going to her head, but more power to her."

"Yeah, I'm not that adventurous." Clea laughs and boops

Archie on the nose. "But I feel prepared for another one of these. That internal clock is ticking."

I rest my chin on an open palm. "You've been dreaming of being a family with Nolan and Tally since we met. I'm almost shocked you're not already knocked up."

Her expression turns wistful and a bit misty. "Do you want more kids?"

"I dunno? Maybe." But the real answer should be yes. Only with a certain quarterback, though. I'll file that under *never going to happen*.

"Clelee," Archie tugs on Clea's sleeve. "Poop."

She blinks at him, as if his literal message isn't quite clear enough. I wait with a grin slowly spreading. When my son sticks his butt in her face, recognition dawns in her expression.

Her expectant gaze swings to me. "Someone made you a present, Mama Bear."

A bull couldn't snort louder than me. "Oh, no. You're on diaper duty. Good practice, right?"

"I've changed plenty," she retorts.

I swat the space between us. "It's been years since Tally was potty trained. Your skills are rusty at best."

She grumbles a bit, mostly for Archer's benefit. He giggles when she plugs her nose. With chubby fingers, he pinches his own to mimic her. I pass her the diaper bag with a grin. Clea scoops him into her arms, blowing a raspberry on his tummy. My kiddo is blessed to have such incredible pseudo aunts.

Once they're bounding out of sight, I glance at my phone. Zero notifications welcome me. The plummet in my stomach is too familiar. Dammit, this wasn't supposed to happen. But there's no denying this empty pang that only my love for him can fill.

After sleeping with Mason, I felt this visceral attachment trying to reform. I often find myself wondering what he's doing, against my better judgment. Allowing him to clog my brain is a sure way to get stuck. That's a dead end I don't need to travel down. It was damn near impossible to move on after he was gone. That daunting task seems to plague me once again.

As if I ever got over him to begin with.

My critical inner dialogue isn't appreciated. I can admit to being disappointed that Mason hasn't called or texted, but that admission will only slightly delay the downward spiral. The urge to bang my head on the table is fierce. I was very specific about no expectations, yet my effing heart didn't get the memo.

With a slow and therapeutic sigh, I roll my shoulders back. The dwelling is done. No more wishing for the impossible. It's time to dust off the gloom and aim for sunny skies. This is what I'm good at. I control my mood, and I choose happiness. There are no regrets—that's not my style.

Clea skips back to the table with a giggling Archie on her hip. Her joyful gait pauses when she looks at me. "Everything all right, Press?"

The smile I offer is genuine, albeit crooked. "Yep, just recalibrating."

"That sounds painful."

I brush off her concern with confidence stabilizing my grin. "Don't worry about me. I'll always be okay."

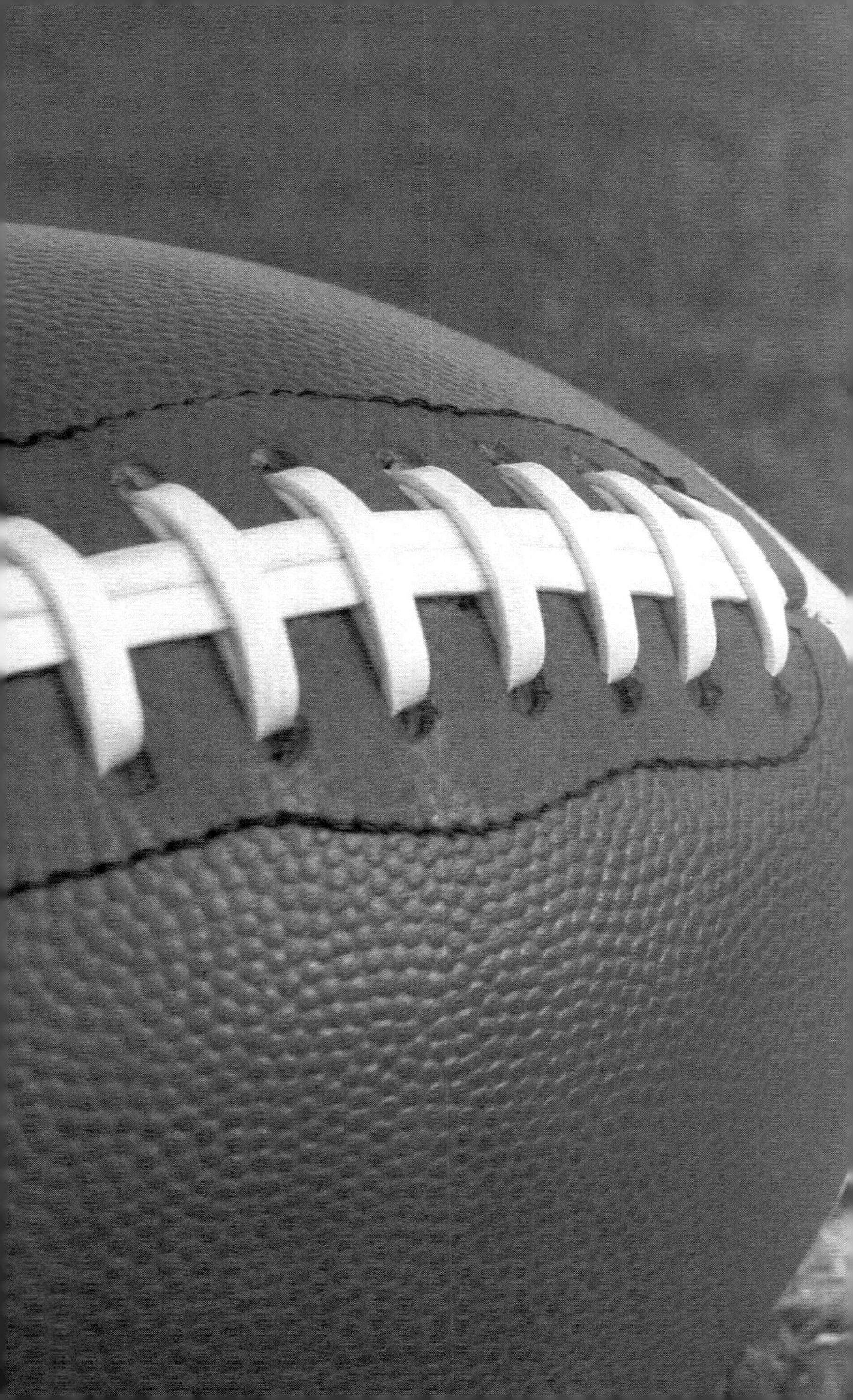

chapter six

Mason

A MID-MORNING HOUR FELT LIKE THE BEST TIME TO DROP BY unannounced. Not that the numbers on a clock will significantly impact how this visit will be perceived. I walk at a pace that suggests a leisurely stroll, but nerves thunder in my pulse. Maybe I should've called first.

This is a bold approach, even for me. But I didn't want to give Presley the opportunity to deny me. How will she react to me randomly showing up at her house? Only one way to find out.

I press the bell, rocking on the balls of my feet. My skin itches as voices from inside threaten to burst into my temples, one in particular edging closer. It's all I can do to keep a lid on my impulses. The door swings open and there she is, far exceeding the vision I've fabricated in my mind. All of the air gets sucked from my lungs and I nearly gasp.

Presley blinks, those gemstone eyes wide and glittering with disbelief. I don't blame her extended silence considering my unexpected arrival.

"Umm," she sputters. "What're you doing here?"

I recall her first words to me at Knotty Knox being quite similar. "In Minnesota?"

Her face sharpens into a narrow point. "At my house, Brax."

The use of my generic nickname is a slight dig at me. She's erecting walls, reinforcing her guard, and trying to keep me at a distance. I've been too far away for too long. When she calls me Ten regularly again, that will be my cue to proceed with the plan. For now, I'll settle with taking baby steps in the right direction.

"I just wanted to say hi." As if this is a completely normal occurrence.

She looks bewildered, jaw slack and lashes fluttering. "What? I thought you were back in California."

My nod is slow. "I was."

"And now you're here?"

"I'm being spontaneous," I reason with a grin that's meant to be charming.

"More like reckless and impulsive." Presley folds her arms, hip cocked at a haughty angle. "You're making a habit of randomly appearing. I have a phone, you know. Feel free to use it rather than just bursting in out of the blue."

"Am I unwelcome?" I frown at the mere idea.

She purses her lips. "You know the answer."

"Wouldn't hurt to hear it."

Her huff reminds me of the teenage girl I first fell for. "I'm glad to see you, of course. This just… isn't a good time."

An unpleasant twinge stabs at my chest. "Why?"

"You don't need a reason." A hint of a smile curves her mouth, even as she tries to remain neutral.

"It might get rid of me faster if that's what you're trying

to accomplish." I won't admit how much the potential of that stings.

"I shouldn't have to get rid of you." Something seems to occur to her, and she pins me with an imploring stare. "How'd you find out where I live?"

That gets a chuckle from me. "I bumped into Millie Jeston while pumping gas. She spilled the beans all on her own, assumed I was heading this way. Saved me a hassle."

"So much for my circle of trust," she mumbles.

I shuffle forward, testing the limits on her personal space. "Have you been here the entire time?"

"What do you mean?"

"In Meadow Creek," I reply.

"Oh," Presley laughs. "No. I went to college near the cities. Once I found out about Archie, moving back was a no-brainer. My parents practically forced me anyway. Just kidding. Mostly."

I grip the back of my neck. "Does his, uh, father live close?"

"About thirty minutes away. Why?"

"Sheer curiosity." Not to mention the secrecy is fraying my sanity.

She squints at me—a thorough assessment being calculated behind her blue gaze. "Jealous?"

"Extremely." But I have no right to be.

A pitchy cackle bursts from her. With amusement wracking her frame, she bends in half to catch her breath. "Wow, that's hilarious."

"I'm glad my discomfort amuses you."

She wipes under her eyes. "There's just nothing for you to be jealous about, Brax. Even if we were anything more than has-beens."

My expression crashes into a fiery pit. I don't care for that term. "Are you going to fill in the blanks for me?"

"How about you tell me why you're on my porch instead."

"There's a lot I need to tell you, Pep. Can I come in?" I jut my chin toward the foyer behind her.

"Now isn't great. I'm not alone," she mutters between clenched teeth.

A fresh rush of jealousy streams to the surface and my posture becomes ramrod. "You have company?"

Presley rolls her eyes with a snort. "Calm down, champ. It's my family."

"Ah, okay," I exhale the tension straining my chest. "That's great. Julie and Jim love me."

Presley smacks her forehead. "My son is included in that equation."

A brick sinks in my stomach. "You don't want me to meet him?"

"Don't sound so butt hurt. He's at a very impressionable age. I'd hate for him to fall in boyish lust with you."

"Why? I'm awesome. Kids love me."

She flings an arm forward. "That's precisely the problem, which circles me back to my initial question. What're you doing at my house, Mason?"

"Mama," a garbled voice calls. Then a toddler is beside her as if appearing from thin air, or my desire to meet him. I'd seen Archer's picture, but this is another level entirely. My legs tremble with the effort to keep me standing.

Presley crouches to greet him while I'm stunned silent. She ruffles his hair, the same midnight shade as hers. "Hey, sweet boy. Whatcha doing?"

"Miss you," he coos at her.

"I miss you too," she returns. "Mommy is almost done."

Archie throws his arms around her neck, clinging on like a tiny monkey. "Love you, Mama."

She snuggles him against her. "Love you too."

I feel like a spy intruding on this special moment with

them. That doesn't stop me from carelessly interrupting. "He's so perfect, Pep."

She rubs a soothing palm down his back. "Yeah, he truly is."

"I can't believe I've been missing out on this."

Presley's gaze swings to mine, concern shining in those ocean depths. "What's wrong?"

My head swivels, the motion disjointed. There's no reasonable explanation for me to be choked up. "Nothing. I've never been better."

Her brow creases. "Um, that's weird."

Our conversation gains the little boy's attention. He implores me with big baby blues. There's no calming the chaos stirring in my mind. I've never felt more inadequate—or unprepared.

"Hi," he chirps. "I'm Archie. Who you?"

The pressure lodged in my chest makes it difficult to speak. I cough over the lump while kneeling to his level. "Hey, Archie. My name is Mason. I'm friends with your mama."

"You play wit me? Trucks go *vroooooooom*." His arms go wild while mimicking a racetrack scene.

Presley sucks in a sharp breath. This is exactly what she was trying so hard to avoid. The conflict stirs in my gut. Do I disappoint him or risk making her angry?

"I would love to, buddy. But—"

"Mason needs to say hello to Gramma and Pop-Pop before he can play," Presley interjects.

"Kay! Come, Mase." Then Archer dashes off into the house.

The breath I release is thick with uncertainty. "Is this okay?"

Presley is studying me through narrowed eyes. "As if I have another choice."

I flinch. "This wasn't my intention, Pep."

"Uh-huh."

"Don't worry. I'll explain everything."

"You better." She steps aside, allowing me to enter.

"Right after I play trucks," I state with conviction.

Before I cross the threshold, her finger digs into my sternum. "Don't make me regret this."

I almost chuckle, considering she said the same thing to me in a very different context last week. Supplying the response I did at the bar won't go over well in this case. Instead, I cradle her cheek in my palm "You won't."

After a hitched exhale, Presley spins on her heel and struts inside. Her swaying hips are hypnotic and I'm trailing behind without conscious thought. The sultry beat pounds through my veins. Nothing else registers until she stops in an open room bathed in bright sunlight. I blink from the haze to take in my surroundings. Two familiar faces are staring back at me. Time hasn't aged them a bit aside from a few extra wrinkles and laugh lines.

"Oh, my stars," Julie gasps. "Are my eyes deceiving me?"

I stride forward, wrapping the woman who's like a second mother to me in a warm hug. "It's great to see you, Mrs. Drake."

"Oh, Mason, you know you don't need to call me that. You're all grown up now." She pats my cheek once I release her. "This is a wonderful surprise."

"It sure is," Jim agrees with a smile. He extends a hand for me to shake. "Mr. Rose Bowl is gracing us with his presence."

I accept his outstretched palm. "Hello, sir."

"Jim," he corrects with a warm chuckle. His light eyes twinkle with mirth, so similar to his daughter. "Did you know about this, Presley?"

"Nope. Mason dropped by without warning." She pops her lips at me.

"That's my style, right?" I recall getting caught sneaking into her window on several occasions.

Julie clucks her tongue. "Ah, yes. You've always been a bit of a rebel."

"And you love me for it."

"That we do." She winks at her husband.

A tug on my jeans has me glancing down. Archie beams at me, showing off a smile that would melt the coldest of hearts. "You sit wit me."

"Sure, buddy."

He drags over a tiny chair and points to the seat. It looks smaller than a postage stamp from my vantage point. "Wight dere."

"Uh, well," I stumble over how to refuse his gesture. The plastic will crumple faster than a matchstick under my weight.

"Archie," Presley swoops in to steal his focus. "Mason can't fit in your chair. Want to sit with Mama?"

He shakes his head with harsh refusal. "No. I sit wit Mase."

I glance at Presley, mostly for permission. She gives me a shrug in return. After pulling out the closest chair, I plop down and pat my lap. Archie clambers up without hesitation. His sigh of contentment nearly does me in. This feels so… natural.

A loud sniff has me lifting my gaze from the toddler. Presley turns away, but not before I notice the sheen in her eyes.

"Pep?"

"I'm fine," she squeaks.

"And I'm Spider-Man," I retort.

Archie whirls to gape at me. "Wha?"

I inwardly curse at my stupidity. "Ah, no. Not really. It was a joke. Funny, right?"

His little nose wrinkles. "No laugh."

"My bad," I offer while ruffling his hair. "I'll be more careful with my choice of phrasing."

At this point, Jim and Julie share a glance. He stands and she's quick to follow suit. "I think we should take Archie for a walk so you two can catch up."

I glance at Presley, but she's still trying to collect herself. "Are you sure?"

He's already moving toward the door. "If this is what I

think, it's probably best for you to talk with Presley in private. We'll get out of the way for a bit."

Intuitive as always, this man. "I appreciate that."

Julie reaches for Archer. "Let's go, sweet boy."

He goes willingly, but glances over his shoulder at me. "Mase come too?"

His mom gasps in mock outrage. "I see how it is, sweet angel. Just call me chopped liver."

His giggle is a jolly sound. "Chop-chop. Come, Mase."

A peek over at Presley keeps me rooted in place. "Maybe later, buddy. I'm going to stay with your mama."

His stricken expression is devastating, a wrecking ball slamming into me. "But, but. Mase come too."

Julie bounces the little boy on her hip. "Gramma and Pop-Pop have Starburst."

Presley snorts. "Bribing my child with candy."

"It works and stops him from crying," her mother sings.

And sure enough, Archie's hurt expression is long gone. He's already grabbing at the treats his grandma is digging for. "Yummy for me!"

"Have fun, sweetie. I'll see you soon.

Julie strolls to the foyer with him in tow. "Say bye-bye, Archie."

"Buh-bye," he coos with a wave.

I watch them go, a dull tug yanking at me to follow. It's such an odd, unfamiliar sensation.

"All right, champ. No more diversions." Presley cuts into my thoughts with her suspiciously cheery tune. "What's your story?"

I get off my chair and join her near the window. "I'm moving back to Meadow Creek. Permanently."

chapter seven

Presley

I'M PRETTY SURE MY BRAIN JUST MISFIRED. THIS IS A HALLUCINATION, right? It has to be. All I'm capable of is gawking at this man I used to know while shock whistles from my slack jaw. The smoke finally dissipates enough for me to speak. "Uh, what was that?"

Mason grabs my hand, threading our fingers together. "I'm home, Pep. Where I belong."

My gaze lowers to our clasped palms. "Why?"

His thumb brushes across my knuckles. "I hate the man I've become. That was glaringly obvious after seeing you again. You reminded me of who I really am."

"Um, okay. That's great to hear, and I'm glad you're in a better place. But what does this hasty relocation have to do with me?"

"Everything."

"Whoa, whoa." I tug free from his hold. "Pump the brakes. Where are you going with this?"

He licks his bottom lip and I'm temporarily captivated by the motion. Then he opens that sinfully delicious mouth. "I'm hoping that we can go on a date. The sooner, the better."

"Oh, no. This isn't happening." I press a palm to my forehead. A wild swarm stirs up a riot inside of me while his intentions settle in.

"Will you hear me out?"

Static fills my ears. "Just because you're back in Meadow Creek doesn't mean we're getting back together."

"I figured you'd say that." His smirk borders on sad.

"Any sane person would say that."

Mason peers at me from lowered lids. "We used to lean more on the crazy side."

"Mostly you," I mumble. "Speaking of those reckless tendencies, you didn't just move back to Minnesota for me, right?"

"There's more to it." But his hesitant tone lacks conviction.

I tuck my arms around my middle, staving off the urge to pounce on him. His undeniable magnetism isn't fair. "What about your life in California?"

"It's over."

"And your parents?"

"They're retiring in Phoenix. I'll see them at Thanksgiving." His answers come too easily, as if rehearsed.

"What about work? Did you find a job?"

He nods with extra enthusiasm. "Carleton is forty minutes from here. They needed an offensive coordinator."

My minds reels while I mentally map the location. "That small liberal arts college in Northfield? I didn't know they had a team."

"Me either, but the program is decent."

"What division is it?"

Mason averts his gaze. "Three."

I cock my head at the number. "Isn't that below your pay grade?"

"Nah, it's a decent gig. It allows me to get more direct coaching experience rather than being the ball boy or something for a big program. Besides, the salary is higher than I thought. That's probably due to the astronomical tuition rates."

"And it's a private school."

"Right, that too." A glimmer of a smile cracks the surface. He appears so earnest and hopeful.

Now that the initial shock has worn off, I take in his appearance. His golden tan reminds me of the beach and lazy afternoons under the sun. Chocolate brown hair frames his face in disarray, a month overdue for a cut. Several days' worth of stubble covers his jaw. He's looking a tad rough and rumpled around the edges, which only adds to his appeal. But it's those weary traces clinging to his gaze that concern me.

My eternal compassion for him—that I'll never shed—prods me onward. "How've you been, Mason?"

Wrinkles form between his brows. "Why do you ask?"

"Aside from this erratic behavior?"

His chuckle is potent enough to curl my toes. "Fair enough."

"This isn't the outcome I anticipated after we hooked up."

"You know you've always had a visceral hold on me."

That confession spikes my pulse. I wage an internal battle to maintain a neutral expression. "Yet you didn't visit."

A sheepish apology flashes over his features. "I'm an idiot."

My eye roll should win a gold medal. "You'll have to do better than that."

"I plan to." The heat behind his words has the power to incinerate my resolve.

But I manage to stay strong, regardless of the tremble in my knees. "This is so messed up."

"It doesn't have to be," Mason murmurs. His finger cuts a fiery trail down my arm.

I swat at the pesky goosebumps that dare to follow. "This doesn't mean we're magically picking up where we left off."

His throat bobs with a heavy gulp. "I understand your hesitation."

"Do you? Because I'm beginning to believe you got knocked in the head too many times over the last six years."

The grin he grants me should be illegal. Those damn dimples. With a seemingly innocent quirk of his lips, he makes me want to do very bad things. "Come on, Pep. We deserve a second chance. I'm serious about this."

"So am I. You don't get to just show up and erase the distance between us." I resist rubbing at the ache in my chest.

"Yeah, I thought that was too optimistic."

"Even for me," I quip. "Did you really expect me to go along with this outrageous idea?"

"I have every intention of proving myself." He circles my wrist, aligning our palms with careful precision. "Let me know you again, Peppy Girl."

The gullible girl inside of me is more than ready to surrender. She's waving a white flag while I fight to reinforce my resistance. A mental wall gets slammed down, each imaginary brick solidifying my decision.

"I'm all for a fairytale ending, but let's get real. We're not in high school anymore. Love isn't nearly as simple. The game has changed."

He's shaking his head. "Not for me."

"That's precisely the problem. I can't blindly dive in with you again. Not this fast. I need to think."

Mason's flinch physically pains me. "What's there to consider? We've got a hell of a foundation built on trustworthy ground. The layers are solid and rooted deep. Plus, we're still explosive together. That's a winning combo."

"Which is clouding my judgment." I hang my head against the pressure. "I'm a different person now. It isn't just me anymore, Brax. Archer is my number one priority. If I let you in my heart, that's it. I can't survive losing you again."

"You won't have to. This is where I'm meant to be. With you and Archie."

I tear my eyes away from him and stare at the wall, cursing the heat that's building in my eyes. "This is too much. You shouldn't even be here. I can't be irresponsible and reckless."

"Not even for me?" The question is quiet, rife with uncertainty.

Damn this man for being my weakness. He's an insistent thrum that won't quit, even after six years. His silence that entire time is the reminder I need in this argument.

"I need stability, for Archie's sake. That's the whole reason I've been single for so long. I can't let you waltz into my life again only to watch you walk right back out."

"That's not going to happen," he vows. The confidence in his tone chills me in the fiery sense.

"You can't promise that. What if you get another job? What if being the offensive coordinator of Carleton isn't enough and you have to leave again?"

"I won't leave again," he insists.

"How can I trust you?"

Mason grunts an unintelligible string of nonsense. Before I can question him, he's reaching for me. A palm lands on my ass and wrenches me forward. I fold into his overwhelming comfort until he's all I register. His arms cinch to swaddle me in a protective hold. Woodsy spice fills my lungs as I get swept up in the past. A spasm clenches my stomach.

He's hushed confessions breathed against damp skin. The answer to every unknown. This is too familiar, a fissure fracturing my protest. Yet I falter with this choice.

"There are too many secrets," I mumble into his shirt.

"I'll tell you everything. Give me a chance."

"Mason—"

He must realize my patience is almost tapped, choosing to interrupt. "I should've called."

I break apart from his warmth with a huff. "Ya think?"

His mouth wilts into a frown. "I'm sorry for ruining your day."

"What did you think was going to happen?"

He puffs out his chest in comedic fashion. "I'd swoop in, regain your affection, and we'd ride off into the sunset."

I twist my lips, choking on a laugh. "You've never been the arrogant type."

"Just a dreamer," he muses with a playful smirk.

A noisy huff flaps my lips. "Did you plan to catch me when I fell at your feet?"

"That's just straight fantasy." Mason beckons me in with a crooked finger. "We'll start slow."

I hold my ground. "I find that hard to believe. Our reunion last week was anything but."

"That was different, but necessary. I might not be here otherwise."

"How reassuring," I grumble.

"It's one of my charms."

"Sure," I relent with a sigh.

He rubs his hands with vigor, a metaphorical drumroll. "I have a job for you."

My eyebrow pitches upward on its own. "Doing what?"

"Organizing."

"Where?"

"My house."

I sputter out a choppy exhale. "You already have a house?"

"Will you help me make it a home?" Mason's smile is humble, a warm bite of apple pie fresh from the oven, yet trimmed with satisfaction.

A slew of expletives attacks me in rapid fire. He's got me trapped. The risk is low. I'll be in my element, controlling our progress or whatever he's trying to attempt. It goes against my nature to refuse him. There's no harm in offering my services. As long as they remain just that.

Another line casts, hooking me with a single tug. "Come on, Pep. For old time's sake?

Eh, fuck it. There's no harm in flexing my expertise. "I'll check my schedule."

"Are you free tomorrow?"

"Don't push your luck, champ."

"Noted," he chuckles and begins a slow retreat. "You'll call me?"

I drum a finger on my chin. "Do I have your number?"

"It hasn't changed."

"You better hope my memory is as reliable as my clutter removal." I tap my temple for emphasis.

Mason holds up a pair of crossed fingers. "My faith in you is undefeated."

Too bad I no longer possess the same confidence in him.

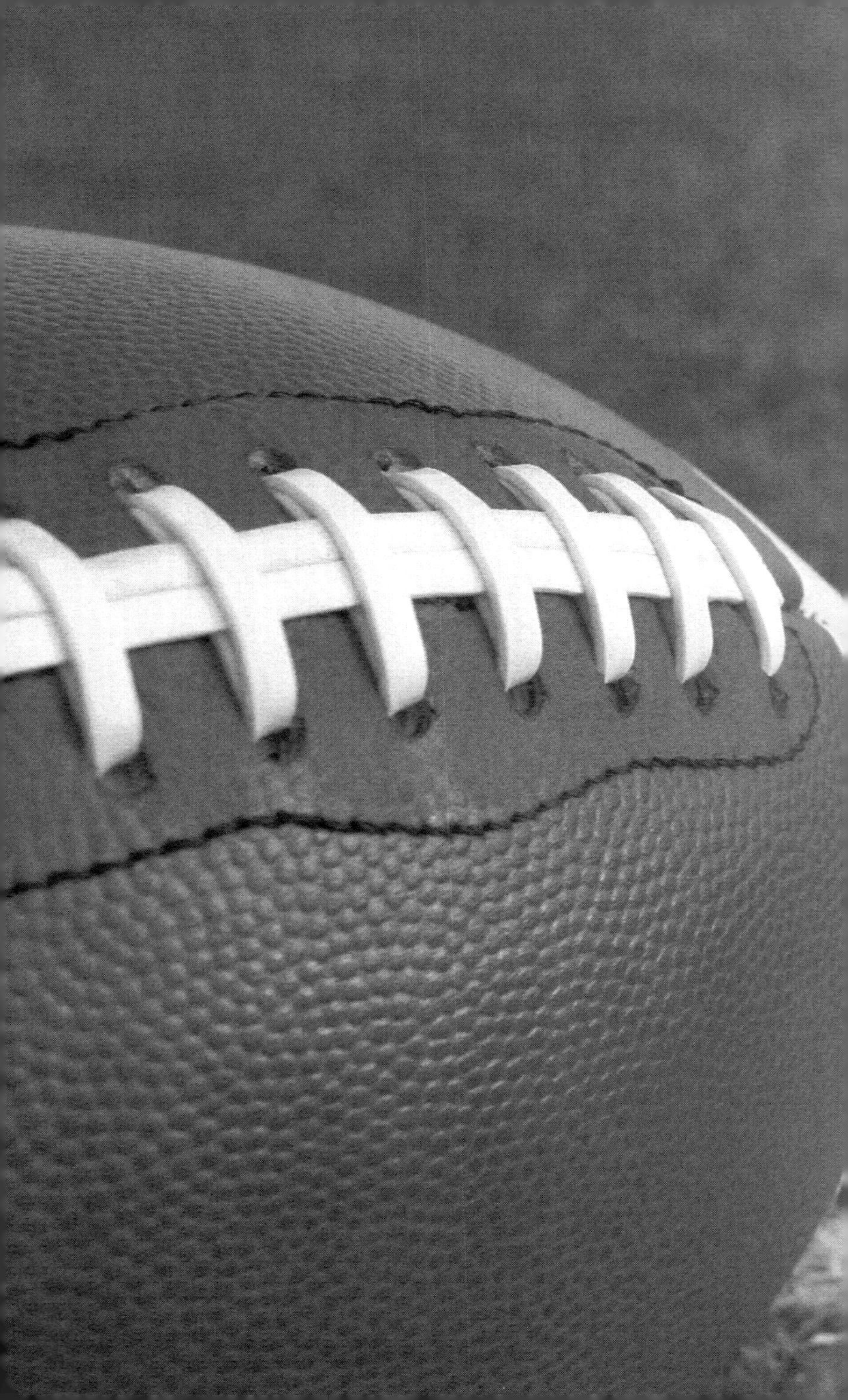

chapter eight

Mason

My steps falter as I step into Pond Alley, one of three lukewarm watering holes on First Street in Meadow Creek. This place hasn't changed. Stale air and dim lights submerge me in the past. The same fisherman relics hang from the walls. Wood beams and an odd assortment of tables interrupt the flow of the wide space. A dozen or so patrons already occupy their preferred spots. But the enormous bar in the center still steals the show.

I drag in a deep lungful as musty memories filter into my system. The scene is eerily similar to so many I invaded as an underage punk. Back then, I'd sit in a corner booth with my buddies and watch the frequent flyers drown their sorrows. I couldn't grasp why so many chose to remain stuck in this place. Now I envy their predictability. They've remained true to themselves while I got lured and lost in the grand shuffle.

Since I left at eighteen, I was never granted the privilege to sit on one of the infamous stools. That's precisely where my feet carry me.

"Well, well. Look who a busted knee and injured pride dragged in. Here to lick your wounds, Braxter?"

I lift my gaze to find Benny—a born and raised local—scrutinizing me with a wary gaze. The smirk I give him in return is gnarled with a confidence that's been pummeled one too many times. "That's one way to greet your customers."

"Good thing you aren't one."

"Give me a chance to order a beer before you assume I'm just gonna hog a seat and breathe the free air."

He tips his head back, a grizzly chuckle mocking me. "That's fucking rich, even from you."

"I see my reputation precedes me." From my periphery, I can see we've gained the attention of those spread across the room. This altercation will be worth more than pure gold to the gossip hounds.

"You're damn hard to miss when every single sports station sings your praises."

"Well, that's over now." That painful throb radiates from my busted joint at the reminder.

"And you can finally grace us lowly folks with your presence." His sneer is a nasty sight to receive as a welcome gift.

"What's with the hostility, Benny? Did I crash your vibe in here?" If I'm being honest, it's rather refreshing. Most break their spines trying to kiss my ass.

He gives me a slow shake of his head, as if I'm being an idiot. "I'm not sure what you're doing in my bar. You're too fancy for our kind."

Heat creeps up my back and I flex against the onslaught. "I'm still the same kid."

"Bullshit," he spits. "But I suppose now that you're damaged goods, you can slum it with the rest of us."

I narrow my eyes, the fire burning hotter in my veins. "Are you about to deny me service?"

"Nah, I'll take your money." He gestures at an empty seat in front of him.

"And ours," comes from behind me.

I turn to the voice, finding a friendly face. My mouth splits into a wide grin. "Gunner?"

My former teammate slaps his chest. "The one and only. Miles isn't far behind."

That name adds another layer to this unexpected reunion. The three of us were part of an undefeated—and unstoppable—dynasty during high school. "Damn, it's good to see you."

I follow his lead and we clap each other on the back in a brief embrace. "Likewise, man. It's been years."

"Too many." That glaring fact has been pounding against my skull for weeks.

"Mind if I join you?" He points at the spot next to the one I had naturally gravitated toward.

"Please do." I slide onto the seat, the worn leather creaking under my weight. A groan escapes me as my ass becomes one with the stool. This feels… right. Along with every other decision I've made since arriving in Meadow Creek.

"So," Gunner drawls. "What brings you to town?"

"This isn't a casual visit. I'm back for good."

"No shit?" His shock is punctuated by Benny slamming down two bottles of Coors Light I don't recall ordering. My friend grabs one without hesitation.

I'm sure as shit not going to complain. After a long swallow, I find myself nodding. "Snagged a place off King, just north of First."

He pauses with the beer hovering in midair. "Why?"

"It's a decent part of town," I reason. "Nice house. Suits my needs."

Gunner snorts, nearly choking on his drink. "No, boner. Why'd you move back?"

Ah, right. I suppose that's the part worth explaining. "It was long overdue."

"I can't argue with that."

Which reminds me. I jut my chin at the bartender. "He's still a salty bastard, huh?"

"Some of the townies are more bitter than most about you ditching your roots without a backward glance. They think you forgot where you came from."

"What's your stance?"

"Fuck what they think. You played in the NFL. Even if you hadn't, your college career broke at least ten records. They should've been cheering for you. We sure as hell did." His considerate words are a balm to my busted spirit. It's nice to reminisce about the highlights, rather than my final play being the focal point. "And now, you're paying homage to your heritage. Welcome back."

"Thanks, man. That means a lot."

He claps me on the shoulder. "Don't mention it. Just being honest."

I guzzle a mouthful of beer. "How was college ball for you?"

"Not too shabby. I didn't have a shot at going pro, but my stats were decent."

"And you moved back after graduating?"

Gunner bobs his head. "I'm teaching at the high school. Just recently took over head coach for varsity too."

"No shit?"

His smile is pure pride. "It's not a bad gig."

"Sounds like a dream." I rub at my leg, the motion becoming a bad habit.

"Another?" Benny's bark lashes at us while he points at Gunner's empty, ignoring me as if I don't exist.

"Yeah, thanks. Let it ride." He doesn't comment on the hostility perfuming the air, but motions between our bottles.

Benny curses under his breath, but turns to fill the order.

I chuckle at his dramatic display. "I was expecting the weather to be frostier than the reception. I'm getting chills here."

Gunner shares my amusement with a smirk. "Don't pay him too much attention. Just a surly asshole."

"Sounds familiar. I remember that from when we were younger."

Benny was two years ahead of us in school and took every opportunity to flaunt that fact. He was the bigger man on campus with several points to prove. The chip on Benny's shoulder was wider than a football field. He never let anyone close enough to discover why.

It must irk him beyond reason that I went out beyond these borders to fulfill my goals. But for all I know, tending bar at Pond Alley is what he aspired for.

"Certain things haven't changed," Gunner says almost absently. Then the faraway look clears from his expression. "How the fuck are you, man?"

"Getting better." I offer Benny a glare when he drops off our fresh round. It wouldn't surprise me if he rubbed a jalapeño around the rim.

Gunner sips from his beer without concern. "That injury looked rough, even from thousands of miles away."

"It fucking sucked," I admit with graceless honesty. "My career ended in a literal snap."

His heavy exhale mirrors my own. "I swear I could hear your bone crack through the speaker. It's an injury you can't just walk away from. We felt the pain for you, if that makes any difference."

"It does, more than you know." The persistent ache has all but ceased. Relief like this will take some getting used to.

He nods in silent understanding. "What're your plans now?"

"Coaching college ball. I just got hired as the offensive coordinator at Carleton."

"In the middle of the season?"

"They were desperate. The position had been vacant since spring." That could've been considered a warning sign, but I've never shied from a challenge. Besides, contracts for the others I found in this area wouldn't start for months.

"Ah, sure." He lifts his bottle. "Then congratulations are in order."

"I'll take that." I tap my Coors against his, tilting it to my lips for a swig.

"Aww, shit. Is that my favorite QB?" The booming voice belongs to none other than Miles Pike.

"That depends." I swivel on my stool to face him. "Is your end still tight?"

"Careful," he warns while planting his ass on the stool to my left. "Or I might think you're flirting with me."

"I could do worse. After all, you're the best tight end that's had the pleasure of catching my balls."

He lounges on the seat like it personally belongs to him, his chest puffing wide. "Now I know you're just blowing smoke up my ass."

"And I'm getting jealous." Gunner winks.

"Just like old times," I joke. This easy camaraderie can't be bought. I had a bond with my fellow 86ers and those from Cal, but it's not quite the same.

"The pack is back in action? Watch out, ladies." Miles releases a sharp wolf whistle.

"Count me out," I laugh.

He recoils as if I punched him. "The fuck? You're spoken for? I can't imagine a woman from California would willingly move to Meadow Creek, even for you."

My chuckle is hollow. "That's a correct assumption. I came alone."

Gunner shakes his head. "I've never doubted your charm. It's been less than twenty-four hours since you strolled in, and some chick already sunk her claws in."

"In a sense," I hedge.

"Presley Drake," they recite in unison.

A groan nearly rips from me. Just her name gets my blood pumping hotter. "Am I that transparent?"

"Yes," comes from Gunner.

Miles confirms with, "Absolutely."

I scrub a palm over my stubble, an image of the raven-haired beauty coming to mind. "Well, shit. There goes my element of surprise."

Gunner scoffs. "That's not a thing where Presley is concerned. Especially in this town. Have you talked to her?"

"A few times."

"And?" Miles motions me on with a spinning wrist.

I toss suspicion their way through a narrow gaze. "Since when do you two care about my dating life?"

"Are you kidding? If I deliver this juicy news to Greta and Jill at Blue Bay, I'll drink free for a year. Maybe a bonus in the staff office too." He looks positively giddy at the prospect, almost bouncing in his seat.

Gunner reaches across me to smack Miles on the chest. "Better pipe down about the competition. If Benny finds out you're about to run next door, he'll piss in your beer."

Good to know my earlier concern was warranted. I glance over my shoulder, more than ready to vacate this frigid environment. "Is the service better?"

"Without question," Gunner spouts.

"Then why'd you come in here?"

"I like to spread the patronage love. That way no one gets grumpy."

"Fucking small-town drama," I mutter. Yet another thing that requires adjusting to.

Miles loops an arm around my neck in a loose chokehold. "Welcome back, Braxter. We've missed you."

On cue, Benny stalks toward us. His scowl is a promise of retribution. "I didn't know we were having a damn ego stroking contest. Your celebration is disrupting my customers."

A glance in each direction proves the opposite, but I'm not going to argue. After slapping more than enough cash on the counter, I swipe along the brim of my hat at him. "Lucky for you, we were just leaving. Thanks for the hospitality, dude. Top-notch."

His brow furrows. "You fucking with me?"

Before I can respond, Miles stands and begins clapping. "May I have your attention? There's a damn legend in our midst, people."

Pride—superficial or not—pulses through me. Their support is a defensive protection I didn't realize I needed. This isn't a game, yet it feels like we're running a well-worn play. I sag into the familiar role without pause.

"You spoil me, Pike."

"Just doing my due diligence." His voice is loud enough to carry across the room. "We're going on tour. Feel free to join."

"That's certainly one way to announce my arrival," I mutter. But the grin I'm sporting reveals my vindication. This is exactly what I need. Meadow Creek is truly where I belong. That's more obvious than ever.

"You're welcome," he hoots. "Now let's go spread the word and get me laid."

chapter nine

Presley

I slide into the booth, frou-frou macchiato in hand. My gaze flicks around the quaint coffee shop while I get situated near the window. We take turns choosing the location for our gabfests. This is a solid pick by my bestie. With rustic accents and homey decorations, comfort exudes from the walls.

A mouthwatering dark roast and caffeinated joy fill my lungs when I inhale. "This place is adorable."

Clea beams as if I complimented her directly. "Isn't it? I swing in at least twice a week."

My lips quirk while I study the vibrant rainbow logo plastered on the cardboard sleeve. The design speaks to my cheery soul. "It's just a short walk for you. I'd be here daily."

"Don't tempt me," she laughs. Her happiness has cranked up several notches since Nolan pulled his head from his ass. The change is a beautiful sight to behold.

"I'm not sure what's all in this, but it's delicious." Audria arrives at our table with a wide grin. She's visiting for the weekend while on fall break. Iowa—and her hunky country fiancé—stole her from us. If she didn't love him and her job so much, I'd be a bit more bitter.

Vannah glides onto the seat beside me with her standard grace and poise. "This has a name I shouldn't repeat with children present."

Clea huffs at her. "As if you don't shout worse than 'Free Me from the Bedpost' on a regular basis."

"Yeah, you're right. I like to pretend I'm modest every now and then," the snarky redhead winks.

"You make my Toasty Delight sound tame," I tease.

Vannah inspects her manicure. "Let's be honest, I don't have to try very hard to accomplish that."

"Yeah, yeah. We don't need to rehash what you and Landon do over lunch."

"I second that." Audria smacks her lips. "Even though I haven't heard most of the sordid stories."

"We aren't that bad. You make it seem like we're sexual deviants." The twinkle in Vannah's gaze might suggest she agrees with that opinion.

"It's more about the graphic retellings." I bounce my brows at her.

She tosses a section of ruby locks over her shoulder. "I'm just trying to keep your lives spicy, you're welcome very much."

"Uh-huh, sure. Anywho," Clea sings. "Thanks for coming my way."

"Not like it's that far," I reason. "I'd happily drive for hours to see my beeches."

Audria winks at me. "Likewise."

Clea sips at her latte, a coy smile brightening her features. "Cuppa Steam is special to me. It's where Nolan and I first started mending our fencing."

"That sounds dirty," Vannah coos. "Tell me more."

"You're such a perv." I nudge her with my elbow.

Her gaze latches swings to mine. "Speaking of, how's your lover?"

I avert my stare, taking a newfound interest in the napkin dispenser. "Mason?"

She snorts. "As if there's another."

"Spill the deets, Press. You promised, and we're all gathered to listen." Clea's reminder isn't necessary. It's a rare treat for the four of us to be together. I plan to take advantage of each second.

Without further delay, I delve into the tale that is my history with Mason. It begins on our first day of middle school when he bumped into me, sending my books and pencils flying. We knocked our heads together while bending to gather the scattered supplies. He snared me with that charming smile. I crushed on him in secret while our friendship blossomed into young love.

After that, it's countless memories that will take months to unfold. I summarize the years in clumps of football games, movie dates, dances, and late nights under the stars. When we used to sneak out after dark and meet at the park. Lazy afternoons at the lake and early mornings watching the sunrise. The first time he held my hand, and sharing every other first we had to give. My stomach is full of flutters until I reach the end when Mason leaves town and doesn't return. They're well aware of his random appearance at the Knotty Knox two weeks ago. The latest revelation is still a secret. For a few more moments at least.

Audria is the first to speak, palms clasped to her chest. "He's your lobster."

I squint at her. "Huh?"

"Like Ross and Rachel. You're soulmates." She's a huge *Friends* buff so the reference isn't surprising.

"But she's not seeing him again," Clea states. Her focus spans to me, a brow lifting in question. "Right?"

"Well," I drawl. "There's been a new development."

The three of them lean in as one cohesive unit. Vannah grips my arm, nails digging into flesh. "You're not moving to California."

Laughter bursts from me. The mere notion is more hilarious than the time Mason's family dog licked my ass during sex. That memory continues to be the best form of comedic relief. I wipe the moisture from my lashes.

"That would be a no." Another giggle escapes. "Never gonna happen."

Clea wipes her brow. "That's a relief."

"Okay, so no one is moving. What's going on?" Audria's imploring gaze searches mine.

"Mason actually moved," I admit. "Back to Meadow Creek."

Three loud gasps choke on my announcement. Hanging jaws and rounded eyes join in the picture of shock. My friends sputter for a few more seconds, deciding who's going to speak first.

Vannah smacks the table, our cups trembling with the crash. "How do you know? What happened? Why are you holding out on us?"

I roll my eyes at her rapid-fire barrage. "He came to my house on Thursday. Just stopped by without warning."

Audria props an elbow on the table, hooked on my words. "What did he say?"

"Mostly sappy nonsense about his plans to woo me," I joke. Although, it's somewhat true. I should probably be more concerned about his stubborn claims. The man is very talented at getting what he wants with a stupid high success rate.

Clea sighs, the sound ripe with fluffy whimsy. "Are you getting back together?"

"No," I blurt. Then logic and my heart scoff. "I mean, probably not."

"That's convincing," Vannah scoffs. Her doubt is warranted.

My resolve is crumbling already, and it's been less than a week since he showed up unannounced. How I'm supposed to remain strong is beyond me. I settle for a lame, "It's complicated."

"You've already used that excuse," Clea chirps.

"It's a good one," I return with a grin.

"How so?" Vannah is an expert on the subject.

"Well, most importantly, I have Archer to worry about."

Audria squints at me. "As in finding him a second daddy?"

"Umm, not quite. I have to be careful about who he meets. The last thing I want is for him to get attached to someone who skips town next month."

"Your kid is too precious. He stole my jaded heart at birth." That's a huge feat coming from Vannah.

"Mine too," I breathe. "I have to do right by him."

"You do," Audria insists while covering my hand with hers. "Always. You're the best mama."

Heat pricks my eyes and I blink to clear the blur. "Thank you."

Vannah rubs my shoulder. "What's bothering you?"

"I feel like I have to be guarded where he's involved. Experience has taught me that. I'm terrified history will repeat itself."

Audria's brows leap skyward. "I feel like that goes against every other core value you possess."

"I'm not trying to assume the worst, but I care about him too much. Those feelings are pummeling me all over again. Our connection hasn't faded, that much is obvious. It will destroy me when he leaves again."

Deep grooves appear on Vannah's smooth forehead. "When?"

"Huh?"

"Why not if? When seems so final."

Clea is busy gnawing on her inner cheek. "Who's to say Mason will leave again?"

"I'm scared to believe otherwise," I confess. The truth trembles my bottom lip.

"Aww, babes." Vannah cuddles me into her side. "I saw the way he looked at you. That guy is a goner, and probably has been all along."

I sniff. "Yeah?"

"Definitely."

"That's nice to hear. Archie already loves him. It was instant, at first sight." Warmth swells in my chest at the memory of my son climbing on Mason's lap.

"Is that a problem?" Clea's tone is soft and sympathetic.

"Not yet."

"But it could be?" Audria reads me like the youngsters she teaches.

"We're spinning our wheels, ladies." Vannah turns to face me. "What're you going to do? You can't ignore him, that much is apparent."

"Help him organize his house?" I cringe while sharing Mason's suggestion.

Clea blinks at me. "Is that a question?"

"Only because that's not the only thing she's planning to reorganize." Vannah wags her brows.

"Already did," I remind with a wink. "He's scratched my itch twice. There won't be a thrice."

Vannah snorts into her coffee. "That's a big pile of crap. Those flames wafting off your loins at the bar nearly singed my eyebrows. If he crooks his little finger, you'll hop on top faster than he can roll on a rubber."

"Whatever. I can't just sleep with him. We're way past that." But the thought of another round makes me squirm. Freaking Mason and his magical penis.

"I think you should go for it. He's serious and making big

moves, quite literally. Nobody packs up their entire life without a damn good reason." Audria flails her arm at me. "And here you are."

A pounding throb attacks my temples. "There's a lot to consider. He told me we'll start slow. Just friends."

"Purely to appease you," Vannah counters.

"I'll declutter him and go from there."

"If that's what it takes to let him score. Touchdown, baby." She gnashes her teeth.

"Whose side are you on?"

"Yours. That's why I'm pushing the issue."

"Exactly," Clea agrees. "He's your one, Press."

"He used to be," I argue.

"Still is," Audria urges.

I'm outnumbered, but the pressure isn't unpleasant. Instead, I choose to let go of the fear. This is Mason after all. He's never caused me pain on purpose. I can trust his devotion to me, but Archie needs to be included in the equation. "Will he accept that I'm a package deal?"

Clea balks. "Hasn't he already?"

Air gets sucked between my teeth. "Not quite."

Vannah taps my phone. "Only one way to find out."

The blank screen mocks me, but I've recently discovered Mason's preferred method of contact. I've left him hanging for five days. His patience is most likely about to expire. If I initiate with a text, that should stave off his impulsive spontaneity. Tingles erupt across my skin at the idea of him showing up unannounced again. A scoff chases off those foolish desires easily enough.

After a swipe of my thumb, I repeat a phrase that's becoming well-versed. "Don't make me regret this."

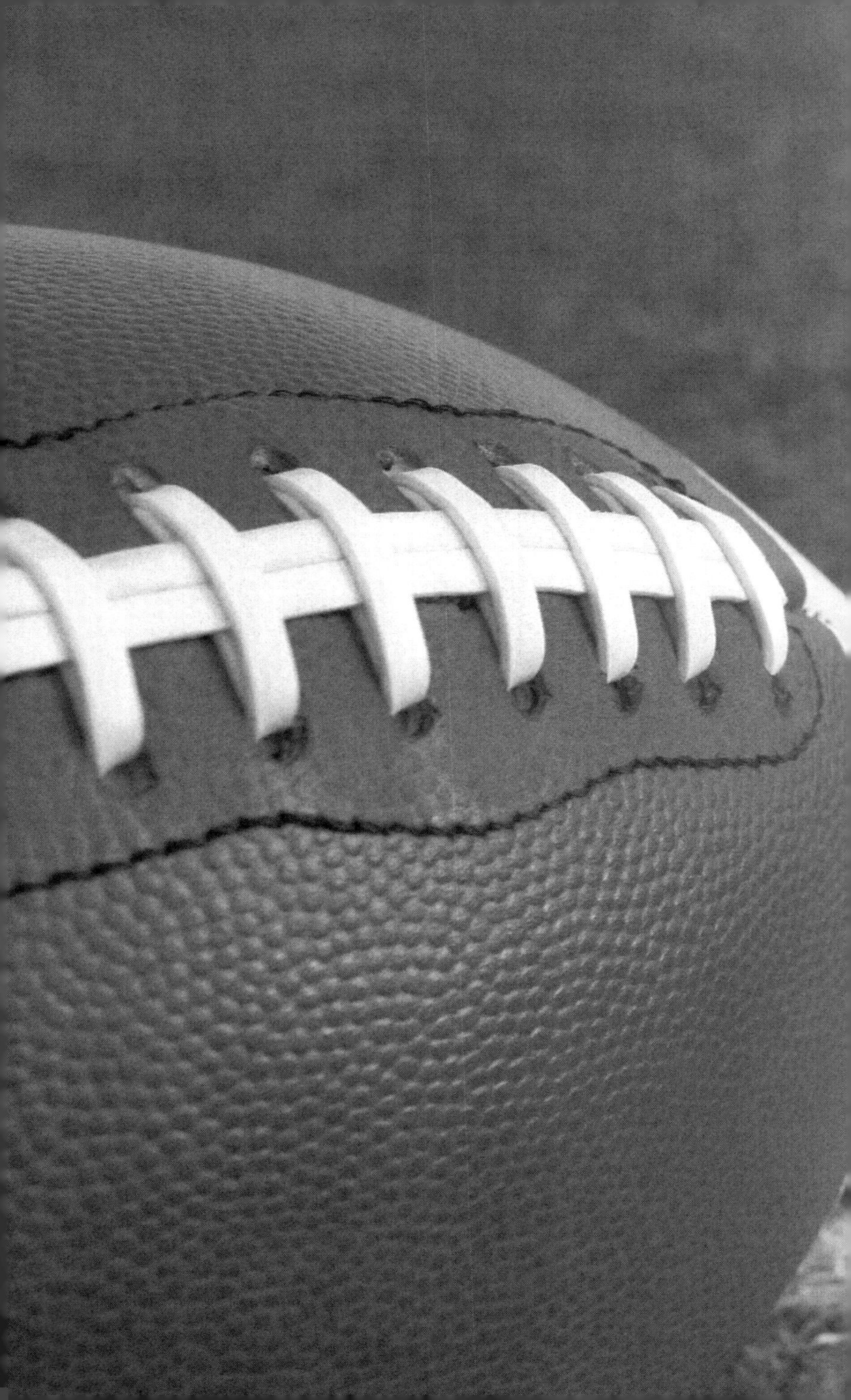

chapter ten

Mason

It's been damn near a week since I pulled into this same spot in front of Presley's house. I throw the truck in park, drag a hand through my hair, and shake off the excess energy. The jitters won't quit. This is just what she does to me. I'm reverting back into an impatient teenager. If I appear overeager, she might find my impulsive tendencies endearing. Or she could think I'm fucking lame. The potential benefits outweigh the risks. I roll the concern off my shoulders with a shrug and step outside.

Presley texted me yesterday about scheduling a date to organize my shit. It should come as no surprise that I jumped at the first available opportunity. This afternoon will kick off our second chance, and I won't blow a moment she's granting me. That's precisely why I'm picking her up.

Call me old-fashioned, but I want to drive her to my

place so we can arrive together. It's more than that, though. This will allow her to infuse my pickup with that addictive wildflower scent. I'll also get a few extra minutes with her in confined quarters. She'll be at my mercy and I'm a sponge, desperate to soak up each second.

As I walk up the cobbled path leading to her porch, my gut takes a slight dip. Archer won't be home to welcome me with exuberance. Presley offered today as an option since her son is with his father. I want him to join us more than anything, but her reservations are warranted. Even so, it stings that Presley is hesitant. Not that I can complain. I'm not a parent, therefore I can't begin to comprehend the level of those protective instincts. But, if I'm being honest, I already feel a soul-deep connection toward the little tyke.

The sooner Presley believes my intentions are genuine, the faster we can move forward.

I'm ready for our future with Archie as an added bonus. She just needs to restore her belief in me, starting now.

I stab at the bell with haste, the twinkling chime echoing my insistence. The door flies wide open a beat later. Presley stands there with a stern expression, yet her twitching lips betray her façade. I can tell she's leaking amusement. Try as she might to hide it, there's no doubt that my appearance pleases her.

She hangs her head with a crisp laugh. "Why am I not surprised?"

"About?" I prop an arm against the wall, bending over the threshold.

Presley's eyes feast on my sprawled position with a downward sweep. She snaps her focus back up to my face and I don't miss the blush blooming in her cheeks. "Um, your early arrival."

An hour is smaller than a freckle in the grand scheme. "I couldn't wait to see you."

My words seem to have the desired impact if her breathy sigh is any indication. "You're too charming."

I take a liberty, lifting a palm to cup her jaw. "And you're too beautiful."

Presley opens her mouth to respond when a masculine timbre smashes our initiate bubble.

"I think we're all set." The owner of the voice comes into view behind her. His broad frame blocks the light streaming from the hallway.

My blink is coated in concrete as I digest the scene unfolding. I stand upright with fire licking at my veins. "What the—"

Presley silences me with a glare, then glances over her shoulder at the man in her home. "Uh, great. Where's Archie?"

"Just packing a few toys." The guy shifts to stand beside her.

That's when he notices me fuming out on the stoop. His relaxed expression tightens into one reminiscent of a predator in the wild. He's built like a linebacker and eyeing me like his next high-caloric meal. I shake off the strange impression when Presley clears her throat.

"I'll bring him to your car if you want to get it running."

"Trying to get rid of me," he rumbles.

"No, of course not." She swats his chest. "I just have... um, company."

"I can see that." His gaze is narrowed in on me while he towers lower over her space. I swear his fucking eyes twinkle while catching my glare. This asshole has the audacity to bury his nose in Presley's neck, groaning with erotic fanfare. The sound is guttural enough to make me avoid my eyes. "You smell so good, Press."

She shoves him away. "Knock it off, caveman."

I have no claim on her, but that doesn't mean I have to watch this display of ownership. "Who the fuck are you?"

"Archie's father." He just stares at me, not threatened in the slightest by the gravel spitting from my voice. "And you must be the elusive Mason."

"You've heard about me?" I lift my chin in his direction.

Presley groans and rubs her forehead. "This alpha peacocking is super cute, but we have things to do. Make nice so we can move along."

"I'm Chad. Nice to meet you." His features crack with a cocky smirk as he extends a hand.

My upper lip curls at his meaty mitt. "We'll see about that."

He withdraws his offer with a chuckle. "Damn, man. You're gonna be fun. A bit muscular for my taste, but I wouldn't feed you to the wolves. Give me a call if you ever want to try playing defense."

"What's that supposed to mean?"

"I guess we'll find out, huh? Tell Archie I'll be in the car." Then he shoulders past me, smacking my ass on the way.

As a lifelong athlete, I barely register the touch. But coming from him, a blood-red flag is raised. I hear the bugle horns blaring as if a duel is about to begin. My fury follows his retreat until he's seated behind the wheel.

Presley clucks her tongue. "Don't mind him. He's overly friendly."

The fire under my skin cools to a low simmer when I turn to face her. "Is there something going on between you two? I don't want to step aside, but I also don't want to get in the way of a family or cause problems for you."

Her smile is a crooked slant. "That's mighty noble of you."

"Sometimes I surprise myself."

"Your knightly surrender is completely unnecessary. Chad is more interested in you than me."

I let my expression go blank. That doesn't compute. Based on their previous interaction a moment ago, I'd safely assume he wanted to bone Presley into next week. "Huh?"

"My kid's daddy bats for the other team." She pops out her hip, allowing a moment to pass while I attempt to process. "Yeah, Brax. Let that sink in."

"Wait," I mutter. "Chad is—?"

"Gay? Extremely," she confirms with a sharp nod.

I'm certain my jaw is hanging a foot from the ground. Here I am, making assumptions. Stereotypes are horrendous for a reason. Everyone is different with their jagged edges and gnarly scars. People don't fit in neat categories and can't be shoved in a certain box. I'm usually not one to judge others, unless a certain someone happens to be drooling on the woman I've always considered mine. Love is free and we're free to love without limits.

Properly chastised, I hang my head. "Okay, uh... that's something. Why did you sleep with him?"

A recognizable *vroooooom* interrupts us, getting louder with Archie's approach. He crashes into his mom's legs with a squeal. "Buh-bye, Mama. I go wit Dada."

Presley lowers to her knees and engulfs him in a hug. "I'll miss you, sweet boy. We'll do a video chat before bed, okay?"

"Tay. Miss you," he mumbles while snuggling closer. His eyes widen when he sees me, the cogs spinning behind those bright baby blues. Archer wiggles to be released from his mom's embrace. "Whut you name 'gain?"

"Mason." I crouch down and lift a palm toward him.

"Mase!" He slaps my hand, sealing the high-five I was aiming for. "You stay wit Mama?"

"Yeah, buddy. Your mommy is going to help me fix my mess."

"You dirty?"

More so than I can ever admit to him. I settle on a simple, "Yes."

His lips twist to one side. "Mama cwean oou?"

"I sure hope so."

"Good." His nod is resolute. "Up, up!"

The invitation is paired with his outstretched arms. I scoop him without pause, spinning round in two fast circles. His shrill giggle is my fuel and I twirl faster.

"Hold on, buddy."

His fingers dig into me. "Wheeeee!"

I do a final lap before slamming to a halt. The landscape wobbles a bit while I gather my bearings. Archie is busy bouncing on my hip, unaffected by the spiral motions.

"Dere," he commands while pointing at Chad's car.

It's a reminder of what just transpired, and the ass I proved to be. Someday in the near future I'll need to apologize to Chad. I bite off a curse but follow Archie's directions. "You got it, buddy."

"Good luck with that," Presley mumbles with a grin.

I shoot her a look—most likely filled with panic—over my shoulder. "Aren't you coming?"

"Yeah, yeah. I'll never leave you hanging, Brax." Presley grabs her purse, pulls the door shut, and locks the deadbolt.

"That's just one reason I love you," I call.

Archie slaps his tiny palms against my cheeks. "Love my mama?"

Dammit, I'm becoming proficient in shoving a shit-soaked boot in my mouth. I glance at Presley for assistance, only to find her expectant gaze locked on me. This is mine to fix.

I ruffle his hair, which does little to flatten the ever-present faux hawk. "I love your mama, buddy."

There might be years of unanswered questions piled between us, and several challenges ahead, but my feelings for Presley remain constant.

"Me too?" His sapphire eyes are filled with so much hope.

The lump in my throat is a fiery ball that demands attention. I can't concentrate on the numerous reasons why voicing his suspicion aloud is a bad idea. Fuck the repercussions. "Yeah, little man. I love you too."

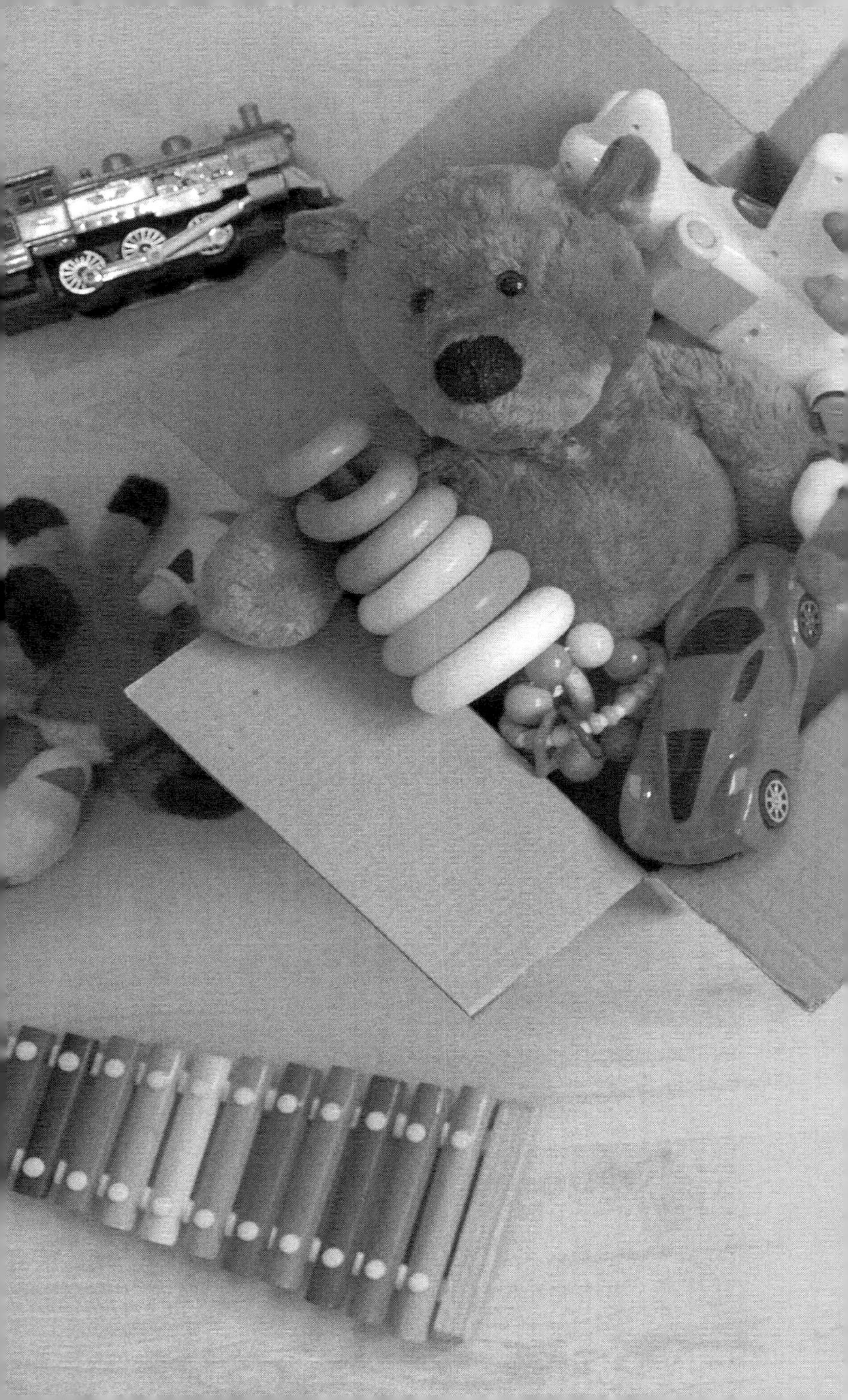

chapter eleven

Presley

King Avenue passes beyond the window in a blur of confusion and disbelief. I rest my forehead against the cool glass, allowing the brief reprieve to soak in. Mason told my son he loves me. But more shocking than that, he openly admitted to loving Archie. What am I supposed to do with that? The stampede booming in my ears hasn't quit since. I should probably be concerned, but the only thing racing through my mind is Mason holding my baby boy.

Meanwhile, the man beside me hasn't spoken. The continued silence leaves me to stew in this vat of unknown suspense. Mason drums an erratic rhythm against the steering wheel. I might be known for my upbeat attitude, but this cloying strain tests the limits. Something has to give.

Five miles has never taken so long to travel. I'm about ready to climb the damn seat to escape the tension.

"Are you mad at me?" His gravelly timbre is better than cucumber slices on my puffy lids.

I sag against the leather with a grateful sigh. "No."

He glances over at me. "I don't believe you."

"Really?"

"The one-word answers aren't helping."

I whip around to face him, arms crossed against my chest. "What would you prefer?"

"The truth."

A fresh wave of frustration burns in my veins. Boundaries were never an issue for us. But now? Mason has blown any evidence of them out the damn windshield. "Fine. Why did you say that to him?"

"I was just being honest."

"You expect me to believe that you love my son?" The notion is outrageous, even if Archie is the cutest thing since puppies and kindergarten crafts.

"Yes." His casual tone rolls over my aggravated nerves.

"How?" The thrum in my pulse skyrockets while I wait for his response.

"He's a part of you, Pep. It's just natural."

My gasp is a gaudy flare in this suddenly cramped space. The air whooshes from me in a quick stream while moisture collects in a steamy mist across my vision. I sniff and drop my watery gaze. There's no describing the comforting warmth his instant acceptance brings forth.

A tremble hitches my exhale. "Damn, that's a good answer."

Mason winks, slinking a hand along the center console to grip my thigh. "Thank you."

"You certainly haven't lost the charm," I tease while fanning my sweaty eyeballs. "I'm not sure what to say."

"Well, I do."

My gaze drifts to his profile without permission. "Okay?"

"After seeing you again, I made a promise to myself. Several, actually. More specifically, I pledged to reveal what prefers to remain trapped within. To be open and honest, especially with you." While pausing at an intersection, he taps his chest. "I feel like Archie should be mine, which makes me sound crazy. But when I look at him, I see us and every wild dream we dared to share. He already has a father—who's great, I'm sure—but maybe I could still be included somehow. If you're willing."

"This is madness," I mutter. The atmosphere tilts and becomes heavy, evaporating our usual carefree vibe. There's no disputing the symphony of flapping wings in my belly, though.

"Told you I sound crazy." The defeated, dejected edge in his voice sets my jaw to steel.

Silence threatens to swallow us again, but I refuse to stay quiet. Especially after his heartfelt confessions. "Do you really feel that way?"

"Presley." He squeezes my leg until I look at him. "I love you just as much today as I did yesterday. And six years ago. That's not going to change. Archie is a piece I didn't realize was missing."

"But your presence has. You've been gone."

"I'm back now," he rasps.

"For how long?"

"Indefinitely."

Then why can't I take the leap and restore my faith in him? I'm nodding too fast. "All right."

"That's it?"

"Yes," I choke.

"Is this too much for you? Too fast?"

I'm moving my head in several directions, trying to chase off the tears. "Kinda? I dunno, but probably not."

Mason sucks in a deep breath. "Okay, that's reassuring."

"I'm not ready to do this with you again. Not yet." If only my words didn't waver in the nonexistent breeze.

"That's fine, Pep. I just need a chance." The hand still planted on my thigh becomes a brand, a permanent reminder that I've always been his.

There's a soul-searing ache spreading through my chest. I'm dizzy from his emotionally tender purge. A glance out the window provides a picturesque view of fall in Minnesota. Red, brown, yellow, orange, and green blend to create a soothing backdrop.

Why am I fighting the inevitable? And seriously, how long does it take to travel just down the road?

As if hearing my silent wish, Mason pulls into the driveway of a modest rambler. He throws the truck in park but makes no move to get out. "This is me."

Pressure melts from me with a sputtering sigh. "Looks like a nice place."

The exterior is basic with no visible embellishments. I don't see any curtains or shutters. Empty flowerbeds and a bare porch. Overgrown grass and stray leaf piles. This is the type of lonely house that's begging for someone to make it a home.

"It'll do for now." The hint at a temporary status hangs in the balance between us.

"Do you own it?" There isn't a sign on the lawn, but that isn't a requirement in this current rapid-sale climate.

"Just renting." The croon in his gritty rasp has me turning my focus to him. Mason is gazing at me with a potent intensity that I'm far too intimate with. That look always had the tendency to strip my clothes off.

"Um, should we go in?" I gulp at the neon green desire swirling in his eyes. Apparently, we're fast-forwarding right to the carnal portion of our relations. That's an area we could always agree on. My palms lift on their own agenda, blocking any attempts he's planning. "We'll finish this conversation after I'm done with your house."

"Stay right there," he commands while unbuckling his belt.

I watch as he rounds the hood and approaches the passenger side. After opening the door, he beckons for me to jump. "You're going to catch me?"

"Always." The memory of him doing exactly this is reminiscent, yet feels so fresh.

I find myself launching forward into his waiting embrace. Mason is solid and sturdy against me, the embodiment of a fierce protector. It's no wonder I feel solace and warmth seeping into my bones. There's a delayed beat where we stay looped as one. Then he ever-so-slowly lowers me to my feet. The hard ridge nudging my belly entices dormant flames to rise. That instant reaction serves as a reminder of how quickly I'll surrender to this man.

His palm trail down my arm. In a fluid motion, his hand drifts to slide along mine. Our fingers tangle automatically, a long-awaited reunion. He clasps on like I'm his anchor. "Is this okay?"

"I guess."

"Even friends hold hands."

I bat my lashes at him, steering us to fluffy ground. The flirty action allows me to regain my composure. "Is that all we are?"

Mason leads me to the garage where he taps a code into the keypad. "For now, if that's what you want."

It's not, but he's giving me the choice. I stare at his bold features while the sun soaks him in an ethereal glow. Dark stubble lines his square jaw. His eyes sparkle with renewed joy. The straight slope of his nose deserves to be traced. He's too tempting. It would be wise to pump the brakes while I still can.

"For now," I echo.

The mechanical grind of the retractable door lifting intrudes on my shameless ogling. I force my attention to swerve forward as the space I assume is used for storage comes into view. But the garage is squeaky clean.

"I'm getting the locks replaced so it's easier to get in this way." He motions to a door along the wall.

After crossing the threshold, my gaze pings around the kitchen and adjoining areas. The open concept floorplan makes it easy to spot absolutely nothing. As in the place is empty. "Do you own any furniture?"

"Not anymore. Sold it all."

"Where's your stuff?"

"In the bedroom." He hitches a thumb over his shoulder.

I follow his lead to the hallway, taking in the pristine condition of the house. There's not a dust particle to be found. It's becoming increasingly more obvious that he's not a pack rat like my typical clients. The brewing suspicion goes nuclear when we reach his room. It's official—I've been duped. Only a dozen or so boxes are stacked against three walls. A bed big enough for five occupies the fourth.

A handful of shirts hang in the closet. Folded jeans and baseball hats rest on the shelf above the rack. Framed awards, accomplishments, and milestones sit in a pile on the floor. His other keepsakes and personal belongings must be hidden from view. The entire scene is strangely concerning.

"How much have you unpacked?"

"Just the essentials."

"And you want me to do what with the rest exactly?"

He shrugs. "Toss whatever I don't need."

"That's… specific."

"You're the expert," he states with certainty. "I want to start fresh."

I stride farther into the room, peering into a box. "Is there a lot of excess?"

His tense expression is my answer. Mason points at a plastic tote near the corner. "Look in that one."

"Why?" I study the container from a safe distance.

He chuckles from behind me. "It's not going to bite you."

"I can't be too sure." But a little nip won't hurt me.

"Can I get you a soda or something?"

"Uh, sure," I mumble while settling on my butt and popping the lid off the tote.

His retreating steps barely register as I consider what might be buried within the last six years for him.

I'm low-key terrified of stumbling across a package with trophies from his other conquests. Mason told me there aren't any mementos aside from my panties, but I find that hard to believe. I can paste a positive spin on any predicament, but uncovering his slew of lovers will challenge my talents.

He's a relatively famous quarterback. Women must've slingshot their thongs at him from the stands. That particular footage wouldn't have been broadcasted on television. With bated breath, I pull out a thin bundle that has a distinct rectangular shape. I almost wipe my brow. It's most likely not underwear.

Now that I'm paying attention, the contents are all carefully wrapped in tissue. This doesn't appear to be a collection of junk, so I could probably move on. Some inkling urges me to keep digging, though.

The edge of a picture frame pokes from the paper. I peel off the corner to see the photo. Our grinning faces appear behind the glass. Heat immediately rushes to my eyes while I smooth a finger over our captured bliss. We were on a ski trip during senior year. It was a freebie sleepover that our parents were forced to approve. He used to proudly display this beauty on his desk.

Several more photos are uncovered next. The Shrek mug

I bought him for his fourteenth birthday. A collage I made him that shows off his best football moments in high school.

Then I find the true treasure chest.

I recognize the shoebox immediately and lose the battle against my tears. The cool tracks race down my heated cheeks as I lift the lid. Highlights from our relationship greet me. I blink against the blur, picking through our past. Notes I wrote him while in class. Movie stubs and receipts for our anniversary dinners. My garter from prom. Dried rose petals from the hotel room we rented for our first time. The fuzzy snapshot of me mirroring his exploding heart symbol after a winning touchdown. A threadbare Meadow Creek Sharks tee that I often wore to bed. The memories threaten to drown me with each item I reveal. My breaths soon resemble hiccups as I attempt to trap a sob.

"Find anything good?"

I startle when his voice shatters the chaos in my mind. There's no point trying to cover my emotional outburst. After an uneven breath, I turn toward him. His eyes widen at the evidence of my upset.

"What's this, Brax?" I gesture to my discovery.

His smile is lopsided, and a bit sad. "All that matters."

My head feels too bloated, and I sag under the weight. How can I resist him? This is romantic catnip.

"You don't have a couch or dining table, but you kept all this stuff?"

"Material crap can be replaced. We can't."

A strangled noise pinches the back of my throat. "Why are you doing this to me?"

He clears his throat, hesitating as if gearing up for something major. "Do you regret it, Pep?"

"What's that?"

"Letting me leave."

"Letting you?" My sorrow flickers to a muted gray. I tip

my head back with a laugh. The newfound amusement sobers with a cough at catching his serious expression. "Um, that suggests I could've stopped you."

"Yeah, and?"

I scoff. "Don't be ridiculous."

Mason shakes his head, the movement slow and calculated. "I shouldn't have left, or I should've insisted you come with me."

My lips part with a wheeze. "How can you say that?"

"That choice cost me what's most important." He crashes to his knees in front of me, reaching for my trembling fists. "Will you forgive me?"

The reality of our situation plows into me. A crossroads materialized, forcing me to go left or right. "I've already told you there's nothing to forgive."

Mason's stare searches mine, delving beneath the heartache and loss. "Then why won't you agree to be mine again?"

"Because I still am." That's when an internal pause button for my doubt gets pushed. I scoot forward until our legs touch. "And that's not going to change."

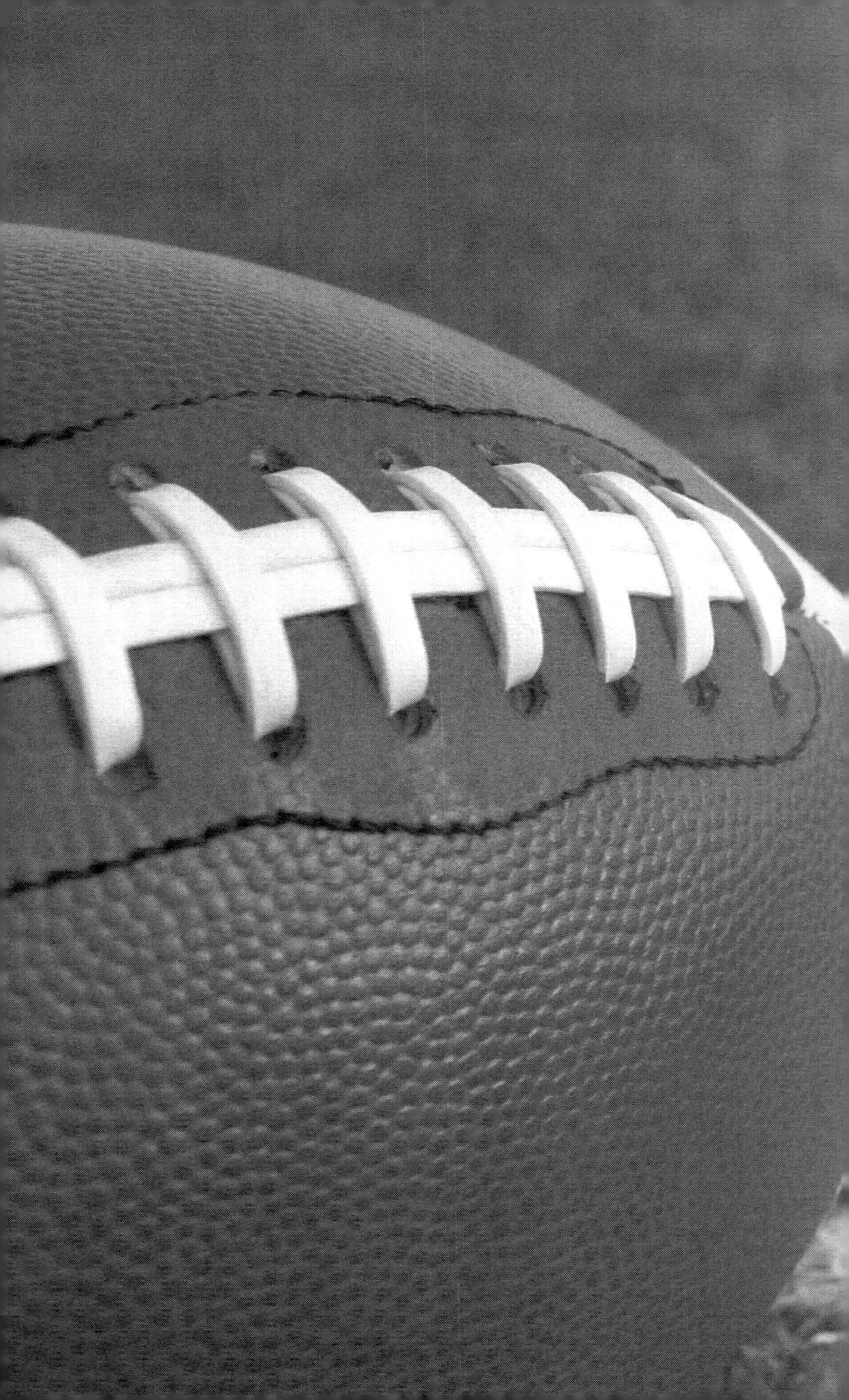

chapter twelve

Mason

My pulse hammers a staccato rhythm while I gape at Presley. "Are you saying—?"

"Yes," she blurts. "You know I can't resist you. Not then, not now."

"You sure you don't want to wait?"

"I've waited long enough."

Then she's launching herself at me, lips smashing against mine in an explosive collision. I almost topple from the impact. That doesn't halt her attack as she nibbles on my bottom lip. Fire bursts in my veins when Presley's fingers tunnel into my hair and yank. That snaps me from the momentary stupor. With a throaty groan, I recover from my fumbling shock to join in the passion-fueled battle she's waging on me.

I open for her with another rumble rising off my chest. Her tongue seeks mine, doling out lashes for every missed kiss. What little was left of my reinforced barriers crumbles with that initial swipe. We erase the distance in every sense. I cinch an arm around her waist while she grips onto the nape of my neck. Presley's nails dig deep enough to leave marks. I absently find myself hoping they'll scar. Then my thoughts return to her body aligning with mine.

She climbs on my lap, legs straddling my waist, and angles further into our kiss. I feel her heat rocking against me. The combustible energy we create from a single kiss is hot enough to set this house ablaze. She clings to me with a fervor that I've missed in the depths of my soul. This push-and-pull momentum is a well-rehearsed dance between us. I fall into the routine without thought, allowing the passion to own our movements. It's a hazy warmth I don't want to surface from. This is how we're meant to be.

Scratches burn along my scalp as she fights to get closer. Desperation surges under my skin and I grip her harder. I've ached for this woman, longed for her against me, and that hollow throb is finally satisfied. She feeds me pure lust with every breath.

In a seamless maneuver, I crush Presley to my chest and roll us until she's tucked underneath me. We don't separate, the constant desire pushing us faster. She arches into me, seeking more that I'll gladly give. My palm skates along her side, over the dips of her ribs, to settle on the soft curve near her breast. Even through the padding, I feel her nipple poking upright for me. I thumb the pebbled point and Presley gasps into my mouth. That spurs me on, increasing the pressure with a soft clamp of my fingers. Then I alternate between flicks and tweaks until she's panting. Pride swarms my veins. She's still responsive to me, overly sensitive in a way that makes me feel like her champion.

Presley's hand curls over my shoulder before shoving at me.

I break from her lips with a groan. "What—?"

"You deserve a blowjob," she explains while reversing our positions once again. She sits astride my waist, hands planted on my chest. "Like a really good one."

My tongue is sticky and incapable of forming words.

She takes my silence as the permission I'd readily grant if my mouth would cooperate. Her fingers toy with the hem of my shirt, dipping under the fabric to tease me. That slight touch is an electric shock to my system, and I squeeze her hips from the onslaught. She doesn't grant me mercy. Quite the opposite while bending to pepper my throat with kisses. I nearly leap skyward when she palms me through my jeans.

"Someone's very excited." Her skillful hand begins an erotic assault on my cock with an upward pump.

"Shit, Pep." My voice is packed with more gravel than a county road.

Presley must feel my control slipping as I go rigid beneath her. With efficient poise, she unfastens my jeans and pulls at the denim. I lift my ass to assist with the downward slide. My efforts are rewarded with a sultry grin as she slinks along my torso.

With just her tongue, she traces the flared head of my dick. I'm already leaking and too eager, which she greedily laps up. Her lips close around my demanding arousal to form a tight seal. Hunger snarls in my gut, that gnawing bellow bucking my hips. A roar gets trapped by my clenched teeth as I try to remain still. This need is fierce, a savage monster devouring a prized meal. It's been weeks since he's been fed, and years before that. She's the only one who can truly sate the beast.

I smack my skull against the floor when Presley pushes me in until the tip tickles her throat. She swallows and I almost bust from the snug fit. With a swiveled retreat, she pays special attention to a protruding vein along the underside of my shaft. I jerk from the unexpected sensation while she follows the bulging trail with her tongue. Then she resumes her intent focus on swallowing me whole.

My muscles burn and strain against the brutal command to remain unmoving. Meanwhile, Presley bobs along my dick with practiced movements. Her pace is just how I remember, the speed slowly increasing to hit my climax. Harsh suction hollows her cheeks and I'm hypnotized by the sight. Her mouth is a haven I'd voluntarily chosen to live without. What a stupid, foolish man I've been. This raw pleasure—her attempt to suck me dry—is a luxury I'll never take for granted again.

"Ohhhhh, Pep. You're a goddess." I thread my fingers into her raven locks, needing another point of contact to keep me grounded.

Her answering moan vibrates straight to my balls and I shudder. When she wraps a hand around my girth and begins stroking, it's game over. A garbled warning spews from me. The beauty nestled between my thighs doesn't pause. I can't outlast her divine methods, and I don't care to delay gratification. A final beat thrums low and I succumb to the relief.

Liquid fire licks along my groin, shooting sparks off my feverish flesh. I lose my vision to blinding streaks of white momentarily. Presley gulps all of me without hesitation.

When she straightens from her hunched position, her lips are puffy and red. She dabs the moisture that's collected at the corner of her mouth. "Finger-licking good without the mess. Just like I remember, Ten."

The nickname flows across my sizzling nerve endings like a cool salve. A tremor of aftershocks shortly follows, and I exhale the smoky tendrils.

"Damn, Pep." I blink at the ceiling with spots dancing across my vision. There's a low buzz in my ears and my brain is congested with cotton. "You're still, uh… way too good at that."

She smacks her lips, a grin peeking at me from the edges. "Thank you."

"Give me a minute and I'll return—"

Presley pushes me flat to my back when I try sitting up. "Nope. That was my selfless gratitude. Take full advantage of my generosity."

"Spoiling me already?"

She crawls up to settle along my side. "You know I don't mind."

I cradle her flushed cheek. "Fuck, I love you."

Her shock sputters out in a choppy exhale. "Diving straight into the feels, huh?"

"Too soon? Should I wait?" The thought of holding back makes my gut churn.

"Nah, there's no reason to pretend we don't." Her lashes flutter in comedic fashion. "Love you too, champ."

"Damn, that's nice. Can I take you to dinner?"

She nuzzles into me, sucking my earlobe between her teeth. "You better after that performance."

A relaxed ease slackens my muscles and I sigh. Comfort like this can't be replicated. My arm tightens around her instinctively. "I've missed you."

"Really? I couldn't tell." Her wry tone gets a chuckle from me.

"Damn," I mutter. "Guess I should've come faster."

"In more ways than one," she laughs. "That would've done the trick."

"Forgive me?" This persistence to have her full faith restored in me borders on obsessive. I have amends to make, regardless of her insistence otherwise.

Presley props herself on a bent elbow. The guarded shimmer in her gaze hasn't faded, not completely. She loves me, but it's not that simple. I can still feel her reluctance between us like an impenetrable force. That shield blocks me. It stands as a third wheel in our fragile restoration.

"I'm getting there. There's just this underlying fear I can't shake," she admits honestly.

The challenge renews my purpose. I readily accept. "You have nothing to be afraid of, not with me."

"If only it were that simple." Then she drums her fingers on my chest. "But I figured we'd be right back in this place once you moved home."

"And yet, you've been torturing me."

Her blue eyes roll at my somber tone. "Just for a week. More importantly, you conned me into coming over to organize your non-mess."

"It worked, didn't it?"

She straightens onto her knees. "You could've just asked me on a date."

"I'm pretty sure I tried that." With a grunt, I get to my feet. "I recall you rejecting my more direct attempts."

Her lips purse in an exaggerated pout. "That sounds slightly familiar, but you didn't have to resort to tricks. You don't have excess anything. I can't believe you don't even own a sofa."

"We can go furniture shopping." I lift her into my arms, planting a sloppy kiss on her cheek.

"That's not in my job description. Besides, you deceived me. I should hold my ground better than this," she protests while melting into my embrace.

"I didn't lie to you. There's plenty of random shit in those boxes. Feel free to toss whatever doesn't belong."

"How am I supposed to know what doesn't belong?"

"Anything that's not personally connected to you," I murmur against the slender column of her throat. "And don't pretend your stubborn ass would budge without greater incentive."

Presley sags deeper into my arms. "You know me too well."

"That's not a bad thing."

Her breathy exhale is a beautiful white flag flapping in a gust. "Fine, I'm willing to overlook your slightly dishonorable methods."

"And you shall be rewarded." I draw her bottom lip into my mouth with a groan. "Muddy Waters is a twelve-minute walk."

"Another convenient coincidence."

"In my favor, if you agree to go with me."

She leans back, quirking a brow. "Didn't I already?"

With that, we straighten our clothes and head out. The late afternoon is warm despite September being an unpredictable month. Idle chatter floats between us with the autumn breeze. Before long, I'm pulling open the door to a restaurant we used to regularly frequent. Muddy Waters was our spot for date night. Might as well dust off that tradition while I'm trying to win her back.

A chime announces our arrival, but it's too busy for the sound to carry far. Much like Pond Alley, I feel a surreal flashback while studying the interior. From the checkered tile floor to rows of vintage liquor bottles perched on a half wall, it's like a still shot from my Meadow Creek highlights reel.

"Even smells the same," I mumble.

Presley tilts her head toward me. "Huh?"

"Garlic bread and fried chicken." Not to mention jittery anticipation. We'd rush our meal to reach dessert. I plan to take my time with her tonight.

She wafts the air to her nose. "Just like our first time."

"Do you come here often?"

Her nod is measured. "Archie loves their buttered noodles."

The searing slash across my chest is brief, but painful. I would already know that if I'd bothered to care. "Wise choice."

"It's a rare delicacy," she jests.

A teenage girl I don't recognize approaches the host stand. "Hey, welcome. For how many?"

"Two." I hold up the number on my fingers.

She glances down at what I assume is a seating chart. "Booth or table?"

"Booth," Presley answers.

The girl nods and jots a note. "Right this way."

After weaving across the dining area, we arrive at a secluded corner near the far wall. The lighting is muted, giving us the illusion of privacy. Presley picks a side and slides in, patting the empty spot beside her. I smirk at yet another reminder of what once was, and will be again.

"Oh, it's like that?"

"Well, yeah. We can't sit across from each other in a booth at Muddy Waters. That would be weird." She doesn't have to prompt me twice.

I drop my ass on the leather seat, stretching an arm across the back to beckon her against me. "This is almost perfect."

"Almost?"

"Archie could've tagged along. Plop him right here." I pat my thigh.

Presley stares at me for a silent moment. "Are you for real?"

"What do you mean?"

"No guy in the history of ever wants a toddler to crash date night."

"I guess that makes me special." My dimples wink at her with my sly grin.

She goes quiet again. "You did talk about us having kids, even when we were too young to see that far ahead."

With a bent knuckle under her chin, I bring our lips together for a chaste peck. "I did, and plan to again once you're ready."

A garbled squeak escapes her. "Okay, wow. Now I'm certain you're just trying to get in my pants."

"More like your heart, but I wouldn't snub a chance to get you naked."

She presses a palm to her flushed cheek. "What're you doing to me?"

I track a pebbled trail along her skin while I drift a finger up her arm. "What I should've been doing all along."

An approaching figure distracts me, further punctuated by a gasp. I turn to see our server—one who has taken our order countless times over the years. Cathy stumbles to a stop, eyes bulging.

After several beats, she seems to collect her bearings and closes the remaining distance to our table. "I'd heard rumors, but didn't believe it. Mason Braxter has returned."

My smile arrives without effort. "Hey, Cathy. The place looks great. Just like I remember."

"Haven't changed a thing, much like the rest of this town. Welcome home, kiddo. And are you two…" She motions between us, bouncing her eyebrows with suggestion.

"I think so," Presley mumbles with far less certainty than I prefer.

A scoff reveals my feelings. "Yes, we are."

She clasps her hands over her chest. "Ah, that's marvelous. Meadow Creek's sweethearts are back in action. My faith in true love has been restored."

"At your service." I tip an imaginary hat.

Presley laughs. "Shameless as ever."

"This just makes me so happy." Cathy sighs in an exaggerated manner. "Can I get you the usual?"

Which I recall being a random selection. I glance over at my date who shrugs in return. There isn't a bad item on the menu, which makes the decision a cinch. I'll eat whatever she brings. "That'd be great."

"Coming right up," she announces before dashing off to fill the request.

With my attention already diverted, I notice a recap from last weekend's game on a television mounted in the corner. The quarterback who replaced me—a trade from Kansas City since Mahomes isn't going anywhere anytime soon—is decent, but our team has a losing record. We're only three games into the season, though. I'll cut the guy some slack. Lord knows I've received my fair share.

The footage reminds me of a not-so-distant memory. It's been months since I held up the scoring symbol for Presley to see. When I adjust in the booth, I find her focus already pinned on me.

"Does it hurt to watch?" She points at the screen.

"The game will always feed my soul, but playing professionally tainted me. I had to adopt a phony persona just to meet their snobby criteria. It took the fun from the sport." Even I hear the bitter bite in my tone.

"But coaching is going well?"

"I've barely started. It's different, in a good way. The responsibility is intense and grueling, but I live for that drive."

"I'm glad." Her smile is kind, a soothing kiss to my tattered edges. "Tell me about your fame and fortune."

The harsh churning in my gut makes me grunt. "I'd rather not."

Her jaw goes slack. "You don't want to talk about football?"

Only a certain aspect. I recall a flippant comment her friend graciously spilled at Knotty Knox. "Did you really watch my games?"

She chews on her bottom lip. "Does it matter?"

"I wouldn't ask if it didn't."

"Never missed one, big shot. You're famous. I'm shocked people aren't constantly hounding you for an autograph."

"That's over now. No one cares about me since my forced

retirement. And what a fucking relief. Being constantly analyzed under the microscope isn't for me."

My phone vibrates with a notification, and a much-appreciated excuse to ditch this topic. The text appears with a glow, and I chuckle.

"Who is it?"

"Gunner. I bumped into him and Miles the other day at Pond Alley." I show her the message.

Presley's eyes sparkle in the dim room as she reads his words. "We can join them later. Unless you're in a hurry to go home."

"That depends on if you're going home with me."

"Buy me a drink at Blue Bay and find out."

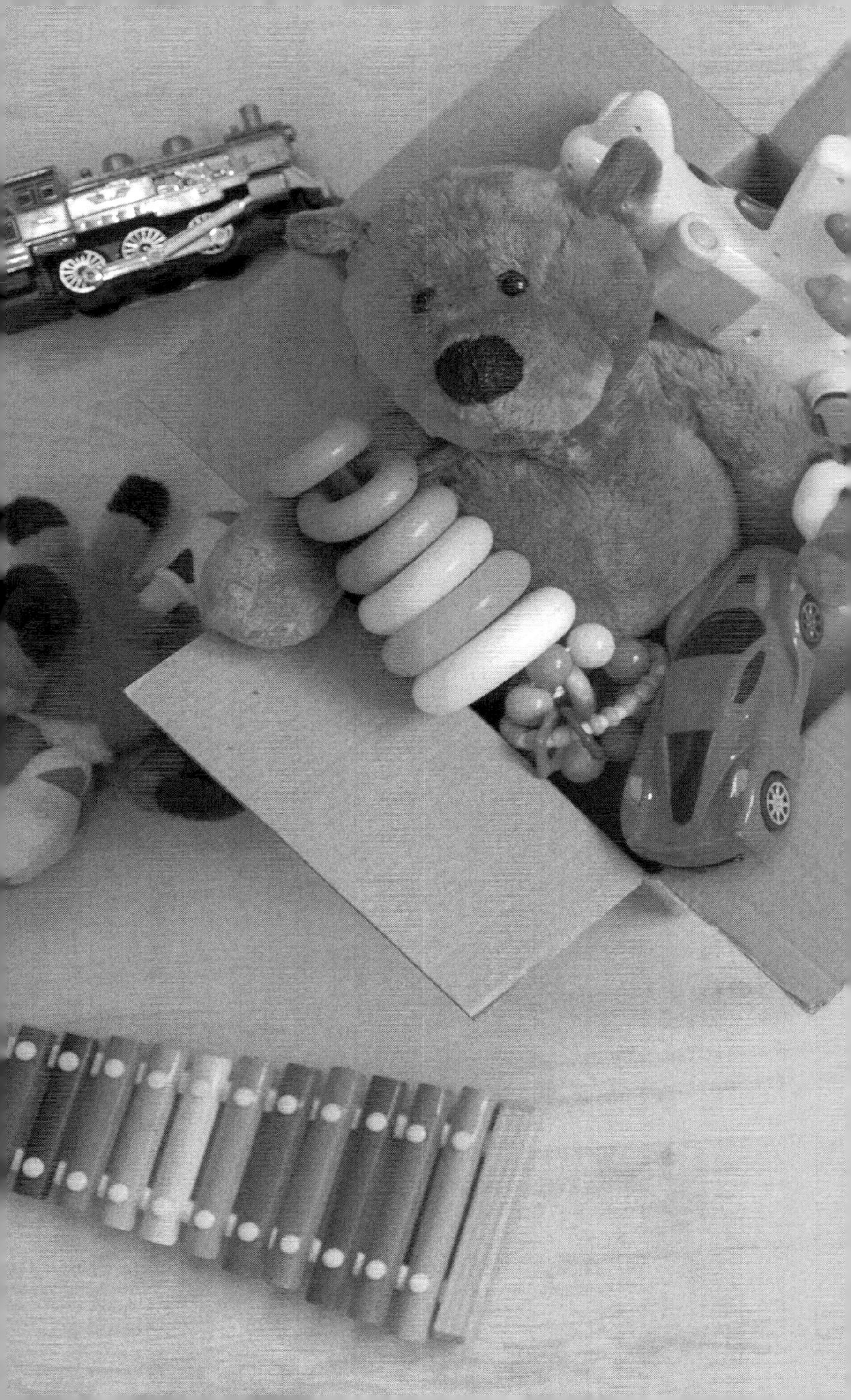

chapter thirteen

Presley

WITH MY BELLY FULL OF PESTO CAVATAPPI AND WARM fuzzies, I allow Mason to lead me along the sidewalk toward our next destination. It's just a few blocks to walk—a huge selling point for this town. Everything is clumped and conveniently located. His palm is a branded presence against mine as we swerve around fellow pedestrians. A chilled gust whips through my hair, alerting me to the evening hour, but the cold barely penetrates.

Tonight has been one of the best I've had in years. The extra bounce in my soles is further proof. I bump my hip into his with my skippy prance.

Mason gazes down at me, that signature smile on full display. "Happy?"

"Very."

He doesn't mirror my sentiment, but his grin tugs higher.

The transformation in his attitude has been rather drastic. A thrill thrums through me at the sight. His eyes no longer appear stormy. He laughs without limits. This infectious energy pours from him and I'm all too eager to drink it in.

"You're staring, Pep." His tone is teasing and light. One more sign that the boy I used to know is nearing the surface. He's still hiding, but barely.

My smile borders on absurd. "Can you blame me?"

"Better be careful or I'll insist we skip this social detour."

I press a palm to my chest in mock horror. "Gunner and Miles will be devastated. I might find gal pals lingering in the shadows too."

"Have you kept in touch with anyone?"

"Not really? I formed such a tight bond with my college crew. But I've had a few nights out with Greta and Jill."

"Those names were mentioned recently," he comments offhandedly.

"Oh?"

"Gunner seems to be a fan."

I snort, recalling his shameless flirting a few months back. "Isn't he always?"

Mason bobs his head. "It was great running into him. This should be fun."

A twinge pinches my chest as I contemplate my next question. I almost cracked a rib while holding my breath during his football speech. "Do you still talk to any of your California teammates or friends?"

"Just a few." His passive-aggressive avoidance on this subject in general is what gives me pause.

I want to believe this can be our future again. Heck, I'm already ninety percent sold. My love for him is absolute. Trust isn't a concern either. It's just this whisper of doubt I can't seem to silence.

My thoughts drift as I get lost in the beat of our steady stride against the concrete. How can he be satisfied with planting roots in Meadow Creek after the whirlwind thrill ride he's been on? My plan is to tread carefully and prod gently until I'm certain. In the meantime, I'm going to soak him in.

The heat swirling from him wraps me in a tender hug. Mason isn't the type of guy a person forgets. I can't deny myself the glorious bliss of being with him, even temporarily. Finding those items he's saved nearly crushed me. I was ready to crumble—and did for the most part. That magnetic impact he possesses is a constant strike against my last shred of hesitation. I'm losing the battle, one small step from hopping on board.

There's an underlying tension radiating from him. That's my fault. He hasn't done me wrong, other than ignoring my presence for six years. No big deal. Sarcasm is evident in my mental musings. He's dedicated to proving himself, and I'm here for it. I wasn't lying about still being his. It's always felt that way deep inside.

"You've gone quiet on me," Mason murmurs into the inky air settling around us.

I study our shadows climbing a nearby brick wall. "Just thinking."

"About?"

"Us."

His cringe is exaggerated. "Good or bad?"

"Mostly good," I offer honestly.

"But there's bad?"

My shoulders droop. "I don't want there to be secrets between us. There are plenty on my end that I'm willing to share, but it needs to be a mutual exchange."

Understanding dawns in his expression under the street lamp. "It's difficult for me to talk about, but I will for you."

"Only if you want to. I'm not forcing you into anything." My curiosity and concern threaten to scald me. This insistent urge to know what pains him is a caged animal pacing inside of me. But pressuring him isn't the route to take.

"We can't really move on unless I do." His muttered response hurts my heart.

I hate that I'm responsible for the haunted gleam crossing his features. I steel myself with a breath and decide to just lay it out there and tell him what I need. "Our time apart feels like a huge question mark. It's a bottomless hole spread between us that could be our ruin if we don't fill in the space. I don't need to hear everything. That's not what I'm asking for, not at all. Just enough to make sure you're okay."

His distance and radio silence flipped so quickly that my head is still spinning. We need to meet in the middle on reliable ground. Together, I hope.

His nod is solemn. "I'll do whatever it takes to win you over."

I flub my lips. "You already have."

"Not completely."

I can't argue with that, considering my internal debate two minutes ago. "It's just hard to give all of me when I don't have that in return."

Mason comes to an abrupt halt, causing me to stumble in my tracks. He draws me against him until we're pressed flush. "I refuse to let anything jeopardize our relationship again, Pep. Nothing is more important than you. Please believe that. My time in California is messy and complicated and better off forgotten, but burying that part of me isn't worth losing you."

The strain evaporates from my limbs and I collapse against him. "You're so suave."

His chuckle rumbles through my lax form. "Oh, you like that?"

"Yes." My exhale ghosts across his lips when he bends to tower over me. "Did I ruin our evening by bringing this up? I don't want to make you uncomfortable."

He brushes his nose along mine. "You're not capable of ruining anything."

"This is precisely why I can't resist you." I rise to the balls of my feet to kiss him silly. My tongue slips out to drag along his bottom lip. A groan reverberates from Mason, fondling the growing heat in my belly. That fire smolders and builds when he palms my ass. His arousal nudges against me and I whimper into his mouth. I'm about to suggest blowing off this pitstop when he pulls back.

"Not to cut you off, but can we finish this later? People are getting a show." He motions to a large window where several faces appear behind the glass.

Flames lick along my neck with a roaring flush. I shove off him with a husky cough. "Uh, yes. Let's go inside."

Mason doesn't let me get far, yanking on my beltloop when I attempt to make a hasty retreat. He rocks his hardness into me again. "You make me crazy, woman."

"Crazy with lust?" I wiggle my brows.

"That's just the tip." Pretty sure he'll tell me whatever I want to hear. Maybe I'll test that theory once we're alone again.

"All right, lover boy." I break from the cage of his arms, patting his chest. "Your friends are waiting."

"I should've ignored that text," he grumbles.

"Too late now."

Mason relents with a grunt and leads me to the door. A humid cloud envelops us as we enter Blue Bay. Friday night tends to create a ruckus, and this is a prime example. Bodies swarm the space, whether sitting or standing or shaking their ass in the far corner by the massive speakers.

A wolf whistle pierces through the rowdy crowd. Gunner stands from his stool with a shit-eating grin aimed at us. "The golden couple has arrived."

Booming applause erupts as we're welcomed into the throng.

A giggle spews from me while I high-five those in my path with outstretched palms. "Well, I guess the news has spread."

"Better late than never." Mason squeezes my hips from behind.

We reach a gap along the bar where our duo becomes a quad.

"It's about time," Miles complains. "Ten more minutes and I would've lost the bet."

Gunner scowls at the reminder, pinning a glare on Mason. "You couldn't have canoodled a bit longer, huh?"

"Apologies, man. I thought you wanted to have a drink."

"Already have one." He holds up a large stein custom-made for Blue Bay.

"No need to brag," Mason jests while moving to get the bartender's attention.

"I hope you don't mind me tagging along to the bro fest," I say in greeting.

Gunner wraps an arm around my shoulders, pulling me into his side. "Are you joking? Our chances of getting laid are much higher with you in tow."

"Ah, well, glad to have a purpose."

Miles tosses me a wink. "Thanks for taking the all-star out of the game. With him off-limits, yet in our circle, we look better by proxy. Like royal knights."

Mason just stares at them. "What?"

"Never mind," Gunner dismisses with a slash through the air. "You have a tendency to wear blinders when it comes to other women. Just stick close and watch the magic happen."

I can already tell this entire ordeal will be a riot. Giddy amusement crackles in my veins, eager for release. "I haven't partied with you animals since high school."

Miles sips from his beer. "Whose fault is that?"

I stick my tongue out in a mature move stolen from Archer. "I'm here now. Let's get a drink."

"Already on it," Mason calls from beside me.

I accept the cocktail he passes me with a grin. "Thanks, Ten."

"Oh, that takes me back," Miles muses with a smirk. Then he turns his sights to Mason, collaring him around the neck. "And you didn't quit with the scoring symbol either. Such a romantic."

Mason's bright gaze whips to mine. The swirling emerald sea is turbulent with unresolved passion. "It's tradition."

His friends fall silent, alarmingly so. The air gains static friction that I could chew on. It seems like a complex puzzle to remember how we fit. I glance between the three men, wondering who's going to crack first.

"Well," Gunner drawls. "I'll cheers to that."

"To Masley," Miles joins in.

I pinch the bridge of my nose. "Nope. We're not resurrecting that."

Gunner leans down. "I just did."

And there's no convincing him otherwise. We toast to years long gone and memories faded at the edges. Minutes blur into hours and I begin to lose track. Next thing I know, Mason is grinding against me on the dance floor. His arms are banded around me from behind while we let the punchy beat guide our hips. The music flows through me in a fluid wave. Warmth courses along my skin, especially when Mason's mouth suckles along the dip between my shoulder and neck. I spin on my heel, spearing fingers into his hair.

"You're about to get so laid," I murmur against his lips.

"Now?" He's probably mentally scrolling through the countless times we've had sex in public. The struggle was real when we lived with our parents. It sure tested our creativity, though.

I toy with the button on his jeans. "Would you rather we wait?"

"That's not a fair question." Mason nips at my jaw, then drifts his nose in an upward path. His groan is punctuated with a sharp inhale. I shiver against him, earning another animalistic noise from deep in his chest. The fact he's smelling me sends my mind straight to the gutter.

My nails tug at his dark strands, holding him close. "What would be a better one?"

"How fast can I strip you bare?"

"Think you can beat your personal best?"

His eyes glitter under the strobe lighting. "Only one way to find out."

chapter fourteen

Mason

THE DULL THROB BASHING AGAINST MY SKULL IS WHAT ROUSES me from a booze-soaked slumber. This painful reminder of my overindulgence isn't appreciated. But it's more than that. As I submerge from the fog, a persistent—albeit soft—tugging against my scalp demands attention.

As I crack my eyes open, a small figure comes into view. Fuck, my brain is so screwed that I'm imagining things. I scrub a palm over my face and try again. Archie's grin offers me a morning greeting.

I jolt alert with my next breath lodged in a strangled gasp. He's inches from my face, fingers tangled in my hair. When his baby blues latch on mine, that smile reaches megawatt levels. Another croak escapes my parched throat. A gruff chuckle—that most definitely doesn't belong to Archer—mocks my surprise.

"Rough night?"

Chad is leaning against the doorframe, seeming completely at ease watching us sleep.

"What the—?" I clamp my lips shut, gaze darting to the little boy still twirling my hair.

His father grunts at my reaction. "Chill, man. I'm not creeping on you. Archie is, though."

On cue, a stubby finger boops my nose. "Mornin', Mase."

Harsh golden rays streak through the slotted blinds. I squint against the penetrating sun while trying to process this situation. Presley is still snoozing as if we aren't hosting unexpected company. My sluggish gaze circles back to the little boy wedged between us.

"Morning?" Gravel coats my mouth and I try to gather some much-needed saliva.

"I wike your jammies. You sweep wit Mama?" Archie's chubby cheeks lift higher as he beams at me, smacking a palm against my torso.

"Uh," I peek over at the woman in question. It's somewhat of a miracle that I kept my shirt and boxers on while in a drunken stupor.

Presley has the blanket tucked up to her chin, concealing her fully clothed form. We took the edge off at the bar with plans for another round after sliding between the sheets. For once, I'm grateful for my wasted dick or we might be in a very naked state. Even so, the man leering from the threshold releases a noise that belongs in porn.

"I've seen it all before." Chad wags his brows at her before turning his gaze to me. "You, on the other hand, are brand-new and extra shiny."

"Dude, I'm straight." I clutch my forehead, which does little to alleviate the marching band practice taking place in my frontal lobe.

"Doesn't hurt to look."

"You kay, Mase? Have owie?" Archie taps my head.

The grin I give is weak at best. "I'm okay, buddy. Just tired."

Sleeping Beauty finally rises to awareness, peeling one heavy lid open to survey the scene. She doesn't move a muscle otherwise. "Why are you talking so loud?"

My jaw goes slack in her direction. "That's what you're concerned about?"

"Yes," she mutters. "There's a stampede of angry horses wreaking havoc on my stomach."

"Mama sick too?" Archie's brow is furrowed in severe concern.

"C'mere, baby. Make Mommy feel better." Presley sneaks her arms out from the covers to latch around Archer's waist, sucking him into a cocoon against her.

"Mama," he protests. "Your bweaf stinky."

"I'm sure it is," she coos while making no move to release him.

The squeaky gears in my brain protest against how normal everyone else is acting. I gape at Chad, who's still rooted on the same spot. "How did you get in?"

"I have a key." He holds up the item in question as if I won't believe him.

My gaze swings to Presley, who doesn't seem bothered in the slightest. In fact, she's looking at him expectantly. "Did you at least bring coffee?"

"In the kitchen," he replies with a knowing smirk.

"You're a saint," she praises with a moan.

I glance between them, my eyes straining from the effort. "What's going on?"

Presley blinks at me. "Huh?"

My focus returns to Chad. "Why are you just standing there?"

"Would I prefer I join you in bed?"

This entire exchange is slowly driving a spike through my temple. I manage to glare at him. "Could you give us some privacy?"

His lips flatten into a firm line. "You're too uptight, man. We just stopped by for Archie's swimsuit. I'm taking him to the pool."

Presley gasps, her palm slapping over her mouth. "With the super huge waterslides?"

"Uh-huh," Archie squeaks. "I go fast like train. *Vroooooom.*"

"You're going to have a blast, sweet angel. I'll miss you." She peppers his face with kisses.

"See you soon, Mama?"

"Tomorrow," she says with a crooked smile.

"Kay," he wiggles in her hold, which is still unrelenting. "We go buh-bye."

But Presley doesn't release him just yet. She gives him a final nuzzle, breathing in what I imagine to be her favorite scent. There's nothing I can do except watch the beauty unfold. It would be a crime to interrupt mother and son in such a heartfelt moment. I find myself feeling like an intruder again. At least I'm not the only one, seeing as Chad isn't budging.

"Love you," she murmurs into his hair.

Archer wraps his tiny arms around her neck, returning the affection. "Love you, Mama."

Presley stretches with a squeal, almost tumbling off the mattress. Her dismount is rather graceful considering our groggy awakening. She tugs at her dress to maintain an overdue semblance of modesty. "Gotta pee-pee. Wanna try going on the potty, Archie?"

"Nuh-uh." He shakes his head with a harsh refusal. "I go in my diaper.

"It will happen eventually, kiddo. Mark my words. Thanks for visiting." Then she trudges to the bathroom.

I'm left sprawled in bed with Chad hovering far too close and Archie gazing at me with stars in his eyes. "Uh, now what?"

Chad scoffs. "You're a sad sight, man."

"What did you expect when showing up at"—I check the display on my watch and wince—"ten o'clock in the morning?"

"You're the outcast in this scenario, big shot. Get used to it or find the door." His warning could be considered threatening if he didn't tack a wink on at the end.

My gut gurgles as I try picking apart the last ten minutes. I almost retch when the whiskey shots that Gunner insisted on beg for an immediate evacuation route. "I'm just… not firing on all cylinders, if you catch my drift."

"Welcome to parenting, Braxter. You don't get to call in sick or sleep off your hangover."

"But isn't it your day with him?" Not that I want to get rid of the little guy. This is just bad timing and slightly inconvenient after my poor decisions the previous night. "I would've made different choices last night if that weren't the case."

His eyes narrow on me. "Prepare for the unexpected when there are kids involved. Trust me."

"Um, all right." There's not much else I can say, even if my tongue was working properly.

"Feel better, stud. See you tomorrow?" His assumption almost chases off my nausea.

"Sure," I mutter before he vanishes down the hallway.

Archie slaps his palms to my cheeks, sending a resounding bang through my head. "You whiv wit me and Mama?"

"Not quite," I hedge with a wince.

His smile doesn't dip. If anything, he grins wider. "You sweep in my room, kay? We cuddle."

A clench radiates across my chest. I'm ill-prepared for these conversations. That inadequacy shrinks my pride into a ball of lint. Changing the subject seems like a harmless strategy. "Do you like football, buddy?"

His lips twist to one side. "I dunno."

"How about we play sometime? I'll toss the ball to you."

"Kay!" His screech is a hammer pounding nails into my skull. "Gotta go. Bye, Mase."

There's no chance to respond, especially in my current condition.

Archer barrel rolls off the mattress and dashes to the door. His small figure disappears in a blur as he goes in search of his father. I'm stunned still for several minutes while the dust clears. Presley emerges from the bathroom looking minty fresh and slightly less rumpled. There are still creases from the pillow denting her skin. Her glossy locks are tangled in knots. But a flushed stain tints her complexion and makes her shine brighter than the Northern Lights.

"Phew," she breathes. "I feel human again. It was touch and go there for a second."

"That's putting it mildly," I rasp.

Her frown is extra droopy for my benefit. "Do you want some ibuprofen?"

"I'd prefer an explanation."

She recoils, but the motion is sluggish. "Whoa. I was under the impression you loved being with Archie. Sure, he was a bit forward with the early snuggle session. It was crazy adorable, though. He's kind of obsessed with you, so you best choose your next words carefully."

I gawk at her, mouth hanging wide. "Do you honestly not understand my issue with what just happened?"

Presley clutches her head. "I'm too fuzzy around the edges for a guessing game, babe."

The springs creak under my weight as I sit upright. "You have to explain the dynamics of your relationship with Chad."

"Oh," she exhales with what sounds like relief. "You're referring to him."

"Yes," I grunt. "The obvious culprit."

She scoffs while padding to the bed, parking her ass on the edge. "Okay, don't be dramatic. It's not like he's a villain or anything."

"I could argue otherwise," I crack. "Is there some sort of guidebook I should read?"

Her forehead wrinkles. "About what?"

"How to handle disrespect of personal space, specifically from an overbearing baby daddy."

"You're still talking about Chad?" Presley's eyes bulge while she sputters. "Don't be silly. He's harmless."

"So you've said."

"That's just who he is." She whips an arm toward the area he'd been standing in not long ago.

"Acting totally nonchalant while watching us sleep? I didn't know he was there until I woke up," I defend myself.

Presley toys with the edges of my unruly hair. "Seems weird, huh?"

"Just a tad." My tone drips with sarcasm.

"I probably should've warned you." She sucks air between her teeth.

"Probably would've eased the initial panic."

Her laugh alleviates the pinch under my sternum. "We're really close, like minimal boundaries. Him walking into my house unannounced is a typical and frequent occurrence."

The pungent stank wafting into my nostrils is rising from a source I don't care to voice. "Please tell me you don't sleep with him on an equally regular cycle."

She stares at me for several beats too many, her expression far too passive. "Did you not hear the part about him being gay?"

Prickles rush across the back of my neck, the discomfort making me sweat. "Clearly that doesn't matter since you have living proof he wades into pussy territory."

"That's crude," she complains while flicking a stiff nipple poking through my shirt.

I dodge her second assault with a grunt. "I'd apologize, but his sexual orientation doesn't make me feel more secure after this morning. You had sex with him, right?"

Her huff is hollow. "Well, yeah. But it wasn't like that."

"How so?" I sure as hell know she prefers manly men. Chad seems to be precisely that, which only adds to my muddled mind. The gnawing in my gut snaps sharp.

Presley's hand curls around my bicep, giving me a gentle squeeze. "He's not a threat to you, champ."

"Then why is he allowed free range of your house? I'm missing a vital piece." The standard for shared custody is not what I witnessed earlier.

"Think of him more like my brother."

"That's not any better."

"Yeah, you're right. It's worse." She wrinkles her nose.

"Am I intruding on a family situation?" It pains me to ask again, but my conscience won't rest.

"No." Presley's grip on my arm tightens. "Not at all."

"How did you end up sleeping with him?" I scrub a palm across my mouth, trying to gather some composure. "I mean, what compelled you to do that?"

"Aside from his charisma and dashing good looks?"

My scowl feels like a vendetta against the man himself. "Seriously?"

"Your jealousy is once again misplaced. It's not that scandalous." Based on her jovial tone, I can tell she's trying to lighten the mood. "It only happened once, and there was a lot of alcohol involved."

"You only did it because you were drunk?" Not sure that satisfies the flames billowing under my skin.

Her flinch is answer enough. "Not exactly."

I groan toward the ceiling. "You're killing me, Pep."

"Excuse me for not wanting to air out my filthy laundry. It's not my finest moment." She pokes my chest. "You're one to talk."

"That's a fair point, but we're not discussing me right now."

"How convenient. Again," she sighs with theatrical flair. "Anywho, Chad is one of my besties. He never got as close to Vannah, Clea, and Audria for whatever reason. That didn't stop me from seeing him daily since we lived in the same dorm. We bonded over *Schitt's Creek* and the rest is history. It's safe to say I know him very well. He was and is gay—firmly—but he wanted to have sex with a woman before graduating college. Don't ask me why, but it was important to him. The topic was brought up enough that I could never forget. We were at a party and his deadline was fast approaching. It seemed like a great idea to volunteer after one too many lemon drop shots. I won't give you the graphic details for what comes next."

"Please don't." The idea of her sleeping with another man—his usual preferences aside—makes me heave. But I wasn't here. I left her. In a sense, I owe Chad for taking care of her when I couldn't.

Presley peers at me from under her feathery lashes. "Chad is a good man. He made me feel safe and cherished and wanted. I was practically starved of sensual contact. Until that night, I'd only ever been with you. No one since either."

Without hesitating, I fling my arms around her and collapse flat onto the mattress. She falls against me with a giggle. My lips seek hers automatically, locking us in a kiss filled with more promise than I can verbalize. I cradle her head in my palm and angle us closer. She parts her mouth for me on a moan, fingers fisting at the cotton concealing my bare flesh. A rumble from me encourages her to grip harder until the fabric shreds. Our tongues coax the passion to build. Blistering heat surges straight to my cock. I buck my hips, letting her feel just how hard she makes me.

Before I can begin stripping off her layers, she pulls away with a gasp.

"What was that for?" Her tone is breathy, eyes glassy and dazed.

My hand sets up camp on her ass, giving a gentle squeeze. "I love you, Peppy Girl. More than ever."

"Are you that relieved I didn't bang an entire football team while you were gone?"

I chuckle, jostling her on top of me. "No, that wouldn't change my feelings. You'll always be the one for me."

Something flickers over her expression, but she doesn't voice it. "Ditto, champ. I've always loved you the most. Well, besides Archie. He gets the squishiest, biggest part of my heart."

"I can handle that."

"You better." Presley pushes herself upright and straddles my waist. "Okay, I'm ready. Tell me your secrets."

"Now? Because the bulge in my boxers has a solid suggestion of a very different variety."

Presley wiggles against me, enticing the heady arousal pumping through my veins. "We have all day. I have nowhere else to be. Do you?"

chapter fifteen

Presley

I don't blink in fear that Mason will balk and vanish. His reluctance swells between us, but I won't be swayed. He needs to even the score. The gauntlet is whizzing at a pace I can't track, but he better snatch.

With a leisurely stretch, Mason crosses his arms behind his head to use as a cushion. His biceps flex for my viewing pleasure. I refuse to be distracted by his mouthwatering physique. The thrum tingling between my legs demands otherwise. A lustful gurgle lodges in my throat, but I gulp around it. I must be strong, dammit.

His fingers skip along my upper thigh. "How about coffee first? Or breakfast. I'll cook."

"Delaying the inevitable," I murmur. "You're not getting off that easy."

"No?" Mason rocks against me. This wouldn't be so problematic if my thighs weren't splayed wide astride him.

"No," I confirm. That might be convincing if my voice didn't wobble.

The predicament I've put myself in is a taunting snicker as I gather reinforcements. I straighten my spine, which just so happens to bump his shaft against me. The resulting whimper is a betrayal of my resolve.

Before I crumble completely, the demand for equality flows off my tongue. "I spilled my sordid tale. It's your turn."

His relaxed pose stiffens. "The story isn't glamorous."

"And mine is?"

"I'd much rather be in your position." He squeezes my hips, adding a double entendre for fun.

"You're just saying that," I call his bluff with a pout.

A heavy sigh corrects me. His rigid posture deflates into the mattress. "I've signed several non-disclosure agreements so you can't repeat any of this."

The eager throb in my chest sputters. "Is that why you've been so tight-lipped?"

"Part of it. More so because I'm ashamed. I already told you that," Mason reminds.

"Okay, I won't share a word. Promise." I dip to seal the vow against his lips with a brief kiss.

His gaze grips mine in an unrelenting hold, as if clutching to an anchor while suffering through the furious tides. "The second I signed on the dotted line, my ass belonged to them. I lost control overnight. They took off on a power trip."

"They?"

"The owners and board members and executives. Those that don't step foot from their ivory towers. Anyone with money or stakes in the game. They're in charge, and took every opportunity to remind me. I made the fatal error of assuming they were in my corner. I really thought they gave a shit about me. Worse than that, I trusted them to be decent and not deceive me. As it turns out, they couldn't care less about my well-being or happiness. All that mattered were the guidelines they established. We had an agreement so long as the profits were made, and I fit the desired mold."

The edge in his tone is razor-sharp, revealing years of unleashed pain that has been bubbling under the surface.

My swallow is thick while I wade through his torment. "And if you didn't comply?"

He strengthens his grasp on me, almost absently. "I'd lose everything. I got fucked by lawyers I never met. My agent and manager were the executors. They told me where to go and what to say. If I wanted to leave town when it didn't involve the team or a game, they'd be on my ass to make certain I didn't step out of bounds. If I was ever found to be in breach of contract, my ass was done for. Worse than it already was. I was miserable while riding high. A fraud, but also a legend. It was a mind fuck. Playing the game was all I had, and I held on tight. It became my only source to escape more than ever."

"What possible leverage did they have to hold over you? How can they get away with that?"

"I agreed to it."

Waves crash in my ears. "What? Why?"

"Take it from me—study contracts like your freedom depends on it. Read the fine print. Don't skip a word. I was a damn fool, Pep. Too fucking gullible. All I wanted to do was play football. They turned me into a pawn." He spits that last statement like a curse.

It takes me several beats to collect my thoughts. "Is this a common practice?"

"They claimed this type of situation was standard. Their treatment was what I should've expected, my gift basket for arriving at the top. I had no concept for the logistics and politics that went on behind the scenes. It's crooked and demented and harbors hate. To this day, I'm not sure why they pick people like me as targets for their perverse entertainment."

"Couldn't you fight it? Go to court?" Or something less ethical. In my head, I'm contemplating strategies to strike these bastards down.

"Sure," he scoffs. "And still lose. I didn't stand a chance against them. It was better to just go along with it."

"What'd they make you do?" A shiver of unease skates along my flesh while waiting for his response.

"It was the image I had to portray more than anything. I'm sure you saw enough online to assume, but I wasn't a reckless manwhore chasing skirts at all hours."

"Really?" I instantly feel guilty about the ripe disbelief in my voice, but the evidence states otherwise. Not that I can blame him. Mason is a famous football player. He was in the NFL, for crying out loud. There's no way he abstained for long. He's a virile man with a lavish appetite. That doesn't mean I have to be happy about his promiscuous actions.

Mason's blank expression sends a tornado of regret swirling through me. "That's what they want you to believe. They thrived on attention and breaking headlines in the media. Meanwhile, my identity was being altered beyond my control. I detached from reality whenever I was off the field."

"So," I mumble, "you didn't have an orgy with the entire cheer squad?"

The noise that rips from him is tortured. "Not even close."

My relief is a selfish splurge, especially at this moment. "Um, wow. That's not what I was expecting."

"I warned you," he taunts. The twitch at his lips is a blessed sight.

"How are you not plotting their demise right now?"

"Oh, I used to. Just internally. Then I got hurt. They released me from all contractual obligations. I was damaged goods and no longer useful."

"That makes you sound like cattle or something."

"Pretty much. My injury is almost a blessing in disguise. That's what I tell myself at least. It destroyed me to walk away, even after their influence dictated my every move prior. I love playing, and always will, but the game got warped. Besides," he trails off. With a wag of his brows, he changes directions with an abrupt curve. "It landed me in this bed with you."

I twist my lips at his distraction tactics. "You could've called me."

"And said what? 'Don't listen to what every station is broadcasting about me? I'm only pretending to sleep with all those women.' It sounds ridiculous." He scrubs a palm over his mouth, trapping a slew of profanity. "They even planted stories about me getting several girls pregnant."

I cringe, recalling the posts I'd accidentally stumbled across. "That was unpleasant to read."

"None of it was real. Quite the opposite." Then he seems to consider the truth in that conviction. "Well, almost."

"Do I want to hear this?"

"It has a happy ending," he offers with a crooked grin.

"Carry on," I exhale.

"For the first year or so, I had zero desire to replace our relationship. It seemed like we were still in love and committed. But I started to realize that wasn't true, and I was making myself more miserable. That prompted me to try chasing off the haunting memory of you. It made me sick to consider, but I forced myself to try."

"That must have been so difficult for you." Sympathy and sarcasm clash in my tone.

He pulls his lips tight in a wry smile. "It was fairly simple in the basic sense. Women were throwing themselves at me constantly. There was no dodging their wandering hands." He must notice the disgust curling my lip, his expression going sheepish. "Sorry."

"It's a necessary evil," I mutter.

"Right," Mason agrees. "That's how I felt. A handful of attempts is what it took for me to accept that getting over you wasn't possible. It only made the pain worse. Fucking others wouldn't get you out of my system. I went through the motions those few times, but it was empty and meaningless and tainted me further. My contract already obligated me to act like a playboy athlete with a bad boy image. I didn't want the reputation to define me. The truth was mine to hold. That's all I had left, if I couldn't have you."

I rub at the ache spreading under my breastbone. "But you could've."

"Yeah, I already admitted to being an idiot. With the way I feel—the way I've always felt—I should have visited. Or insisted you visited me. At the very least I should've called."

"I won't disagree with you."

"It was impossible to convince my heart that we were officially over. My brain and dick got the memo, but I couldn't erase the impression you stamped here." He pats the space over the beating organ that wouldn't let him forget me. "That mark is forever."

In a seamless motion, he sits upright and reaches back to yank his shirt off by the neck. Up until now, I haven't seen his bare chest. A tattoo on his left pec smacks me in the face. It's just text scrawled in his choppy handwriting. *If she isn't Peppy, I don't want her.*

Heat immediately springs to my eyes, clogging my vision with a fiery blur. "Oh, Ten. What did you do?"

"Just a reminder of who I'd never forget. I did this three years ago. No regrets. You're forever, Pep." Mason's palms make an upward trek along my sides, eliciting a path of pebbled bumps. "And with me always."

My fingers pet his inked skin. "I can't believe you did this. You should've told me sooner."

"I should've done a lot of things. Maintaining contact with you is at the top." His thumb drifts over my cheek. "My list of failures is long, Pep. I have so much to atone for. Above all else, nearly losing you will be my greatest regret."

The drum in my pulse goes silent. "You didn't fail."

"I did," he rasps. "I failed you."

"You didn't. Not really." My trembling palm lifts on its own, cupping his scruffy cheek. "But lucky for you, I'm the forgiving type."

Mason's eyes widen into vast green depths I long to drown in. "Just like that?"

"Well, there have been several other reasons leading up to this point. The box of memories earned you a blowjob."

"What does my sob story get me?"

I curl my fingers in the curve of a heart, fanning the shape outward in our exploding symbol. "A touchdown."

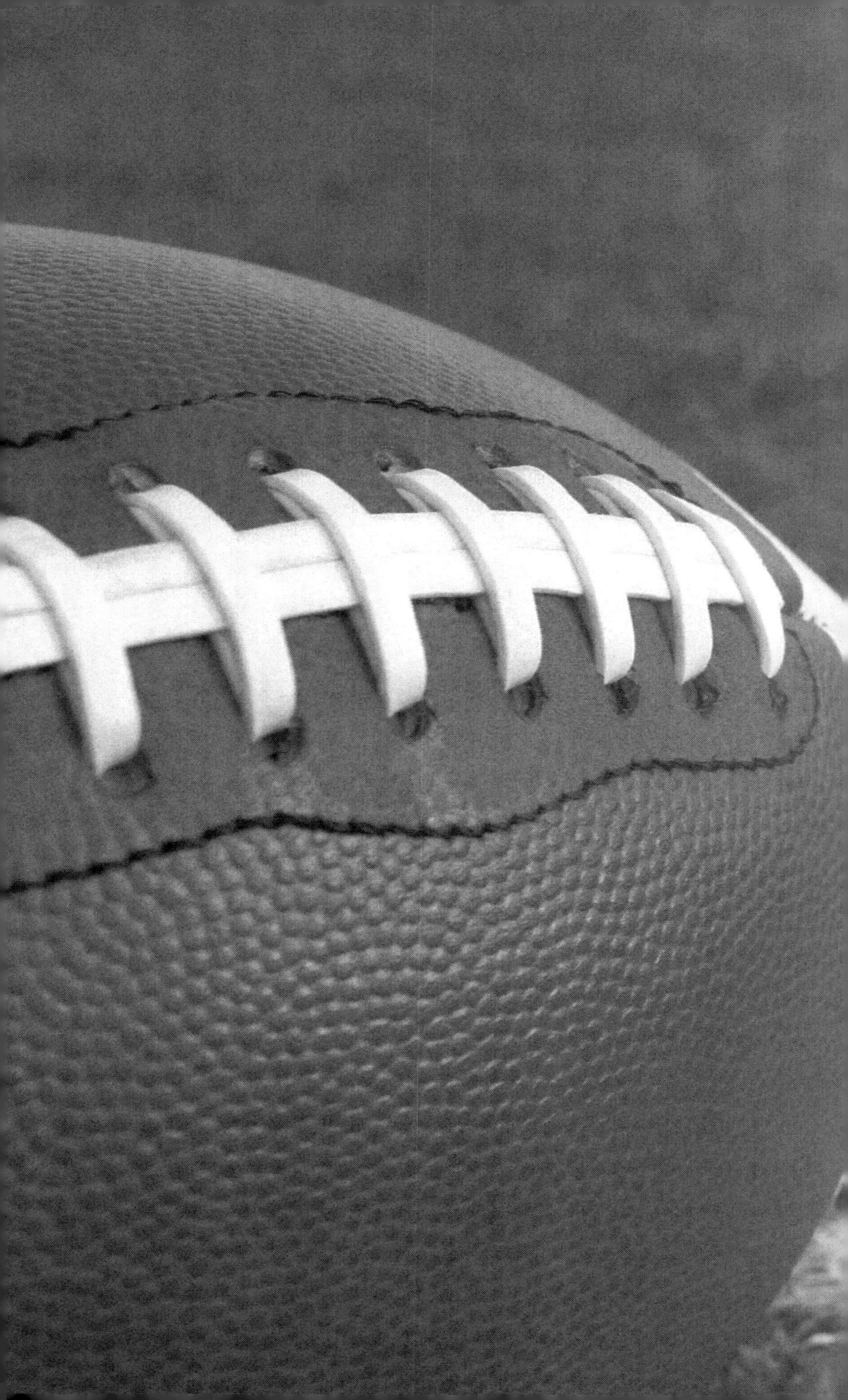

chapter sixteen

Mason

Ferocious desire ignites in Presley's gaze, morphing the calm waters into a bubbling hot spring. Her thighs cradle mine, an arm cinched around my shoulder to hold me against her. Not that I'd move a muscle. The fiery lust sizzling beneath my skin demands I answer her siren call. There's no reason to delay. That doesn't mean I don't enjoy hearing the request spill from those pouty lips.

I draw in a slow breath, finding that action far easier than it has been for years. The bricks that have built a damn brownstone on my conscience are suddenly gone. I didn't tell my overpriced therapist a fraction of what Presley now knows. She's the only one I can truly trust. That gleam in her eyes reminds me that it's time to switch focus. Easy enough, considering my cock has been hard for her since she sauntered from the bathroom.

"You want me to toss my ball in your end zone." I dip down until my nose brushes the delicate column of her throat.

"Yes," she urges in a rush. Her hips punch forward. Only the fabric barriers are keeping us apart. "Please."

Desperation perfumes the air in a heady scent. Presley knows all she needs to do is ask nicely to get me raging hard. Her mouth forming the word is a surge of fire to my groin. Always has been.

I trace the curve at her waist with my palm. "Top or bottom, Pep?"

She scrunches her features in contemplation. "I'd like to ride you for the first round. Then you can bend to my whore-igami folds for a change."

The breath gets caught in my lungs and I choke. "What?"

Her lips dust mine in a tease. "You may be an expert in the technique, but I'm not quite as limber as I used to be. We'll see how flexible you are, champ."

Amusement sputters from me, jostling our notched forms in a disjointed beat. "Whore-igami?"

The twinkle in her expression mirrors my humor. "Yeah, you're always folding me just right. With a few expertly placed creases, I'm contorted into a pleasure position."

"I'm happy to fold you again."

"Ladies first," she purrs.

"Busy day we have planned?"

"Extremely."

My hands wander higher, skimming the outer curve of her breasts with my thumbs. "We better get started."

Presley is straddling my lap with our chests nearly plastered as one. Her clothes need to go. I tug at her dress, and she gets the hint. With a whoosh, the garment meets the floor. The detriment to my common sense is left in just a lacy bra and thong. Saliva pools in my mouth while I trace a frilly cup that keeps her concealed. Her cleavage is inches from my face, in perfect range for motorboating. Before I can bury myself in her ample tits, she lifts slightly to tug at my boxers. I dip my thumbs under the elastic and shuck the restrictive cotton with a downward swoop. My cock springs free with an enthusiastic bob, waving to get her attention.

Slim fingers wrap around my length, offering a gentle stroke. "Good morning to you too."

"It sure is." I strain into her touch as a fiery longing propels through me.

Presley releases me in the next beat and I almost bellow. Then I'm distracted by her slinky movements as she slides off the bed with a graceful tuck and roll. Her feet plant on the floor with practiced finesse, reminding me of the routines she used to perform on the sidelines. She reaches back to unclasp her bra, ditching the sexy scrap from around her hips next.

There's a brief pause once she's exposed for my eyes to feast on. I'm about to slap my thighs and tell her to join the huddle. The naughty sparkle in her gaze stops me.

"How about a cheer for the sake of tradition?" Presley rolls her fists in front of her, reading my filthy thoughts from mere seconds ago.

My throat struggles with a thick swallow while the fantasy unfolds into reality. "If I'm scoring a touchdown, it's only logical."

"Call me superstitious." She winks.

"I'll never stop you, Pep." My sole focus is latched on her naked form while she begins to shimmy.

Presley's breasts sway with the rhythmic tempo and I'm ready to forgo this delay. Then she bends into a tucked position. In the following step, she springs up and shakes her hands for makeshift pom-poms.

"Give me a T!"

"T," I chant.

"And an E!"

"E," I echo.

"Now an N!"

"N," I nearly growl the letter.

"What's that spell?" She wiggles her fingers for emphasis, not waiting for my response. "Ten, Ten, Ten! He's going to give me all of them."

In a seamless drop, Presley spreads into the splits. Her legs are splayed wide and giving me a juicy preview. But the hiss rattling from her cools the fever in my blood.

Her face crumples with a grimace. "Oh, shit."

"What's wrong?"

"I might've just sprained my vagina." She stands on wobbly legs, peering between them to inspect for any noticeable damage. "Nothing looks broken or torn. I should've prepared better."

"Need a hand?"

"At the very least." Her husky tone threatens to destroy the small semblance of my control that remains intact.

"This doesn't bode well for our sex marathon."

"I'm fine." She bends in half, immediately popping down into a stretch. "Just need to shake it off."

"Are you sure?"

"Absolutely."

"We can postpone," I try again.

Presley rotates her pelvis, working the joint at her hip. "Are you trying to give me a complex? No delay necessary, champ. You can soothe the ache with your long drive."

I watch for another moment, but she only serves to fuel my arousal with these obscene motions. With a blind swat, I gesture to my jeans behind her. "There's a condom in my pocket."

A rosy blush stains her skin while she shifts in place. "Let's play without defense. I want to feel your score. All of it."

The meaning strikes with a resounding whack, and I widen my eyes on her. "Are you sure?"

She's already nodding. "I have an implant. If you're being honest about your lack of conquests, we have nothing to worry about."

"I've never gone without protection. That's only reserved for you."

"See? We're good."

Emotion steals my voice momentarily. I beckon her forward. "C'mere."

I scoot until the wall is flush with my back, allowing me to hold this upright position without effort. She returns to the mattress and resumes her straddled pose on me. Her flesh caresses mine with sultry purpose. There's a bated breath where she hovers above me, my body nearly trembling with the force to remain still. Then the pressure snaps taut as she begins lowering herself at a pace meant to breed madness.

She fully seats herself on me with that sensual glide. Her sheath is snug and slick, granting me entrance with a slow stretch. It's been years since I've felt her bare against me. The memory didn't keep me warm at night.

Presley mewls and curves her spine, notching us impossibly closer. The wrath in my veins crackles when she lifts until we nearly separate. I curl my hands into fists, fighting the urge to take control. Temptation is a feral beast snarling in my gut, demanding I thrust balls-deep with a savage punch. The patience pays off. In the following breath, Presley impales herself on me. A single downward slam and she's filled to the brim. My eyes cross at the intense sensation. With that purposeful move, she tames the chaos bubbling in my gut.

There's a silent command to buck my hips faster. This deafening order to hoard the powerful thrum under my skin. That desire spreads until my lungs burn. The smoky tendrils swell and retract on a fluid cycle. But I allow her to maintain the lead.

Rather than surrender to my natural instincts, I cinch an arm around her waist to erase any remaining distance. She's secure against me, rocking forward and back at a steady tempo. Her skin is hot and feverish sliding along mine. That friction prods at the blistering flames spreading to my limbs. The slippery sensation coils around my cock while she clenches her inner muscles. I'm captured in her depths until she deems me worthy of release.

Yet Presley is pliable against me, mine to take and mold. The whore-igami term resurfaces and I almost laugh. I thrust upward with punishing force, silently cursing the years that kept us apart. I won't feel the need to look back with regret one day.

For now, every second plunges me deeper into the clutches of her seductive wiles. Vines crawl around my limbs, dragging me below the surface until all I see is murky lust. The only thing that can release me from these binds is tipping over the edge—and based on the pinched desperation covering her expression, Presley is delving into the depths right alongside me. I want to free her from the restraints as well.

She rotates her hips in a seductive swivel. I'm hypnotized by this erotic dance she's performing on top of me. The invitation is a blaring fog horn—one I'm eager to accept with equal enthusiasm. I grind into her, meeting that insatiable desire with my own. Our lust burns hot enough to scald my skin. She's the gasoline to my flames, soaring me higher.

Musk coats the air, thick in my nostrils. I inhale our combined essence with a pleased rumble. Her nails pierce my flesh as I pump into her harder. I tweak her pebbled nipples and she gasps for more. She pushes against me, a sturdy pillar to lean on. I accept her brunt force with a groan as our pleasure cranks hotter. The fire is reaching boiling limits.

Sweat covers our skin, creating a slick glide between us. My body sticks to hers with feverish friction. A dibble of sweat trickles down her neck. I lick an upward path along her throat to catch the stray drop. Salt and wanton sweetness bathe my tongue. That unique flavor is the cure to my unyielding thirst, yet I'm instantly parched for more.

With my nose buried in the crook of her neck, I release a feral groan. "I could never replace this."

"No," she agrees.

"Not even close."

"Tell me more."

"You own me, Pep. From that first moment you smiled at me, dousing me in eternal optimism."

"I snared you."

"You did, and always will." There's no uncertainty in my tone. Only the sure demand that our hunger be sated.

After that, we become an erratic flurry ready to wreak havoc. She soaks into my bones, down to the very marrow. Her hands lay claim to me with each scratch and pull and demand for more. My fingers dig into the toned flesh of her ass, hauling her tighter against me. We get lost in the throes, chasing this promise just inches from our grasp. The restless ache requires sustenance.

Palpable want curls off my tongue, tantalizing me. We double the speed of our grinding motion as we race toward the peak. My hips are a hammer trying to nail her into submission. Slapping flesh accompanies our hounding need. That pulse lulls me into a trance. The past no longer exists. Nothing else matters in this vortex she's created. All I feel is her.

Presley's whimpered cry punctures the billowing lust and I tumble after her into the expanse of climax. The relief is instant and calms the rage with a final plunge. Her limbs wrack with spasms. I drain all I have into her until I'm wrung dry. For several breaths, we're suspended in blistering heat. A static buzz fills my ears. I'm barely aware of the tension leaking from my muscles.

She rests her forehead on mine, exertion heaving our huddled forms in the afterglow. I'm thoroughly spent and satisfied, but my appetite is a ravenous pit. The reprieve will be short, especially with her pussy still fluttering around me.

A sloppy palm lands on my shoulder, offering several pats. "Well done, champ. You never disappoint."

"I agree. That might deserve a spot on the charts."

Presley's labored exhales puff against the sweat dappling my chest. "It definitely deserves another cheer."

"You're not going anywhere," I chuckle against her lips. "If anyone is spraining your vagina, it's me."

chapter seventeen

Presley

"Could Meadow Creek be any cuter? I mean, this entire street belongs in magazines and blogs selling small-town living. And this store? Adorable." Vannah's gaze is devouring the shelves cluttered with random knick-knacks and novelty items.

"You act like you've never been here before." I swipe a glass figurine from Archer's reach, turning the stroller a bit more to the left.

"Let's be honest, it's been a while."

"Whose fault is that?"

"Mine, obviously. And what a tragic mistake." She picks up a Dammit Doll, laughs at the description, and passes the stuffed coping mechanism to my son. "That will come in handy. My treat."

"Pebbled Stones is a sight to behold." I'm only being mildly sarcastic.

We're treating ourselves to a random mid-week outing. My bestie lives almost an hour away in Minneapolis. To say I was shocked when she suggested we spend the day in Meadow Creek is an understatement.

"I made the right choice driving all this way. Just look at this. Who doesn't need a House Mouse?" Vannah studies the small rubber animal with a smile. "I'm going to scare the shit out of Landon with this little treasure. He's going to scream like the city boy he is."

"You're so sweet."

"How kind of you to notice." She skips her manicured nails along a display of handcrafted mugs. "The hubs is a bit more creative with his praise. He invented a few new words last night. I banged him hard enough to puncture the wall and it sent both of us over the edge at the same time. That just goes to prove how *sweet* I really am."

"Please don't use inappropriate language. We're in the company of innocent ears." I point a meaningful finger at my son.

Her wince is paired with a stumbled as she slams to a halt. "Oh, sh—crap. He's repeating stuff now, right?"

Archie beams at her in answer.

I snort and roll my eyes. "Like an echo."

"Echo," he repeats with a giggle.

"Smart kid. I need to watch my mouth." Vannah pouts.

"That'd be a first."

"Well, this must be child-proofed." She begins digging in a sticker box. "What we lack in population, we conquer with community."

I smile at the bold letters in a doodled design. "That's our motto."

Vannah coos at the die-cut, tucking it under her arm. "See? Freaking charming. I get the appeal."

"The free daycare doesn't hurt."

"Not a selling point for me."

"Do you want kids?" This is the moment I realize we haven't discussed the baby topic lately.

She swats at the air with nonchalance. "Sure. Once I'm thirty, we'll start trying."

"Oh, you're one of those planner types. I forgot."

She nudges me. "Hush. We can't all be blessed with a beautiful accident."

Before I can respond, a rapid flurry of whispers catches my attention. Three women I recognize from frequent sightings around town are darting glances over at me. They look young, maybe on the cusp of twenty. That's old enough to hide their shit-talking better. The scene reeks of gossip. My suspicion is confirmed when I overhear part of their conversation.

"Do you think she actually believes he's going to marry her?" The blonde wrinkles her nose in my general direction.

Her carbon copy scoffs, tossing golden curls over her slim shoulder. "That would be supes depress. She's like twenty-five and can't be that naïve at her age. It's just sad, though. I almost feel bad for her."

The first purses her lips in an exaggerated pucker. "Right? What single man of his status wants to be saddled with a frumpy chick who has a kid? Especially in this tiny town?"

"Well, he was raised in Meadow Creek." The meek voice from the third girl pipes up.

The bitchy duo pin her with seething glares. The second spits a fiery retort through clenched teeth. "Don't be ridiculous. She trapped him in a dead-end situation. No way a guy like Mason wants that baggage."

This is the moment my bestie loses her composure.

Vannah drops her purchases on the floor, lunging forward to throw a hissy fit. I grab her elbow at the last second.

"Oh, those bitches are gonna meet my fist. Let me near them." She gnashes her teeth.

I almost let her loose while steam spouts from my ears. "My son is the furthest thing from baggage."

Our notice doesn't stop them. The longer they talk, the more I'm convinced that they're speaking loudly on purpose. This is so reminiscent of high school. Nausea bubbles in my stomach. Girls were always jealous that Mason couldn't be swayed from my apparent clutches. It seems that opinion hasn't changed.

"Mason is the lucky one." Vannah counteracts their volume with a boisterous tone of her own.

"Mace?" Archer sits forward in the stroller, searching the store for his new favorite person.

"He's not here, sweet boy. We'll see him later." I pet his faux hawk with a gentle caress.

"How traumatic," a blonde bimbo coos. "Her son thinks Mason will be his daddy."

"That man can pretend to be mine," the other cackles.

Vannah gags. "Gross. What a pack of immature hussies. Mason isn't old enough to be their dad. And if he was? Disgusting. Hard pass on those twat waffles."

But their poisonous venom highlights the fear festering in my gut. It's just shallow trash they're spewing, but my insecurities feed on that garbage. I don't let the pain show, keeping my shoulders straight and glare even. Inside is another story. My stomach is somersaulting while I try to ignore their hateful stares.

My bestie still appears to be seconds away from tackling the trio to the ground. Her gaze swings to me, probably seeing the ashen hue covering my complexion. "Don't listen to them. You're not frumpy. If you have a daddy kink, that's totally fine. I'm sure Mason will roleplay with you."

I laugh, but the noise is hollow. "Thanks, Van. I'm trying not to."

"Do you want me to say something?" She bristles as the catty girls continue their dissection of my downfall with Mason.

"That's not necessary. I don't want to make a scene." That's the last thing I need after this horrific demonstration.

"They need to be taught a lesson in respecting their elders."

"Now you're being ridiculous. Like you just said, we can't be that much older than them."

"It's the principle." She smacks a fist against her flattened palm.

"I'm comfortable in my relationship, no matter what others say." But that's a lie. These girls are just sprinkles on top of a steep doubt mountain.

Vannah turns to face me, effectively shutting out the villains still spewing shade. "You love him, right?"

"I've never stopped."

"And he confessed his secrets?"

"Yes," I say automatically.

Her eyes narrow slightly. "Which must be extra dirty since you won't share them with your bestie."

"I've already apologized."

"Yet still won't spill the tea."

"Not my story to share."

"Whatever," she huffs. "But that confirms the truth. Those women are just jealous they don't have a hot man doting on them."

"I know that. Truly. But it just hurts hearing my fears out loud from another mouth."

Vannah's frown is so fierce it could convince me to agree

with anything she says. "Have you talked to him about these feelings?"

I'm nodding before she's done. "Probably too often."

"I'm sure he wants to soothe your worries. Let him rub you down with all those soft touches."

"I actually prefer it rough." My wink signals the joke, allowing the light to crack through these stormy clouds.

She whistles under her breath. "Oh, damn. You get laid once or twice and the tigress is off-leash. Bravo to Mason."

"He's good for me, and Archie."

Upon hearing his name, he abandons the toy in his grip. "Mama sad?"

I lean over to plop a kiss on my son's cheek. "I'm happy so long as you're near."

That seems to appease him, and he returns to the collection of stuff within reach. If only I could be so easily distracted. The chatter still buzzes in my ears, feeding the worst negative assumptions.

"You're going to need a lot more than a Dammit Doll to wage this war." Vannah sneers at the girls, most likely preparing to hiss if necessary. "Let's go get an alcoholic beverage like the sophisticated ladies we are."

The thinly veiled jealousy spearing from the gaggle confirms they can't legally drink. The urge to stick out my tongue is fierce. My friend grins in victory, looping an arm around my shoulders.

"Come on, Press. You can regale me with tales about the massive penis Mason Braxter carries around in his pants. No one else will ever have the privilege."

"Penis!" Archer squeals, clapping loudly.

"Vannah," I groan toward the ceiling.

Her mouth pops open, seeming perplexed about my scolding. "What's the big deal? The little man has one."

I scrub over my forehead. "But he doesn't need to be shouting about it in public."

"Could be worse. I could've said—"

I slap a palm over her mouth, muffling whatever choice word she was about to spew. "Please don't. We're leaving. I'll tell you about the sausage loaf Mason feeds me on the way."

"That's my girl. Lead the way."

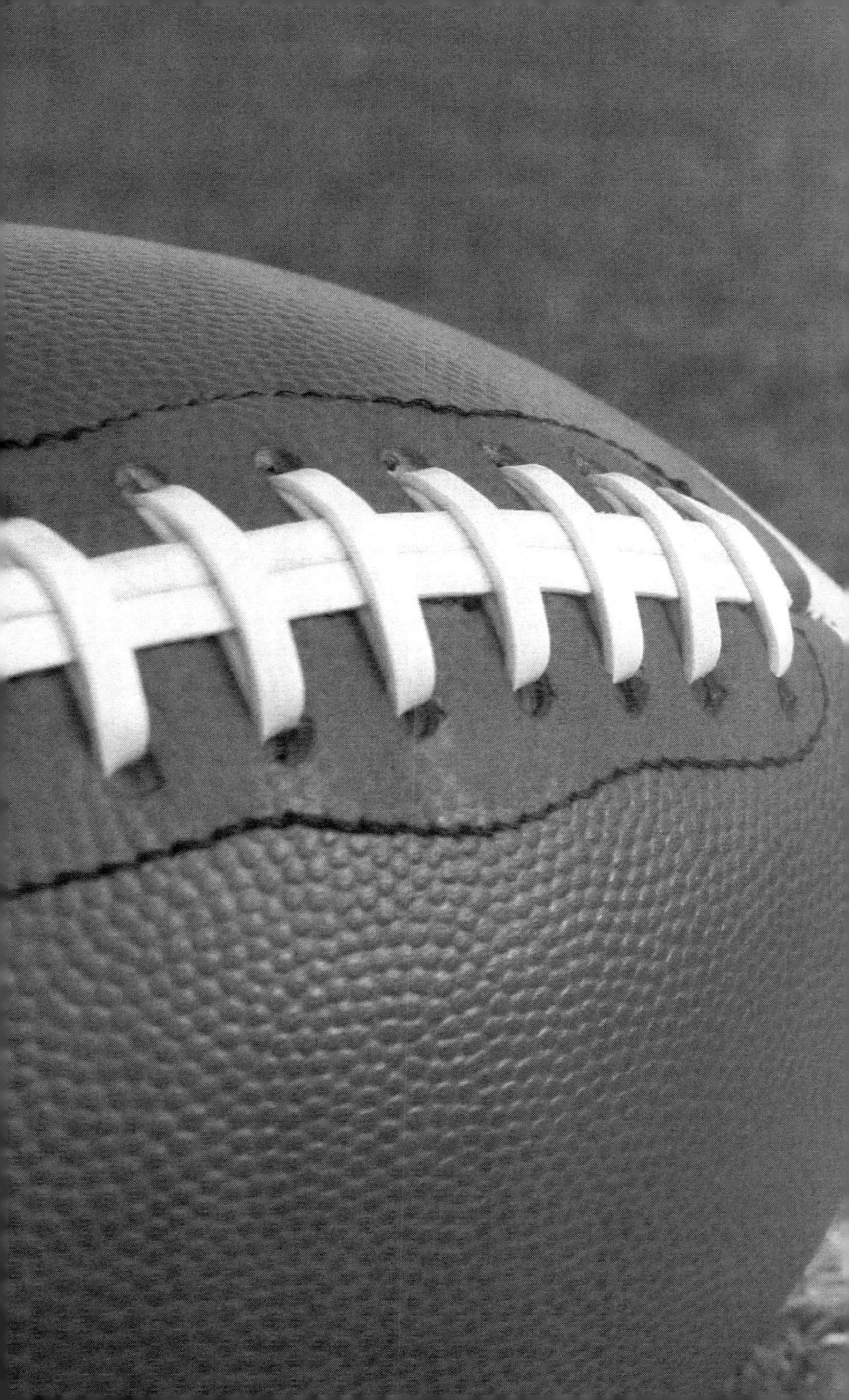

chapter eighteen

Mason

"SOLID EFFORT," I CALL FROM MY SPOT ON THE SIDELINES. "Let's run that again. This time, more pressure from the front line. I don't want to see the pocket jeopardized."

My players nod, dropping into position to run the drill. I study their formation with an assessing gaze. Any hole or weakness will be exploited by our opponents. Colt—the quarterback—snaps from the bent squat, his feet light and quick. The linemen are a different story. Their response is sluggish and sloppy. A defense with any sense will plow right through them and get the sack.

"Tighten the line," I bellow.

The play screeches to a halt with my command. A dozen helmeted heads swing to face me. I clap in rapid succession, then spin my wrist to signal they should go again. Their commitment comes with jerky nods. Even though fall is halfway done, the grass is still green, and fresh enthusiasm pumps into the atmosphere. These boys are eager to learn—and win. I'm ready to prove my worth. Not just to the players either.

It's been a month since I started as the offensive coordinator at Carleton. The other coaches have been generous enough to give me a wide berth while I get accustomed. There are plenty of knots and snags to work through. That's to be expected, especially since I got hired after the season had already begun. We're making the most of what's left. My style differs from what they were used to. The blending method has been bumpy at best. But I'm determined not to fuck this up. Coaching is giving me purpose, along with my girl and her hilarious son.

The past two weeks with Presley have proven to be a lesson in patience and sacrifice. Those are two traits I struggle to obtain. She remains cautious, even after we laid our secrets bare. I've been spending the days since trying to mend the damage. The wound is years deep and scabbed over. Eventually I'll remove the scars my silence and absence created. That's my main focus, above all else.

There's a sudden commotion, resulting in several guys colliding. This is just offensive practice. We don't tackle to the ground. Yet a fumbled pile on the turf suggests otherwise. The others stumble to avoid impact, still successful in tripping over their damn feet.

I search for the distraction through narrowed eyes. It only takes mere seconds to spot the culprit. The shapely figure of every man's desire is sauntering toward the field. A furious cocktail of lust and protective instincts surges through my veins. Wind blasts in my ears even though the air is still. We're in the thick of October, but the weather is uncharacteristically warm. That doesn't mean I approve of the expanse of skin she's showing off. These guys are getting an eyeful of what's mine.

Like a predator tracking his next meal, I stalk Presley's every move. Her dress is a tad too tight for my liking. She's seduction wrapped in midnight fabric. The shade represents filth and sin and every depraved act ramming into me. I'm tempted to shrug off my pullover to cover her curves. Before that intention settles, my mind circles the drain into the gutter. The sway of her hips demands attention. Each captivating swing is a yearning I'm desperate to answer.

Then I recall where we are, and the other men who have their thoughts on a similar trajectory to mine. Based on the dumbstruck expressions spreading across the masses, each one hopes they'll get a chance to strut their shit. They'll all catch more than flies with their jaws hanging so wide.

I whistle through my teeth, corralling their strayed focus. "Five laps. Now."

That's the equivalent of two miles—a leisurely stroll in the park for them, even in cleats. It will keep them occupied while I handle Presley's scantily clad presence.

A chorus of grumbled protests greet my demand, but no one dares to argue. Colt is sporting a grin that's too familiar. The uneasy twinge in my gut can't be ignored. He could easily succumb to the lavish spoils forced upon me. The thought is fleeting and disappears within moments. That's not my problem to solve. Besides, it takes hellish force to rip my eyes from Presley.

The team shuffles off to the outer track as a cohesive unit. Except one. After a pointed glare from me, Colt gets his ass moving with the herd. That gives me ample opportunity to devour the sight before me.

"Hey, Pep." I stride across the field to meet her. "This is a surprise."

She sidles up beside me, puckering her lips for a kiss. "I

just finished with a client in the area. Figured I'd stop by to see you in action."

"You organized someone's house wearing that?" I lean back to grant myself another once-over of her lush body. Wildflower blossoms and supple dreams waft in the open air. That only serves to pummel me with a visual of her delectable curves withering from my tongue's torture.

Presley glances down at her dress. "Is there an issue with my outfit? I thought you'd like it."

"It's how much I like it that's the problem. Me and every other pair of functioning eyeballs on the field."

A naughty gleam flashes in her baby blues. "Ah, feeling a bit possessive?"

"Extremely."

"Don't worry, champ. I'm all yours." She presses against me, close enough that her mouth brushes my ear. "I changed into this little black beauty just for you."

"Thank you," I croak. This woman has the power to tip me off-kilter with a quirk of her pinky.

"That's what I thought." Her tone is smug—and has every right to be.

Our three best receivers approach from around the far end. Their necks almost break while trying to keep Presley's ass in sight. I can barely decode their muffled voices.

"Fine as hell," is mumbled loud enough to carry.

"Coach is a boss beast. That honey is pure gold," comes from another.

"No wonder he's always in a good mood," trails from the last one.

"Aren't they sweet?" She wiggles her fingers in their direction.

My scowl is aimed at them while I address her. "Are you flirting with my players?

Presley knocks her hip into mine. "Just saying hi. There's nothing wrong with being friendly."

"Uh-huh. Looks like it."

"What? You know I've always had a thing for guys in jerseys."

"Trading me in?"

"We'll see how the season goes." At least her wink is sent in my direction.

"I don't like my odds."

"Why do you think I wore this dress?" Her lips pepper my jaw. "A little incentive for what you get later."

"You're a wicked woman." It takes titanium-grade willpower to stop myself from groping her where we stand.

"I'm well trained in how to motivate a star athlete. Should I demonstrate another cheer?"

A harsh grunt scrapes from the depths of me. The routine in her bedroom plays on repeat even weeks later. "Those strategies are better kept private. Just for me."

Presley walks her fingers up my chest, toying with the zipper. "I love when you turn into a caveman for me."

"That makes one of us." The pinch in my chest is a strange mixture between discomfort and satisfaction. She's the only one who gets this type of reaction from me.

"All right, I'll go easy on you. How are the dynamics?" She lifts her chin at the jogging offense.

The tension releases from my limbs. I'm grateful for the reprieve in subject matter. "Decent. I've seen worse."

"And better."

"That's obvious." Not to sound like a pompous ass, but the statement rings true. "Most of these guys have what it takes. The drive and potential are there. It's the confidence that's lacking."

She hums while nodding to a favorable beat. "I'm sure

you'll help with that. Such a big shot gracing this tiny campus with his presence. Do they treat you like royalty?"

A distinct memory from my first day rises to the surface. Anyone even distantly related to the team had gathered to greet me. The hoots and hollers were so damn loud that my ears are still ringing a month later. They just about rolled out the red carpet.

"I put the kibosh on that. There's no reason to idolize me."

"Um, okay. Did you forget about the two years you played professionally? That's unfathomable to these young bucks. Let them drool over you." The pride in her voice scrubs at the toxic rust that tarnishes too many of those memories.

"I'm just glad to have a job."

"You're happy coaching here?" The uncertainty in Presley's tone gives me pause.

"Yeah, of course. Do you still doubt me?" I already know her answer, but the confirmation motivates me.

"Not on purpose," she rushes to say. "I can't seem to help it. There's just this tiny sense of dread plaguing me. I might be optimistic, but I'm not foolish."

This is a conversation we'll repeat until every last shred of skepticism disappears. "You have every reason to be wary. I'm the one who left. That's on me. You aren't the one who has to prove his place. It's my burden to reclaim the trust you've lost. I won't leave you again."

She nibbles on her bottom lip. "Yeah?"

I tug the tortured flesh free from her teeth. "Yeah, Pep. This is forever."

Her sigh is still too heavy. "I believe you, but I also refuse to hold you back. The last thing I want is for you to ever resent me."

"I could never."

"You could. What if a major offer with the NFL comes through?"

"I've made my choice."

"But you can change your mind." Her renewed doubt clangs like a gong against my skull.

"No." My tone is resolute.

"Stubborn as ever," she mutters.

"You used to appreciate that about me."

"Still do, Ten." She goes quiet for a moment, gaze skittering to some distant point behind me. "I've been meaning to ask you something."

"That's terrifying," I chuckle. In truth, my gut plummets just hearing those words. I hate this unstable ground we're still stumbling on.

"It's not bad. Just curious why you stayed in California after your injury. I can't imagine you wanted to stick close to those who made each waking moment miserable."

Regret leaves a sour taste on my tongue. This is a hole in my story that I meant to cover sooner. "Rehab and physical therapy were provided by the team. I couldn't seek treatment elsewhere—that was another clause in my contract. Once the dust settled and I was back on my feet, it didn't take long for me to set my sights elsewhere. I just wasn't sure where I'd land."

"You didn't plan to move back to Minnesota." Her statement lacks any note of question.

"I did," I retort. "Honestly, I didn't see myself anywhere else. But shame held me hostage. Instead, I let chance roll the dice. That conference in the cities couldn't have been timed better."

"That's awful fanciful of you. I'd like to know what would've happened if we didn't cross paths at Knotty Knox." She's echoing something eerily similar to what she said that very night.

"I would've found my way home. It gets lonely in the dark. Only one girl has ever shared her light with me. Regardless of my waning pride or fear of rejection, I wouldn't be able to stay away for always. There's no other choice for me, Pep. You're it, along with Archie. One day, your faith in me will be restored too."

"That will be wonderful," she exhales with what I imagine to be relief. Her use of a definite connotation is a giant step in the right direction.

"It certainly will." I bend to rest my forehead on hers. "Just promise to love me. That's all I can ask of you."

Her breath blends with mine, cementing our words into a vow. "As if I have another choice."

"Then it's official. You're stuck with me."

"Wasn't I already?"

"It doesn't hurt to remind you."

"Determined as always."

"Another trait you appreciate." I wag my brows, earning a laugh from my captivated audience.

"We can finish this later. They're almost done," she muses.

My gaze shifts from her momentarily to check on the guys. "Counting laps?"

"Something like that. I don't want to distract you." She smiles at me, her eyes sparkling under the afternoon sun.

"Too late."

Presley links our fingers together, giving me a squeeze. "Dinner in town tonight?"

"Sure."

"Can Archie tag along?"

"That shouldn't be a question." This is another frequent cause of doubt I'm eager to eliminate.

"It's hard to comprehend how open you are with having him around."

"Get used to it, Pep. I want your son to be part of my life. Our life. Together."

"Damn, that's romantic. You're tempting me," she teases.

Her sudden upbeat attitude compensates for the shrouded guard in those soulful blue depths.

"To do what?" If she suggests sneaking off for a quickie, I'll put Colt in charge for a few plays.

Presley beats my assumptions to a pulp. "To be reckless and foolish and let love speak the loudest."

My arms move on their own, hugging her tight against me. "I'm ready when you are."

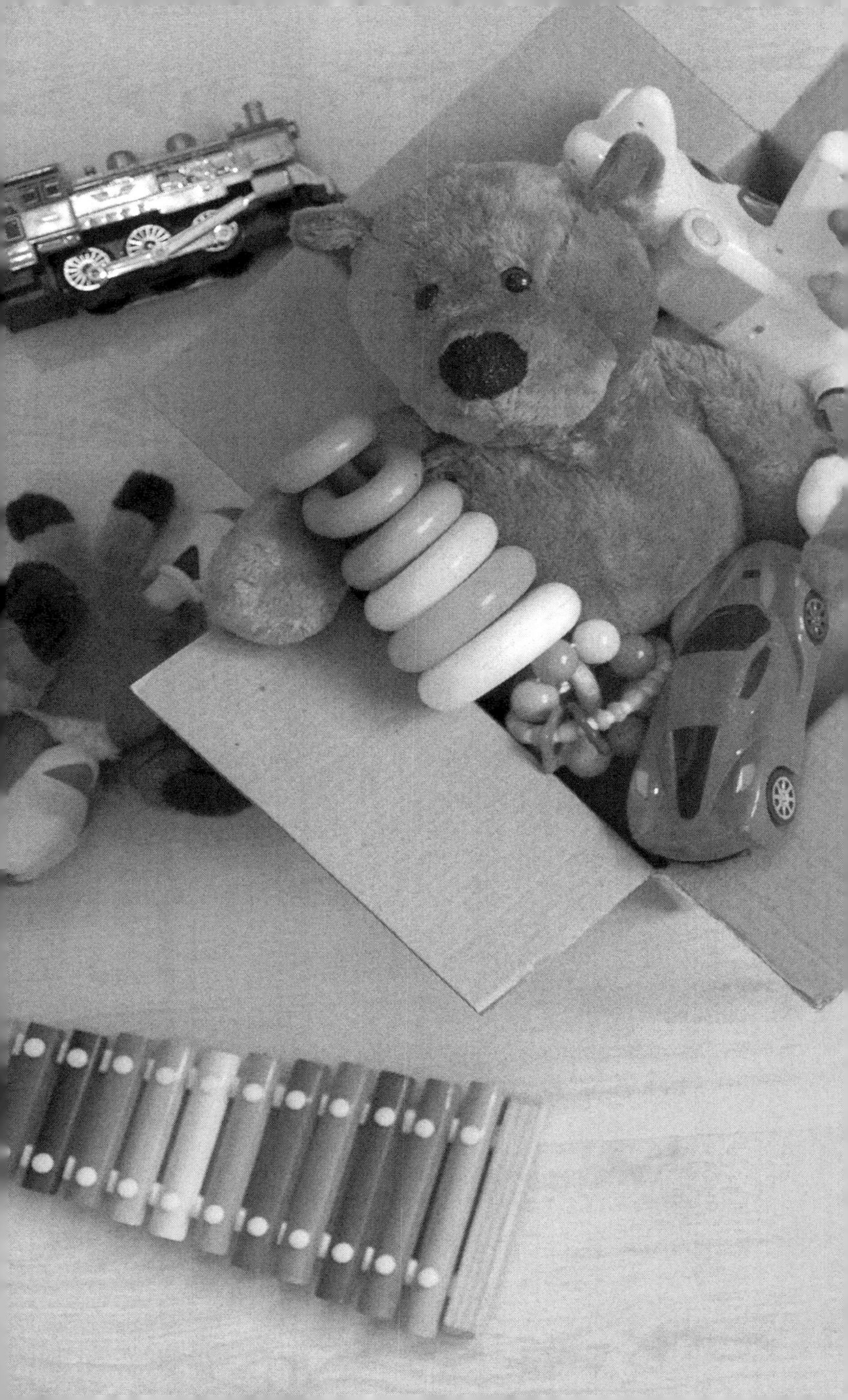

chapter nineteen

Presley

Muddy Waters is fairly calm as we walk through the double doors. The restaurant was a no-brainer with Archer in tow. My mouth instantly pools when I inhale the savory scents filtering through the space. Six o'clock on a Thursday seems to be ideal to drop in. Only half the tables are occupied, giving us plenty to choose from. There's a sign instructing us to seat ourselves.

"Booth?" I glance over at my boys, a thrill zinging through me at that plural term.

"Boof!" My son's adorable pronunciation gets a smile from me.

"Does that work for you, buddy?" Mason tickles the toddler latched onto his hip.

The picture they create gets my engine thrumming hot. I swear my libido runs wild whenever Mason is near Archie.

If I'm not careful, I'll be suggesting we add more babies into our mix. My belly warms in preparation. I mentally scold the irresponsible impulse. At this rate, I'll be willingly knocked up before Christmas.

Our favorite server skids to a stop on her way to the kitchen. "Well, look at this happy family."

I grin at her special greeting. "Hey, Cathy."

"Glad to see the little one joining you tonight." She waves at Archer when he shifts his focus to her.

"Hi, Caff. Butta' noodews for me?"

"We need to sit down first, okay?" I tap his nose.

He nips at my finger. "Kay. Let's go, Mase. Giddy up!"

Mason neighs, then takes off at a choppy gallop. "Hold on, buddy. My horse is fast."

I'm left swooning in the entryway, palm clutching my throat. "Oh, my."

"You're in trouble," Cathy muses.

"I'm well aware," I exhale.

She gives me a nudge from behind. "Go get 'em. I'll be over in a few."

My feet seem to glide across the floor in my haste to catch them. That is until I catch several other women admiring the view. I chance a longer look across the room and find most eyes pinned on Mason's sculpted butt. Green tinted fumes stream from my nostrils with a harsh breath. He's providing mommy porn of the finest caliber, and every female in this joint is taking notice.

I stomp the remaining distance to our booth, set on staking my claim. Bunch of deprived beeches. The lot of them. Another slow sweep reveals that the shameless gawking hasn't ceased.

Rather than salivating over the meals on the menu, these horny toads want the special dish served just for me. I can empathize. Almost. Not too long ago, I was beyond frustrated of the sexual variety. Mason eased each empty ache with exquisite methods only he's capable of. These women want the same treatment. He's a juicy steak when they've all been barely surviving off lettuce and stale crackers. One after the other, they catch sight of my cutting stare and wisely return to their own conversations.

"What's wrong, Pep?" Mason must hear my teeth grinding, or notice the fierce glare I'm still pointing toward our fellow patrons.

I drop onto the empty seat with a huff. "You're single mom catnip."

A choked chuckle spews from him. "What?"

My arm blindly motions to his adoring audience. "Actually, scratch that. You're bait for every woman. They all want a piece of you, as in steal a bite or lick."

His eyes track my not-so-subtle flailing. There are still a handful of brave souls peeking at him from under their false lashes. Understanding flashes in his emerald eyes, that charming smirk firmly in place. "Oh, is someone jealous?"

"Yes," I blurt. "Extremely. It's bad enough people think I'm trying to trap you in this tiny town with my baggage."

The amusement lifting his features falls flat. "Who thinks that?"

A sour bubble expands in my stomach. "I overheard these girls flapping their chaps at Pebbled Stones. But I'm sure all the other spiteful wenches in Meadow Creek agree."

"Wenches," Archie giggles. His focus doesn't shift from the coloring page in front of him, but he keeps babbling. "Wenches are spitty. Wenches, wenches."

I smack my forehead at my careless ranting. "Great, I'm no better than Vannah."

"Auntie Van has potty mouth," Archer announces with pride.

Mason ruffles his hair, the action coming naturally. My son

nudges into the affectionate touch. It serves to defuse most of the aggravation stabbing at me.

"She does, buddy. Far worse than your mom, right?"

"Uh-huh." His tongue peeks from the corner of his mouth while he draws a circle.

"Maybe I should move," I comment almost absently.

Mason's hand stills halfway to adjusting his hat. "What?"

"Not far. Just away from Meadow Creek."

"Why?"

"A fresh start somewhere new. Before Archie is enrolled in pre-school."

My son perks up. "I go to shoowl?"

"Soon, sweet boy. Once you're three."

"How many dat?"

I hold up my fingers to show him.

"Fwee?" His blue eyes widen.

"Yep. You'll be three on your birthday in January. Four months to wait."

"Yipppeeee!" He wiggles in his seat. "I'm gonna get pwesents."

"So many," I confirm. His grandma alone spoils him rotten.

"But your parents live here," Mason interjects.

"So does our past. And the rumors we can't escape."

"Like what?"

My exhale is forced. "You left. I stayed. We broke up. You're an all-star athlete. I'm a single mom who got knocked up by her gay best friend. We're dating again."

He squints at me. "Those are facts."

"Not helping," I clip.

"I gonna color good. Gotta get better for shoowl." Archer refocuses on his paper, crayon flying across the page with his erratic strokes.

Once my son is properly distracted, Mason switches his

attention to me. His gaze is a spotlight trying to expose my darkest insecurities that I've buried deep. "There's something you aren't telling me. I don't believe you're this upset from just a few catty women being rude, or when they try to get my attention. People are bound to point and stare. They'll say things that aren't nice. That's just how it goes."

"Especially when you're involved."

"What's that supposed to mean?"

"You're Mason Braxter," I deadpan. I'm tempted to tack on a *duh*, but refrain for maturity's sake.

His brow furrows. "I always have been."

"But you're the famous version now."

"Hardly."

"You don't have to play the humble card. It's fine to admit your ego has been adequately pampered over the years."

"Not by the only one who matters."

"You flatter me." I can't help batting my lashes at him.

"Just returning the favor."

"Even if you weren't, you're too sex—hot." I wince, my eyes flying to Archie.

He's too busy scribbling to catch my near slip.

I clear my throat, regaining a margin of composure. "Girls wanted you like their next fix in high school. I remember that quite well. But this is different. These women are worse than piranhas after a fleshy snack."

Mason grimaces. "That's an exaggeration. And unappetizing."

"Yeah, okay. You shouldn't have to be constantly reassuring me. What's happened to my positive outlook? It's safe to say my confidence has been shooketh."

"But why?" His gaze is pleading.

"Stupid insecurities. I need to get over the gloom already. This isn't a recipe on how to make a successful relationship last." I roll my eyes, mostly at myself.

"Hey," he grabs my hand. "We've been over this. You have every reason to hesitate. But I love you, Pep. Only you. That's how it's always been. That's how it always will be. You stole my heart in seventh grade and I don't accept returns."

"That's not really how stealing works," I tease.

"There's my girl."

And cue the flutters. I melt against the booth in a puddle of sloppy mush. "You have the right words for every occasion."

"It's a talent I take very seriously." He blows against his nails.

"Phew, sorry for the wait. There was a spill." Cathy appears out of seemingly nowhere.

Mason flashes her a grin. "No problem. We've been keeping ourselves busy."

"I bet you were." She winks. "All right, who wants a milkshake?"

"Me!" Archer lurches to his feet, stomping on the wooden beneath as if we're not already looking at him.

"You got it, sweet pea." Cathy winks at him. "How about the adults?"

"Just an iced tea for me," I reply.

"Same," Mason drawls.

"Coming right up. Do you want to order food yet?"

"Butta' noodews, Caff!" Archie bangs on the table with a fork and spoon. The sharp clatter pierces my eardrums.

"And what do you say, Archie?" I remind him.

"You we-come?"

"No, the other thing."

"Oh. Pwease?" He turns to Cathy and lights up a grin so bright it could outshine the sun, then bangs on the table again.

Mason chuckles at his antics, calmly snatching the utensils from his grip. "The usual is good for us."

She taps a pen against her lips. "You make it too easy on me."

I prop my chin on a flat palm. "We're not picky."

"That's why you're my favorite. Be back in a jiffy with your drinks." Cathy dashes off, weaving between tables with expert grace.

"Mase," Archer tugs on Mason's shirt. "I go pee-pee. Too wet."

I cluck my tongue at him. "That wouldn't be a problem if you went in the potty like a big boy."

"No, I go in my diapew." He points at the puffy area in his pants as if I don't recognize the signs.

"I can take care of that for you, buddy." Mason makes grabby-hands at the backpack hanging on a hook beside me.

The swoop in my belly distracts me momentarily. "Uh, actually you can't."

He frowns and lowers his arms. "Why not?"

I blow out a heavy breath. "There's no changing station in the men's room. Chad complains about it whenever I suggest coming here."

Mason reels backward. "How can they not have one? Isn't that illegal or something?"

I snort. "That'd be a no."

"This is unacceptable. I'm going to talk to Roger." His neck swivels with the urgency to find the manager.

My shoulders bob with a shrug. "It's actually super common in restaurants, especially in this town."

A muscle pops in his cheek. "I'm offended on your behalf. You shouldn't be expected to always do the changing just because you're a woman. What if I came here without you? How would I change little man's poopy butt?"

"Butt!" Archie laughs and points to his. "I have butt here."

"You sure do," I giggle. "And it's such a cute tushy."

"So?" Mason prods.

My brain boomerangs to his previous question. "Uh, I don't know. On the… counter?"

"That's ridiculous. I'd do it right on the bar until Roger takes this problem seriously." He stabs a finger into the table for emphasis.

Amusement tickles my chest at his outraged dramatics. "You're being very passionate about this."

Mason's jaw goes slack. "Why aren't you more upset about this?"

"It is what it is. I'm used to it. The mommy is expected to handle the mess."

"What an archaic practice," he mutters.

"Don't waste too much breath. Archie will be potty-trained eventually."

"But I should be able to change the next one wherever we go," he mumbles almost absently.

I whack my chest. "Come again?"

Humor dances in his eyes. "That will be part of the process, yes."

My vision from earler rewinds to play again. "Oh, my. You're talking about having a baby?"

"If that's all right with you." Sweet temptation pours from his raspy tone.

"It is." My voice is too breathy in return. "Wouldn't be the first time we've discussed kids."

"Or the last," he adds. His gaze is a fire set to incinerate all logic and sense.

I'm liable to fling myself across the distance separating us. That's highly inappropriate, considering the toddler in our midst. "You should talk to Chad about these bathroom grievances. He'll be happy to hear another guy is fired up about the subject."

Mason smacks his tongue as if something tastes bad. "I don't think he likes me very much."

"He does," I say. "He's just testing you."

"Why?"

"To make sure you're legit."

"Everyone believes I'm going to cut and run?" The defensive crack in his tone makes me wince.

I reach for his hand, threading our fingers together. "Not at all."

Mason's thumb traces over my knuckle. "Sure seems that way."

"It's an adjustment. I've already expressed my concerns. You've given me no reason to doubt you. Chad hasn't had that luxury. We're getting accustomed to this new normal, and the addition of you in our circle."

His eyes search mine, a shimmer of relief evident. "That sounds promising."

"As it should." I squeeze his hand. "Besides, Chad is a huge Mason Braxter fan. He drafted you in his fantasy league last year."

"Ah," he strokes his chin. "There's my angle."

"Just don't forget that he's also wildly attracted to you."

His eyes bulge. "What?"

"Nothing. Time to fix this diaper disaster." I beckon for Archer. "Come to Mama."

Mason scowls. "I'm still mad about these gender roles."

A tingle skates along my spine. I wink in an overt fashion. "You can take that frustration out on me later."

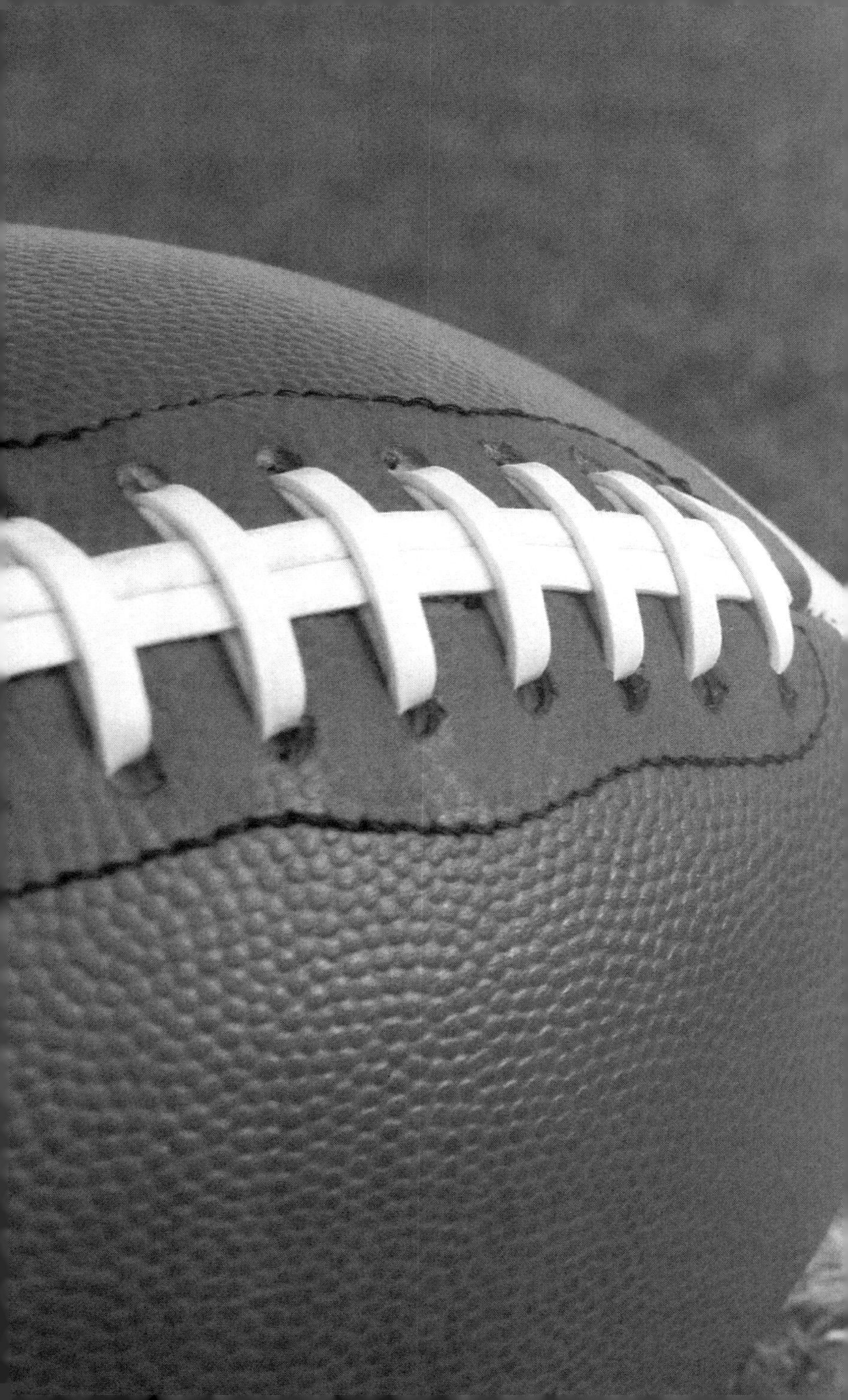

chapter twenty

Mason

"Are you sure about this?" Presley is wringing her hands, knuckles white from the pressure.

I watch her fidgeting through narrowed eyes. "Are you?"

"Yes?"

"That's not convincing. I'm about to develop a complex."

"Okay, okay. You're right." She shakes out her fingers, palms up in surrender. "Sorry for being a spaz."

I sling an arm around her waist, pulling until she's flush against me. "Deep breaths, Pep. I can handle watching the little dude for a few hours."

She's nodding too fast, as if trying to convince herself. "Do you want me to go over the diaper changing process again?"

"I've got it memorized from the last dozen demonstrations. Besides, the one I just did is still on."

Presley combs through her hair. "I'm being overly paranoid, huh?"

"Just nervous, which is understandable. He's your baby. The most precious cargo. I'm honored that you trust me enough to leave him in my care unsupervised." There's a noticeable comfort enveloping me as further proof. Not that she can see what her confidence does to me.

Her exhale is a long stream, as if the strain is slowly evaporating. "It's a necessary step. I want to prove I trust you."

"This is a huge leap. I feel the faith." My hand lifts on its own to cradle her cheek.

"Good," she says with a wobbly grin.

"You better go, or you'll be late."

Presley wrinkles her nose but doesn't argue. "Archie? Mommy is leaving."

The little man zooms over from his stack of toys and crashes into her legs. She crumples to her knees, cuddling him close. Warmth spreads through my chest at the tender embrace. These moments are always precious. I'm privileged enough to bear witness.

"Buh-bye, Mama. I get snack now," he wiggles from her hold.

She releases him with a laugh, straightening to address me. "That's another thing. He's a major—"

"Snack monster," I finish for her. "You told me."

Presley lets a silent curse fly free. "I swore I'd never be one of these mothers."

I squeeze her shoulder. "I've got this. Go do your thing, then we'll meet you for lunch."

Her lips capture mine for a brief—albeit intimate—farewell. "My client is only fifteen minutes away. Whatever you need, just call and I'll be here."

"Understood," I mumble against her pouty mouth. After

another kiss, this one with a dash of tongue, I guide her to the door. "Don't worry for a second. I'll treat him like my own."

That's precisely how I see him, strange as that may seem.

She squeaks when I pat her on the ass as a parting gift. "Thanks again for doing this. It means everything."

"That's exactly how I feel about the two of you."

"Love you, Ten." Her breathy tone causes an inconvenient spike in my pulse.

I widen my stance, keeping my mind firmly G-rated. "Love you too. Go bring home some bacon, woman. Leave the men to do their bonding."

With a wiggle of her fingers, she retreats to her car. I watch her ass sway in the stretchy leggings she's wearing. The sight is appetizing enough to last me until lunch. With one last lingering glance, I close the door with a resounding click. Then it's just me in charge of another human.

"Mase," Archer calls from the kitchen.

My steps clap as I stride forward to meet him. "Yeah, buddy?"

"I poop." He turns to stick his butt toward me.

His timing is impeccable, not that I'd pass off the duty. Literally. "Ah, just for me. I'll take that as a compliment."

"It's stinky." He plugs his nose.

"Even better. We're hitting the ground running. I like your style, kid."

Archie beams at me, the picture of pride. Then he takes off for his room. I follow the fumes while mentally preparing to unwrap this nuclear bomb. He's already lying down and has assumed the position by the time I cross the threshold.

I kneel and begin tugging at his jeans. "Did these get tighter, buddy? They're stuck like glue."

His giggle is sharp and full of joy. "Tickles, Mase."

The war between me and denim ends a second later. Next

is the assault on my nostrils. I swallow a gag as the stench wafts over me. "You weren't kidding. That's stinky."

"Told you," he laughs.

With caution hedging my movements, I peel back the tabs. I grab the wipes and whip out a few to have at the ready. "This is probably going to be messy."

"Uh-huh."

"Holy sh—," I croak. "That's a lot of poop."

"Big load," he agrees.

"That's an understatement. How did all of this come out of your body? I'm going to need more wipes. Probably an entire pack."

As if to prove my point, Archer grunts and a shart tops off this shit storm. Projectile fecal matter flies from his butt to spray all over the already full diaper and changing pad. By some miracle, I manage to remain unscathed—only just so. The carpet and his clothes appear to be free from damage as well.

"Trial by fire," I groan. "I hope there isn't more coming."

"All done, Mase." He sounds rather satisfied, and rightly so.

"This is quite impressive, buddy." My hands are a blur of motion as I wipe every speck of residue. The smell is making my eyes water. Another heave threatens to empty the contents of my stomach while I scrub at the pad beneath his bum. A few more swipes for good measure and I'm finished. I fall onto my ass with an exaggerated sigh once he's dressed again.

"Tanks, Mase. Much better." Archie springs to his feet with renewed energy.

"My pleasure, I suppose. We have to get you going on the potty. It's part of the learning curve."

"Like big boy?"

"Yep, like a big boy. I go on the potty. Your mom and daddy do too."

Wonder reflects in his expression. "I go on potty too. You help me?"

Shock ripples through me, but I recover easily enough. "Of course, buddy. Next time you feel the urge to pee or poop, let me know."

"I gotta go pee-pee now."

"Again?" I could've sworn there was plenty in that disaster I just dumped.

"Yep, I gotta go." He holds himself between the legs, knees wiggling.

"Okay, okay. Let's try." I steer him to the bathroom, open the toilet lid, and get his pants off again. "Sit or stand?"

He blinks at me. "I dunno."

"Sitting is safer." Lord only knows his garden hose will douse the walls. After removing the diaper I just meticulously fastened, I hoist him onto the seat.

His little legs swing in erratic circles while he concentrates on the task. It only takes a second for the telltale tinkle to patter into the bowl. He gasps, gaze dropping to see the evidence. "I did it!"

"You did it!" I share in his enthusiasm, lifting a hand for him to slap.

He doesn't leave me hanging, giving me three high-fives in a row. "You pwoud of me?"

"So proud, buddy. I can't wait to tell your mom."

Who hopefully won't be too disappointed she missed it. A sliver of unease worms under my skin, but I chase off the creeping sensation quickly enough. She wouldn't want to dissuade him from going on the potty, present for the event or not.

Archer seems unaware of my internal battle while I get his lower half concealed. He has an unpredictable cannon that can't be left uncovered for long.

Maybe I should take a picture. I stare at the piddle job

with a cringe. Presley might want to document this moment. Couldn't hurt, even if it's gross.

After digging out my phone, I motion to him to get near the scene of the achievement. "We can take a photo to show your mom and dad what a big boy you are."

"Kay!" He strikes a pose, both thumbs straight up.

I capture the memory with a laugh. "You're one amazing kid."

He nods, soaking in the praise. "Snack?"

Amusement bursts from me in a booming clap as if from a snare drum. My deflated state is instantly rejuvenated after the crappy incident moments ago. I suppose he deserves a reward. "I bet you're starving after dropping that load."

"Uh-huh."

"How about we pack a treat and go to the park?"

"Yes!" He takes off faster than I can track him.

My stride is slightly more sluggish. After flushing the piddle and washing my hands, I find him waiting in the foyer. Not positive how long I took to catch him, but the kid moves fast. His Marshall—a character from *Paw Patrol*, I recently discovered—backpack is overflowing with graham cracker pouches. The tiny bag doesn't stand a chance of zipping. He's smiling so wide. That expression is bursting even wider than the backpack with pride. I fold in half with a rough chuckle.

"Are you sure you grabbed enough to feed both of us?"

He studies his mountainous stash with pursed lips. "No more weft. Box is empty."

"Well," I drawl. "Then this will have to do."

"Kay! We go?" He points out the window.

After taking a few packages off the top, I manage to get the ultimate snack pack shut. "Guess it doesn't hurt to be prepared. Should we take the stroller, or do you want to walk?"

"I ride up 'dere?" He points at my shoulders. It's his

favorite mode of transportation, which puffs my chest out to comical measures.

"Yep, once we're outside. Just call me the little man chariot."

"Yipppeee. C'mon, Mase. We ready." He flings the overstuffed Marshall onto his back, an added bounce in his step.

I reach for the bag Presley pre-packed for me, along with a football. Archie has taken to playing catch since I introduced him to the sport a few weeks ago. After I lock the deadbolt and get him secured, we set off along the sidewalk. There's a community park just down the road with plenty of space to run.

The weather is once again cooperating for an October afternoon. It's warm with a slight breeze. Archie chatters the entire trek about the latest *Paw Patrol* episode in one long run-on sentence. Without breathing. Honestly, I'm not sure how he does it with those tiny lungs. The kid definitely isn't shy or afraid to fill the silence. He reminds me so much of Presley. Her sunny disposition radiates from him.

When the first signs of sprawling green grass come up on our left, Archer squirms in my grip. "We here! Hurry, Mase."

I increase my pace to a light jog to appease him. "Okay, buddy. Hold on."

"Faster," he squeals.

"Where should we stop?" The field seems endless. Several large patches are available for us to toss the ball the short distance he can handle.

"Over 'dere!" His tiny fingers dig in my hair, using the short strands as reins to steer me in the chosen direction.

Just as I'm moving that way, a conversation between two women catches my attention. The pair are huddled close, but their voices carry on the wind. My name filters between them like a dirty secret. Presley is mentioned soon after.

The brunette is scowling, the expression pinching her face. "I can't believe she isn't with them."

Her friend—a plastic-looking redhead—scoffs, disdain curling her upper lip. "How pathetic. She has him watching her kid. Is he trying to compensate for the real father being gay?"

"How long do you think this will last?"

"I give them until Christmas."

"No way," the brunette spits. "He'll come to his senses by Thanksgiving."

The redhead quirks her brow. "Wanna bet?"

No wonder Presley thinks people in this town are plotting against her. These women are vicious. If they're not bothering to hide their true colors, I shouldn't either.

"One sec, Archie. I need to ask these two a question." Then I'm striding toward them with purpose. With each foot I erase between us, their eyes expand to saucers. "Do you ladies have something you'd like to share with us gents?"

They flounder like fish out of shallow waters. The brunette finds her voice first. "Uh, no. We just think it's... cute how you're babysitting."

My eyes roll so hard that I get a cramp. "It's not babysitting when he's my kid."

Am I taking a liberty with that deliberate claim? Absolutely. Should I discuss this with Presley later? Most definitely. Will she be mad about me spouting off to these rude vipers with poisonous tongues? Probably not. Does that free me from blame if Archer decides to repeat that he's mine? It's too late now. There's no turning back.

Archie rests his chin on my head. "Uh-huh, yeah. I'm wit Mase."

"But, uh," the redhead stammers. "Chad is his father."

"And your point is?" The frustration in my tone is a harsh blow against their bold behavior.

Her mouth snaps open and shut, unsure how to proceed. "You can't be his dad?"

I spread my stance, the epitome of not backing down.

"You're saying I can't step into the parenting role? He can't have two fathers? Seems pretty ignorant to me."

"That's not... uh," the brunette fumbles.

"Save it," I clip. "As in don't put our names in your mouths, especially if it's only to fling insults."

And that's all my patience can handle. I turn away before they can attempt to make nice or retaliate. Besides, Archer doesn't need to be subjected to their type of hate.

Aside from Benny at Pond Alley, my reception from Meadow Creek has been fairly toasty. I'm realizing now that my head might've been buried in the clouds, or maybe I was blinded by the residual bliss from reuniting with Presley. Maybe she was right to consider relocating to a different city. Just so long as I'm included in the equation.

"I'm getting a kick running into you this often, Braxter. This is becoming a habit."

My gaze seeks out the familiar voice, tension still straining my posture. I force a grin while watching Gunner stride toward us. "Hey, man."

He recoils with a grunt. "Who pooped in your pants?"

"Poopie pants," Archie babbles. "Extra stinky."

"Well, thanks. That answers my question, dude." Gunner smiles at my companion, then shifts his focus to me. "Is this your chaperone, Brax?"

I bob my head. "Presley had to work. Archie decided I was up to snuff in the cool-enough-to-chill department."

"Solid choice." He offers Archer a fist bump. "But why do you look like a crab with his pinchers glued shut?"

That gets a laugh from me, easing the lingering pressure from my chest. "It's not worth mentioning."

"Okay, I can take a hint. What's on your fun-filled agenda?"

"Just got here. We're going to toss the pigskin a bit."

Gunner's expression brightens. "Heck yes. Is this pre-training camp?"

"Something like that. He loves to throw."

"Mind if I join the huddle?" He juts his chin at the ball in my grip.

"You'll have to ask the little man. He's in charge." I hike a thumb at the toddler who's ducking into my periphery.

Archie regards Gunner with a shrewd gaze, taking this responsibility very seriously. "You pway football?"

"I do," Gunner responds. "I used to be on the same team with Mason."

That gets a gasp from Archie. "Cool. I wanna be on same team with Mase too. You frow to us, kay?"

"You got it, dude. I'll even let you have the ball first." He begins running in place, knees striking high.

I appraise his enthusiasm through narrowed eyes. "You know this is amateur hour, right?

Gunner scoffs, setting off across the field to get in position. "Don't dampen the dream, man. I'm about to play catch with the greatest quarterback this town has ever seen."

And with that, I'm back on Team Meadow Creek. The nasty rumors about me leaving are what have to move on.

chapter twenty-one

Presley

"I can't believe I missed it." Chad's sour expression matches his surly tone.

"So did I," I remind him for the umpteenth time. "That's a parental hazard with having a job. Don't forget shared custody. Unfortunately, we can't be with Archie every second to catch each milestone."

He scowls. "That's different."

"How so? It's as if he was with my parents."

"But he wasn't." His clipped tone grates on my frazzled nerves.

We've been bickering about this subject for an hour too long. Chad's usual mellow attitude shifted to sullen after discovering Mason took care of Archer a few days ago. The fact that our son had his first successful potty on the toilet during that period only adds to his ire.

I comb through my hair, a huff tacked on with the agitated motion. "What's your problem? I'm failing to see the major malfunction with letting Mason watch after Archie."

"You wouldn't," he snips.

My tolerance for this grumpy version pulls taut and I hiss between clenched teeth. "Okay, seriously? Quit being dramatic. We've survived co-parenting this long. Just spit out the problem so we can solve it. This passive-aggressive crap is annoying."

"Crap," comes my favorite echo. Archer giggles from his spot on the carpet, toys spread around him in all directions.

Chad's thunderous expression cracks with a crooked grin. That break in the clouds allows me to take a decent breath. "He's such a goofy kid."

"That's all from you," I tease.

"Ha," he barks. That smile spreads a touch wider. "Blame the dirty talk on me."

The pinch in my chest loosens. "It's well deserved. I knew you in college and saw more than my fair share."

"You even got a slice of the action." His wink is ridiculously exaggerated.

"Once again, that was your fault. You got us into the pickle that night."

"But you were the one who sat on mine."

I gag, completely for his benefit. "See? You're bad."

"As if I could let that low-hanging fruit dangle for long."

My lips curl on their own. I've missed this effortless banter. Chad is one of my closest friends, but our circumstances put too much pressure on us. Things haven't been the same between us since I got pregnant. There's this unspoken fracture that can't be fixed with simple words. But moments like this make me feel like we're getting on the right path again.

I pause for a beat, assessing his calming mood. "Are we going to be okay?"

A crease dents his forehead. "I thought we already were."

"Sure, a strained version."

He relents with a drawn-out exhale. "We've never had to deal with this since neither of us has dated anyone worth bringing home to meet Archie."

"I'm aware." The noise I emit is slightly manic. My dry spell still haunts me, although the only one who could end it did so with a bang to eclipse the lapse.

"There's just been a lot of change very quickly," he adds.

My nod mirrors his. "It's been a whirlwind since mid-September."

"When Mason Braxter barreled back into town."

"Yeah, he kinda took me by force. I didn't get a chance to prepare."

"It's fine, Press." But his tone suggests otherwise. "He's not some rando you picked up off the street."

My scowl rivals his from earlier. "Give me more credit than that. Pretty sure that's your area of expertise, stud muffin."

"Oooh," he whistles. "Here come those sassy claws. I figured those were solely reserved for Mason these days."

I swat at his arm. "Perv."

Chad's gaze slides to our son, who is blissfully unaware. "Careful, or you'll be labeled the naughty one."

"Well, I suppose it's only fair if I share credit." A zip skitters through me at just how filthy I've gotten with a certain someone lately. "I'm back in the game and off the market."

"Lucky girl."

I sigh, the sound dipped in satisfaction. "He's pretty hot, huh?"

His lips smack. "My mouth literally waters whenever I think about what he's packing down below."

"Eww, quit picturing my boyfriend naked." Is it possible to get jealous of a hypothetical? Especially when it involves my gay baby daddy?

Chad wags his brows. "Too late. If you ever want more sausage in your bedroom meal combo, please don't hesitate to call me."

I choke on my spit. That visual is wrong on too many levels. "Knock it off. That's just… no. Please hold while my brain scrubs the image from memory."

He grunts. "Now who's being dramatic?"

"This conversation took a sordid turn. We were making real progress."

"Until you got us off track."

"Fine," I relent and shoulder the blame for this so-called detour. "Are you feeling better about our situation?"

"Mostly. Archie is already very attached to Mason. That's what worries me most." He strikes at the concern that was plaguing me with that statement.

"Mason seems just as attached," I defend. Their bond is what it took for me to finally relinquish my fear.

"Isn't that strange? How can he feel such a significant connection to a kid who isn't his?"

Disbelief is a putrid cloud that slackens my jaw. The insistence to rush to Mason's rescue balloons inside me. "They have a special bond. Within minutes, it was clear that they just clicked. Mason told me after they met that Archie already felt like part of his life."

"It shows, even if I've only seen them interact once or twice." The somber notes in his tone stab at me.

"That doesn't mean Archie loves you less."

"I know that," he mutters. At my pursed expression, Chad heaves a defeated breath. "I do, Press. It's just happened so fast. I've never had to compete with another man for his affection."

"It's not a competition."

His snort resembles a bull ready to charge. "Obviously. If it were, Mason would be a goner."

I don't encourage that petty remark with a response, right as he is. "Besides, Archie has enough love in his heart to have a dozen daddies."

"Don't even go there, woman. I'm in a fragile state."

My stomach somersaults with a turbulent spiral. "I hope this isn't upsetting you too much."

Chad seems to consider that, the tension slowly seeping from his frame. "How can I really be upset with Mason showering Archie with love? I couldn't ask for more from the guy helping you raise my child."

I squint at him, fist parked on my hip. "You're handling this really well all of a sudden. That's pretty incredible."

"What can I say? I'm warming up to the idea. It will be good for Archie to have another strong role model." He's definitely gaining perspective after his initial outburst.

"I agree. He can have the tie-breaking vote."

"Let's not give him more power." Then he goes still, his gaze flitting from me to our son. "Mason is sticking around, right?"

"Yes." Unwavering confidence punctuates that singular utterance. The power behind it feels like delivering a punch.

Between Mason and Chad and every Negative Nancy in Meadow Creek, this topic is a broken record I'm ready to use as a frisbee. But I can't brush off his concern. Eventually we'll look back on these moments of doubt with a laugh. That's the upbeat spin I'm putting on this overplayed tune.

"You really love him." Chad is studying me with that keen eye he's known for.

"Is that a secret?"

He hums and rubs his chin. "For what it's worth, I approve."

"Did you want me to ask for your blessing?" The notion is comical, earning a laugh.

"Regarding the man who will be around our son on a regular basis?" He shrugs. "It wouldn't have hurt."

"I didn't think about it that way."

"Just picture the catastrophe if I hated the guy."

A dull throb pulses at my temples. "Oh, Lord. Now *you* don't even go there."

What remains of his stern resistance melts, and he props himself against the wall. "You don't need my permission. I was just screwing with you. My jealous fit was misplaced. It's not as if I'm losing precious time with Archie."

"Look at you being mature. This change of heart looks pretty on you." The thought sparks another. "Are you seeing anyone special?"

"Nah, no one is holding my interest."

"He'll come along."

"And I'll be eagerly awaiting his arrival." Chad might seem brash and broody, but the dude is a total romantic on the inside.

"I'm glad we cleared the air."

"Same, and that's my cue." His attention shifts to the boy still happily playing on the floor. "Are you packed, kiddo? It's time to go."

Archer glances at the mess he made of my living room. "I clean up?"

"I'll do it, sweet angel. Your daddy is ready to go."

Chad rocks on his feet. "Need to go potty before we hit the road?"

I scoff. "Real smooth."

Our son frowns. "I only go wit Mase, like a big boy."

"What's that man's secret? He's got you both whipped. I need this magic to snag my own Mr. Wonderful."

I roll my eyes. "I'll be sure to ask him for the potion recipe."

"Please do." He pats my head in a patronizing manner.

I'm almost afraid to broach the next subject with our truce freshly mended. But steel straightens my spine. "Would it be all right if Mason comes trick-or-treating with us on Tuesday?"

His smile dips ever so slightly. "Dang, Press. Already inviting him to joint holidays?"

"I feel like Halloween is a safe one to share with him at this point."

He crosses his arms. "But you're altering our traditions."

"Is it really that big of a deal?" My posture stiffens as I brace for his answer.

"Not at all," he jests. "I can't ignore a chance to screw with you."

"You're so funny."

"This will really get the town in an uproar." Chad's smile resurfaces to megawatt proportions.

"Eh, screw 'em. We've always prided ourselves on being unconventional."

"And I gladly accept any opportunity to prove that point."

"Then we'll see you Tuesday."

"Tell Mason to wear something s-l-u-t-t-y." He spells the word to avoid nearby listening ears. It proves to do the deed while Archie continues bashing two trucks together. "Feel free to dress the part as well. Tarzan and Jane could be super cute."

"It's supposed to be windy and in the fifties. More importantly, this is for the children."

"The kids get candy. I deserve a tasty treat too." He folds his hands in a pleading gesture.

I swat at him. "Maybe one that doesn't objectify my boyfriend."

"Don't pretend you wouldn't try sneaking peeks under his loincloth."

"I've seen his mighty python plenty. Spoiler alert—that beast won't be contained by a scrap of fur." The theory should be tested in private with just the two of us. Strictly to see Mason in the getup, of course.

Chad scowls. "Such a brat."

"Don't be salty. We'll find you an anaconda of your own, but stop trying to steal mine. He's taken."

Archer chooses that moment to tune in. His baby blues ping-pong between us. "You talkin' 'bout snakes?"

"And on that note," I shove at Chad's shoulder. "You can discuss slithering serpents on the way to your house."

chapter twenty-two

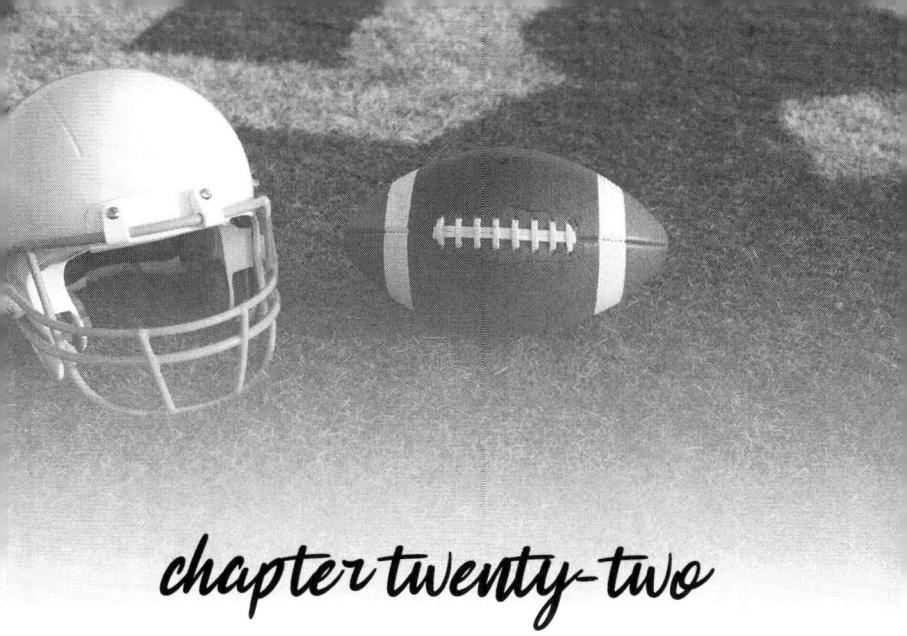

Mason

A BITTER CHILL BITES MY NOSE AND I DUCK TO AVOID ANOTHER blast. There's a telltale scent that the cold drags in, as if nature is shivering and sending off warning signals. The temperature on Halloween in Minnesota is a gamble at best. There were several years growing up with blizzard conditions. Others provided us with surprisingly summery weather. Usually it's somewhere in the middle.

This is bordering on a wintery introduction.

"Are we sure he's warm enough?" My gaze slides to Presley tucked beside me.

"Yes," she laughs. "He's fine. We're only stopping at a few more houses. Your concern is admirable—and adorable—but several notches over the top. Archie currently has more layers than an onion."

And that's not an exaggeration.

His Chase—another character from *Paw Patrol* that I've recently discovered—costume is stretched to the seams thanks to multiple shirts and pants. He looks like a roasting marshmallow one rotation away from bursting. The sight is comedic relief and placating comfort pumped into my veins, serving constant amusement. Especially with his waddling stride thrown into the mix.

My fists jam deeper into my pockets. "I appreciate the Shrek reference, Pep."

"Thanks, champ. That was special, just for you." Her hip bumps into mine.

Chad doesn't comment, only offering a smirk while shaking his head. Pretty sure he mutters something about freaking love potion under his breath.

I'm still wary of the guy. Mostly due to the fact that he seems determined to test my patience at every opportunity. My buttons have been pushed by far worse trying to intimidate me, though. I dodge each trap he tries to set while launching one of my own. We can spar all night.

Meanwhile, Archer is twirling on the sidewalk in front of us. The little man rarely stops moving, a constant motor running on full tilt. He doesn't pause or stand still. That energy and excitement is infectious. It spreads between the adults, warming us as well.

His body heat is probably readying to boil any second from the combination of extra clothes and sugar content. That's the best protection he can get from this nasty wind.

"Dis one?" His tiny arm flails to a three-story monstrosity that resembles a haunted nightmare.

Spooky sounds stream from hidden speakers. A witch cackles, followed by a terrified scream. Then a masculine timbre booms like thunder. Creepy organ music pierces my eardrums. Cats hissing comes next. The loop is meant to strike fear. But that's just the start.

Smoke billows from a fog machine. Spotlights flash shadowy images on the garage. Spiderwebs cover every available surface. Ghosts and pumpkins and scary statues frame the path leading to the porch. More decorations than I can track adorn the yard.

Archie is a foot from the driveway, vibrating in place as he prepares to race up the steep incline. His pillowcase is already stuffed with sweets. I'm about ready to call it quits for the group. The last thing I want is for some terrifying object to lunge out and traumatize him.

Presley's jaw is hanging slack. "Wow, they went all out."

"It looks like Halloween vomited on this place," Chad laughs.

"With no chunk left behind," I add.

"You two are gross," Presley complains. "I'll take Archie to the door while you continue talking about puke."

"You're really going to that one?" Uncertainty leaks from my voice like chicken shit.

She blinks at me. "Why wouldn't we? They give the best treats. Last year, it was an entire bundle of candy and crafts."

That comes as no surprise, considering the overachiever effort they put in with appearances. "All right. We'll just, uh… wait here?"

Her brow quirks. "Are you afraid?"

"For Archie," I explain.

The firm line from her lips calls me a liar. "He's super brave. Right, sweet angel?"

"Uh-huh. Not scared." He tugs at her arm.

Presley allows him to lead her away. "We can probably head home after this. Archie will want to open whatever they give him."

We watch them go from our rooted post on the sidewalk. Archer doesn't hesitate, more than eager to approach the freaky display. Presley, on the other hand, is practically walking on eggshells. Her apprehension bellows to me. Maybe I should've brought him to this one.

Before I can move, I catch Chad staring at me from the corner of my eye. The impulse to ask what he finds so fascinating burns through me. With teeth clamping my tongue, I manage to resist. He can be the one to break the silence.

"I like your costume."

A chuckle rumbles from me while I glance down at my 86ers jersey. It was a no-brainer after Presley whipped out her cheerleader uniform. "Might as well put this relic to use. Halloween is the night to play pretend."

The ache in my knee barely flares with that remark. It's almost laughable how the cure was just waiting for me. I probably should've dressed like a fool instead.

"Clever, mate." Chad taps the patch covering his left eye, an essential piece for the pirate he's portraying.

"Thanks. Yours is more creative."

"I know," he agrees with a smug grin. "But you're not just faking it. That's authentic merch."

There's no use denying facts, outdated or not. I recall a detail Presley mentioned in a previous conversation. "Do you want one?"

"Sure."

"I can sign it for you." Fuck, that makes me come off as an entitled douche.

He nods. "That'd be cool."

This exchange couldn't be more awkward if I was naked. I'm content to allow the silence to reclaim the yawning space surrounding us. That makes one of us.

"Do you miss it?"

The question almost startles me. "Football?"

"Yeah." His wry tone suggests I missed some obvious context clues.

"I'm coaching."

"That's hardly the same."

As if I need to hear that. "I'm exactly where I want to be, if that's what you're getting at."

Chad studies me with an unwavering focus that I imagine is similar to being under a magnifying lens. After several beats too long, he gives a sharp dip of his chin in acknowledgment.

And that's where our tension snaps.

Archie is barreling toward us at what must be a record pace for his toddler legs. He crashes into his dad without making any attempt to brake. "I gots lotsa goodies!"

Presley arrives an instant later, huffing slightly with the exertion it took to match her son's speed. She hefts his pillowcase up for us to see. The bulging sack is almost overflowing. "They topped us off. We're done."

"Uh-huh, I wanna eat candy. Right now!" He stomps his foot for emphasis.

I yank at the brim on his police cap. "You have a huge haul, buddy. Are you going to share with us?"

Archer tips his head to the side. "I fink 'bout it."

Presley boops his nose. "Only a few pieces tonight. It's almost bedtime."

He peeks in the pillowcase she's still holding. "King sizes."

Chad snags Archie's hand, swinging their joined palms. "I'll be the judge of that. You're staying at my house tonight, sugar baby."

He pouts at his dad. "Big boy, not baby. I went on potty."

"That's true. But I haven't seen you do it." Chad winks at him.

Archie narrows his eyes. "I fink 'bout dat too."

"Good enough for me."

Presley snuggles close to my side, linking her arm with mine. "What a picture we make. My son, gay baby daddy, and on-again boyfriend all in a row."

I laugh at that description, true as it might be. "Someone better capture the shot. That's a priceless portrait."

"So priceless."

We allow the ruckus from passing kids to serenade us for what remains of our return trip. The streetlights and stars above guide us. A soothing sensation drifts over me. That contentment has been embracing me more often than not lately. My resulting exhale gets swept away with the breeze, taking any lingering strain with it.

Presley must feel the change in me as we near her place. "You okay?"

"Outstanding," I correct.

"Oh, that's fancy."

"It's fitting for the event."

The edge of her mouth twitches. "Trick-or-treating?"

"Being included."

She sniffs, a glassy sheen visible in her gaze under the porch lights. "I always want you with us."

"What a coincidence," I murmur against her lips. "That's where I always want to be."

"All right, kissy faces. There are innocent eyeballs in the direct vicinity." Chad's scold barely makes an impact on the intoxicating high I'm floating in.

Presley gasps with mock horror. "Oh, Chad. I didn't see you there. Sorry if our peck was too dirty for you."

His eyes roll skyward. "Real rich, Press."

Archer skirts around us, grabbing his bag of loot from Presley. His knees hit the floor a moment before he dumps the entire load over the carpeted area. He licks his chops, arms open wide as if to hug the pile.

Chad groans. "I was really hoping to avoid this."

"It's getting late," Presley notes. "He can sleep here."

Chad seems to mull over the options. "That would save me the chore of helping pick up this disaster."

"I done finking 'bout sharing," Archie interrupts. "Mase go first. Then Mama and Dada."

I wince, my gaze bouncing to Presley and Chad. They exchange a look, followed by matching shrugs. He's the one to speak.

"No worries, man. We can't be mad that he's loving on you."

Presley nods. "You're the exciting one with all the pizzazz."

"But eventually that will wear off?" Not sure if I'm trying to convince them, or hope that isn't the case.

She makes a noncommittal noise. "Maybe, but not for me."

I dip down to brush my nose along hers. "That's reassuring."

"Mase," Archie reminds me insistently. "You gotta choose candy."

"Oh, right." I smack my forehead, then pluck a Reese's from the pile. "Thanks for sharing, buddy."

"What Mama want?"

Presley inhales deeply, as if sugar is ripe in the air. "Skittles for me."

"Dada want Snickers," Archer relays with confidence.

"You got my number, kiddo." Chad accepts the proffered candy bar.

A minute passes in silence while we munch on our treats. Then Archie peeks up at me from under his lowered lids. "You love my mama?"

I recall him asking this when we first met. My answer will never change. "I sure do."

"And you love me?"

"Lots and lots."

"How 'bout my daddy?"

I glance at Chad, who's waiting expectantly with wiggling brows. "He's growing on me."

Archie squints as if trying to decipher my meaning. "Kay. Let's eat more candy."

"Only one more piece," Presley interjects. "It will be bedtime soon wherever you're staying."

"Fine." He pouts but doesn't argue further.

"Thanks again for letting me partake in the festivities." My smile is for Presley, but I extend the gesture to Chad as well.

"You belonged out there with us. Besides, it was Chad's idea." She tilts her head toward him, batting her lashes too fast.

"I find that hard to believe," I murmur.

"As you should," he replies. "But in all honesty, you're not a terrible addition."

I suppose that's the best I can hope for coming from him. "Appreciate that."

"You got this handled?" Chad motions to the treat stash, then his son.

Presley's nod is instant. "Yeah, of course. I can bring him over tomorrow."

My head bobs to mirror hers. "I look forward to seeing the little man hopped up on sugar."

"You're going to regret that," she murmurs.

"How bad can it be?"

"You're about to find out, Braxter." Chad's gaze is too penetrating. I almost feel violated. Just as I'm getting ready to show him the door, Archer gasps from his spot near the stairs.

"Mase, is dis treat for me?"

A horrible, slimy inkling worms its way through my stomach before I even look to see what he's found. The sight of the bottle in his grip is all the confirmation I need. My head hangs as I desperately search for a plausible explanation that will appease him.

Chad beats me to the punch, striding to where his son stands. His eyes widen once he snatches the item from Archie's grip. He reads the label aloud to further humiliate me, no doubt. "Tropical Glide."

"This isn't happening," I mutter.

He continues as if I didn't speak. "Strawberry daiquiri-flavored lube."

"Okay, that's enough. We get the point." There's a fury brewing in my gut, ready to strike at a very particular target.

"Oh, I strongly disagree." Chad is doubled over with laughter at this point. "I think it's best I take Archie with me, Press. It seems Mason has big plans for you this evening. This is an edible treat to share with your partner."

"For me?" Archer tries to grab the bottle from his dad.

"No," I blurt. Then I regain my composure with a calming breath. "I mean, there's something else in the bag that's for you."

"Really?" Wonder clangs from his pitchy voice.

"Yeah, buddy." I kneel beside him to search the contents, finding the small package easily. "Here you go."

He stares at the gift with a blank expression. "What dis?"

My eyes seek out Presley, finding her already staring at me. Tears shimmer in her gaze again. I suck in a breath, that fear of overstepping a harsh pain gnawing at me. "Is this okay? I was worried it might come across as weird. He feels like a son to me, so I thought…"

The words dry in my throat. Uncertainty sweeps overhead like a murky cloud crackling with doom.

She shakes her head, black hair whipping in all directions. "It's sweet, incredibly so. I love that you act like he's your responsibility too. That's super special to me."

Chad agrees with a grin. "Really thoughtful. Don't doubt yourself with these gestures."

"Just do what feels natural. That's paying off very well so far," Presley adds.

With their permission granted, my focus returns to the little man eagerly anticipating an explanation. "I bought you a pack of undies to try. Maybe these bad boys will motivate you to go on the potty more."

"Huh?"

I open the plastic casing, holding up a pair with Chase decorating the cotton. "See, Archie? You use this slot rather than pull them all the way down. My dad taught me that when I was your age."

He grabs the underwear. "Peek-a-boo penis!"

I choke on my tongue. "Uh, yeah."

"That's a fun game he likes to play without clothes on," Presley explains with a laugh. "Not sure where that started."

"Might've been my fault," Chad mumbles. "Penis talk flows free at my house."

Archer is practically beaming. "I want on. You help me, Mase."

One look at Chad provides the definition of crestfallen. He averts his gaze, shoulders hunched inward. The expression knifes me in the chest, even if we aren't on the greatest of terms.

"How about you give them a try with your dad? You're going to his house now. Maybe you can slip on a pair over your diaper before bed."

Chad almost looks shocked by my words. Maybe he should be, but I have no intention of stealing his thunder. This should be a bonding experience for him to share with his son. I already had my moment with him.

"Can I, Dada?" Archie waves the undies in his face, fast enough that the fabric is a blur. "I wanna go in potty like big boy."

"Sure, whatever you want." His tone still holds notes of bewilderment.

I shove upright to my feet. "We're on the same team, right?"

"I wish," Chad mutters.

"What?"

"Never mind," he rushes to say. "I guess we should go. We've got huge plans of our own now."

Presley has been busy repacking the candy and passes the full sack to him. "See you Thursday?"

"Yep. I'll relay all the potty success."

"You better keep me in the loop before that."

Chad scoffs as if the other option is insulting. "Always."

After several hugs and kisses, Presley releases Archer. "Be good for your daddy."

He taps her nose. "You be good for Mase."

We all share a laugh as they leave. Then Presley launches herself at me.

"That was a good thing you did for Chad," she purrs along my jaw.

"Yeah?"

She nips at my earlobe. "Really good."

"Am I about to get a reward?"

Presley snatches the lube still cradled in my palm. "Big-time, champ."

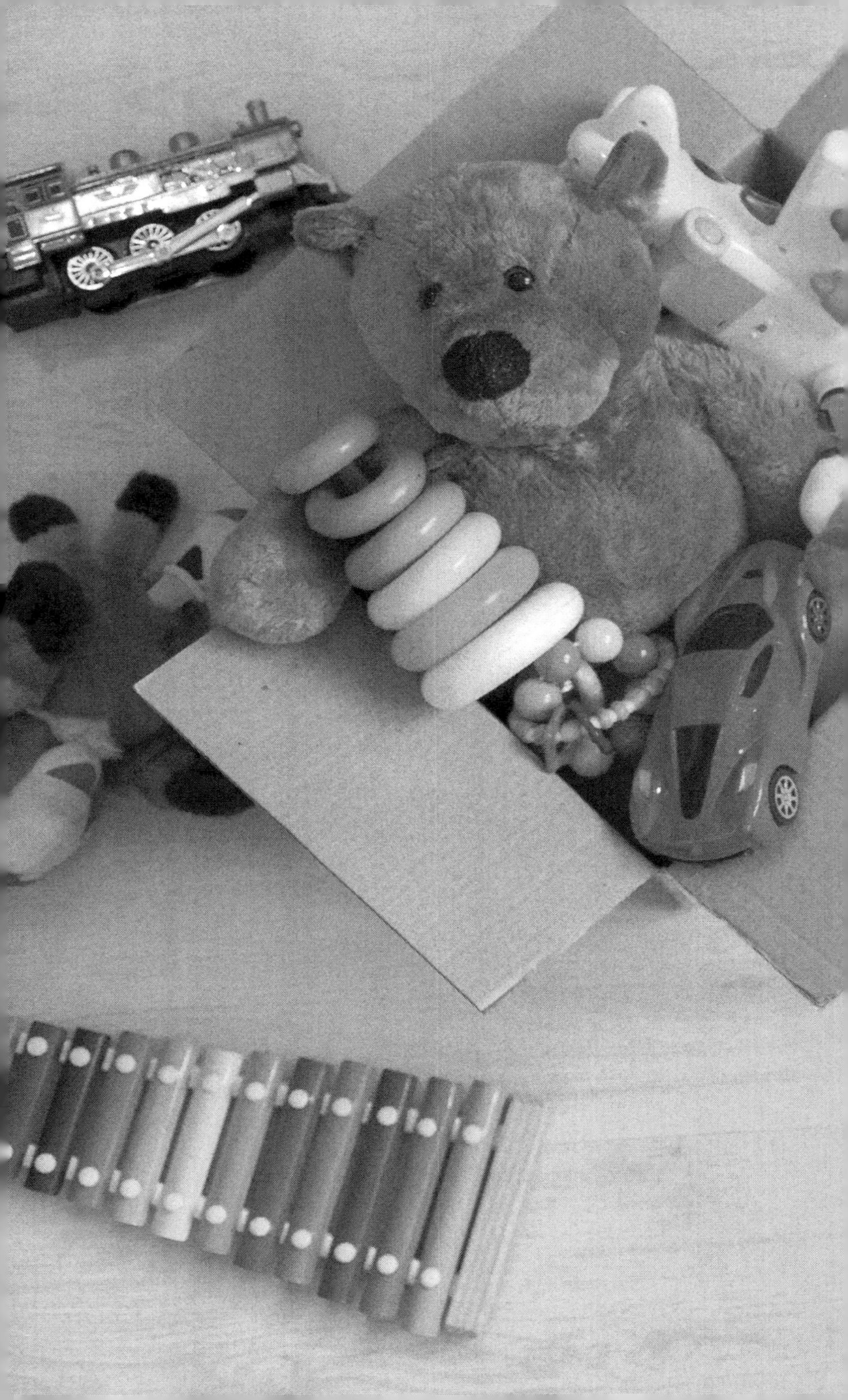

chapter twenty-three

Presley

THE PIPES CREAK AFTER I TWIST THE KNOB AND WATER STREAMS from the nozzle in a wide spray. Steam begins to billow and rise. I test the temperature with a quick swipe, stepping into the shower with a satisfied moan. Warmth penetrates my weary limbs, chasing off the clutches of sleep. That heat swaddles my exhausted muscles. Each second drenches my body and pumps me with rejuvenated energy.

I tilt my face into the steady flow just as the door opens. The accompanying cool blast interrupts my serenity, but only momentarily. Strong arms wrap around me from behind. I sink into his hold with a smile tugging my lips. This tender embrace is even better than the cleansing relaxation of the cascade.

It reminds me if our intermission last night. A bathing session was required after he did me extra dirty. My ass clenches at the reminder and I nearly moan.

Mason nuzzles against me, his stubble a coarse rasp on my cheek. "Why didn't you wake me?"

The mist swirling in inviting tendrils grows thick with lust. That tangy desire saturates my tongue. "I didn't want to break the peaceful spell you were under. You looked very happy."

"I was dreaming of you," he confesses against my flesh. "And this."

A gasp rips from me when he cups my core. We had too much fun with that lube. The evidence from our final round is still sticky between my thighs. "Already?"

"Did I wear you out?" Deft fingers slide along my folds.

A shudder wracks me. "Almost."

He circles my clit, fondling the smoldering embers with an expert touch. "Can I eat you for breakfast, Pep?"

"You already had me for dessert," I remind him. "Several servings."

"Will you deny me?" His fingers continue strumming my arousal.

My head thumps his chest as I surrender. "Never."

Then Mason is in motion, pressing my back against the tiles. I hiss and arch my spine against the chilled onslaught. A raspy chuckle bounces off the ceramic as he lowers to his knees, tracing my dips and curves on the downward trajectory with that sinful mouth. My fingers blindly stab into his hair, gripping for purchase. I'm already throbbing for him.

A twinge yanks at my inner walls when he drapes my thigh over his shoulder. The dull ache is instantly forgotten with his initial swipe along my slit. That taste test has a groan spilling from him.

"You're better than a strawberry smoothie," he rasps across my exposed center.

"Not a surprise since we drained the entire bottle." My voice is a breathy exhale.

"Fuck the lube. This flavor is all-natural. It's just you."

As if proving a point, he coats his mouth in my essence. He waits for my gaze to settle on his before slowly licking my arousal off his lips.

The garbled nonsense that spews from me matches the mush in my brain. I finally manage a hoarse, "More."

And he delivers.

Mason feasts on me with broad strokes from that wicked tongue. His precise actions are laced with purpose. Each silky glide through my sex ends with a lap around my clit. I bang my head against the unforgiving surface behind me. The ache gnaws until an opening rips for the pleasure to flood.

A tremble attacks my legs, the floor becoming unstable. My grip on him tightens as I search for an anchor in fear I'll shoot straight to the stars. Sensation submerges me while he sucks and nibbles and devours. These direct methods are meant to send me reeling. The mission is almost accomplished as the prickling tingles begin to spread.

Then Mason pulls away, just an inch. That gap is wide enough to calm the clawing need snapping inside me. But the lust pooling in his green eyes feeds my own until I'm ready to beg again.

"Ride my face, Pep."

I'm all too eager to comply, already rocking my hips. My head knocks against the tiles with a jerky nod. "Yes, please."

His responding groan is decadence coiled in filthy intentions. "That's my girl."

Mason returns to his task in the next breath, adding more suction the faster I grind. The intensity propels through me with a punching force. I wobble while trying to keep pace. His fingers dig into my hips, assisting the disjointed rhythm I'm helplessly spiraling on. The water pelts me with fiery drops, only serving to fuel the flames raging inside my lower belly.

"You'll give me all I want," he demands.

I'm nodding, lost in the desperation to reach relief. "Yes. Take me."

"You'll feed me until I'm full." That fierce command comes with rapid flicks against the thrumming bundle currently controlling me.

"Don't stop," I whine.

Mason must hear the hysteric edge in my tone. With meaningful focus, he finishes the job. I'm hurtling over the cliff before I realize the orgasm is crashing down. Waves rush in my ears while he drowns in me. My eyes slam shut against the flash of colors streaking from all sides. Spasms erupt as I fling into the abyss. Rigid bonds from the mounting pressure hold me hostage until the climax wanes. The relief is potent after that, allowing me to sag against the wall. I watch the rise and fall of my breasts while dragging in gulps of oxygen. Mason rises to stand and clutches my trembling form against him. After that brief reprieve, I'm ready for more.

"My turn," I purr.

With a palm to his chest, I swap our positions until he's plastered to the wall. I'm kneeling in front of him before the implication registers on his features. My fingers curl around his jutting length, giving a swift tug to set the stride. He's the only man I've done this for, and quite often. That means I know every ridge of his cock. Each sensitive spot and bulging vein. I use this knowledge to my advantage. His flared tip becomes a lollipop as I swirl my tongue in teasing circles. Without warning, I take him in until he hits my throat. I swallow, forcing the remaining inches to fit.

A strangled noise flees him. "Fuck, Pep. Too damn good."

I moan around his length, bobbing in and out eagerly. He collects my soaked hair into his fist. I almost expect him to guide me with this makeshift handle, but it seems he just wants a clear view. That assumption is confirmed when I peek up at him from under my wet lashes. Barely restrained rapture is written in his expression. The smoky intensity wafting from his gaze spurs me on. I hollow my cheeks, pulling him deep inside, forcing him to bite off a muffled curse. A smug grin lifts my stretched lips while I preen under his rapt focus.

The motions play on repeat. I get lulled in this fast tempo while striving to hit his release. Salt greets my tongue, hinting that he's close. That confirmation sends me in a flurry. Just as I'm about to bring my hand back in the game, Mason pulls on my hair.

"Enough," he bellows.

That doesn't mean I stop. Not until he scoops me off the floor by my armpits. My mouth is still slack, tongue lolling, when I'm facing him again.

His expression is a tad crazed, eyes blown wide and dilated. "You didn't listen."

I dab at the corner of my lips, only to have the spray launch a cleaning cycle at me. "Does that make me a bad girl?"

The untamed beast ebbs sightly while he digests my words. "Do you want to be?"

"For you," I murmur and nip at his lip.

Mason crushes his mouth to mine, palm cupping my jaw until I open for him. Our tongues thrash in a wild race for control. I loop an arm around his neck to bring him closer. He growls and deepens the kiss. His steely shaft bumps my mound, insistent and starving. I reach down to stroke him, my palm glancing along his velvety skin. That's when the last restraint snaps.

He rips his lips from mine, panting with labored breaths. "Wicked temptress."

"You didn't let me finish." I pout while giving him another leisurely pump for good measure.

He plucks me off his girth, dropping my hand on his shoulder. "I need your pussy."

I shift to trace his nose with mine, foreheads glued as one. "You know where to find it."

Mason bends and hoists me up in a fluid motion. My legs wrap around his waist while he spins us. A startled squeak puffs from me when my back meets the tiles. The cool smack is to be expected, but is too sharp of a contrast to ignore. He just smirks with a palm firmly planted on my ass. His dick nudges my entrance while he adjusts our position. That's all the preparation I get.

There's a slight pinch in protest when he enters me in a single stroke. He's buried to the root, stretching me wide enough to sting. I cross my ankles against his ass to haul him tighter against me. He's already notched in deep, but there's an empty pang demanding more. Our connection is a burning torch gaining momentum. I feel that fire with each powerful drive from his hips.

"You're so wet," he rumbles against my shoulder. His mouth suckles a path to my neck, sipping at me to quench his thirst.

I tilt my head to grant him better access. "That's the entire point."

"But this is all you."

"It's what you do to me."

"Too hot. Almost scalding."

"That's just us. Together," I murmur along his temple.

"Nothing can beat this. I belong inside you." His rasp is a sacred vow against my hypersensitive skin.

"Yes. Always."

"Feel this, Pep?" He punctuates the question with an upward jab, sending his cock to tickle my womb. "You're only fit for me."

"Only you," I agree.

With a hand pressed to my tailbone, Mason angles me forward to strike an area that curls my toes. A whine flows from my parted lips. Plumes of salacious lust waft from us. My nails scratch at his arms while he thrusts to a pounding bang. Our joined friction brews and builds until static sparks along my skin.

An animalistic growl ripples from him. "Can I take control, Pep?"

"Please," I rush to surrender. Whatever eases this blistering cramp in my core.

Mason tucks an arm under each of my legs, hauling my knees up and out. I'm splayed to obscene measures and rendered immobile. That loss of agility makes me feel trapped and caged, but caught in capable hands. In this moment, I'm letting him dominate my pleasure. Mason doesn't take the opportunity for granted. His pace resumes without mercy. While spread this far, he sinks impossibly deeper. A silent scream clogs my throat as he repeatedly shoves to the hilt. I'm forced to accept all of him and I love it. My clenching walls beg for more.

I buck into him to test my limits. That only succeeds in sinking lower on his length. His raspy laugh mocks me.

"Nice try," he grates from clenched teeth.

"I'm stuck." The moan is almost pitiful.

Mason's eyes gleam with primal satisfaction. "Right where I want you."

"Are you going to let me come?"

"You're not going anywhere until I do." He pistons deep, making his meaning clear.

That fact shouldn't thrill and excite me, but it cranks my inner thermostat to boiling. I trust this man. With everything.

Even though Mason has me spread and twisted in a whore-igami pretzel, we move to a languid beat. There's no hurry. He draws in and out in lazy strokes, punching forward with a harsh thrust every other turn to keep my head spinning.

His stare bores into me, just as mine does to him. We're

connected in far more than the physical sense. I can almost feel his thoughts as he whispers a kiss across my lips. This man owns me in mind, body, and spirit. He gets all of me. Forever.

The water lashes us, dousing the flames in furious hunger. We require sustenance and our pleasure buffet is about to arrive. I grip his shoulders with curved palms and tug, as if that will speed up the delivery process.

A jolt shoots through me when he stoops to take a pebbled nipple into his mouth. I mewl and arch as far as this position allows. He grants me more suction, his tongue swiping across the sensitive tip.

"Are you done being bad?" The question is murmured against my breast.

The demand for relief pummels me. I'd agree to any terms at this point. "Yes, totally done."

His lips make a scorching path to my other nipple. "Promise?"

"Uh-huh."

"That's right, Pep. You're gonna be good for me."

"Please," I beg. "I need you. Harder."

He digs his fingers into my ass, smacking us tighter together. "How can I resist such pretty words?"

"You don't." My lashes flutter as the heat becomes unbearable.

"I don't," he agrees.

With a final plunge, Mason propels both of us into euphoric gratification. I become the spasms locking my limbs. Sight, sound, and smell cease to exist. All that's left is the sensation of him filling me. Humid moisture fills the room as I get pulled under his endless depths.

The valve opens and pressure pours out. Our combined relief spills from our lips, shattering the silence in this intimate place. We're suspended in bliss as one entity. I melt into the afterglow, only held by his strength.

We're spent in a tangled heap as the lingering ecstasy twitches our extremities. Mason is drifting his palms along me, as if drawing me back to reality. I slowly allow his touch to ground me until my feet are planted on the floor.

He doesn't release me, gaze searching mine. "Good?"

I sway slightly, pure delight wheezing from my weary form. "Fucking fantastic."

His smirk is steeped in pride as he grabs a loofah. He dumps on a generous amount of soap and works up an impressive lather. The dots connect when he begins washing me, the heavy bubbles and suds popping along my skin. I watch the warm bubbles through bleary eyes, then shift my focus to him.

"What're you doing?"

Mason pays special attention to cleaning my breasts. "Taking care of you."

"I can do that." The protest is weak, even to my own ears.

"So can I."

Who am I to argue with that?

Comfort and adoration flood from his doting motions. His sensual ministrations feel better than a pampering session at the spa. Once he's done, I let him rinse me with thorough concentration. Not a single spot remains soapy.

"You're going through an awful lot of trouble." I grip the knob in preparation to shut off the water.

"Why wouldn't I?"

My lips brush his ears as I crank the nozzle. "I plan to get you dirty all over again."

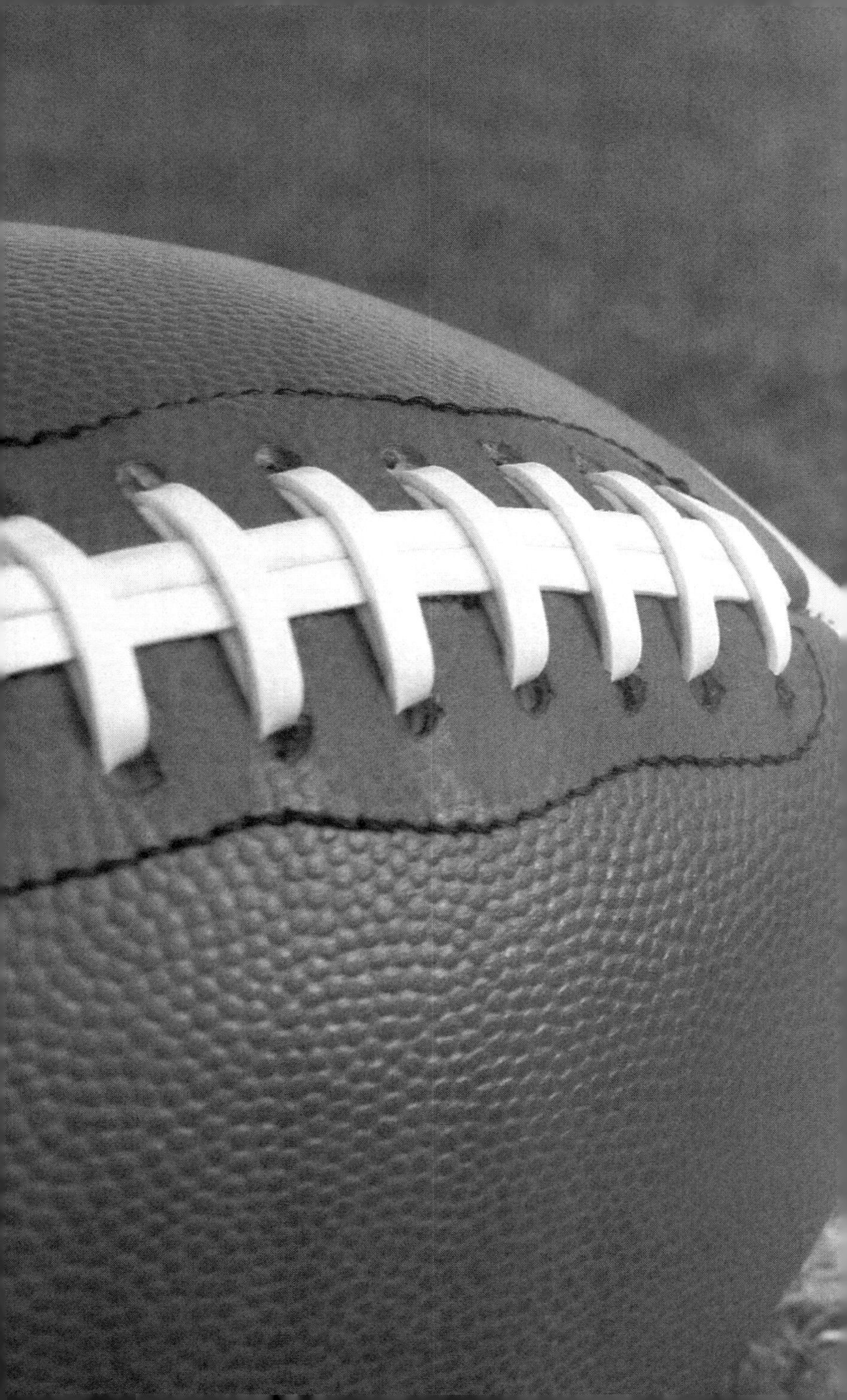

chapter twenty-four

Mason

Presley shields her eyes while gazing up at her son, who's gladly perched on my shoulders. "You're spoiling him."

My smirk is an appropriate blend between acceptance and confidence. "And you don't?"

"Touché." She inspects our surroundings with a lopsided grin.

I do the same, allowing the infectious energy to infiltrate my system. The Tri-Tide Fall Fest is in full swing. Set on a repurposed field, the event sprawls across at least fifteen acres. Most of that is reserved for the hayride and corn maze.

The grounds are arranged in three sections. To our left are inflatables, a mega slide, some standard rides, carnival games, and mini-golf. The corn pit and maze are on the right. Concessions and a few random booths frame the main area straight ahead. Hay bales and piles of colorful leaves litter much of the center, along with a stage for the band. There's so much to choose from, I don't even know where to begin. Fortunately, given the sheer excitement written across Archie's face, that won't be a decision I'll have to make.

We'd been stalking the forecast all week for the most optimal time to attend. It's early enough to avoid the peak hour crowds, but the morning chill has already been chased away. An outdoor event in November is dicey, but this season has been milder than most. Pretty sure the latest reports mentioned that Minnesota is warmer than Texas right now. We can't complain about that. The sky is cloudless and sunny. With minimal wind and the temperature in the low fifties, we're set for success.

"Did you bring Archie last year?" It almost hurts to ask, knowing I wasn't here to join them.

Presley links her fingers with mine. "Yes, but he was too young for most of the stuff. He mostly stayed in the stroller."

"Ah, so this is a whole different experience." The cramp threatening to squeeze loosens marginally.

She rolls her eyes. "Don't fret. You didn't miss much."

A boulder drops in my gut and I wince. "Only where the festival is concerned."

"Nope," she clips and wags a finger. "Turn that frown upside down, champ. We're done wallowing over the past. The present is where we live and thrive and look ahead to our glorious future."

I take her chin between my thumb and finger, tilting until our lips seal. "You're so wise."

Archer makes kissy noises from his VIP seating. "Mase loves Mama."

"That wisdom is hereditary," I chuckle while patting his leg. "Where to first, buddy?"

"Face paint!" His answer is a shout to be heard across the entire festival.

My ears ring from the blast. "Did you say pumpkin slingshot?"

"Nooooooo," he cries. "Face paint!"

"Oh, you're thirsty? How about chocolate milk?"

"Whisten, Mase." His fingers yank at my hair with his insistence. "I wanna be Marshall. Woof, woof."

Then he breaks out into the *Paw Patrol* theme song. I can't help singing along—in my head, of course. Pretty sure I catch Presley mouthing the words while we stride toward the tent where Archie's demands will come true.

He tugs at me every few steps as if to guarantee I'm going in the correct direction. I swear the kid has a special sense when it comes to sniffing out his activities of choice. Not that I blame him for following his nose. The air is crisp and ripe with fair fun. I inhale a greedy whiff, an easy smile curling my lips.

"You look pleased," Presley notes in a twinkly tune.

I swing our clasped palms while keeping a steady hold on Archer's shin. "How could I not be? I'm with my two favorite people in a land of family entertainment."

She hums, pure joy sparkling from her baby blues. "You're made for this."

"I really am."

Her hip nudges mine as she edges closer. "Have I told you lately how happy I am you came back?"

"Maybe," I drawl. "I could stand to hear it again."

"Mason Braxter," she recites with exaggerated seriousness. "Once again, you've changed my life. I had no idea how lonely I'd been until you reminded me how it feels to be loved. Cherished. Wanted. Desired."

"Worshipped," I add in a whisper.

A shiver trembles through her. "Yes. You're the only one for me."

"We here!" Archie's sharp excitement pops our intimate moment.

I go still, blinking slowly at the sudden return to harsh clarity. It's too easy for me to fall under Presley's spell. With a cough, I scan the interior of the canvas structure mere feet away. Two women are seated inside at separate tables. Vast arrays of painting supplies are scattered across the surfaces. There's no one sitting in the empty chairs beside them.

"Hi," Presley greets with a wave. "Are you open?"

The one closest to us nods and beckons us forward. "Just finished getting everything laid out. You're smart to arrive early. Come on in."

Archer doesn't pause, zooming toward her and plopping down on the available seat. "I wanna be Marshall."

"From *Paw Patrol*," I fill in the blank with a grin. "It's his favorite show."

"You're adorable," Presley murmurs.

I furrow my brow. "What'd I do?"

"The fact you don't know makes it even better."

My mind whirls over the possibilities, but nothing obvious comes to mind. Rather than question her, I return my attention to Archie. The white base for the half mask option already covers his forehead and cheeks. Black dots to complete the Dalmatian signature are in progress. He's sitting on his palms, but still wiggling. The lady clucks her tongue in reprimand. His reaction is instant. For a child whose motor rarely idles, it's almost shocking to witness his ability to freeze on the spot.

"Is she a witch?" I mumble the question from the corner of my mouth.

Presley huffs. "Might as well be. She has the magic to paint his face."

"We need to learn these tricks."

She nods. "He's starting to get wise to the countdown warning."

Our observation session ends with a final spot over his eyebrow.

"All right, kiddo. You're all set." The woman reaches for the mirror, spinning it for him to see his reflection.

Archie's gasp is answer enough. "I whook wike Marshall!"

"You look just like him, sweet angel." Presley is about to tap his painted nose, but thinks better of it. Her fingers ruffle his hair instead.

Archer's focus swivels to me, waiting expectantly for my praise. "Wat you tink, Mase?"

I let a low whistle loose. "Perfection. I wish my face was painted exactly the same."

His smile soars to his eyes and then some. He turns to the lady currently preparing for the next customer. "You do Mase too?"

She glances at him, lifts her gaze to me, then lowers back again. "Sorry, kiddo. There are too many waiting. I can't let him budge."

Presley follows the woman's gesture toward the tent entrance. "Holy shitake mushrooms. Is that the line?"

My jaw goes slack upon seeing the wait that seemed to form in an instant. There must be a dozen kids gathered in single file with their parents lingering on the sidelines. "Wow, you're popular."

The two artists release mutual sighs, exhaustion already heavy on their features. "This is our busiest event. Thankfully it only runs on the weekends or we wouldn't get any rest."

"It's only getting started," the other mentions absently while she colors in a blue splotch on a child's cheek.

"Okay, we'll get out of the way." Presley digs out some cash, but I halt her movements.

"I've got this." After handing over the money, I stuff extra in the tip jar. "Thanks for making his day."

The woman smiles in acknowledgment. "I think you're doing a fine job of that on your own."

I open my mouth to respond, but words fail me.

Presley elbows me on her way out. "Don't look so dumbfounded. I already told you."

"Up, up." Archie flings his arms in the air.

My lips twist to one side while I study him. "Is that Archie? You kind of look like a dog."

He growls, snapping his teeth. "I'm Marshall."

"Oh, right. But do pups ride on shoulders?"

His features scrunch in concentration. "I dunno."

As if I could deny him for another moment. I scoop and deposit him right where he belongs, dipping low to clear the exit. Presley is waiting for us with a warm grin.

"Where to next?"

Archer is too busy barking to answer.

I erase the space separating us, avoiding the growing line waiting to get their faces painted. "We could do the hayride. I think the entrance is near that dinosaur bouncy house."

"Or the Ferris wheel," she suggests while hitching a thumb in that direction.

Archie wiggles above me, hands slapping against my temples. "I wanna do da wheel!"

The rapid thump in my chest reveals my hesitation. "Is that safe?"

Presley just stares at me. "Wow. You're seriously adorable."

The confusion reigns higher than ever. "What does that mean?"

She reclaims my palm against hers, threading our fingers. "You're protective and super chatty and just plain giddy when it comes to Archie."

"Why does that make me sound like a fluff puff?" More so, why shouldn't I be all those things?

"You mispronounced adorable." Then she lifts onto the

balls of her feet to whisper in my ear. "And incredibly sexy. You love my son like he's yours."

Realization dawns with the flip of a switch. "Oh."

"Yeah," she laughs. "Oh. You're extremely appealing. Single mom catnip, remember?"

I tighten my grip on her hand. "You're the only single mom I want to attract."

"Even better," she purrs.

A pat on my head demands attention. "We go on wheel now?"

The reminder is a cold smack to my chilled skin. I almost flinch. Presley's cool-as-a-cucumber state corrals my impulse to outright deny his request.

"Doesn't he have to be a certain height to ride?" My concerned gaze meets Presley's calm demeanor.

She flicks my arm, adding a pinch for good measure. "Don't be a worry wart. It's literally the slowest ride in existence. The carousel goes faster."

"But the height," I insist.

"He'll be wedged between us."

That appeases the queasy knot in my belly. "Okay, okay. You know best."

Her smile slips into a tilted slant. "You're capable of deciding."

"But I'm not his parent."

Presley gawks, her lips parting to berate me. A figure emerges from the fray before she can.

"Is that Mason Braxter I see?"

My shoulders hike to ear-level at the meek tone, jostling Archie in the process. "That's me."

When I turn, recognition is a sledgehammer to my skull. It takes a second for the dust to settle. Her silhouette stands proud through the haze.

"Sloane?" Shock pulverizes my voice into gritty pulp.

"You remember me." Her timid expression doesn't reflect the shock her words suggest.

"Why wouldn't I? We graduated together," I reply.

"You don't need to remind me. I've been here the entire time." Her wary gaze snakes to the woman beside me. "Right, Press?"

The neutral temperature cranks to sweaty levels as she reciprocates with her own guarded stare. "I'm not in the habit of keeping track."

Sloane winces. "Oh, sorry. I wasn't trying to be a—"

"It's fine," I cut in. There's no reason for her to continue with more useless slander. "We're used to receiving opinions of all shapes and sizes."

"That's a nice way of putting it," Presley mutters.

Sloane's expression crumples. "I've heard the rumors. People can be brutal, especially the jealous hags."

"Wut a hag?" Archer's chin rests on my head.

Her eyes whip to him. "Hey, cutie! A hag is—"

"A word that rhymes with rag," Presley rushes to explain.

The other woman pauses, confusion fading into understanding. "Right. Tag and bag too."

Archie squeaks with a jolt. "I gots a bag! Wooks wike Marshall."

"Just like you do," I tell him. "Let's get fired up."

Presley sighs while I jog in place, Archie squealing with glee. "Too adorable."

"I didn't mean to interrupt your day. Just wanted to say hi. You make a super sweet picture." Sloane holds up a fake camera formed with her hands and clicks.

"Thanks." I offer a crooked grin, too skeptical to let the other half lift.

"Speaking of, would you mind?" Presley holds her phone out.

"Not at all. It's an honor to capture this moment."

Without further prompting, Presley plasters herself to my side and rests a palm on Archer's leg. I wrap an arm around her while maintaining my grip on the little man. We're in tight formation as Sloane lifts the device.

"Say cheese," she coos.

"Cheese," pours from us in unison.

"Absolutely precious." Sloane passes the cell back to Presley. "Don't listen to what anyone says. It's obvious you belong together. All three of you."

Warmth spreads from my chest in an outward sprint until I'm sweltering. "Appreciate that."

"You're awesome," Presley agrees while proofing the images. "These are great."

"I smile good?" Archie leans over to get a look, almost sending me off balance.

"The best," his mom chirps.

"Okay, that's my cue. This has been a chocolate-dipped treat. Have a great Fall Fest!" After a wiggle from her fingers, Sloane wanders off into the throng.

Presley watches her retreat with a grin spreading. "That was… unexpected."

I snag her hand to engulf it with mine. "Maybe we won't have to move after all."

"That would save a lot of trouble," she muses.

"What's next on the agenda?"

"Da wheel!" Archer flails his arm toward the ride, almost knocking me sideways again.

"How could I forget?" I smack my forehead.

"I have a few guesses," Presley jokes.

"Okay," I relent. With our palms clasped, I guide her forward.

"About time," she murmurs. Her coy smile reveals the tease behind those words.

The line is short and passes quickly. I pay the attendant,

who doesn't give our tiny toddler a second glance. Metal creaks as we step on, get settled on the narrow seat, and pull down the lap bar.

As our cart leaves the station, rocking slightly, Archie squeals in delight. His legs kick wildly. "Wheeeeee! We go high."

"This was a good idea," I murmur while we rise to the top. From this vantage point, I can see how the corn maze slices into the stalks.

"I'd say I told you so, but… oh, who am I kidding? I totally told you so." Presley blows me a kiss.

"My doubt will never be aimed at you again," I vow.

"Ditto," she whispers.

With that small promise, old scars suddenly vanish as if those marks never existed. I relax on the bench as comfort washes over me. The breeze dusts my face, countless more memories to be made skipping along the horizon.

"Wow, look at the view." Wonder radiates from her voice.

My gaze remains locked on her and Archer, the scenery barely a blip on my radar. "It's the most beautiful sight I've ever seen."

chapter twenty-five

Presley

THE STEERING WHEEL SLIDES IN MY GRIP AS I PULL INTO Mason's driveway. His house looks exactly the same as it did months ago. I find myself questioning—for the hundredth time—why he hasn't bothered to decorate. There isn't a single plant or flower in the dirt beds. No drapes shielding the windows. Not even a welcome mat on the porch. My eyes sweep over the grass to find he's at least been mowing the lawn. Or most likely paying some teenager to do it.

Those ponderings vanish when I catch sight of my boys in the yard. Mason is crouched low to be at Archie's level. They haven't noticed me yet, too engrossed in their game of catch. I step out quietly with every intention of continuing to watch their exchange as an unannounced bystander. It's a small miracle that the door doesn't creak.

There's plenty of space separating us, but I have a direct

view. Mason holds the football with both hands, preparing a light toss to Archer. My son thrusts his arms forward, stiff as a board. Mason lobs the pigskin directly into his waiting hold. The joy that radiates off them is infectious. A smile threatens to split my face while I become mesmerized by their game.

Mason's voice carries across the distance. "You did it, buddy!"

"Frow to you, Mase." My son chucks the ball at him without further warning. He hasn't quite mastered the spiral yet, and it careens off in an odd direction, falling woefully short of the distance required.

Somehow, Mason still manages to dart forward in time to catch the wild toss. He pumps his fist in the air. "Great job!"

"'Gan, 'gan!" Archie is bouncing in place with his arms extended, signaling for another round.

They repeat the process with the same results. I remain firmly rooted in place, afraid to miss a second of the action. The sight brings fiery heat to my eyes, and I sniff. This is what I've longed for, more than I can ever admit. It's a single mother's dream to have her son accepted by a man who isn't his father. Mason did so from the first instant. He provides boundless affection where we needed it most. This is just another example of how wonderful he is for us. More so, he's given my son the gift of sharing his favorite hobby.

Chad—bless his heart—isn't athletic. While trying his darnedest, he could maybe throw a ball straight. Not that he needs to be a pro at Archer's current skill level. He just probably hasn't thought to try, and that's totally okay. This can be Mason's thing with Archie.

My son launches himself at Mason, thin arms winding around his neck. "I love you, Mase."

"Love you back, buddy." Mason returns the embrace with enthusiasm, eyes sliding shut as if to immediately cement this moment to memory.

Tears trickle down my cheeks. The lump in my throat makes it difficult to swallow. I feel like a voyeur in this scene, intruding on a private moment meant for just them. That doesn't stop a muffled sob from escaping.

Mason's eyes snap to me lingering on the outskirts of their bubble. A grin curves his full lips, the sight stealing my breath. Pretty soon I'll faint from this emotional onslaught.

I clutch a palm to my chest. "You two are so stinking cute."

He narrows his eyes while crooking a finger at me. "You mispronounced manly."

My feet follow his silent command, delivering me into their space. "I'll show you what I meant later, and how grateful I am."

"I'll take that gratitude, but rewards aren't necessary. I love being with this little guy." He tugs on the wool hat covering Archer's head. I belatedly realize it matches the 86ers one Mason is wearing.

A fresh sting attacks my eyes and I swat at the resulting streaks. "Consider it a bonus then."

"Mama!" Archie puts an end to his silent participation in our conversation with that sharp squeal. "You see me? I frow ball far!"

I kneel and open my arms for him. "You really did. Very impressive, sweetie. I can't throw a ball that far."

Archer flings himself at me, nearly tipping us over. "Mase teach you."

"I'm sure he will." I wink at the man in mention.

Mason sits on the grass beside us, ripping at a few random blades. "How was work?"

A satisfied hum rolls from me while I rub my hands together. "This client is a jackpot. She's living in a hoarder's paradise."

"Only you would be excited about that." He chuckles and

drifts a thumb along my jaw, catching a stray droplet. When he sucks the evidence of my happy tears off his digit, I'm certain another wave is about to crash over me.

I focus on what he said to keep the emotion clogged. "She's going to keep me busy, and well-compensated."

"You better still have time to spend with your two favorite guys." His meaningful gaze latches on Archie, who nods along in moral support.

"Mama be home for us." He sticks out his bottom lip in an exaggerated pout.

I scoff. "As if I'd ever be gone longer than necessary. I only accepted these extra hours because a certain someone insists on spending quality time with a specific buddy of his."

My son furrows his brow. "Huh?"

"What your mom means is I ask to hang out with you. When it's just you and me, we get to have male bonding," Mason explains.

"Whussat?"

"Like when we play catch or hang out. Male bonding."

"Ohhhhh," Archie exhales. "I wike male bondings with you, Mase."

"But it's also really great when we're all together too," he adds for my benefit.

That's the moment my stomach grumbles in protest. I flinch from the obnoxious sound. "Guess I'm hungry."

"Want me to make you something?" Mason moves to stand.

I accept his outstretched palm, and he hoists me upright. "Like what? Chicken nuggets or a corndog?"

"Hey, don't knock Archie's cuisine of choice. He's the only reason I have food to offer."

That reminds me of my earlier musings. "Do you even have three chairs for us to sit on?"

"I have two and a lap that's always available." He gestures to the aforementioned area. "Take your pick."

Archer scrambles to his feet. "I sit on Mase."

"See?" Mason's grin is too smug for my liking. "Problem solved."

I park a fist on my hip. "Don't you see the issue, though?"

His extended pause leads me to believe he doesn't. He confirms with a hesitant, "No."

"It's been two months and your place is still bare-bones. You should probably get some furniture."

He crosses his arms with an unflinching stare. "Why? What's the point?"

"To be comfortable," I press.

"It's not supposed to be."

Archie chooses this moment to grow bored of us, dashing to a nearby tree to run circles around. His fast pace almost makes me dizzy by association. My thoughts scatter into smaller pieces than confetti.

With a quick shake of my head, I get back on track. "I'm really confused. You're living in a skeletal environment on purpose?"

"Yes."

A baffled noise shoots from me. The tone is sharp, nearing shrill levels. "When are you going to turn this house into a home, Mason?"

If I'm being honest, I thought this was due to low priority or laziness. He's at my place more often than not, especially lately. According to him, he just doesn't care.

He shrugs, the motion very noncommittal. "I don't plan on sticking around here very long."

My breath hitches, the following inhale a struggle. "What?"

"I figure it's only a matter of weeks until I convince you to let me move in."

"Oh." The pressure clamping my chest ceases immediately.

Mason studies my slack expression with raised brows. "What'd you think I was going to say?"

"Nothing?" Dammit, that wasn't meant to be a question.

"Pep," he urges.

I groan, almost ready to stomp my foot. "Well, what do you expect? It's very suspect that you haven't settled in."

"There's a reason for that."

"Yes, I understand that now." Two months too late.

He rocks forward on his shoes. "So, how about it?"

The flutter in my pulse skitters faster. "Is this you asking to move in with us?"

"Yes," he states without a second of delay.

"Just like that?" I snap my fingers for emphasis.

"I was ready after Knotty Knox."

A very unladylike snort flares my nostrils. "You would be."

Mason entwines our fingers, giving a gentle squeeze. "Don't pretend you didn't feel the same."

"Bulldozer," I mutter.

His chuckle is gooey chocolate left in the sun to melt. "You love it."

"I do." But a vital member of this decision has been left out. He just so happens to make a reappearance by my side for the announcement. "I'm not the only one you need to convince."

He gets my meaning, of course. Mason drops to his knees in front of Archer, palms folding in a silent plea. "Would you like it if I lived with you, buddy?"

My son lifts his gaze to mine, uncertainly swirling in those blue depths as if Mason is playing a joke. When I nod, he swings his stare to the man waiting for an answer. "In my woom?"

"At your house," he hedges.

"Yes! I wanna wive wit you." His wide eyes pong back to me. "Okay, Mama?"

I'm busy biting my lip. "Can I think about it?"

He peers at me from his crouched spot on the grass. "Do you need to?"

"Not really." A giddy zing floods through me with the admission.

"That's what I thought."

"So confident," I murmur.

"About us?" He wraps one arm around my legs. The other sandwiches Archie in the middle. "There's never been a doubt."

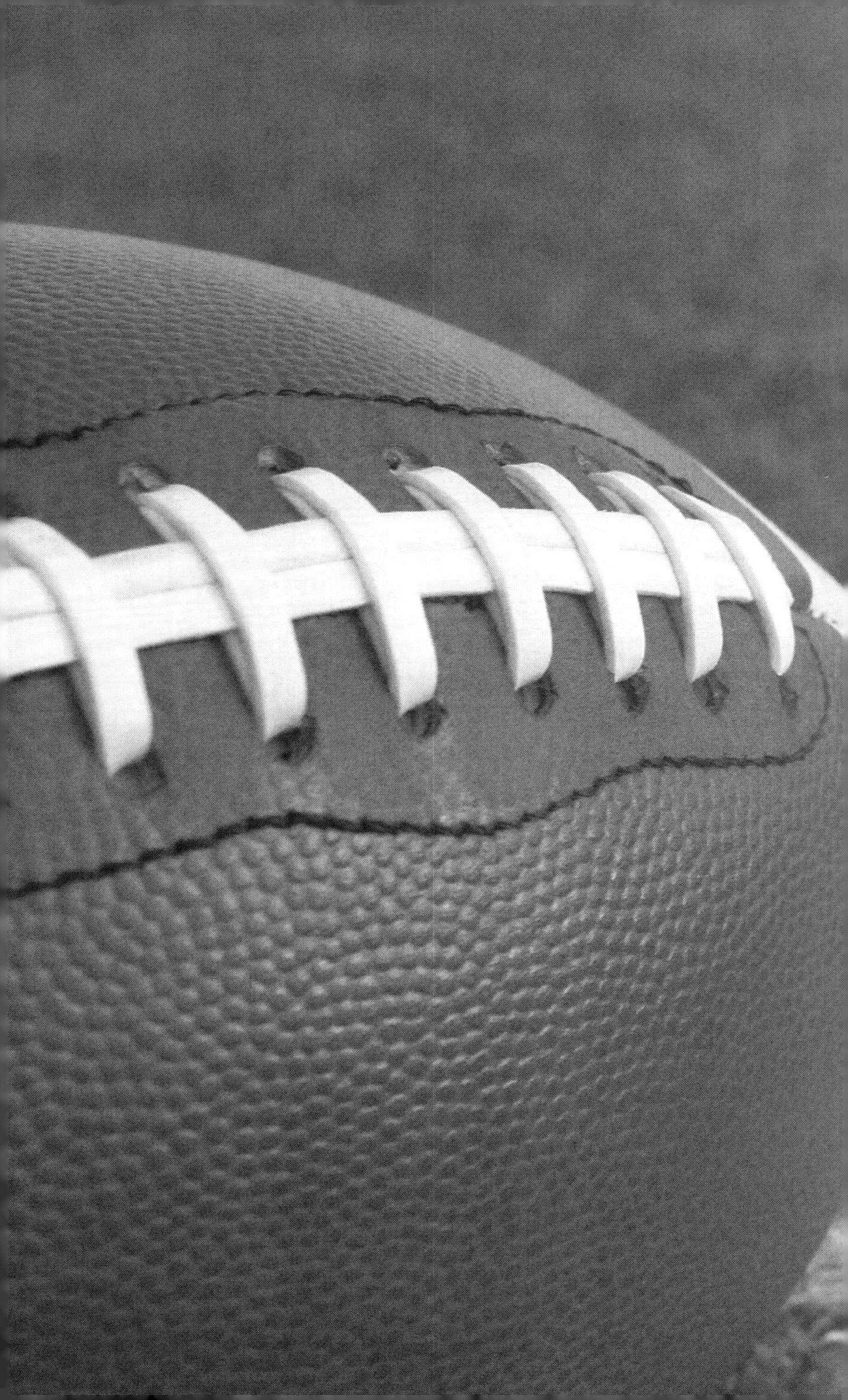

chapter twenty-six

Mason

THE AIR GAINS A FROSTY BITE AS AFTERNOON SURRENDERS TO evening. Another long day at practice has run its course. I roll my neck to release the kink. My muscles ache and I'm not even the one running drills for hours. It's just the natural result of maintaining such intensity on the sidelines. The players and other coaches compliment my methods. It feels good to be needed, and vital, on a team again.

"Hey, Coach." A jogging stride slaps the concrete behind me. "Wait up."

I pause my retreat, turning to face Colt. "What's up, Wylder?"

He quickens his pace to meet me on the path. "Thanks for that personal session. It was brutal, but appreciated. I can barely feel my legs."

Yet he's hardly winded. I pushed him hard on purpose.

The guy is talented, and that skill is reflected in each throw he launches. He's the type to thrive on a challenge.

Once again, I'm reminded of my own experiences. Nothing wore me down while on the field. It was just everything that happened once I stepped off the turf.

I brush off that ancient history with a grunt. "Just doing my job."

"Ah, don't be modest. You're going well above and beyond the standard. This feels like an entirely different offense since you started. We have a winning record, Coach. You can't deny that." Pride thrums from his square posture.

"It's dedication and determination," I recite. Fuck, how many times did I hear that growing up? The phrase was hammered into my skull until it became a permanent stamp.

Colt squints while digesting my words of wisdom. "Can't take credit, huh?"

"Not when you're doing the heavy lifting."

He holds up a pacifying palm. "All right, fair enough."

The pause extends into a silence that's not getting me home any faster. "I'm assuming you didn't stop me just for that."

"Nah, there's something else on my mind." He scrubs the back of his neck. "I'm hoping to get your opinion."

"Sure, I'll do my best."

His chest expands with a deep breath. "Not sure if you're aware, but several D1 schools are showing interest in me."

Murmurs and rumors were starting to trickle down about potential offers, but I wasn't sure about their authenticity.

I have a sinking suspicion about where this conversation is headed. My gut reaction is to suggest he stays put. That's not fair to him, though. He's not that much younger than me, but our circumstances set us on separate paths. His situation isn't mine. Most athletes in this sport don't have the slightest clue about the dark hole some are shoved into.

The grin I manage is limp but genuine. "That's great, Wylder. Are you thinking about transferring?"

He bobs his head. "Yeah, for sure. It would be a smart move. If things go well, I might get a shot at playing pro."

"What's the problem?"

"My girlfriend won't follow me."

The air stalls in my windpipe and I cough. That scenario is far too familiar. An ache spreads while I gather my bearings. "Ah, that makes the decision more complicated."

Colt sighs, resignation slumping his stature. "What would you do, Coach?"

A rough chuckle scrapes from my parched throat. "You mean, what did I do?"

His eyes blow open to saucer size. "No shit?"

The advice bubbling on my tongue is jaded and tainted after years of being a pawn. "I had a similar choice to make—career or love. Center Cal could make my football fantasies come true. My girlfriend didn't want to move. In the end, I chose the game."

Colt's focus doesn't waver from me. "Do you ever regret it?"

This is a topic I've covered with Presley, and my opinion won't change. "It's a sore spot—I won't lie to you. I can't be sorry for accepting the opportunity to play the sport on that level. Those stadium lights are just… better than a dream. Beyond anything I can articulate. There's no other thrill quite the same. But if I could go back, I'd handle my priorities with great care. I would've fought harder to stay with my girl."

"Damn," Colt spits. "That's what I'm afraid of."

"Not the perspective you were hoping for?"

His momentary frustration fades into another casual smile. "I prefer a simple solution."

My laugh is pitched with disbelief. "That's not a luxury you can afford in this case."

His expression dims at the edges, but the center stays illuminated with perfect resolution. "Maybe I can have both. The U of M has been sniffing around campus."

"I'll put in a good word," I offer.

Colt's energy bounces back with a whoop. "That'd be awesome, Coach. Then I can have the best of both worlds."

"That would be the optimal outcome." Even I catch the dejected note in my tone.

"What aren't you telling me?"

"Just don't assume the battle is over. Nothing worth striving for is going to be simple to achieve."

"Well, shit. I kinda thought the worst was over after talking with you." That naïve outlook won't protect him against the forces waiting to feed off his potential.

Something Presley said once materializes. "You'll figure it out, Colt. Make the right choice for both of you. The last thing you want to feel is resentment."

He drops his jaw. "How could I? She's my girl. We've been together since high school."

The pain in my chest intensifies and I rub at the inflicted area. "You just never know what might happen. If it comes down to you choosing her over the game, or the opposite, there might be lingering guilt. That doubt can plague you."

Colt is nodding, seeming to digest the weighty decisions in his near future. "I have a lot to consider. See? You go well above and beyond."

"Just doing my job," I repeat.

"Yeah, yeah. Making it look easy."

If only that was the truth for every aspect. "Just follow your gut."

"Not my groin," he tacks on.

"Correct," I chuckle. "That would just cause unnecessary heartache."

His gaze tracks my features, which I try to smooth into a neutral mask. "Sound advice. Thanks, Coach."

"My door—or sidewalk square—is always open for you."

"Means a lot," he murmurs.

"Good luck." I tug at the brim of my hat.

"Thanks, I'll need it. See you tomorrow."

Just as Colt begins walking away, a vibration buzzes from my pocket. I dig out my phone while a smirk grows. The carefree expression instantly fades when I read the name on the screen.

"Paul," I grunt in greeting.

"Hello, Braxter. I'm glad you answered." His smarmy tone sends a chill slithering down my spine. "There's news you'll want to hear."

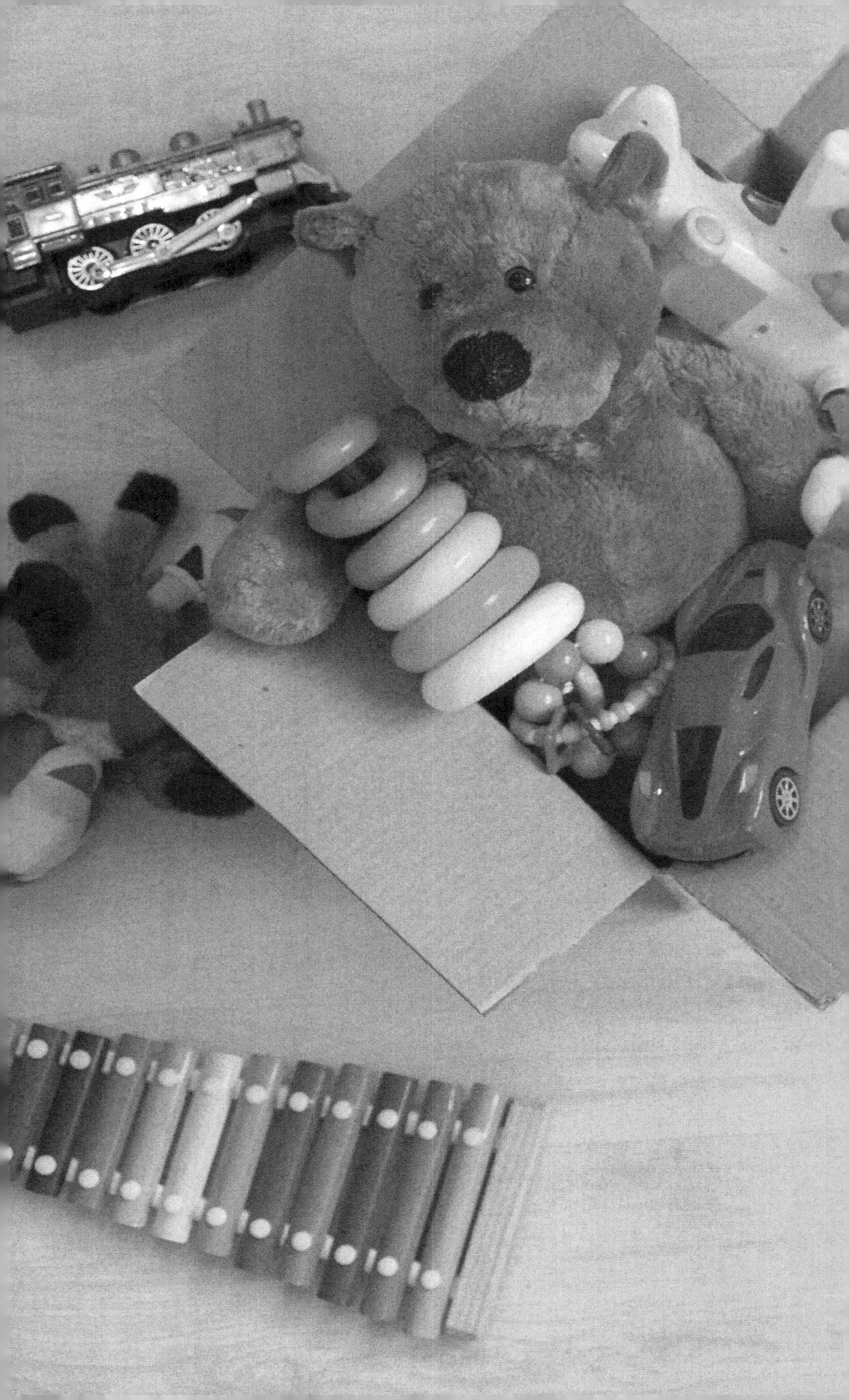

chapter twenty-seven

Presley

The happy hour crowd at Knotty Knox provides upbeat background chatter. I slouch on the tall stool—cushioned backrest included—and expel the residual stress from my last client. Clea and Vannah mirror my actions, synchronized sighs passing through their slack lips. Then they're reclining for optimal comfort while we wait to order drinks. We paint a picturesque portrait—a trio of bad-ass boss bitches.

The fact that we snagged a spot in the first place is a testament to our mad skills. Our high-top is in the bar section, which is packed to the max with like-minded folks trying to let off some steam on a Friday afternoon. People resemble lumps of clutter in the smaller, sectioned area. Employees attempt to fight against the flow, dodging and dipping wherever there's a sliver of free space. It's a congested traffic jam of human proportions.

A frazzled server slams on the brakes at our table. I can almost feel the impending panic wafting from her.

"Apologies for the wait. We're slammed." She blows several loose strands of hair off her forehead. "My name is Sara. Feel free to yell across the room to me. In the meantime, can I grab you ladies anything to start?"

"Alcohol," Vannah practically shouts. "Margaritas. An entire pitcher. Make it tall and wide."

The woman's frantic gaze passes over Clea and me. My bestie beside me requests three glasses. "Otherwise the redhead won't share."

Vannah huffs, tossing some fiery locks over her shoulder. "I'd consider it."

I lean forward to add, "Chips and queso, please."

The server taps on her handheld device. "Got it. I'll get the booze out right away."

I watch her vanish into the throng, sympathy careening in my pulse. She's going to need something strong to decompress after this shift. Something very strong. The word leads me to an image of Mason and his bulging biceps. Then his almost-eight pack that trails to an even more impressive package. I swat at the air to dissipate the hussy fumes. Lord only knows what will happen if Vannah catches a whiff.

As if sensing her name in my mind, she releases a loud groan. "Damn, it's good to be out with my girls."

"Long week?" My stare is pointed at her as she practically chomps on the proverbial bit.

She lets a snarky snort loose. "Yes. Very. Landon has been riding my ass about these new contracts. It's a mess."

"Why do I get the feeling you're being literal?" Clea

doesn't bother masking her wince, wiggling a bit on the seat.

"No, prudette. When he's actually riding my ass, it's cause for celebration. You should try it. That position really… forces you to relax and accept the intrusion." She taps Clea's squirming thigh.

My platinum blonde friend scoffs. "I'll never understand how your mind works."

"That's probably for the best. It's terrifying to unsuspecting onlookers." Vannah puckers her lips, the visual far too graphic after what she just suggested.

Sara returns in a wind-whipped flurry of precision and jitters. She puts the pitcher in the middle, passing us each a flared rimmed glass. "Would you like me to pour for you?"

"No, no. I'll do the honors. You're very busy, and probably needed elsewhere." Vannah's manicured nails are already latched on the handle, dragging the margarita mixture to her side.

The server sags with a relieved exhale. "Thank you. I'll be back to check on you soon. The chips and queso should be right out too."

"All right, ladies. Let's do a toast to us." Vannah pushes a nearly overflowing drink to me, then repeats the process for Clea.

The balancing act of getting the liquor to my lips is proving unsuccessful. A puddle is already forming from the sloshed contents. "I can't lift this without spilling."

"It's called a leaner." She demonstrates sipping from the rim without picking up the glass.

"Okay," Clea laughs. "Cheers to us!"

Then we treat ourselves to a hearty gulp. Tart goodness bursts on my tongue and I eagerly swallow another round. The strong slap of tequila is barely detectible under the sour lemon-lime tang.

"I'm glad you chose this place, Van. Lots of good memories." Clea sips at her margarita while looking to be lost in thought.

The saucy redhead follows suit, polishing off another swig. "I figure it holds sentimental value. How's wedding planning?"

"Really fun." The bride-to-be inspects the glittering rock on her finger. "Really, really."

"It shows. You're positively glowing." I swipe at the salt-dipped rim, sucking a few granules from my thumb. "Still thinking about August?"

She nods. "Yep. We've narrowed the location down to three venues. Just waiting to tour the Minneapolis Golf Club before making a final decision."

"I can't wait for all the festivities." A breathy sigh whizzes from me. "Celebrating love is the best."

Clea clasps her palms against her chest. "And it's not just me. We're all getting a happily ever after."

"That's a perfect segue." Vannah's gaze boomerangs to me. "Don't think you're off the hook, Peppy Girl."

Clea giggles. "Oh, I almost forgot about that nickname."

"Supes adorbs," Vannah coos. "How does it feel to be back at the scene of the crime?"

With feigned enthusiasm, I fan my face. "I'm tickled pink. My va-jay-jay is fluttering at the reminder."

"That's my girl." Vannah blows me a kiss.

"Pervasaurus." Clea elbows her, then casts her gaze on me. "Are you still planning to host Friendsgiving? Mason just moved in, right?"

Giddiness spirals through me at the reminder. "My place is set for the occasion. He owns four possessions. One is his truck. We've already unpacked and organized."

Vannah refills our half-full drinks. "Not surprising with a professional on call."

"Audria and Reeve will be in attendance, unless another blizzard hits." Clea holds up a pair of crossed fingers.

"We've been lucky with the weather so far," I mention while glancing out the nearest window. Sunshine filters through the pane, but the temperature is a brisk forty-one.

"Hey, be careful. You better knock on wood." Vannah pounds her fist on the table.

I steady the trembling glasses from her abrupt superstitious beating. "Pretty sure you handled that for the three of us."

"Oh, shit." Vannah's concentration is glued on a spot over my shoulder. "You should've knocked. This is what I was afraid of."

"Huh?" I swivel in my seat to follow her rapt focus. Clarity replaces confusion as my gaze latches on the television screen. Shock and dread and a flurry of other mixed emotions quickly follow. "What the—?"

A garbled squeak comes from Clea, and I assume she's watching too. "They're talking about Mason, right? Your Mason?"

I squint, trying to read the scrolling captions. It only takes a few sentences for confirmation. For a moment, I'm paralyzed. My vision tunnels on the bold words that have the power to destroy me. "Yes, they certainly are."

"He's being considered for the Stampede's offensive coach? As in, the Montana professional football team?" Vannah's questions are like static against the pounding in my ears.

There's a rapidly brewing storm inside me. My pulse is hammering at a level that should cause concern. Everything fades into a muted gray while I gape at the segment being aired on ESPN. "I don't know."

"Does he want the job?" Clea's voice sounds like she's underwater.

"I don't know." My tone is weak and brittle.

"What does this mean?" Her gentle prod is a hushed murmur, as if I'm about to spook.

"I don't know." There are too many thoughts racing in my brain.

A soft hand rubs along my arm. Vannah's soothing voice accompanies the comforting touch. "Based on your reaction, I'm guessing Mason didn't tell you."

I shake my head. A queasy cramp seizes my stomach and I gulp against the rising lump. There must be a misunderstanding.

"What are you going to do?"

"I don't know." Those three words feel safe while I fight the urge to overreact.

Clea is suddenly beside me, wrapping us in a side hug. "Maybe you should talk to him before assuming the worst."

"How could I assume anything else?" The evidence is still playing for all to see. A major network wouldn't run the story if it wasn't true.

"This is so predictable," Vannah snips.

"How so?" I force the prompt to the surface. Engaging in conversation is the only thing holding off the impending doom just waiting to sweep me away.

"They're always firing and hiring coaches. It was only a matter of time—and not long at that—before they poached Mason." She flicks a wrist at the TV, referring to the NFL update reel.

"He's happy at Carleton," I mumble.

Vannah winces. "Really? It's such a tiny college."

I shoot a glare over my shoulder at her. "Quit being negative. Size doesn't matter."

"That's a good one." She chokes on seemingly nothing. "Don't forget who you're talking to."

"Mason just wants to coach. He doesn't care about the salary or level." Which is precisely what he's spent the last two months convincing me of.

My so-called bestie spies on my insecurities. "Is that what you want to believe?"

"Savannah Simons," I scold. "Now isn't the time to be your snarky self."

She makes the gesture of zipping her lips and tossing away the key. Yet her mouth still moves. "I just don't want you to get hurt."

"And I appreciate your concern. Mason won't do anything to jeopardize our relationship. Besides, he would never leave Archie." Not willingly at least.

"Are you sure?"

"Yes," I force out from a fake smile. Insistence vibrates from my posture just to be sure.

"You can't blame me for assuming otherwise." Vannah bats a hand at the sportscaster still prattling on about the subject. "Especially after your initial worries with Mason."

"That was then. We're solid now."

"It just said he's a top contender for the job," Clea repeats the devastating blow.

Vannah appears on my left, flanking me in resilience. "Let's be honest, he's probably the front-runner."

I scowl at her. "You're so sweet. Thanks for the moral support, Van."

"Just being realistic." She offers a limp shrug.

"There has to be an explanation." I'm already grabbing for my purse, eager to get the truth from Mason.

Clea rests her hand on mine, offering a show of solidarity. "Will you ask him to stay if he gets picked?"

"He won't leave." I'd be willing to confirm that with

absolute certainty. That doesn't mean he shouldn't. This could be huge for his career.

"How positive are you about that?"

"Absolutely." But the confidence has dimmed from my earlier conviction.

"But?" Vannah motions for me to spill. "There's something you're not saying."

"Mason is the only one who can fill in the rest."

chapter twenty-eight

Mason

The drive to Knotty Knox passes with a steady beat of tires on asphalt and the tap from my thumb against the steering wheel. That's the extent of what remains calm. My mind is a jumbled mess. There's an insistent throb at my temples. A hollow pang chases me while I try to focus on the unknown miles ahead. Any prediction I attempt ends with a blank.

This is the scrambled state I find myself in while approaching the parking lot. It's a small mercy that I find an empty spot near the front. The engine is still puttering to a halt when I fling my door open. I replay the few details on repeat with my rushed footfalls breaking apart each repetitive cycle.

Presley sounded frantic when she called me an hour ago. That immediately set me on edge. She claimed it wasn't an emergency, and assured me Archer is safe. He's with Chad this weekend. The possibilities that remain are endless, pummeling me on an excruciating loop. She refused to tell me more until I got here. The only semblance of comfort that's securing my sanity is knowing this discussion can be held in a public place. That leads me to believe whatever this is can't be too bad.

The roar of Friday night assaults me as I cross the threshold. From my paused position at the entrance, the crowd billows outward in each direction. A quick scan reveals the thickest bottleneck is located in the bar area. As I stand and study the scene, people are trying to force their way into the already overpopulated section. Thankfully, that doesn't hinder my ability to seek Presley out within seconds. There's an invisible tether connecting us. That internal navigation came in handy on my first visit to Knotty Knox too. I've never appreciated that automatic detection more than right now.

Without taking my eyes off her, I barrel into the throng. The sole purpose of reaching her propels me faster. That determination must be visible on my features. Nobody stands in my way, scattering the moment I'm about to shove past them. The distance shrinks until only a few paces separate us. I see Presley fidgeting at the end of this makeshift path, even with numerous bodies still blocking my view.

Unshed tears glisten in her eyes, the sight gutting me upon arrival. "Why didn't you tell me?"

"Tell you what, Pep?" The pressure in my chest eases when she allows me to hold her hands.

Presley swipes at the droplets staining her cheeks. "About the job offer with the Stampede."

I freeze, my brain stalling temporarily while processing this information. "How did you hear about that?"

"It was just on ESPN." She jabs a finger at the nearby television.

"ESPN," I echo.

"Yes."

"Like the main channel?"

Her glassy gaze narrows. That glare is a hot poker searing into sensitive flesh. "Does it matter?"

"No," I hedge. "I just don't understand how that's possible."

Presley pinches her lips tight enough that the surrounding skin turns white. "I watched the segment, Mason. There was no mistaking your name plastered all over it."

I tick my jaw forward. "They used my name?"

She's nodding too fast. "Said you were a front runner."

My tongue is tied around disbelief and betrayal. "I can't believe this. They're still trying to fuck with me."

Her lips part, only to close again. She appears to be reconsidering her argument. "What do you mean?"

"I had no idea they were running a contender reveal already, especially with me included."

"Why didn't you know? You seem like a vital part of the equation." Presley flings an arm toward the bank of screens, but the network has transitioned to a hockey game.

The past twenty-four hours rewind on slow motion. I'm searching for an error—no matter how minuscule—that could've led to this. But there's nothing. Just as I originally suspected.

"Pep," I start. "This is a massive clusterfuck, not to mention totally false."

She snorts. The sound is a sharp contrast to how rigid strain melts from her stance. "No shit. What's the truth?"

I rip the hat off my head, yank at my disheveled hair, and attempt to collect the tatters that are my thoughts. "My agent Paul called yesterday and told me about this upcoming opening, that my name was being tossed into the mix. I told him that I wasn't interested."

"Really?"

"Really, Pep. I specifically told him no. Loud and clear. That didn't deter him. He's called and texted to the point of obsession. Just hounding me. I've probably told him no a dozen times." My tone is nearly a growl. "And I can assure you he is no longer on my payroll."

"Why didn't you tell me?" This time, her question holds a lot more meaning.

"There was nothing to tell."

A slim eyebrow quirks at me. "Seriously? "

"It's insignificant," I bark. That ire blistering my veins is misplaced. I blow out a long exhale to release the fury they've ceremoniously dumped on me.

"This is far from insignificant."

"Not to me. It wasn't even worth a second of consideration. And if I'm being completely honest, I didn't want to give you any reason to lose faith in me again. Not over something that doesn't matter."

Presley's chin trembles. "How can it not matter? They're considering you for an NFL coaching position. That's huge."

"I don't want it."

"But your career—"

"I don't care about my career."

She peeks at me from moist eyes. "How can you say that?"

My hands collect hers again. The need to touch her is an agitated fiend that doesn't settle. Not until our skin meets. "I was very honest with my ex-agent. He's probably fielding calls to keep his hope alive, but there is no amount of money they could possibly offer for me to leave you."

"What?" Shock is a smoky fog billowing from her.

"I don't want the job." I leave no room for argument in that statement.

"Why not? It's your dream."

"You're my dream, Pep. You and Archie." I allow a small grin to crack through the murky skies. "Maybe we'll even add to our family one day."

She returns my smile, the pressure in my chest nearly

ceasing to exist. "I want that too. That doesn't mean you need to sacrifice your career. We can make this work long distance."

I'm already shaking my head. "No, we can't. I don't want that. You don't either. Besides, I'm not going anywhere."

"You should apply, or whatever the process is." Hurt flashes over her features with a wince. It's obvious that the suggestion is painful for her to voice.

I admire her in this moment. Selfless consideration and sincere commitment radiate from her resolved frame. My girl is brave—and too damn stubborn. I bend to rest my forehead on hers. "That could lead to me moving to Montana."

Her breath catches, ending in a muffled cough. "I know."

"You'd let me go?" It's my turn to go still. The air transforms to toxin in my lungs with every second I hold steady.

"I don't think I could," she whispers after the longest beat known to man. "But if you stay, you'll be hurting your future job prospects."

"No, Pep. I'm gainfully employed. If I leave, I'll be sacrificing my happiness. Surrendering my soul. I can't do that again. I can't truly live without you. I'd just merely exist and survive." My lips tease over hers with my next conviction. "If I go, you and Archie are coming with me."

"That's not possible."

"Exactly. The coaching position was never meant to be mine. I said no for a reason. The only reason that truly matters."

"Okay. I'm going to be selfish," she blurts. She shakes her fingers loose from my grip, only to fist my shirt and haul me in.

"Yeah?"

"Stay with us." The plea in her tone is still too heavy with conflict for my liking.

"That's my plan. Indefinitely." I'll repeat it until we're old and gray if necessary.

"Really?"

"What is it you think I need to be satisfied, Pep?"

"If I knew the answer, you wouldn't be asking it."

The solution is burning a hole in my pocket. I practically rip the velvet box free from its hiding spot. Presley watches my movements without blinking. I'm certain there's cautious optimism floating in the atmosphere. Maybe that's just the playlist reverberating in my mind.

Her lashes begin to flutter, framing the surprise with sheer wonder. "What are you doing?"

"Something I can't stop thinking about. Something I should've done years ago." I lower to one knee, snatching her left hand on my descent. "Making you mine. Completely and officially and for always."

Her baby blues are almost circular. "Now?"

I pause my impulsive reveal, my thumb rubbing along the thin crack that will expose what's cushioned inside. "Should I wait for Archie? In all honesty, I planned for him to be present. But this just feels more like our style. In the moment."

She seems to consider that, her bottom lip clamped between her teeth. Then her head gives a wild toss. "No, it's okay. He's probably too young to understand the significance. We'll do a mock performance for him later."

With that, I snap open the lid and hold the offering for her to see. Her gasp is a strangled noise. The gallop from my heart strikes another gear, taking off at a breakneck pace. Heat gathers across my vision in a watery blur. My stingy gaze finds hers wet, tears already streaming in a downward flow.

"We're doing it right this time. No more leaving or separating or sacrificing." I slap the tattoo that's hidden beneath my shirt. "It's always been you for me, Pep. You're the only score that matters. My touchdown pass to win the game. Every single one. I love you."

Then I kiss the second knuckle on her third finger. If all goes well, she'll be wearing a permanent reminder of this promise.

"Um, wow. Okay. I don't even... holy crap." She gawks at

the sparkling sapphire cradled by diamonds, still cushioned in the satin pillow. "It's beautiful."

I find my usual knack with words faltering while I stare at the girl who's meant to be mine. There are only four that truly matter. Maybe six if I want to be extra. "Will you marry me, Presley Drake?"

"Yes!" she squeals. "Yes, yes, yes!"

A second fiery wave attacks my eyes. Before my sight is further impaired, I slide the platinum band on. The shiny metal loop glides along her digit without a hitch. "Fits just right."

Our personal exchange expands and shatters with rowdy cheers. Deafening applause seals Presley's answer into the record. That reminds me we're in the center of Knotty Knox. It seems everyone went silent to watch our intimate moment.

My fiancée tugs me upright into a warm embrace. "I love you so much, Mason Braxter. My champion for life."

"I'm going to make you so happy." The vow is spoken directly in her ear to be heard over the continuous celebration.

Trembling fingers cup my jaw. "You already do."

Two figures materialize from the sidelines. I recognize them as Presley's friends—Clea and Vannah. Their slow clapping is drowned out by the crowd's standing ovation.

The redhead waves her phone in the air. "I got the whole thing recorded! Excellent improv, All-Star. I approve."

Presley scoffs. "About time."

"Oh, hush. I was just protecting you."

I glance between them. "Am I missing something?"

"Nah, we're golden. Congratulations, love doves." She draws us in for a joint hug.

"Let me see the rock." Clea wiggles her fingers in demand.

Presley thrusts her arm forward, the biggest grin in history stretching her lips. "Isn't it stunning?"

"Matches your eyes," Vannah coos. She glances at me for a brief pause. "Well done, Braxter. You're a keeper."

"I sure hope so." The chuckle rolls from me with ease.

"Have you just been carrying this bad boy around, waiting for inspiration to strike?" Clea looks ready to devour every detail.

"Something like that," I drawl. "I was at an antique store with my mom a few years ago. It wasn't necessarily by choice, but I'm damn glad she insisted I join her. This beauty spoke to me from behind the display case. She didn't have to ask who the ring was for."

Three matching sighs swaddle the story in whimsical flair.

"That's a serious two-point conversion," Presley exhales while lacing her arms around my neck.

A groan spills from my lips, quickly stamping her with a kiss. "I love when you talk football to me."

"All right, that's our cue." Clea giggles and nudges her friend.

"Fine by me. All this emotional turmoil makes me miss my husband." Vannah makes a lewd stroking gesture with her hand. "See you at Friendsgiving!"

Then she zig-zags through the packed space like a professional dodgeball player with an agenda.

"There's always one filthy outlier in a bunch. She's ours. I better catch her." Clea wraps Presley in a tight hug. "Congratulations, Press. I had a feeling this would happen."

Her friend pats me on the shoulder. "Stellar proposal, Mason. Top-notch."

Presley plasters herself to me while we watch them disappear. Once they're out of sight, her glittering blue depths latch on mine. That blinding smile hasn't wavered. "We're engaged."

I trace the lifted curve of her cheek with my thumb. "Finally."

"Have you thought about the wedding?"

"Since our fruitless teenage planning, you mean?"

Her brows bounce. "Uh-huh."

"Whatever your heart desires, Pep. There's a way to sweet talk a woman. Downgrading her dream isn't the correct approach."

"I don't think it's possible for you to ruin anything." She plants another kiss on my mouth for good measure.

"Those are great odds," I mumble against her pout.

"Especially if you're the betting type."

"Well, in that case. Are you in the mood for a little whore-igami? It's somewhat of a tradition—or should be." I nod toward the dark hallway where we became intimately reacquainted.

Presley's eyes don't leave mine, a coy expression replacing the dazzling jubilee. "It's another yes from me."

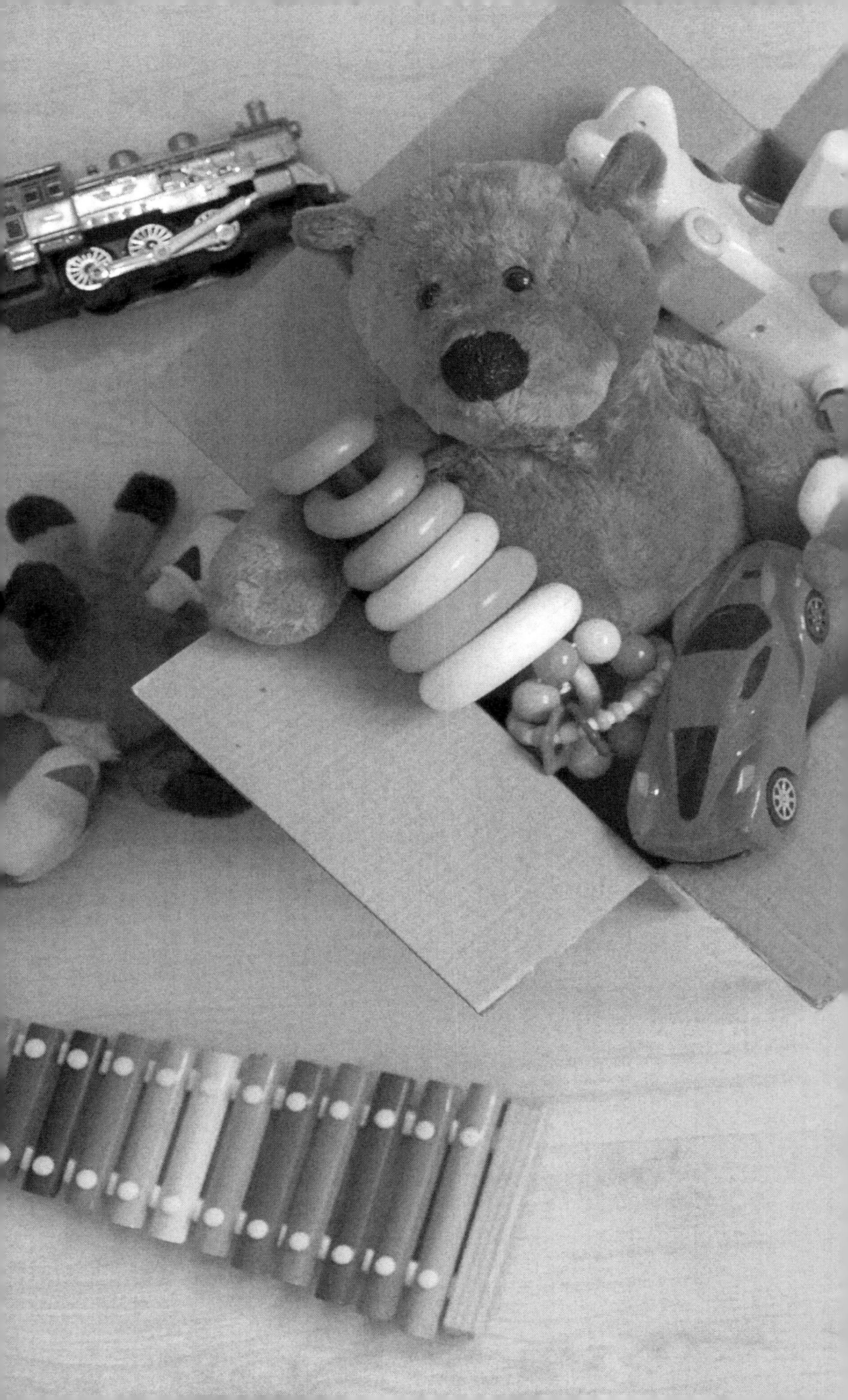

chapter twenty-nine

Presley

MASON SWINGS OPEN THE PASSENGER'S SIDE DOOR AND catches me with ease. Once my feet hit the pavement, he locks the truck and kills the dome still illuminating the cab. My eyes strain to adjust against the pitch black swallowing us.

"Why are we here so late?" My boots crunch across the snow-covered grass. The inch we got yesterday has managed to stick.

"I don't want to be disturbed." Mason's palm is notched securely in the dip of my spine.

A plume of fog appears with my pitchy laugh. "At the Shark's football field in mid-November?"

"You'd be surprised." He guides me to a gap in the fence where the players usually enter. Security is really firm around these parts.

"Who else is crazy enough to loiter at the high school?"

"Didn't want to take any chances." His amusement is visible with that statement.

"Nobody in this town is fierce enough to fight the elements." After a full-body shiver, I snuggle tighter to his side. "But I feel like the risk of getting caught is higher in the dark."

The stars and moon join us on our trek to the turf. All other signs of activity are tucked safely in bed at this hour.

"Ah, that's where you're wrong. It will be bright soon."

As if on cue, the floodlights buzz with incoming electricity. Then the stadium is bathed in an artificial glow. Shadows linger on the outskirts, beckoning us into the unknown.

My focus skitters to the small building that houses the controls. "Oh, you called in a favor from an inside source. Gunner?"

"Gunner," he confirms.

"That was nice of him."

"He owed me one or two."

Curiosity tickles my tongue, but I swallow the urge to pry. That debt was probably years old. "Will he get in trouble?"

"For what? We aren't going to debase the property. I just want to sit with you on our home bench for a bit."

Memories resurface with hurricane strength. It takes willpower to remain in the present. The past is too tempting. If I'm not careful, I'll be lost in the reverie and miss whatever he has planned.

"That's reasonable." I toss out a grin.

"Then I'll take you someplace warm."

Humor bursts from me in another steamy cloud. "Now you're just spoiling me."

"That's my goal in life."

"Sweet-talking me so smooth," I murmur against his cheek.

Mason leans in, pressing deeper into my touch. "Just take it all in."

If he insists.

I scan the quiet area, once like a second home to me. The typical enthusiasm and infectious energy are noticeably absent. Instead of rowdy fans and clashing rivalries, vast stillness claims the space. An all too familiar scene appears from years long gone. Mason hoisted high after launching a killer throw that earns us a stunning victory. His gaze seeking mine, our symbol molded between his palms. Pom-poms rustling with my glee.

Without even meaning to, my gaze travels to the section I often occupied. The grooves on the sidelines are worn from cheerleaders rooting on our team. I was right there with them at every game beginning freshman year. It feels like an eternity since my sneakers scuffed the gravel. I dig my toe into the frozen ground on pure instinct.

The bulky arm around my waist pulls me closer. "See? Not even the frigid frost can freeze out those memories."

I shake free from those faded recollections. "Is that why you brought me?"

"Sure," he rumbles across my temple. His lips are a roasty brand against me, the chill chased from that small patch. "Figured why not reminisce in a place that has some of our best?"

"I do have a fondness for our reunion specials."

His hand clutches my hip. "That's the spirit."

Mason steers me to the very bench he mentioned earlier. The metal is cold, practically burning my ass. I jerk upright with a curse. He doesn't hesitate to deposit me on his lap.

Warmth beats the nippy bite when he engulfs me in a hug from all angles. "Better?"

"Much." I snuggle deeper into his embrace.

"I should've brought hot chocolate."

My belly heats at the thought alone. "That would've hit the spot."

"Next time," he murmurs.

"Oh, we're making this a regular thing?"

"Sure, why not? Our youth is rich in the soil."

I stare down, imaging the secrets swirling just under the surface. "Good thing the dirt can't talk."

The tip of his nose resembles an icicle as he traces my jaw. "No shit."

Something prods at me, demanding to be voiced. "Have you spoken with Paul since the false reveal?"

"He's tried," Mason grunts in confirmation. "My lawyer—the only decent one left in my corner—is handling this little mishap. It's best if there's only one point of contact for all the prying media questions. Hoyt used a bunch of fancy words I can't remember."

"But Hoyt is going after the person responsible?"

A shrug jostles our tangled position. "If he can pinpoint who that is. I doubt this was Paul's big idea."

My upper lip curls. I've never met Mason's former agent, and I have zero interest in doing so. Just thinking about that sleaze makes my skin crawl.

"Why did they think going public with the news would sway you?"

"Maybe I'd be convinced to reconsider if it went viral. Maybe they'd try to push me as an influencer or something. Those people only care about fame and fortune and causing drama. It's inconceivable to them that I'm content without the glamorous position they were generously willing to grant me." The bitter blade in his voice could slice deep.

"I'll never understand that logic," I mutter.

"Me either. That's why I didn't belong."

"You're meant to be here." I press against him with a sigh.

"Yeah, Pep. Wherever you are." Mason tightens his hold until breathing is a chore. He must catch my wheeze and eases off a second later.

"Well, their efforts were in vain. It's over and done."

His nod bumps into my head. "At the very least, Hoyt is contacting the network to set the record straight. They can't run a story with my name splashed all over it after I vehemently declined."

"I'm glad he's handling that for you." I gnaw on my inner cheek, indecision weighing heavy on me. "Aren't you worried about how this will impact your reputation? How about your future with coaching?"

"No," he scoffs. "If there's backlash, it's just bad press. I can handle that. Besides, a job is just a job. What I choose to attach to my name is my choice."

"You can do whatever you want, huh? The sky has always been limitless for you."

"I'm going to focus on making you my wife and being the best stepdad to Archie."

Warm fuzzies erupt along my already pebbled flesh. "Gosh, you're too much. I truly am getting spoiled."

"As you deserve to be."

"Does that include the reason we came out tonight? Is there a special occasion?" I recall his persuasive methods with a pleasant shiver. That last orgasm is still tingling my lady bits.

He crosses his arms over my abdomen, increasing our joined heat. "It's our anniversary."

I do a quick mental calculation, but my numbers are way off. "Huh?"

Mason nuzzles into the crook of my neck. "Our first official date as a couple, Pep."

My body melts into his with the consistency of sentimental mush. "Oh, Ten. How do you remember that?"

"How could I forget?" He nips at my earlobe. "Too bad I was a day early with the proposal."

I scoff. "This just gives us another date to celebrate."

"Each day with you is one to honor."

"Why are you so freaking romantic?"

"Because I have you."

I twist to face him, palm cradling his scruffy cheek. "You and that thoughtful, panty-melting mouth."

"What a fan-fucking-tastic combo." Mason lifts my chin with a bent knuckle, claiming a kiss to stoke the internal flames. "It's landed me in a very sweet spot with you."

"Since the beginning." My breath minges with his between the narrow sliver separating us. "November eighteenth in seventh grade."

"Remember when I won that plastic ring for you at the arcade?" He fiddles with the sapphire and diamonds glittering on my finger. "You acted like it was worth millions."

A giggle puffs from me. The bubble-gum token was gaudy and didn't fit. That didn't stop me from wearing it on a chain around my neck. "I still have it."

"Really? Even after I upgraded you on Valentine's Day our sophomore year?"

That was a legit purchase from a jewelry store at the mall. Pretty sure it cost him several paychecks. I'm still bitter about the discrepancy in how much we spent on each other after setting a price cap. After he raved about the scrapbook I made for a week straight, the sting was more of a dull jab. I got even on his birthday that summer.

"You never forget your first. But I've saved them all. Couldn't part with the treasures you bestowed upon me."

"Damn, Pep. I thought you make a living tossing out clutter."

I lightly punch his arm. "Nothing you buy me is junk. Every piece is precious, even the plastic ring with all the gold paint flaked off."

"It's probably an heirloom by now."

"We can pass that priceless relic down to our children."

Mason stills beneath me. "Interesting you should mention that."

"Oh?" My stomach flutters into a whirlwind.

His hand drifts along my thigh, adding gentle pressure with each pass. "I was thinking we could add to our team."

"Already?" Damn, my voice is desperation personified.

"But Archie should be included in the process." The giddy thrum in my pulse—premature as it might be—screeches to a halt with that addendum. His mind must be on a different wavelength.

My smile wavers at the edges. "Um, okay."

"This might seem crazy," Mason warns while threading our icy fingers together. "What's the likelihood you'd be interested in getting a puppy?"

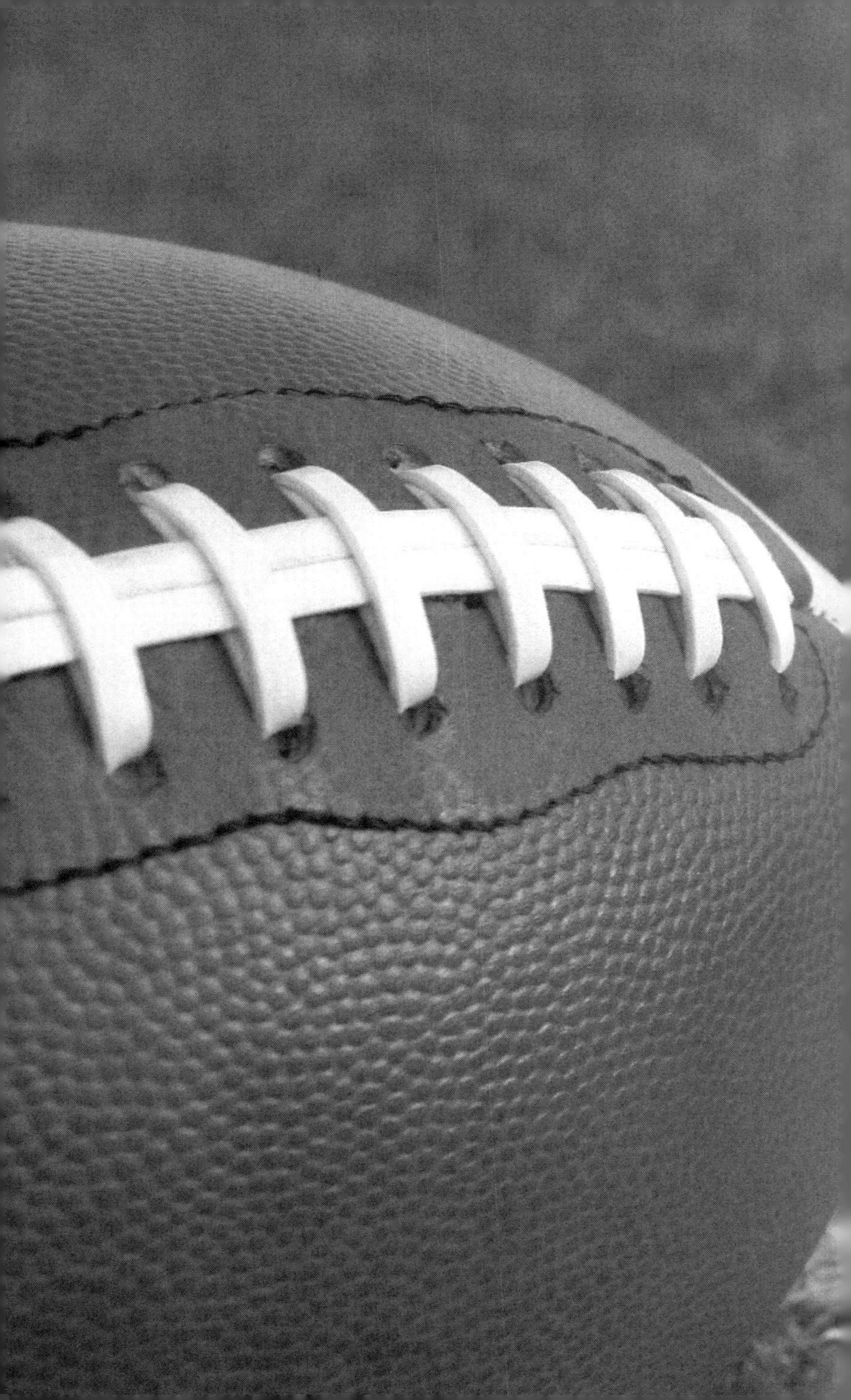

chapter thirty

Mason

Presley's knee is bouncing at an erratic tempo that almost sparks my own nerves. "I wasn't sure about this idea at first. Honestly, I thought your screws were loose. But now? I'm totally sold."

I rest a palm on her leg, calming the jitters with a light squeeze. "They should be pulling in any moment."

"How did you find out about this litter again?"

"Colt's sister is the breeder. Bettie lives way up north with her husband. I think they have something like three hundred acres. Their operation is small, but reliable. Definitely not a mill situation."

She's distracting herself by swiping through the most recent pictures that were posted online. "But these puppies aren't for sale?"

"Nope. Rescue only."

"Why?"

"Their health can't be guaranteed. Seven out of eleven had to be put down." My gut cramps at the reminder. Colt has been pretty bent out of shape this past week at practice. This experience has traumatized their entire family.

A deep furrow creases Presley's brow. "That's awful."

"It is. That's why we're alleviating stress by giving one a good home."

"Pretty sure every other person would take a golden doodle puppy for free." She twists her lips to one side, seeming to compute that fact.

I lift her hand, threading our fingers together. "But Bettie is afraid to let just anyone take one. This situation has never happened before. She's had more than a dozen litters over the past four years. This male and female have been bred before without issue. It was a freak occurrence. I guess they're retiring those dogs after this too."

"They sound like good people," she says almost absently.

"Exactly." I see the vehicle Bettie described in her last text turn into the lot. "And we're about to meet them."

Presley straightens in her seat. There's still a jerky beat squirming through her. "Did we buy everything she needs? Are we ready? This is a huge commitment."

"So is agreeing to marry me. You said yes faster than I could slip the ring on your finger."

She sends me a flat stare. "That's different."

"You're right. The dog will be harder to deny. Far more irresistible too."

"Until she piddles on the carpet," Presley mumbles.

"We're already potty training a toddler. The dog can join in without a hitch. Maybe that will be a motivator for Archie. We could make it a competition."

"I'm not sure they make a sticker chart for that."

"Maybe we move forward with a different strategy."

Remembering to put a star on the sheet after each successful potty is harder than I ever thought possible.

Presley's brows rise. "Tell Archie that and see what happens."

The little man chooses that moment to wake from his spontaneous car nap. "Where's pup-pup?"

I smile at him in the rearview mirror. "Hey, buddy. We're about to get her. She's right over there."

His eyes pong to the Ford Escape beside us. Then he begins struggling with his seatbelt. "I wanna get out. Out, out."

"Okay, sweet angel. Hold on." Presley steps out and rounds the truck while I shut off the ignition.

Once our feet are all firmly planted on the ground, we walk to where Bettie and her husband are waiting. There's a wriggling fluff ball with toffee-colored fur and white markings bumping into their legs as we approach. Her tongue is lolling out and she's practically leaping up and down with excitement, matching Archer's enthusiasm.

She'll fit right in.

"Hey there," Bettie greets and steps forward. "Mason, Presley, and Archer?"

"That's us." I extend a hand for her to shake.

"It's a pleasure to meet you. I'm Bettie and this is Stan." Bettie takes my offering while gesturing to the man at her side. Then she moves to welcome Presley and Archer in the same regard.

My fiancée is all smiles. "Thanks for driving such a long way."

"Just part of the process. We always include delivery."

"Even under these circumstances?" Presley's shoulders are hunched to frame her ears.

"Yes, it's important to us that each family receives the same quality of care. We can't control everything, but that's something we can provide." Stan's tone is firm, yet brimming with sincerity. It's clear they love these dogs.

"Thank you," I say.

"Pup-pup," Archer squeals and instantly drops to his knees. The puppy hesitates only long enough to give him one good sniff before scampering up into his arms and lavishing him with sloppy kisses. We're serenaded by the sound of his giggles.

"They're going to be best friends," Bettie exhales. Relief is evident in her relaxing posture.

"It seems they already are," Presley comments. "She's perfect for him."

I wag my brows in her direction. "Totally called it."

"Yeah, yeah. You're always right."

We're entertained by Archie and his new bestie playing tag in the small boundary our bodies create. After a few minutes, Bettie reviews the contract with us. She explains—again—that this is an adoption, and they will not be accepting money. It's outlined in writing about the puppy's health not being guaranteed, even though she's showed no signs of having the defect most others had. Presley and I sign on the dotted line, claiming her as ours.

"All right, that should do it." Bettie passes us a bag full of essential supplies to get us started. "We'll leave you to get acquainted. Long haul back home. If you have any questions, feel free to send a text. Otherwise, I've provided detailed notes of our routine in the folder."

"You've made my son—and us—extremely happy. I'm not sure how to repay you." Presley's voice wobbles with emotion.

Bettie clutches a palm to her chest. "That's the greatest gift you could give us, and all the gratitude we need."

We wave as they leave, the puppy's leash held tight in Presley's grip. Archer hasn't stopped rolling and racing since we got here, the fur ball hot on his heels and barking joyfully. I find myself wondering which one's tank will hit empty first.

"Ohhhhh," Presley's voice is several octaves higher than normal. She lowers into a crouch, holding wiggling fingers out for the puppy to sniff. "She's beautiful."

Our pooch is busy giving her a tongue bath in exchange for the close proximity. Her tail is whapping in a circular motion, almost a blur. She's ready for liftoff at this rate.

"Someone is so excited," I coo and scratch her soft ears.

"Me!" Archie flings an arm straight in the air. "I love the pup-pup."

Presley peeks over at me. "I hope you're ready, champ. Puppies are worse than infants. They're rambunctious and don't sleep. Worse, we can't just strap a diaper on and let them free."

"I wouldn't know." The somber notes radiate around us.

She rests her head on my shoulder. "You will."

"Soon?"

Her eyes find mine after she shifts upright. "Oh, now you want to discuss babies?"

"When have I not wanted to?"

"I thought you were referring to a baby when you brought up the puppy last week."

"She's the gateway to get you agreeable, and to keep Archer busy. That will allow us to stay busy, if you know what I mean."

"Incorrigible." But there's no hiding the smile tilting her pouty mouth.

"For you? Absolutely. I can think of little else than seeing you round with my baby." I trap a moan that was ramping to indecent levels.

Presley's arms loop around my neck, drawing me down against her. "Oh, Mason Braxter. When will you understand I've been ready for the whole shebang since I was thirteen."

I chuckle. "We might've caused a serious stir getting started at that age."

"You know what I mean." There's no doubt her eyes are rolling with that statement.

"I do, and I feel the same." I pepper her cheek with kisses. "So, we'll start trying?"

"Once I visit the doctor, we'll be good to go."

My nose buries in her hair. With a long inhale, I pull intoxicating satisfaction and potent bliss deep into my lungs. This woman feeds every craving. "I look forward to practicing with you in the meantime."

"Hi, Teddy. Love you." Archie's chirpy voice draws us back to reality. His tiny fingers are combing through the doggie's thick fur. "So soft."

Presley's gaze shifts off me and lowers to him. "Teddy? That's a cute name."

"Uh-huh. Dis Teddy. My pup-pup."

I pull all three of them against me in a move that's becoming a signature. "It's settled. Welcome to the family, Teddy."

chapter thirty-one

Presley

A HAND SLIDING INTO MINE STARTLES ME FROM THE DAZE I'd fallen under. Mason's eyes shine bright green under the dim dining room lighting. "You okay, Pep?"

I glance at our guests seated around the table for Friendsgiving. It's a tradition I started with Vannah, Clea, and Audria in college. Now there are a dozen grinning faces gathered to give thanks. I had to buy an extra section for my table to accommodate our expanding group.

"This is wonderful," I murmur. "I'm glad you're here to help me host. Not sure I could've handled this without you. We're a big crew now."

"And we'll only grow in number." He brings our joined palms to rest on my flat stomach.

The action is clear, but far too early. I just got my

implant removed two days ago. Even Mason's all-star super sperm can't get the job done that fast. It doesn't hurt to be hopefully optimistic, though.

"We should take a trip," Vannah cuts the idle chatter between couples with that suggestion.

"You love those vacations, Sugar." Landon's face disappears into the curve of her neck.

She takes a purposeful glance down, then glances over her shoulder. "There are children present, Lannie."

"Hasn't stopped you before." His tone dips with scandalous intent. Her husband used to be a strict, no-nonsense corporate suit. Then Vannah came along.

"They already think I'm a s-e-x addict," she complains. That doesn't mean she dodges his somewhat hidden advances. In fact, I'm pretty sure she shifts closer.

"Might as well prove them right."

Landon would be nearing eviction status if the kids previously mentioned weren't preoccupied with Teddy in the den downstairs. Chad was feeling like the ninth wheel and elected to keep an eye on them. My next order of business is finding a guy to treat him like the king he is.

Audria snorts, fork stalled inches from her lips. "Aren't we a vibrant bunch?"

"I prefer salacious," Vannah mumbles around a mouthful of French silk pie.

"You would," Clea huffs.

"Speaking of," she scoops another bite of whipped chocolate mousse. "This is delicious."

"That rhymes," Clea and Audria blurt in unison. They crack up in the next instant.

Nolan kisses his fiancée's cheek. "Tally is rubbing off on you."

Clea gives him one in return. "Hasn't she always?"

"Much to my benefit." Love practically smolders from

his gaze. He might've been stubborn initially, and almost lost her, but his groveling efforts proved to be Olympic gold standard.

"She brought us together. You should probably get her that pony she's been begging for." Clea barely masks the humor ready to burst from her features.

Nolan's sigh is a loose tendril wrapping around her pinky. "I'll consider it in the spring."

"Seriously, though." Vannah groans around the utensil locked between her teeth. "This is incredible."

"I didn't make it." That confession should come as no surprise. I can cook almost any dish, but baking is a skill that escapes me.

"The credit goes to me." Mason waves a finger in recognition.

Vannah flutters her lashes in apparent euphoria. "Well done, All-Star. You're beginning to amaze me. Forget that chic boutique in town. I might drive to Meadow Creek just for your dessert."

"Should I be jealous?" Landon's focus is rapt on his wife while she devours the next portion.

"Don't worry, Lannie. No one can satisfy me like you can. Not even French silk pie."

"We could pick one up on the way home. I can offer you a personal serving surface."

Vannah's lips part with a garbled wheeze. "Don't tease me."

"I wouldn't dare."

"And I thought we gave folks something to gossip about." Reeve winks at Audria.

She snuggles into her husband's side. "Bampton Valley still doesn't know what to do with us. Mrs. Mayberry doesn't miss an opportunity to glare at me in the grocery store."

"Only when you ram into me with the cart." He mimics the motion for us to witness.

"It's a ritual steeped in force of habit. We wouldn't have met otherwise."

"That's extremely false. I would've found a way to make you mine no matter what you hit me with."

"Damn, that's smooth. Well played, farmer." Her chef's kiss hits the mark.

I push my plate away, belly aching at max capacity. "When are you two heading back to Iowa?"

"Probably Sunday night. We have dinner with my family tomorrow. Might stay there for the weekend. Reeve could spend an eternity with my brothers."

He skates his nose along her cheek. "Don't have my own. Thanks for letting me borrow yours."

"Anything for you, babe. Keeps them off my case." She brushes her nails on her shirt—a task done well and complete.

My gaze grows a tad weepy while digesting the heart-happy scene. "I'm really glad we're all together. Priorities shift. Demands grow roots. Time is precious. We've managed to stay tight. That's something special. Not many can hold onto friendship like this."

"Ah, heck yes. Here come the glitter sparkles. I love when you get sappy, Peppy Girl." Vannah motions her onward.

Mason snorts. "That's straight thievery."

"I didn't see a trademark," she laughs. "But that's beside the point. Where are we traveling to?"

Clea and Nolan exchange a glance. "Are kids invited?"

"Yes. I don't think we have a choice in the matter since at least one of you has a bun in the oven. Might as well let all the rug rats tag along." Her pointed stare targets a specific individual.

Audria winks at me, her glass very much full of sparkling juice. They're expecting a little cowboy or cowgirl in late summer. "I'm good with a beach resort. Just give me a lounge chair and I'll be set."

"Easy as always," Vannah praises. "I like your style, preggers."

"Always at your service." She tips an imaginary hat.

"To the beach," Landon boasts.

"To the beach," we all repeat.

"Let's do a toast," Mason says.

We all raise our drinks, suspended in air while waiting for his sentiment.

"To whatever comes next and living our best."

A chorus of whoops and hoots rings out as glass clinks against merriment.

Then he leans in until his lips tickle my temple. "And to loving the one you're destined to be with, even if you need a second chance at doing it right."

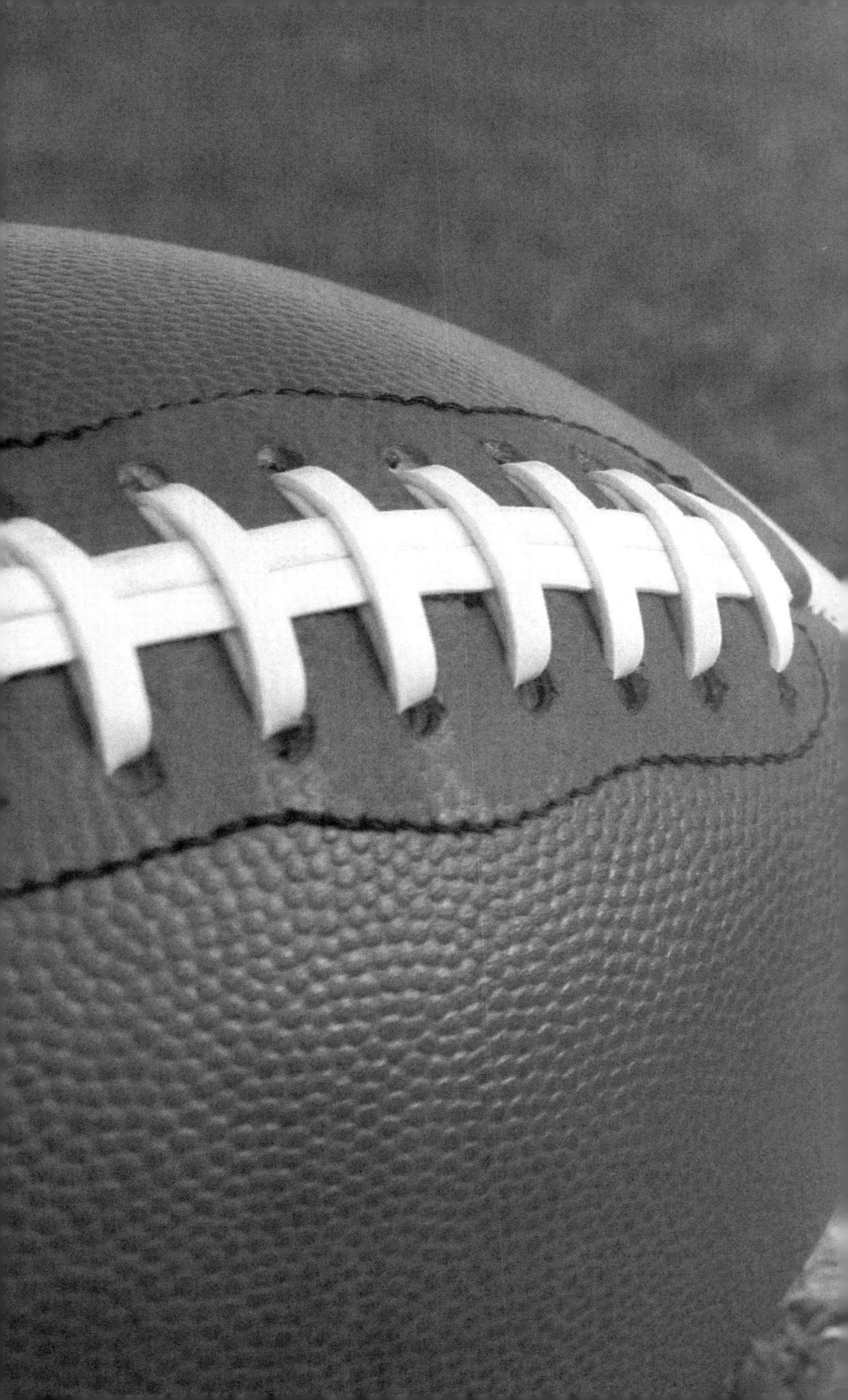

epilogue

Mason

Heat prickles along the base of my spine. I'm close, but Presley needs to tip over the edge first. Her pleasure fuels mine more than ever while I pump my hips. Our tempo is lazy, yet hypnotic. Each push and pull lures us further into the grip of temptation. I want this to last, but I can only hold back for so long.

A sharp sting bites my shoulders when Presley digs her nails in. With her chin tipped to the ceiling, I'm granted a direct view of the captivating passion she has on full display. Her smile is an enticing beacon dipped in irresistible warmth. I follow her demand to bask in her glow with each thrust. Her mouth parts with intoxicating pleasure and she expels a breathy sigh. A thick swallow bobs her slender throat. Her flushed features are highlighted by the sunshine streaming through the curtains. For a moment, I get lost in the serenity pouring from her. This woman is my peace and certainty. Just being in her presence grounds me.

Presley must notice that I'm momentarily stunned. Her body writhes under me. "Do it, Ten."

"Let me enjoy you." I sink lower, fire infusing my veins.

A smoky exhale puffs from her as if to extinguish my flames. "Aren't you already?"

"Extremely," I rasp. "I don't want this to end yet."

"We can go again. It'll help our chances."

A shudder wracks my frame. "I love when you talk dirty to me."

She bites her bottom lip, her hands drifting down my back. "I'm going to get so round with your baby in me."

I let my lids droop. "Fuck yes."

"Everyone will know I'm yours."

My cock glides in, bottoming out to the hilt. "Always mine."

She nods while clenching her inner muscles. "Make it happen."

I kiss the euphoric bliss she's still flaunting, sipping at her soft and slow. Her tongue sneaks out to skim along mine, our lips slanting higher with the connected joy. I swivel my hips as she accepts me deeper, seducing me with each subtle motion.

Our arousal and desire join with a fluid motion. Flesh slaps together in a tantalizing melody. I pump forward with a smooth thrust and she welcomes me in her slick depths. Her legs lift to frame my hips, tilting our angle to an upward glide. She rocks against me as I sink in and pull out. I don't falter when she clenches tighter. Our willpower clashes with the raging sea roaring between us.

Presley curves in an enticing arch, serving her irresistible tits to me on a buffet platter. I don't hesitate to feast on her offering. My mouth waters while I dip to pull a pebbled peak into my mouth. Her nails rake along my scalp as she whines.

"Yes, more." Her hips wiggle and shift with impatience.

I slam my entire length inside of her with brutal force, pushing us across the mattress. "Like that?"

"Uh-huh. Again." Her thighs squeeze my waist while she holds on.

"You want it all?"

Her head thrashes with her frantic lust. "Give it to me."

"Gonna ask nice?"

"Now," she demands.

I bury my face in the crook of her neck, inhaling salvation and lust. "That's not what I asked for."

"You're not filling my request either."

I plunge forward, grinding my hips into her. "Pretty sure you're full of me."

"But I need more. Give me what I want. Please," she whimpers.

It's the baby juice that she's truly seeking, and lucky for her, I'm fully stocked and ready to deliver. A muffled curse drips from her when I still haven't reached my own climax.

Another harsh plunge from me shoves us impossibly closer. "You'll get every drop."

"Please," she repeats.

That's all I need to find another gear. Pleasure shimmers from her heavy-lidded gaze. She slays me with that heated stare, cranking my pace to a feverish level. Sweat brews between us. The slippery friction allows me to maintain this steady momentum while an erratic thrum floods my veins. That throb nearly sends me off course until her arm cinches around my neck to tug me down for a kiss. Our lips meet in a brief exchange, just long enough to tease me. I've barely caressed her mouth when she breaks apart with a moan.

"Too good. Gonna burst."

"That's my job," I rumble.

"Then get to it."

"My girl is bossy."

"I'll be whatever it takes for you to surrender the score. Just let go. I'll catch the pass." And she means that.

Ever since we started trying, Presley has been nearly desperate to get me in the sack. I almost chuckle at the insanity of that statement. That woman barely has to hitch a brow in my direction, and I come running, clothes strewn along the way. As if she ever has to do more than crook her pinky at me.

Then she tosses in some football lingo and I'm grasping for the shreds of my control. I can't resist that level of temptation. My speed becomes frenzied while the pressure becomes too much. We're chasing that promise beginning to crest over the peak.

Speaking of catching passes, I feel my balls tighten. It won't take much more. "You wide open for me?"

"I'm ready. Put a baby in my belly, champ." Her palm smacks my ass while she bucks against me.

"What Peppy wants, she gets."

Our eyes lock and hold. The flood of emotion flowing from her gaze burns into mine. My motions turn jerky as I hurdle to the goal line. Then we're into the end zone. She clenches around me, the kickoff to her release. Another spasm shoves me over right along with her. Liquid warmth wraps us in utter contentment as relief rushes through our heightened awareness. I can feel the comfort flooding over Presley along with mine.

With what little strength remains in my gelatinous limbs, I prop upright to avoid collapsing on her. My clammy forehead rests against hers, our mingled breaths expelling at a labored rate. "What do you think?"

She pinches her features in concentration. Then a shimmy shifts her hips beneath me. My dick nudges deep with her movements and she gasps.

"Oh, it definitely worked." Her eyes twinkle. "I'm feeling extra fertile."

"Yeah?" I'm certain my gaze reflects the same giddy optimism.

"Yep. Your swimmers are heading in the right direction and I'm ready to receive them."

"It just takes one," I tease.

"But he needs the others as motivation."

I nod and cluck my tongue. "The competition is fierce."

"They all want the girl," Presley agrees.

"Only the fastest and strongest claims victory."

She giggles against my cheek. "I bet they're racing."

Before I can respond, the knob rattles. I fling my gaze in that direction while Presley goes rigid beneath me. Her palm nudges my chest in the next beat. Air gets trapped in my lungs as I flop over.

"Mama? Mase? Why door locked?"

Breath sputters through my slack jaw as Archer's voice registers. "What's he doing home?"

"Chad," she grinds while scooting to the edge of the bed.

I manage to circle her wrist, pausing her retreat. "Don't you need to elevate your pelvis?"

"No time."

I chuckle at her furious stomping toward the bathroom. It's damn convenient we have an attached one. "Still don't think it's a huge deal that he drops by announcement whenever?"

"I'm willing to admit it's slightly inconvenient as of late." Then she disappears from sight, leaving me to handle our company.

I dive off the mattress in search of my discarded clothes. Cool cotton sticks to my sweaty chest, providing a slight reprieve. That does little to calm the thunder pounding in my ears, though. The waistband of my sweats is barely settled around my hips when I flip the lock. Archie doesn't hesitate to burst inside. If he notices my labored breathing, he doesn't comment.

"Hi, Mase. Guess what?" His smile is broad and toothy.

I comb a few fingers through my disheveled hair, granting myself another second for composure. "The Vikings won the Super Bowl."

His features screw upward. "Huh?"

"Never mind. Tell me what," I urge him.

Archer does a little dance, delaying to increase my anticipation. "I went poop!"

"That's great, buddy. Congratulations." I hold out a palm for him to slap.

He leaps and connects our hands in a resounding smack. "In dah potty. Like big boy. No skids in my undies."

"Ohhhh," I exhale. "That's even better."

"I push so hard." He grunts as if to provide an instant replay.

Any lingering post-coital bliss from my recent release fizzles out with a hiss. "That's important. You have to get it all out."

"I did! Lotsa poops. Daddy didn't a picture." He pouts at Chad.

"Not sure anyone else needed to see that. Be glad you didn't smell it." His narrowed gaze is pinned on me.

"So stinky," Archer giggles.

"I'll buy nose plugs," I drawl.

"Good idea," Chad adds with a laugh. "He's really getting the hang of holding it."

"I'm glad you stopped by to tell me." It's then I realize he didn't ask where his mom is. That's definitely for the best. "I'll tell your Mama once I find her."

Archie gives me a thumbs up. "Kay, Mase. I go play wit Teddy. Bye!"

Chad and I watch him zip off down the hallway without

another word. I can almost see dust billowing behind him. Maybe I should vacuum later.

"Had yourself a nooner, eh?" The man doesn't bother to appear sheepish for interrupting.

I haven't completely adjusted to the lack of boundaries between us. That doesn't mean I can't fake it. "What gave us away?"

"It smells like a humid brothel in here."

Bile rises in my throat at the visual that creates. I gulp the queasy churning in my gut. "When the mood strikes, man. Besides, we didn't have any reason not to. There wasn't supposed to be anyone else home until tomorrow."

He doesn't react to my dig. "Glad you're putting that Tropical Glide to good use."

A snort streams from me. "Oh, we used the entire bottle that same night. Now we've got Blow Joe. Tastes like bubble gum."

Chad shakes his head. "You're a weird guy, Braxter."

"Thanks for noticing. Always happy to provide entertainment for you."

A squeal from the bathroom interrupts us. The door bursts open a second later, a disheveled Presley stumbling out. It's a relief that she took a moment to throw on a shirt, which must be mine since it almost hangs to her knees. I breathe a bit easier with her naked ass hidden from view. That thought is fleeting once I catch sight of what she's holding. There's a plastic stick in her grip, the type I've recently become all too familiar with since we started trying. Standing in the aisle while agonizing over the endless choices is a thrilling way to pass time.

"Pep?" I prompt after her bewildered silence stretches to concerning lengths. My feet are moving while I reach to cradle her jaw, my thumb drifting along the smooth skin.

Presley blinks and gives herself a little shake. "I decided to take a test."

"And?" I barely hear the word over the drumbeat in my pulse.

"There are two lines." Her voice is a mere squeak while she bounces in place.

My muddled brain struggles to recall the simple directions I've read a dozen times. "That means—"

"I'm pregnant!"

"You're pregnant." The awe in my tone rings out an instant before I'm scooping her flush against me.

Moisture pools in her baby blues, reflecting the sheen covering mine. "It's just one positive test, but it feels real."

The knot in my throat makes it difficult to speak. I croak on the first few attempts. "We're having a baby?"

Her tears flow over my fingers. "Yes."

I kiss salt from her lips, then crash to my knees. With a tremble wracking the motion, I press my face against her abdomen. "I'm going to figure out how to be the best dad. This is such an incredible gift you've given me, Pep. I'm going to spoil you rotten."

Presley runs her nails along my scalp. "You're already an incredible father."

A blubber rips from me and I bury the emotion against her shirt. "I'm already a mess."

"That'll do just fine. Babies are very messy." Humor tints the wobble in her tone.

Chad begins clapping, piercing our intimate exchange. I'd forgotten he was here. It feels right that he's with us for this, though. I'm going to need all the advice he's willing to give me.

"Bring it in, man." I lift an arm in invitation.

He's beside us in the next instant. The embrace is somewhat awkward considering my face is still smashed to Presley's stomach. That doesn't stop us from leaning on each other.

Warmth spreads through my veins as the magnitude of what's to come burrows beneath the surface.

"What goin' on?"

We separate from our strange formation, yet I remain crouched. Presley lowers to a kneel while Chad gives us space to announce the news. Archie is hovering over the threshold with a question lifting his features.

As a cohesive unit, Presley and I beckon him to us with open arms. He plows into our waiting embrace without pause.

"You're going to be a big brother," Presley tells him once he's returned to his feet.

A groove indents the skin between his brows. "Wha?"

I ruffle his faux hawk. "Your Mama is going to have a baby, buddy."

His eyes flare open to ocean-spread standards. "Where?"

"In her tummy." I rest a hand flat on Presley's stomach.

Archer gasps and tries to lift her shirt. "Wanna see."

"The baby is very tiny. We can't see him or her yet." I create a small sliver between my thumb and index finger.

He wrinkles his nose at the minuscule size I'm presenting. "Why?"

"This is probably going to take further explanation," Presley mumbles from the corner of her mouth.

And this situation could go sideways fast. "I'll research some best strategies."

She cups my cheek, gaze shimmering with affection. "See? Already incredible."

"You make it easy for me," I murmur while tilting into her touch. Then my focus slides to the little man who remains perplexed by this discovery. "We'll find a book to read, buddy. Maybe a cool shirt for you to wear too."

That seems to appease him, a smile returning to his face. "M'kay."

"We'll get going. Congrats again. You two need to

celebrate." Chad begins steering Archer from the room. He pauses for a moment to glance at us once his shoulder. "With a bang."

"Bang, bang, bang," Archie calls while walking away.

Shared amusement tumbles free as we stand and watch them leave. I peek over at my fiancée—the woman made for me—and let a grin run wild. The action tugs at my cheeks and probably borders on megawatt. Presley's features dance with joy while her fingers trace the grooves of my dimples. Somehow, my smile manages to notch upward several more degrees.

"Ah, there he is." Her body melts into mine with a sigh.

I drop my forehead to touch hers. "And who might that be?"

"All mine."

Ready for more from Mason and Presley? I whipped up a bonus epilogue and find out what happens with the Tropical Glide if you dare. Get both scenes for free here!

what to read next

Did you know Clea, Vannah, and Audria have their own books? They're all available to read now!
Here's an excerpt from *There's Always Someday*—Nolan and Clea's emotional journey at finding love.

As we approach the line of grass separating our adjoining properties, the door of the truck pops open. The interior light reveals the silhouette of a lone man behind the wheel. He unfolds himself from the vehicle and goes to retrieve something from the backseat. When he straightens, a pink bundle is wiggling in his hold. It's not just him after all. He's cradling what I assume is a baby, mostly covered in a fuzzy blanket.

The guy moves from the vehicle's shadow and turns back around—only to gasp, startled as he sees us cutting a path toward him. "Oh, hey. I didn't notice you there."

My brother waves. "Didn't mean to sneak up on you. We just wanted to say hello."

This is probably the point where I'm expected to join in the conversation, but I'm struck speechless. The man is handsome—dare I say, gorgeous. My naïve heart takes off in a punishing sprint. The rapid rhythm sounds foolish, even to my own ears. But those doubts can't stop this hopeless reaction from thrumming through me.

The ground quakes as I suck in a shallow breath. My lungs refuse to expand further than a quick inhale allows. For a moment, I believe the storm has found a second wind and is attempting to knock me sideways. But my feet are steady.

I attempt to clear the fog with several measured blinks. That does little to dissipate the immediate trance he's put me in. I always thought that meeting the man of my dreams would be a special occasion. An elegant gala or a fancy dinner party seems more appropriate. But here I am, standing in the mud, and it's all I can do to stop my jaw from falling open in shock and admiration.

From what I can see in the pitch black, he's extremely attractive. Strikingly so. He's tall, with a strong jawline and hair that's somehow both unruly and perfectly styled. His eyes, even in the dark, have a soulful hue. It's as if he's already seen too much and his inner spark took the brunt. I almost recoil from that haunting gleam, but I stand firm. Mama didn't raise me to shy away from the tough stuff.

A closer inspection reveals that his neutral expression is forced and brittle. His lips are drooped in a solemn frown. Creases and shadows linger around his eyes. Harsh lines across his forehead scream of strain. There's a noticeable hunch in his broad shoulders. The weight of something extremely heavy appears to be crushing him. He seems to be running on empty, seconds from collapse under some unknown pressure. The energy surrounding him is dull, with a listless quality. I can't stop myself from wondering what brought this stranger so close to being drained dry.

But none of that interferes with his appeal. If anything, he's more attractive in spite of it all.

He's young, probably early twenties if I had to guess. Thick stubble covers his square jaw. His features are sharp and sculpted. The artist hidden within me discovers a muse in this statuesque man. Rugged angles that threaten to leave a mark, either on the surface or far more permanent. Probably both. I get the impression he's complicated with countless protective layers. The image of a beautiful rose cocooned in thorns appears in my mind. That's too ridiculous and I gulp against the tickle in my throat. Laughter won't be appreciated in this instance.

Rather than getting lost in the flutters he spontaneously

creates, I find myself heading straight into a bleak abyss. It's obvious that this guy is the furthest thing from emotionally available.

A tiny wail cracks into the silence. That's when I remember he's clutching a baby against his chest. I can't imagine having a child at my age, and he can't be much older than me. To further remind us of her existence, a tiny fist thrusts into the air and swats at the air blindly.

I've never felt such a powerful urge to capture the moment behind my lens. My index finger twitches with the desire to click the shot. The picture they create deserves to be displayed.

He begins to shush her while bouncing in place. "Uh, sorry. It's past her bedtime. We've been on the road for hours."

His words finally break me free from my mesmerized bubble. I start talking without conscious thought. "Oh I don't mind. Ha ha. She's adorable, by the way. Long drives can be really hard even for grown-ups." I internally scream at myself to get it together, but my mouth is moving too fast for my brain to catch up. "Hi, um, I'm Clea, we live here—not like 'we' as a couple. That would be super weird since this is my brother. We live right over there. Sorry, I already told you that. Where did you come from?"

Kody gives me an elbow to the ribs to shut me up. "What my nosy sister means to say is that we're glad to have new neighbors. This house stood vacant for too long. I'm Kody."

Fire singes my cheeks. I find myself grateful that it's dark out, or this handsome stranger would see me turning redder than a beet.

"Nolan," he offers. "It's nice to meet you both. Oh, and we're from Madison."

It's safe to assume he's referring to the city in

Wisconsin. "What brings you to Minnesota? It's the lakes, right?"

Kody pins me with a glare. I almost wither into the soaking lawn. The last thing I want is to chase him away with an insulting inquisition, but Nolan squashes any concern that I've potentially overstepped. "A fresh start. That's the plan, at least."

I wait for him to say more, biting my tongue to get ahold of myself before I invade his privacy any further. When only the crickets answer, I decide it's safe to proceed. With caution, of course. "Well, you really picked a great place to live. Excellent choice."

Face meet palm. I'm beginning to sound like a welcome wagon on too much sugar and caffeine.

The harsh lines exposing his sorrow lighten just a touch when he glances at me. "I really needed to hear that ringing endorsement. It's a good thing you stopped by."

Whether he's being sarcastic or not isn't important. I'm not ashamed to admit that the hint of a smile on his face sends me reeling all over again.

"Can we help with anything?" I paste on what's meant to be an encouraging smile.

Nolan wears defeat like a familiar cloak. His glassy eyes lift to mine. The man looks close to tears. "Could you hold her for me?"

My tongue sticks to the roof of my mouth. I have zero experience with kids, but that doesn't mean I'm not intrigued by the little pink bundle snuggled against his chest. Denying him, especially in his current state, is impossible. "Umm, sure."

Nolan deposits the squirming bundle into my outstretched arms. My movements feel wooden and odd. The corner of his lips hitch, just the slightest bit, and only briefly. "You'll get the hang of it."

I nod, believing his words deep in my gut. "What's her name?"

"Tallulah." The word is choked from him. "We call her Tally for short."

I stroke a finger down her satin cheek. "She's absolutely beautiful. Aren't you, precious girl?"

"She gets that from her mother." A single tear rolls down his cheek with that broken statement. A tight knot dips in his throat as he swallows. "If only she were here to appreciate the similarities. It's just us now. Tally's mom isn't… in the picture."

The urge to ask tickles my tongue. There's clearly a story there. I'm curious enough to tug at the thread, but guilt would instantly gnaw at me. This isn't the moment to pry. For now, I'll give him the comfort of holding his little girl while he unpacks.

"I'm just going to grab a few sleeping essentials, if you don't mind keeping her occupied." He hitches a thumb toward the trailer.

A disgruntled noise squeaks past my pursed lips. "Not at all. Take your time."

"I'll help carry stuff inside." Kody's features are screwed up into a tight pinch. My brother rarely frowns, but this entire evening is dragging us into unfamiliar territory.

"Thank you." Nolan sniffs and wipes at his face. "You have no idea how much I appreciate this."

"That's what neighbors do. You'll see." I send him another comforting grin to pair with my sentiment.

He yanks at his shaggy hair. I find myself wondering if he's let the length go astray on purpose. "Yeah, okay. You might need to be careful, or I'll take advantage of that kindness."

"Oh, whatever," I scoff. "If you need me, just give a holler. I'll be right over."

His rigid posture eases at the edges. "Don't say I didn't warn you."

"I wouldn't dream of it." The reflex to wink flutters my lashes, but I hold off at the last second.

My brother nods his agreement before following Nolan behind the truck. Then it's just me and the baby. Soft coos and gurgles fill the quiet enveloping us. Good thing my mom isn't nearby to catch sight of this. It might be enough to speed up her grandmotherly instincts.

As I stand there with Tally in my arms, the fog finally lifts as clarity returns. A solid mass settles in my belly soon after. But this sinking sensation isn't laced with dread. It feels more like divine intervention. Just thinking of some magical forces at play makes me giggle. That storm must've put something goofy in the atmosphere.

Yet I can't ignore my sneaking suspicion. It would take very little effort on my part to fall for this man and his little girl. There's no doubt that I'm about to find out just how easy the tumble will be.

Read *There's Always Someday* today—available with Kindle Unlimited!

Leave Him Loved (Audria and Reeve)

Something Like Hate (Vannah and Landon)

novels by HARLOE RAE

Reclusive Standalones
Redefining Us
Forget You Not

#BitterSweetHeat Standalones
Gent
Miss
Lass

Silo Springs Standalones
Breaker
Keeper
Loner

Total Standalones
Watch Me Follow
Ask Me Why
Left for Wild
Leave Him Loved
Something Like Hate
There's Always Someday

Screwed Up (part of the Bayside Heroes standalones)

acknowledgements

This part is somehow the toughest. What can I possibly say that will be enough to show my endless thanks and gratitude to everyone who deserves it? Virtual hug time! You know who you are and you're incredible.

I need to start by thanking my family. Writing a book requires a lot of time that often spreads into hours meant to be with my husband and kids. Especially as a deadline looms. I'm eternally grateful for their patience and support so I can continue following my dreams. You're my favorites. I love you to a galaxy far, far away. Also, a special shoutout to my little man for providing hilarious material for Archie. Peek-a-boo penis was totally his idea!

I need to thank my brother-in-law, Gary, for the whore-igami term. He'll never read this, and that's for the best, but he gets the credit for that one.

To YOU, my readers. Thank you SO MUCH for choosing Doing It Right to read. Out of all the books you could read, mine is one you picked. That alone never ceases to boggle my mind. I greatly appreciate your support. Thank you, Thank you!

I should probably thank to Mason, Presley, Archie, and the Quad Pod Babe Squad for filling my head with awesomeness. These characters have brought me so much joy. I hope you enjoyed them as well!

Renee is my right and left hand support system, but she's also my bestie. She keeps me going, even on the worst of days.

Thanks for being everything I need without having to ask. I'm so thankful to call you mine.

Kk and Heather—my bestest beeches. There isn't much I can say that properly conveys my never-ending love for you two. From sharing nachos to falling down escalators and losing our voices from singing too loud, we're in this together. Forever and ever. You're stuck with me.

I always receive so much praise about my covers. That's all due to the extremely talented Talia with Book Cover Kingdom. Ever since the beginning, she's been there for me to share her crazy-amazing skills. It's the best day whenever we get to create magic together. I can't wait to see what we whip up next!

Kate the great for being… well, great. Day after day, you're there for me. Sprinting with you is almost as fun as talking nonsense. Thanks for creating my gorgeous special edition cover too. Lovely!

I have been extremely fortunate to find genuine friendships in this super-duper book world. Whenever I need a positive boost or words of encouragement or to share a laugh, these ladies are there for me. I know I can turn to you, no matter what, and that kind of supportive comfort is priceless. Thank you to Tia, Shain, Annie, Leigh, Amy, Michelle, TJ, Suzie, Kandi, and many more. Your friendship is irreplaceable. Thank you, thank you.

An extra loud shoutout to my reader group—Harloe's Hotties—and my review crew. Because of you, I always have a warm and happy place to turn. You're my people. That means everything to me. I'll never be able to thank each of you individually, but please know how much your support means to me. I love you all!

Thank you to Candi Kane and her team at Candi Kane PR. She's such an unstoppable force and works tirelessly to ensure each release goes off without a hitch. I'm forever grateful. Also, a big thanks to the wonderful ladies at Give Me Books. Once again, your help for this release is invaluable and very much appreciated.

Thanks to Rafa, the very talented photographer who shot the stunning image of Victor to become the muse for Mason. Doesn't he make you a bit breathless?

There are so many vital individuals who assist in the writing and publishing process. Renee reads as I write and keeps me on track. Thanks to Patricia, Kayla, and Keri for beta reading. Sending a huge thanks to Alex with Infinite Well for editing and polishing Doing It Right until the story sparkled. To Lacie and BB for proofing. A massive thanks to Stacey from Champagne Book Design. As always, she once again created the most stunning interior for my book baby. I cannot recommend her formatting services enough!

I need to send out another huge round of thanks to all the readers, reviewers, bloggers, bookstagrammers, BookTokers, and romance lovers out there. Because of you, authors like me get to continue writing and doing what we love. You're who we strive to reach and aim to be better for. Thank you to infinity for continuing to be there for all of us!

And last but definitely not least, if you enjoyed Doing It Right and want to do me a huge favor, please consider leaving a review. It really helps others find my books. Thank you for reading!

about the author

Harloe Rae is a *USA Today* & Amazon Top 5 best-selling author. Her passion for writing and reading has taken on a whole new meaning. Each day is an unforgettable adventure.

She's a Minnesota gal with a serious addiction to romance. There's nothing quite like an epic happily ever after. When she's not buried in the writing cave, Harloe can be found hanging with her hubby and kiddos. If the weather permits, she loves being lakeside or out in the country with her horses.

Harloe is the author of the Reclusive series, *Watch Me Follow*, the #BitterSweetHeat series, *Ask Me Why*, the Silo Springs series, *Left for Wild, Leave Him Loved, Something Like Hate, There's Always Someday, Screwed Up,* and *Doing It Right*. These titles are available on Amazon.

Stay in the know by subscribing to her newsletter at
bit.ly/HarloesList

Join her reader group, Harloe's Hotties, at
www.facebook.com/groups/harloehotties

Check out her site at www.harloe-rae.blog

Printed in Great Britain
by Amazon